CHAMELEONS

Junctions Murder Mystery Series

Book Four:

CHAMELEONS

L. E. Fleury

The reader should be aware that the characters in the *Junctions Murder Mystery Series* are fictional. While most of the historical locations and events are accurate, the writer has taken artistic license on certain issues to enhance the plot or to paint a more beautiful mental picture. Enjoy the books!

Copyright © 2024 by L. E. Fleury.
All rights reserved.

First paperback edition July 2024.

Editing by Joyce M. Gilmour.

Cover design by Heylea, LLC.

Cover photo: iStock credit: mihtiander

Cover photo enhancements by
Kelly Rainbow Butterfly.

Published by Heylea, LLC.
cabininthewoods2021@gmail.com

Special thanks to contributors:
R.W. Shelden, 117 Ranch, and A. Urbaniak.

ISBN: 979-8-9890236-4-6 (paperback)

I dedicate this book

...to the Father: Thank you for giving us eternal life.

...to the Son: Thank you for your Blood Covering that gets us back Home.

...to the Holy Spirit: Thank you for enriching our earthly sojourn.

"Pride goeth before destruction, and a haughty spirit before a fall."

Proverbs 16:18 (KJV)

CHAPTER ONE

Drama

He thought it was one of those "guy" dreams, because the bed was undulating, over and over, but the frantic grasp of his wife's hand on his arm brought him quickly back to reality.

"Don! Wake up!" Connie Collins shouted at her husband. "The house is shaking!"

He recognized it immediately, pulling her from the bed. "It's an earthquake," he whispered hoarsely. "Grab your pillow and follow me, babe." He reached out in the dark, heading for the hallway. "Cover the top of your head with that pillow," he commanded. "We're going under the kitchen table!"

The crash of dishes hitting the kitchen floor stopped them at the bedroom door. "Dining room table!" he yelled, pulling her in the other direction. Suddenly, the shaking shifted in another dizzying direction. Something tumbled to the floor in the living room, but he kept going. He was dragging a chair out of the way when wooden structures in the roof started to groan and crack. Grabbing the pillow as she slid down under, he followed, pushing her to the floor and placing his body over hers. There was a long, ominous shudder, moving the table legs across the floor.

Then it was quiet.

Connie remained under her husband's protective body. "Is it over?"

"Maybe, maybe not. There are always aftershocks." The retired Army Air Corps pilot went into extended survival mode. "Stay put. I'm going to grab a blanket and another pillow."

"Are we sleeping under this table all night?" It was almost a whine.

"Don't know yet," he called out as he groped his way back down the hall.

They dozed through the rest of the night, not knowing what to expect, but the small city of Winooski remained quiet. At four in the morning they arose to clean up the damage.

"I'll check on the attic," he informed her, once the glass was swept up in the kitchen. A few minutes later he came back with the report that all things seemed to be holding; a professional inspection could be arranged later.

"Good," his schoolteacher wife replied. "We need to get ready for work, then." She looked up from where she was putting books back in the living room bookcase. "What shift are you driving today?"

"Good old Burlington Transit has me on day shift," he said, as he turned on the radio. "Let's see what the WJOY morning news has to say about last night."

"Sure. But don't forget, we have a counseling session at six this evening." She wiped the dust from her hands.

"Oh, I forgot about it, in all the excitement. Do we have to do this one? Maybe we could reschedule."

"Don, we are certified Christian counselors, and we agreed..."

"...quite an earthquake we had last night, folks," the announcer was saying. "We have been informed that it was a six-point-three, and that's a pretty big one. We've also been told that the epicenter seems to have been in the Jericho township area. This has not yet been confirmed, but we can tell you we've also received reports from residents on Browns Trace Road that the rivers were running backwards. It seems folks ran outside for safety and were eyewitnesses to this very sight. Meanwhile, we are waiting for details on structural damage in all of Chittenden County. So far, there have been no reports of injuries or deaths. This quake will be remembered as 'the big one in the summer of 1950,' for sure. WJOY will keep you up to date as we get further information. In the meantime, we can all be grateful this scare is over, and there will be no further damage."

He was wrong about that.

***

Five years before the big earthquake, another great shifting was going on in Germany. Professor Abraham Schuler's family had managed to stay ahead of the Nazi thugs, moving from one house to another, then from one city to the next, and finally, into Spain, where this couple and their two young children finally received sponsorship in the United States. The word came early in 1948, although it was another year before they actually got on the plane. It was primarily his professorship that saved them, providing employment in the USA, and before long, they had been transported to Burlington, the "Queen City" of the Green Mountain State, where he immediately joined the staff at the University of Vermont. Temporary housing was found in the ground floor apartment of one of the two cottages on the grounds of the Children's Home, at 555 Shelburne Road. This particular cottage was located just behind the Big Girls' end of a large, brick triplex structure. The Big Boys were located at the other end of the dining room area which separated the two living quarters.

The little family was probably also missed by their German pursuers, in part, because of their pale red hair — almost blond in the sunlight — and the explosion of soft freckles over pale skin. They did not fit the stereotype of what German soldiers thought a Jew should look like. Then, too, the fortyish couple was exceptionally educated and lived a quiet, non-political lifestyle. Still, even though now safe in America, a residual fear permeated their existence and the tall, slender mother kept her children quietly in the Children's Home apartment for weeks. Eventually, the need for healthy social interaction with their peers overcame her caution, and sometime in July the two young ones ventured out onto their postage-stamp-sized lawn. The Home Kids, of course, were curious, and so Mrs. Bushey, the Home's director, talked with Mrs. Schuler, and the German-born joined the American-born. Nobody in the play yard even had a second thought about it. Eight-year-old David went to the Big Boys' ball field and eleven-year-old Esther — called "Essie" — eagerly joined the girls at the other end of the complex. The Home girls quickly learned a lot about this new playmate: She could speak English very well, and she was going to be a ballerina when she grew up — something they doubted as she demonstrated how to stand on her toes, for she was lanky and awkward and got a funny look on her face when she did that. But she was full of stories and asked a lot of questions about American books and fairy tales, and then one day she said, "We should write a play."

Her closest friend, Jenny Roth, was delighted with the suggestion. She went inside and asked for paper and pencils from the downstairs housemother, Mrs. Ferndale, who seemed amused, watching from her private room's window as the two playwrights sat on the summer grass, creating their masterpiece. The creative duo hadn't any idea what they were getting into. It took only a couple of afternoons to come up with the complete drama, which, Essie informed them, her mother would be happy to make into a real script on her portable typewriter. A couple of days later, the finished play was presented to Mrs. Bushey, who got back to the girls the next day.

She laid out the rules: Costumes would be made during playground time, and rehearsals, as well. Yes, the play could be presented in the third-story music hall in the main building. There was to be no tomfoolery, or the whole thing would be called off. One of the older girls would supervise to make sure no damages were done.

The supervising girl turned out to be Jenny's almost eighteen-year-old sister, Donna. Indeed, it almost became a family effort, with the two Roth sisters and their younger brother, Eddie, all having parts in the twenty-minute production. Still, it was an experience that sealed a friendship between Essie and Jenny, one that would prepare their journey through a real-life drama, over the next twelve months.

***

For most of that summer, the play-writing amateurs enjoyed a position of quiet honor at the Children's Home. Wherever they went, young heads nodded in respect, even stepping aside to allow these celebrities to be first in line into the dining room, because everybody wanted to be friends. But Professor Schuler was anxious to get his family into housing closer to the university, and get it done before the school year began, so Essie was gone by the first of September. By then, the three Roth children had been in the Home for over ten years. The older sister, Donna, would turn eighteen in August, so when she graduated from Burlington's Edmunds High School, she applied for a job at the telephone company, right there in the Queen City. Sure enough, she got the job in late August, two weeks after doing the play. She moved immediately into an apartment on Winooski Avenue, with two other operators who were looking for a roommate. For her, the long stay at the Children's Home had come to an end. It was late summer of 1949.

That was a lonely winter for the other two Roth children, although they got to sit together in Sunday school at the First Methodist Church in Burlington, where there was opportunity for family talk. It was well into the month of March — and 1950 — when one such conversation took place. Miss Green, the Sunday school teacher, was called from the room, and the youngsters immediately took up whispered communications. Back in the corner, Eddie leaned closer to his sister. "Donny Dague called me a freak," he said with a pout.

"What for? There's nothing wrong with you. You're handsome."

"He said I have a big nose and buck teeth."

She peered more closely at the angular face with the deep-set eyes. "You and me look a lot alike, but you're the lucky one. You look like the famous actor in *The Wizard of Oz* movie. Um…" She paused to remember the name. "Yeah, Ray Bolger, the dancing scarecrow, remember?" The boy didn't seem impressed, so she went on. "Now me, I look like Margaret What's-her-name, the wicked witch of the west, or whoever." She laughed. "But you know what? Everybody loves them, and I mean *everybody*. You know why, Eddie? Because they're part of a story that makes people happy." She folded her arms resolutely. "So that's what I'm gonna do, and that's what you should do, too."

"What are you gonna do?" It was the culprit, himself, sitting two chairs away.

"Just never you mind, Donny," she snapped at the rascal. "This doesn't concern you."

The Dague kid screwed up his nose. "Well, I don't care what you do, you stupid girl." He was suddenly inspired. "Anyways, I know something about you two, and you don't."

"No you don't, Donny." Eddie's twisted grin exposed his curiosity. "You're just saying that. You don't know *diddly*."

"Yes I do."

She jumped right in. "Don't either. You don't know diddly-squat, you fibber."

"Do too!"

"Oh yeah?" Eddie prodded him. "Prove it, then. Just you go ahead and prove it."

"Don't have to," the mean kid muttered.

"Uh-huh, just what I thought," Jenny said with a smirk. Then she went into a sing-song taunt. "You don't know... did-lee squaw-hot! You don't know... did-lee squaw-hot!"

That did it.

"Oh yeah? Oh yeah? Well..." The braggart's withering look established his superiority. "...your uncle is taking you both out of the Home, and he's gonna use you for slave labor on his farm in Jericho!" There was a little waggle of the head. "I heard the housemothers talking."

CHAPTER TWO

Jericho

Uncle Mark Roth's 1948 Ford truck rumbled along Vermont Route 15, gently rocking the three of them on the cab's bench seat. Behind them, the children's two suitcases thumped under the tarp that kept this battered baggage inside the pickup's open bed. Sitting next to the passenger door, Jenny sneaked a sideways peek at her brother, then at the driver, noting the family resemblance: the dark hair, prominent nose and ears, and even the eyes set deeply inside shadowy sockets. There was no doubt about it — this was a blood relative. She looked down at her hands, folded politely on her lap, before clearing her throat. "This is a very nice truck you have, Uncle Mark." She looked for support from her brother, who turned toward the man.

"Did it cost a lot of money, Uncle Mark?" the boy ventured into what he thought was "man talk."

The man laughed. "Ah-yuh. It cost a lot of money, kid." He glanced at the boy. "I worked hard for this truck, let me tell ya."

"Yes, sir," the hapless lad murmured. It was difficult to know what was okay to talk about.

She came to the rescue. "Well, I can tell you, Uncle, that Eddie and I know how to work. If there's one thing we learned in the Home, it was how to work." She patted Eddie's shoulder. "Right, Eddie?"

Her younger brother nodded, and then there was only the rattle of the bright red truck moving off the main highway. As they drove slowly through Jericho Corners, then picked up speed on Lee River Road, her thoughts went back to her last talk with big sister, Donna.

"I really like my job at the phone company; why should I want to move up there to Jericho on a farm, of all places? Of course I don't want to come with you and Eddie."

Jenny had looked around to see if anyone else could hear this exchange, right there in the middle of the Burlington Transit bus terminal's waiting room. "Listen, I only have ten minutes before my bus back to the Home. I asked you to come here, because I thought we should all three be together. Together, Donna." She moved in closer to the soft, round face of her older sister. "Don't you want to finally be a real family, Donna?"

The telephone operator shook her sandy pageboy hairdo. "Oh my gosh, Jenny. You may be kind of a 'Plain Jane,' but you think like a fairy tale character; like, you're going to wake up and live happily ever after." Her lips went into a tight line. "You need to get real, kiddo. Quit looking at the world through rose-colored glasses, will you? Our chance to be a real family went out the door when our mother went ditsy. Can't you get that through your head?"

"No, no. Don't say that. She has a brain tumor, for heaven's sake." Jenny pulled her coat together, as though to protect herself against a cold wind. "It just took so long to catch up with her. She was married and had three babies before it all came crashing down." Indignation rose up within the girl. "You should know this, Donna. You got to see her on the way to get treatment in White River Junction, remember?" She bent in, again. "I missed seeing her, because my bus got stuck behind an accident. Remember? You and Eddie got to see her that one time. What do you mean, she was 'ditsy'? You should have respected her. You should have seen what was going on with her. You should have seen it!"

"Oh, I saw it, alright. I saw it plain and simple." Donna's face reflected the solemn memory. "She didn't even know who we were. Eddie just leaned on her shoulder like a lost soul, and I was just

somebody sitting in this very same bus station. In this very same bus station, Jenny." She blinked slowly. "Our mother didn't even know who we were. You didn't miss a thing, kiddo. She was gone." The oldest child needed to make that point, again. "I mean, gone. Not there anymore. If you ask me, the sooner she kicks off, the better. She's nobody. Lost. Confused. Sad. Not Anna Roth any more. Not doing anybody any good, I swear." Her voice dropped to a whisper. "The only thing left is her life insurance policy. At least us kids will get something, after all." Jenny's head was bent low. "Hey, little sister, I'm sorry I have to be so blunt, but it's just the way it is." She stood to leave. "Meanwhile, I'm going to make a life for myself. I have a good job with good benefits, and some new friends, and I'm even on the company softball team."

"The telephone company has a softball team?"

Donna laughed. "Yup. And I'm one of the pitchers — in fact, the best one they have."

Jenny stood up to hug her sister. "Well," she said, "thanks for meeting me here. I can't say I agree with everything you said, but I'm glad we got to talk." She pulled back, trying to make it an amicable departure. "So... a softball pitcher, huh?"

"Hey, and a damned good one. I can really zing 'em in there!"

When Jenny came back to the present, the truck was moving off Lee River Road, passing under an arced sign which read, "Roth Ranch." The driveway, which was two ruts with a grassy ridge in between, hair-pinned slowly down before them, passing a field of Hereford cattle on the left and a cornfield on the right. Farther below, a large, faded, red barn came into view. Behind it, just past a small grove of trees, a ribbon of sand held back the movement of shimmering water.

"Is that a river, Uncle Mark?" she asked.

"Ay-yuh. Called the Lee River, 'though some folks got other names for it."

"Like what?" Jenny asked.

"Like that sandy strip we can see from here. It's also called 'Crocker's Sand Bar.'"

"Can people fish there?" Eddie's eyes sparkled at the thought.

"Sure can," came the answer.

They turned one last curve, past a stand of birches on the right, and there was the house. Its white clapboards shone brightly against the background of what appeared to be a bare-limbed orchard behind it.

"Oo-oo," Jenny cooed. "That's a big old farmhouse!"

"Jiminy crickets! That's a big, old *porch*," her brother exclaimed, as he turned back to his uncle. "Do we get to sit on it?"

"What?" The man was surprised. "Of course. That's what it's for."

Jenny explained: "We had a big porch in front of the dining room at the Home, but we weren't allowed to be on it."

Mark's eyebrows rose again, then dropped. "Well, I'll be damned," he mumbled. Moments later, he slid his lanky body out of the truck, motioning to a woman and a young girl standing on the steps. "Kathy! Rhonda! Come meet Anna's kids."

The two were escorted into the home, where, just inside the front door, a large staircase led up from the living room to the four bedrooms on the second floor. Eddie was given the smallest one, right at the top of the stairs. Opposite his doorway, Jenny walked into a large, cheerful room with twin beds. She would be sharing a room with Rhonda. Next door, another space which had been converted into a spacious bathroom stood between the girl's haven and the master bedroom. There was, the children were informed, a guest room across the hall from the master bedroom, and a linen closet between that amenity and Eddie's private sanctuary. "There's stairs up to the attic in there," Kathy cautioned them, "and they're old and dangerous, so whatever you do, stay away from them." The two Home Kids nodded in obedience. They could not be bothered with an insignificant restriction like that. No, they were impressed, for this was no dormitory. This was a real house, a *real* home.

Kathy's rosy face glowed under the crown of her ebony hair as she and her daughter, Rhonda, served a supper of steaks and mashed potatoes, followed by homemade applesauce, raisin cookies, and vanilla ice cream. "We wanted this to be a special dinner," the woman said.

Rhonda, who was a fifteen-year-old version of her mother, nodded in agreement. "We're beef ranchers, just like when we were in Texas," she commented. "Lots of meat on the table."

Dishes were done, and they all retired to the evening glow out on the large front porch. It was there that the two children began to get the whole picture.

"Anna married your father, right out of high school," Uncle Mark said. "After I got out of the Army, I got a job offer in Texas. They wanted to stay here in Vermont." He pulled a puff of smoke from the pipe in his hand. "I took off, anyway. Never thought it would break up our family." There was another puff. "Anyway, it turned out I had some stuff to work out, about that damned war." He tapped the tobacco down into the bowl of the pipe. "Took me a good five years to get out of my shell down there in Texas." He smiled at Kathy. "Then I met this lady, and things turned around for me."

"Now tell the rest of it, Mark. You know, how you learned about Anna's health, and her kids in the Home," Kathy urged him, as she shifted her bottom on the porch swing.

"Well yes, I was notified that my brother, Edward — her husband — had passed on, that she was sick, but there wasn't a whole lot I could do about it. Up until I married Kathy, I was an ex-GI, with no qualifications to take on three kids." He drew out a match stick, igniting it by scratching it along the thigh of his denim pants. Two puffs later, he continued: "Once Kathy and Rhonda came onto the scene, it was okay to get you kids back into the family. So we packed up and came back to Vermont. Found this place. Liked it, and even Thunder liked it."

"Who's Thunder?" Eddie asked. "You got a dog?"

Mark was amused, but it was Rhonda who laughed out loud. "Thunder is a big old bull," she informed him.

"Not so old," the man corrected her. "More like a big *prize* bull."

"How big?" the boy wondered out loud.

"Oh, about eighteen hundred pounds, I'd say." He enjoyed the awe in the teenager's eyes. "I'll introduce you to him tomorrow."

"Me, too?" Jenny wasn't sure she wanted to do that.

"Sure. Like it or not, he's part of your new family." Mark studied the bowl of his pipe. "Aw, he's okay. Just don't get him riled up, and you'll get along just fine."

Kathy spoke up. "And that's what it's all about — getting along. After all, we're all you kids have got, now."

Jenny blinked behind her imaginary rose-colored glasses. "Oh, but Mama isn't going to leave us kids high and dry. Did you know that she has a life insurance policy?"

Suddenly it was very quiet on the porch, while the Texas ladies waited for the man to take the lead.

"Ay-yuh," Mark Roth finally answered. "Just another reason why you kids needed to have family watching out for you, as far as I was concerned." He tapped the bowl of the pipe with one finger. "After all, that's what my brother would have wanted for his children, and I take that responsibility very seriously."

"I think we need to get ready for bed," Kathy said, with a yawn. "Eddie will be up early to start learning how to take care of beef cattle." The two Home Kids rose immediately and prepared for bed. Once properly under the covers, they waited, each in their own room, but nobody came to pray with them. Finally, because they were so grateful to at last be

13

in their family, they each prayed on their own, then snuggled down for some much-needed sleep.

It was a loud thump.

Jenny lifted her head from the pillow, straining to hear where it may have come from. There is was, again. She sat up, thinking maybe Rhonda had fallen in the bathroom next door. But there was no cry for help. She sat quietly. There it was, again. This time she zeroed in on it. It seemed to be coming from up there in the attic. Rhonda walked in to find her roommate staring at the ceiling.

"What are you looking at?" Her own light brown eyes scanned the top of the room.

"Something is thumping. Did you hear it in the bathroom?"

"Uh, maybe. Thought you bumped your head against the wall or something." The teenaged Texan kicked off her slippers. "Maybe something blew onto the roof. It's kind-a windy out there."

A light knock on the door brought Jenny face-to-face with Eddie, in his nightshirt. "What's that noise in the attic?" His eyes reflected the worry in his voice.

"Probably something got blown onto the roof. Don't worry about it, Eddie."

"Oh. Well, okay," he said, turning back toward his room.

"I guess we're both just a little nervous," Jenny reassured the other two, as she softly closed the door.

With that, the three children cuddled into their feather pillows.

But the thumping continued off and on throughout the night.

***

The next morning, Uncle Mark kept his promise to introduce Thunder. The huge animal was standing a sparse ten feet from the fence where he, Eddie, and the two teenaged girls were draped in various positions. The two Home kids took in the immense rectangular body, mostly a reddish brown, with a band of white that spread like a dress shirt down his chest to the whole length of his underbelly. A patch of curvy white on the end of his tail perfectly matched the glistening crop of curls between the long, forward-lateral curve of the trimmed horns.

"How come there's no points on his horns?" Eddie asked.

"For safety reasons," the herdsman replied.

The boy looked back up. Thunder's wide, white face was punctuated by dark eyes with long, silvery lashes. Still, this was no "pretty boy." Further examination revealed that, although the stubby, muscular legs didn't look like they could hold all that weight, this was truly a rough hunk of masculinity. Rhonda noted how Jenny looked, then quickly looked away from the appendages under the fellow's white shirt-tail. She bent close to whisper into the innocent girl's ear, "Now, *that's* a lot of bull..."

Because it was a Saturday, the children were free to get acquainted after morning chores. Uncle Mark led them around to one side of the red barn's interior. "We keep our goats in here," Rhonda informed the other youngsters. "They graze up in the orchard during the day."

"I have a surprise for you two," Mark said, pointing to a couple of bicycles leaning against the wall just under the hay loft.

"Bikes!" the brother and sister exclaimed together.

"They're secondhand, but in good shape," the uncle reported.

In minutes, they were out in the yard, wobbling back and forth with great determination. By lunch, they were doing very well. Rhonda hauled out her own bicycle and did a fast spin around them, before Kathy called them in to wash up. While they were sitting at the table, she asked her mom the big question: "After we clean up the kitchen, can I lead them on a bike ride to the Center?"

Kathy looked to Mark, who answered, "Just don't be getting lost. And be home for chores."

The road stretched out before them. Careful to keep single file, the trio traveled from one spot to another, with Rhonda as tour guide. Their first stop was at an intersection where Lee River Road met Browns Trace Road. Before they turned right toward Jericho Center, the girl explained the history of Browns Trace. "This is named after the first folks to settle hereabouts. The Browns got captured by Indians and a whole bunch of stuff happened, but they got back and started all over again." There was a wave of her hand to the left. "If you go that way, you can find where they lived back then. But today, we're going to the Center."

"Wow!" Eddie exclaimed. "Captured by Indians, huh? Did they get scalped?"

Rhonda rose to her position as expert. "I don't know about that, but," she chirped, "there's a lot of famous people who lived here in Jericho." She turned at the waist from her straddled stance as she steadied the bike. Looking back at the two listeners, she went into full performance. "Have you ever heard of Snowflake Bentley?" The siblings nodded their no. "Well, he was a perfesser who took thousands of pictures of snowflakes, and guess what? Not one of them looked the same as any other. He proved all snowflakes look different."

The bike ride recommenced, leaving the Lee River behind. Rhonda pointed out houses and the view of Mt. Mansfield and then another river to their right. "Browns River," she called out over her shoulder — and then they were in Jericho Center. The lead bike came to a stop in front of a two-story building on their left, set back away from the road. "Here's where you start school on Monday," she announced. "This is Jericho High School." The two looked at the clapboard building's wide front doors, and swallowed hard. A new school. They hadn't thought about that. Rhonda pointed to a one-story building just left of the school. "And that's the gym." Again, the Roth siblings gulped. Gym classes with new people... who knows what that will be like? "Both buildings have a really neat, old stone foundation. I think it's slate, but I'm not from Vermont, so I'm not sure."

The Home kids peered more closely. "Yup. It looks like flat pieces of slate," Jenny spoke up, hoping she was right. Actually, it didn't matter, because the tour guide was moving on.

Farther down the street lined with budding maple trees, she came to a stop in front of the Jericho Center Country Store, leaning her bike against the building. Jenny and Eddie followed suit. Inside the store, the two newcomers stared in fascination, until Rhonda revealed that their Uncle Mark had furnished enough loose change for each of them to buy a Fudgesicle. They went outside to lick the things down to the flat wooden stick, all the while listening to Rhonda talk about the village green across the street.

"Now, that's the Congregational Church on the left of the circle. There's a sign that says it was built in 1863, or thereabouts." She leaned forward, to point out the building where the first high school was supposed to have been. "They had different names for those schools back then," she pronounced wisely through her pale, creamy chocolate mustache. "I can't remember all of it, but there's a lot of history right here in the Center."

"Like what else?" Eddie was licking the wooden stick, already.

She grinned. "Well, like, when they first had this village green, some pig farmer let his hogs root and roll around on it, like it was a pigpen, or something."

Eddie enjoyed that thought for a moment, then threw the stick into the trash barrel at the side of the store's front door. "So, what's next?"

Jenny was wiping the drippings off her blouse. "Wait a minute. What time is it? We have to get back in time for chores."

"Let's head back," Rhonda suggested. "I have only one more place to stop. It's on the way."

Somewhere along the Browns River, right there in the old mill district of the Center, she slipped completely off the bike, letting it down carefully in the roadside grass. Jenny and Eddie followed, curious as to what the girl was up to. Immediately, Rhonda pulled a y-shaped stick from her dungaree pocket, shaking out the attached heavy rubber band.

"Hey! You got a slingshot?" Fourteen-year-old Eddie was instantly captivated.

"Yup," came the nonchalant answer, as she drew forth a handful of stones from her other pocket.

The crumbling stone foundation of some long-forgotten mill was being sculpted by the roaring spring waters. In the midst of this noisy, unrelenting onslaught, a high rock stood, its saber-like top dry and bright in the sun.

The tour guide took a step closer to the edge of the river, then pointed to this huge white target several yards away. "See that rock?" She made sure they saw it, then turned back to lift the weapon. "Watch this." A stone was placed on the rubber sling, then she drew it back, took aim, and let the band go. A sharp ping accompanied the puff of white residue that rose from the large stone. The impact was surprisingly violent. Something inside Jenny's being actually cringed.

"Wow! That's something else!" Eddie turned to his sister. "Isn't that something?"

But Jenny did not answer.

Rhonda demonstrated her skills for a few minutes more, and then, of course, Eddie wanted to try it. "Heck no," the shooter replied. "You'd probably pop a rock into your own eye." She put the slingshot into her pocket. "But, tell you what, mister, I'll show you how to do it without hurting yourself... after school or something. How's that?"

"Is that okay with your folks?" Jenny wondered.

"Sure. I give slingshot lessons all the time."

"To everyone? I mean, to girls, too?"

"I would, but girls don't seem to be interested."

"Well, *I* might be."

Something changed on Rhonda's countenance. "Really? Well, I guess I probably could do that. We'll see."

With that half-hearted promise, the three teenagers moved on down the road toward home.

It wasn't until after her prayers and Rhonda had once again trailed in from another lengthy stay in the bathroom, that Jenny thought to ask, "So, Rhonda, if you moved here from Texas, how do you know so much about Jericho?"

There was an attempt to be casual. "Oh, we've been here over a year, now. And I have friends who like to study that stuff."

"Oh yeah? What friends? Somebody from school?"

"Uh-huh." Jenny thought it was just a Texas drawl, but Rhonda's reply was purposefully vague.

"So do I get to meet them? What are their names?"

This time it was an exasperated sigh.

"Kids in Mr. Taft's Vermont History class. Sometimes we go on field trips." She yanked the covers up to her chin. "Okay, no more questions. I need to go to sleep."

Jenny was a surprised at Rhonda's prickly put-down... like maybe there was a whole lot more to the story. Suddenly, Jenny felt that inner cringe, again; Rhonda was a bit scary. Or maybe just hard to live with. Or maybe she had a secret.

"*But never mind,*" the soon-to-be-sixteen year old thought. "*That describes most of the kids in the Home.*" It was nothing new, so she rolled over and closed her eyes.

But it took a while before she finally dozed off, because of the thudding coming from above the ceiling.

CHAPTER THREE

Secrets

On Sunday morning, Eddie and Jenny were also surprised to learn that their new family didn't go to church; it was just another work day on the ranch, except what they claimed was their usual late Sunday morning breakfast. At the table, Jenny asked if she could earn some money to buy postage stamps so she could write to her sister, Donna, and to her German-born friend, Essie. Kathy said it would be nice to have someone help with the ironing, and so it was arranged. Jenny wrote her first two letters that afternoon. Each one was a page long, filled with hope, although she did mention the odd noises coming from the attic. At the end, almost like an afterthought, she added a cautious word about Rhonda's odd moods:

"She's sort of like a chameleon. It's hard to know who she really is. Sorry to say, I don't trust 'chameleon' people."

On Monday morning, Uncle Mark drove them to school, where the two registered and took seats in classrooms filled with new faces. That discomfort was somewhat alleviated in the last class of the day, however, when Jenny took her seat in Mr. Taft's Vermont History class. She recognized him immediately, for he had always reminded her of the cowboy movie star, Roy Rogers... only, shorter and his eyes were more beady than twinkly. He was an alumnus of the Children's Home. She dug deeply into her memory for that one, coming to the conclusion that he'd been one of the older boys, just a few years older than Donna. Suddenly, she was filled with hope. "If some kid from the Children's Home can leave that place and become a real honest-to-goodness teacher, well then, so can I." She didn't really want to be a teacher, but that wasn't the point.

After class, she approached him. "Excuse me, Mr. Taft, but aren't you Walter Taft who used to live in the Children's Home in Burlington?"

He tilted his head in surprise. "Why yes, I am." He looked more closely at the girl. "Have we met before, Jenny?"

"More likely, you'd remember my older sister, Donna Roth."

A light came on. "Oh my goodness! Of course I remember Donna. I had a big crush on her!"

She laughed out loud. "On *Donna*?" When he nodded, she laughed again. "You know what she is now? She's a telephone operator in Burlington, and she has to be all nice and polite to everybody over the phone. Can you believe that?"

"Still the feisty little lady, I take it?"

"Heck, yes! She's even on the company's softball team."

"Oh, is that so?" He squinted. "Let's see... she would be around nineteen now, so that sounds about right."

"How did you guess her age?"

"Because I'm twenty-four, and I was five years older than her."

"Oh."

Rhonda's glaring face appeared in the classroom's doorway. "Hey!" she yelled at Jenny. "You gonna take the bus, or," she bumped her fist against the doorjamb as she said, "*walk home*?"

Jenny snatched her books. "Coming." She paused at the door to say one more thing. "I think it's great what you have done. I hope sometime you will tell me how you did it."

Rhonda grabbed her arm, shot a curious look at her teacher,

than yanked the new kid in school right straight out to the waiting school bus.

***

Five days later, twelve students who were fortunate enough to have bicycles participated in the last spring bike tour — they were always on a Saturday — during which time, Mr. Taft opened their eyes to some rather troubling tidbits of local history. The group had taken a break, relaxing in a semicircle on a patch of spring grass sloping down to the banks of Browns River. It was a question from one of the youngsters that opened the can of worms.

"Whatcha doing this summer, teacher?"

"Studying for my master's," he answered, blinking in the faint April sunshine.

"Oh, I know what that is," a fellow named Andrew piped up. "You have to write a paper or something, right?"

"Right. It's called a thesis."

"Yup. That's what it's called. My big brother wrote one about horse breeding in the United States. He wants to be a vet. I don't know why he needs to have a master's for that, but he did it, anyways." The youngster was curious. "So, what're *you* writing about?"

"The History of Secret Societies."

All eyes fastened on the teacher.

"What are you talking about?" Andrew asked. "You mean, like in the college frat houses?"

Mr. Taft leaned back on one arm. "Well, they are included, for sure, but it goes way back before the fraternities and sororities, believe me."

"What the heck is a secret society?" one of the girls asked.

Andrew was ready to show off a bit. "Aw, you have to swear allegiance and never tell the secret password and the secret handshake... that sorta thing."

Mr. Taft smiled, again. "That's part of it, but there is really a lot more involved, and some of it is very serious stuff. I wouldn't recommend it, myself."

"Why not?" the same girl asked. "Do they do scary things to you?"

"I heard they might make you eat worms," Andrew said with a snicker.

"I heard that was part of the initiation ceremony," another boy added.

The rest of the group waited for Mr. Taft to take the lead. He pursed his lips, then sat up cross-legged. "Okay, listen. Secret societies always involve more than keeping secrets and keeping other people on the outside of their exclusive club. They always involve rituals." He glanced around to be sure they were all listening. "I prefer to use the word 'rituals,' rather than 'ceremonies,' simply because 'rituals' seems to denote something of a deeper, darker nature when it comes to secretive activities." There was a faint smile. "So, please indulge me as I make that distinction. I feel that any ceremony that must be performed in secret, well, it has a more sinister nature. After all, an open celebration, like a birthday party, is a lot different than an initiation into the depths of hidden practices and secret promises." The teacher was encouraged by the rapt attention of his class. "I seriously, *seriously* advise you to avoid those types of organizations."

The girl was right on top of it. "So, can you tell us who these guys are?"

"Um..." He was reluctant, but they deserved an answer. "Listen, I don't want to make anybody mad, but they're all pretty well-known, right here in Chittenden County, and yeah, all over the United States." There was a quick biting of the bottom lip. "I'm sorry to say, the Grange is one of them." The collective gasp was mostly from the girls. "I know, I know. The Grange does a lot of good in the rural areas of our country, but they do participate in rituals, and those rituals involve the honoring of ancient goddesses." He noted all the open mouths, but kept going, citing the Grange's involvement with four female Greek and Roman deities. "There's Ceres, the Roman goddess of grains — that's where we get the word, cereal — and Pomona, also a member the Roman Dil Consentse, who is fruit producer and protector. Then there is another Roman, Flora, goddess of flowers, and of course, Demeter, who is the Greek goddess of the harvest."

The girl challenged him. "So what? It's only pretend."

"Is it? Tell you what: I'll let you be the judge: Four real women 'become' these goddesses during the rituals. They take their place, speak for them, and act for them. It may be just pretending, but it's very likely a lot more real than they all think."

She was persistent. "Well, if they're just pretending, it doesn't mean anything."

"Unless," Jenny suddenly interrupted, "those goddesses are like ghosts or something, and they can come and make trouble." She turned to Mr. Taft. "Do we have any granges in Vermont?"

"Yes. The first one was in St. Johnsbury, around 1871 or so, and there are granges all over the state now, still performing rituals involving these goddesses." His next words came solemnly. "You have a good point, Jenny, because these deities, if they were real, would have been operating for all this time, right under our Vermont noses."

Rhonda needed to get into this conversation. "Wow, Mr. Taft! That's a disturbing thought." She cleared her throat and tossed her dark hair in the sunlight. "It makes me wonder where all these secret rituals and stuff came from." She winked at him. "I just bet you know that answer, too."

The rest of the group saw the flirting, the boys gleefully snorting, the girls rolling their eyes, but the teacher came through it with a straight face and a straight answer. "Like a lot of these secret societies, the Grange based its rites and rituals on those of Freemasonry."

Andrew was suddenly alert. "Hey! You talking about the Masons?" When Walter Taft nodded affirmatively, the boy exclaimed, "My grandpa is a Mason. You saying my grandpa worships goddesses?"

"I don't know about your grandpa," Mr. Taft wisely replied, "but the Masons recognize all forms of religion and respect their various gods, because that's their goal: They want everybody to get along, and nobody's religion is right or wrong."

"What's wrong with that?" the grandson wanted to know.

"It means they don't believe there's one true God," a boy's voice said quietly. The others turned to look at Eddie. "Well, it *does*," he insisted.

Mr. Taft needed to wrap up this delicate subject, for the afternoon was nearly gone. "I think we can just leave it at this: The Masons deal with all sorts of gods, including ancient ones, and this is evident in their secret practices. Just stay away from it."

"But they do so much good," Andrew objected.

The rattle of a rusty truck drew the small group's attention as it slowly passed on the road. Mr. Taft waited until it was quiet again before answering Andrew's comment. "I know they do, and we are all glad about that, Andrew. But these folks don't have to be secretive about their other activities. That's the part that bothers me." He rose slowly, glancing at his watch. "It seems to be more about having power and superiority over all the others — the outsiders who don't belong inside those sacred walls — than anything else. You know, these organizations are all over the world, and they have been out there for centuries... the elite. They see themselves as the special ones who possess special knowledge — just for them." He addressed the whole group. "That's a very telling thing, about the nature of man, don't you think?" Seeing they still didn't quite get it, he went a step further.

"Look, they seem to be a good thing, but they are hiding the fact that they are something bad, as well. The reality is, they switch back and forth, according to what they need to look like at any moment, always making sure they appear good at all times. They're like sophisticated versions of chameleons, changing color whenever they need to hide something from the general public." He wasn't sure they got it yet, but it was time to draw this outing to an end.

The youngsters mounted their bikes in silence, then followed their teacher back to the school's parking lot, where their folks were waiting to load bikes and head out in all directions of Jericho township.

Sure enough, on the way home those parents got an earful. It birthed a disturbance down deep in their bones.

***

It was also around that same time in April when Uncle Mark was forced to investigate the thumping and bumping that seemed to be coming from the attic. The noise had not stopped since Jenny and Eddie's first night, somewhere around the last week of March. He checked out the roof first, and there were no flapping shingles nor bumping slats in the round vents at each end of the attic... at least not that could be seen from the outside of the building. He came down the ladder for the last time, early on a Thursday evening. Eddie and the three ladies were waiting. "Well," he drawled like a cowboy, "looks like I'm gonna hafta take a good look inside the attic." He wiped the end of his nose with the back of his hand. "Probably some critters." He shook his head. "I hate dealing with critters."

The three youngsters didn't get to watch him check out the attic the next morning, because it was a school day. Furthermore, there was a delay in their getting home that afternoon because the bus was late picking up the kids after school. It was two miles down the road, with a flat tire. Some of the students piled into the gym for a quick game of basketball. Others stepped outside for some batting practice. The rest hung out to talk near the wide front steps. Jenny however, sought out Mr. Taft, who was still at his desk.

"Could I bother you for a minute?" she asked.

"Sure. What's up?"

"I just wondered how you got to be a teacher. How did that happen?"

His Roy Rogers smile crinkled the crow's feet to the outer edges of his eyes. "I joined the Army and got the GI Bill. After I got out, I went to UVM, and now, here I am!"

"What's the GI Bill?"

As he was explaining it, Rhonda walked in. She looked at him, then at Jenny, before sauntering up to get in on the conversation. "You planning on going to college, Jenny?"

"Boy-oh-boy, I sure would like to!"

"Well, it's not that simple." The light brown eyes revealed a mocking spirit. "You have to join the Army, kiddo, and you know what they say about women in the Army..."

"No, I don't, but it doesn't matter, because Mr. Taft says women can join the Navy or the Air Force, or even probably the Coast Guard, before too much longer." She gave her history teacher a quick salute. "Thanks, Mr. Taft. That's what I needed to know." She grabbed her books and headed for the whine of the school bus engine.

But Rhonda was not happy. She decided Jenny was getting to be a royal pain in the butt. Still, the Texas cowgirl figured she could stay a minute longer at the teacher's desk. After all, those kids had to put away all that gym equipment before they could get on the bus. She had a few minutes to spare, and she intended to make every second count, for Mr. Taft was far more than just one of her teachers, and she wanted to be sure he was aware of that. There was a slight batting of the eyelashes as she prepared to say something, but Walter was looking out the window and grinning. The frustrated flirt turned to see what was so amusing. It was Eddie, making funny faces at the girls on the front steps. Suddenly, Rhonda didn't like Eddie so much, either.

Evening chores were late because of the tardy school bus, and so supper was just before bedtime. During the meal, Mark let the young ones know he'd checked out the attic, and there was nothing up there except for a bunch of dusty furniture. "I figure it can't be squirrels, 'cause they're not night critters. Most likely coons or a feral cat or maybe even rats thumping around."

"So, how are they getting up there in the attic?" Eddie asked.

"I'm still trying to figure that one out, son." The man pushed away from the table. "Meantime, don't be worrying about it." He looked at his watch. "In fact, it's bedtime right now. Get to it!"

Once the trio was upstairs, Kathy turned to her husband. "You didn't tell them about the rocking chair," she whispered.

"And just how do I explain that?" he murmured back. "A rocking chair that starts and stops rocking all on its own. Now tell me, how do I explain that to three impressionable kids?"

***

In May, during the last school bus field trip of the academic year, the subject of secret societies and ancient deities came up, once again. It was the bikers who brought it up, of course, and even though Mr. Taft tried to keep the attention on the little ski village of Stowe, the idea of ancient gods having influence in their communities far out-weighed the fact that the Von Trapp family, who, like Professor Schuler's family, had escaped Nazi Germany. "The Von Trapps now live here in Stowe. I hear Maria is still leading the singing," the history teacher announced. But the kids would not be distracted.

"Are there gods in Stowe, too?"

He tried to soft-pedal it, but the upshot of his answer was "maybe," since he had been told there was a grange in the area, but he hadn't found the time to check it out.

When word of this got to the rest of the students' parents, a cry went up for him to back off. They would not have such things said about their home towns. This teacher's credibility took a serious blow, although no disciplinary action was taken. The man would remain on staff, but under scrutiny.

Jenny made mention of this rather sticky situation in her letters to Essie and Donna, commenting that it could be pretty interesting to see how this history instructor could keep being honest and captivating, and still keep his job. Connie didn't seem to have much to say about the situation, but Essie definitely had some questions in her own letters:

"Wow! Looks like you have lots of drama going on up there. So, how are you getting along at the ranch, itself? Is it big? Do they have a lot of cattle? Is there a garden?"

Jenny wrote back long letters, mentioning the latest on the history teacher's plight, then describing the Lee River, the small herd of cattle, and, of course, all the rumblings of Thunder, himself. She wrote about the big house, and the orchard that covered several acres behind it.

"We have five goats, who keep the orchard mowed. And there's a greenhouse, kind of tattered, because nobody uses it anymore. I guess the trees are different types of apples, but they don't look all that healthy, either. Aunt Kathy said the lady who used to live here was a scientist, or something. Anyway, right now, there are lots of pretty blossoms, and if the bees do their job, and the worms don't take over, we should have some apples in a couple of months. Maybe I will make a pie."

Essie wrote back:

"I am curious about your Mr. Taft's situation. It could get interesting. Keep me posted on that one, for sure. As for the neglected apple trees, there're usually a few good apples. I have not made an apple pie, but it sounds like so much fun. Maybe I could come up and make pies with you on a weekend, sometime. What do you think?"

Jenny decided to see if her friend could come for a visit, just as soon as she felt comfortable asking. *"Surprising, though,"* she thought. *"Essie has never seemed like the pie-making type."*

***

Meanwhile, Rhonda, who had been doing a slow-burn over the last few weeks, was hatching some plans of her own. The presence of the two Roth siblings was more complicated than she had anticipated. Eddie was a nuisance, and Jenny was just too darned cozy with Mr. Taft, and *something* had to be done about that. It would have to be handled carefully, but those two had to be kept under control, one way or another. However, about the third week in May, Jenny announced she'd landed a job at Maude's Nursing Home for the whole summer. The job included board and room, so she'd be staying in the Center for all that time. She apologized for not being there to help with chores at the ranch, but here was a chance to make some money for college tuition, just in case she couldn't get into the Air Force or the Navy. "It works out perfect, since I turn sixteen in June," she explained.

Rhonda was overjoyed to get rid of her competition, even if only for a few weeks, but she had to do something about that pest, Eddie. It wasn't long before she hit upon a plan. Eddie was pretty much in charge of feeding and caring for Thunder, who was held in a spacious enclosure between the barn and the river. It was far enough away to keep Thunder from the cows until breeding season, and there were lots of trees to keep the big guy comfortable whenever he ventured from the shed where he bedded down at night. It was here that Rhonda would execute her plan to put the bothersome boy in his proper place.

She started annoying the bull whenever Eddie was in the area with him, sling-shotting small pellets into Thunder's backside at just the right moment. Hiding behind the trees, she had a free hand to upset the big animal whenever she wished, and that was whenever the boy was in the enclosure and vulnerable to an attack. This activity continued for a few days, until Thunder associated his discomfort with the physical presence of the boy. On the fifth day, Eddie was greeted with a snort and the shaking of that massive head. He looked up, surprised, but then continued his chores. On the sixth day, Rhonda waited until just the right moment, then sent a sizeable stone slamming into the bull's face. The head went down and sharp hooves dug furiously into the ground. Eddie turned to see eighteen hundred pounds of wild rage coming at him, full speed. He barely made it over the metal fence.

"What the heck?" he whispered, wiping the dirt from his clothing.

It was a flicker of color that exposed the girl's flight back toward the house.

Now, Eddie was mad. When he got back to Uncle Mark in the main barn, he told on the girl. Uncle Mark said he would take care of it. The WWII veteran's face flushed with the revelation of his stepdaughter's true nature. "Aw, hell. You sure about that?" Eddie swore he was telling the truth. "Well, I'll be damned," the man said. At the end of the day, Rhonda was forbidden to use her slingshot on the ranch property.

But the damage had been done, for Thunder no longer trusted Eddie. Taking care of that big bull was going to be touchy from then on. Still, Uncle Mark urged him to stand his ground against the prize bovine. "Nobody wants to be a quitter, boy. Make sure he knows you're the boss." The lad wasn't sure how he would be able to do that, but knew better than to argue. After all, Uncle Mark was still at war with all those critters in the attic, and the man's patience was running out.

That very same Friday night, the thumping was heard above the master bedroom.

"What happened when you went up there *this* morning?" she asked her husband.

He sighed. "I got ticked and grabbed the damned thing and tried to take it down from the attic, but it's too big. I couldn't get it down through the door opening."

"What? Then how did it ever get up there, in the first place?"

"I guess it must have been built up there, or taken up in pieces." Another sigh. "I don't really know."

She stared at the ceiling spot where the thumping seemed to be coming from. "So how come *we* can hear it now? Only the kids could hear it before this."

This time there was a low moan. "Aw, I got really frustrated and threw it down this end of the attic."

"Did it break?" She was hopeful.

"Nope. Just rolled over to an upright position, and started the damned rocking, again."

"My god, Mark. What're we going to do?"

He rolled over, his back to her. "First, I'm gonna get some sleep. Then tomorrow I'm gonna go up there and chop the hell out of it."

Connections

Jenny hopped onto her bicycle and headed for Jericho Center the very next morning. She arrived for her job orientation appointment at Maude's Nursing Home precisely at eight thirty, just before shift change at nine o'clock. Mrs. Hannity, the director, led her back to the kitchen. "Alice, here's your brand new helper," the boss called out to the head cook. Alice backed off from the stove and nodded at the girl.

"Alright then, you ready to get to work?"

"Yes, ma'am."

The next few hours flew by; a mixture of dishwashing, loading trays and delivering meals in the dining room, finding linen closets and the right storage areas for pots and soaps, and directions on how to treat the residents in a firm, but kindly manner. It was two o'clock when she finally sat down on the front porch with a cool glass of lemonade. Mrs. Hannity spotted her from the office window and went out to keep her company. "How'd it go, Miss Jenny? Are you holding up okay?"

She laughed. "Yes, ma'am. I'm getting the hang of it."

"Uh-huh. That's good." The fiftyish lady tucked a dyed strand of red hair back behind her ear. "I do have to let you know that the doctor is making rounds today — he usually sets his own schedule — just routine check-ups. He came over this morning, but then he got an emergency call and had to wait to make his rounds here, until this afternoon. Matter of fact, he's here right now."

"Oh!" Jenny sat straight up on the slatted bench. "Should I hop to it, then?"

"No-no. This is only your orientation day. Anyway, it's not all that complicated; we can cover that on your first real day of work." She leaned back as if to think about what to say next. "But you should probably have a word with the doctor before he leaves."

"Of course. I should meet him. I understand."

"Um, well, that's true, but you need to talk to him about your uncle, Jenny."

"Really! What's up?"

"Your Uncle Mark was the emergency call that Doc got, honey." She turned to explain. "It seems he was chopping wood this morning, and the axe hit a knot or something, and came smashing back against his forehead." She held up a calming hand. "Not the blade, dear, only the back side of the axe head, so..." The woman clasped her hands on her lap. "So, we just need to know if you're going to be needed at home. That would mean you couldn't work here, after all." She forced a smile. "So we just need to hear that from Doc, okay?"

"Sure." The youngster couldn't help wonder why Uncle Mark was chopping wood, since he recently remarked just a few days ago that he ordered the usual two cords from somebody in Essex Center. She decided not to mention this to Mrs. Hannity. Anyway, two ladies were coming up the steps onto the porch, and the director was rising to greet them.

"Hello there, Mrs. Short!" She was obviously addressing the one with the soft brown curls which framed a peachy complexion.

"Oh, please call me Greta," the pleasantly plump woman urged her. Then she turned to her companion. "And this is my friend from church, Connie Collins."

Mrs. Hannity reached out to grasp the school teacher's hand. "Nice to meet you." Noting that Connie's gaze had gone to the young girl who had risen to her feet out of respect for the arriving guests, she quickly introduced Jenny, who nodded graciously, much to the delight of the two visitors. Clearly, this young lady had been brought up with exceedingly good manners. "We're hoping Jenny will be joining our staff for the summer," the director started to explain, stopping because the doctor emerged from the front door onto the porch. "Oh, Doc," she said, "please take a minute to let us know if we get to keep Jenny. Is she needed at home, what with her uncle being injured?"

The two visitors paused, half out of sympathy, half just plain curiosity.

Doc Horton's golden owl eyes peered at the girl through his special order, gold-rimmed glasses. "You his new daughter?"

"Uh, well, I'm his niece, sir."

"Whatever. Doesn't matter." He shifted his doctor bag to the other hand. "I delivered your uncle fifty-some years ago. He grew up stubborn and left for Texas stubborn, and came back last year... just as stubborn. He'll be up and at work first thing in the morning." He moved the crick in his aging neck. "You're good. Be here right after school's out for summer. It'll be fine."

The three ladies smiled broadly.

At the three o'clock shift change, Jenny found herself once again on the front porch, this time taking note of other workers arriving. Surely, she would be working with some of those, as well. This time, she took a seat in the faded porch swing at the south end of the verandah, which was closest to Jericho Center's village green. Suddenly, two somewhat familiar women were leaving the building — Greta Short and Connie Collins. She rose automatically to her feet. "Hello again, ladies!" she called out, with a little wave. The two women exchanged a pleased look, and then came over.

"Got room on that swing for a couple more girls?" Greta asked in her usual robust manner.

"Of course." There was a quick look around. "Tell you what, you two take the swing, and I'll take..." she pulled a small spindled straight chair around to face it. "I'll sit here, so we don't have to crook our necks to talk to each other."

The ladies chuckled and took their seats, relaxing into the cushions.

"I guess you were visiting somebody today," Jenny opened the conversation.

"Oh yes. My mother," Greta informed her. "Her name is Millie. Have you met her yet?"

"Maybe. It's been pretty hectic." The teenager bent forward. "What room is she in?"

"I still haven't memorized the number," Greta confessed, "but it's on the second floor, the last one down the hall, on the back side of the building."

"Oh! The lady who wants a three-minute egg. Got it." Her head nodded as she finished the mental picture. "She seems to have a lot of spunk."

Greta's head jerked backwards with glee. "I guess you could call it that."

Intrigued, Jenny pursued the subject. "If you don't mind me asking, what do you talk about with these patients? I mean, they have lost so much independence. You know, having to wear diapers and all that."

Connie Collins spoke up. "Not all of them have to do that, but, yes, there is a great sense of loss in their lives. So the thing is, visitors have to keep the subject matter on upbeat, hopeful themes."

"That's good, but, well, it has to be hard. Now, for instance — if you don't mind," Jenny carefully asked, "what subject did you choose to talk about today? How did you keep Millie upbeat?"

The ladies exchanged another look.

"We talked about *you*," Greta candidly informed her. "We talked about what good manners you had when we met you and how we wished more young people would know how to be polite and respectful."

Connie was eager to add the details. "And Millie just jumped right in there, about how young people didn't know how to fold a napkin or even use one, for Pete's sake, and that kept her alert and energetic for the whole forty-five minutes."

"Wow. That's very interesting. I need to remember that," Jenny murmured.

Out on the street, traffic was swishing slowly through a light rain. For a minute, the three sat in silence, then the Christian counselor in Connie prodded her to ask the question. "Yeah, it was an interesting conversation with Millie, but I, personally, am wondering, Jenny: You didn't greet us so well without some proper training. Where did you learn all those good manners? I mean, you must have had extraordinary parents."

The girl was surprised. "Oh, well, thank you, but I didn't get all that from my parents." She paused to figure out a face-saving answer, but there was none, so she just blurted it out. "I was brought up in the Children's Home at 555 Shelbu —"

The gasp of the two women interrupted her.

"Oh my goodness," they seemed to say together.

Greta took her usual lead. "That's just around the corner from our church on Swift Street. We are very familiar with that location."

"My-oh-my," Connie declared, "isn't it a small world? Who would have thought we would come across one of the young ladies who actually grew up there?"

Jenny suddenly remembered another connection to the Home. "Speaking of a small world, I can top that one. Would you believe one of my teachers here in Jericho also grew up at the Children's Home?"

"No!" Connie exclaimed. "I'm just finishing my first year of teaching at Essex Junction High School, and we had a meeting with your coach about girls' basketball games." She tilted her silvery head to one side. "Maybe I've met her."

Jenny smiled softly. "Actually, it's a man, and Mr. Taft only coaches the boys' team." She hastened to point out that he also taught Vermont History.

"I see," Connie replied, "but it happens that he was there, also. And I do recall commenting on how we teachers serve triple duty. I teach Social Studies, conduct gym classes, and oversee the cheerleading program."

"They wear a lot of hats," Greta concurred.

"I'm beginning to see that," the teenager replied. "Mr. Taft is also studying for his master's this summer. He's doing a paper on secret societies."

The ladies' eyes showed a spiked interest.

"Do you know exactly what secret societies he's studying, dear?" Greta asked carefully.

"He mentioned the Grange, and that they take their lead from the Freemasons."

"They let him teach that?" Greta was suspicious.

"No-no. He just happened to mention it on one of our bike trips." She sucked her lips into a tight line. "He paid the price for that. Got reprimanded. I'm guessing he could lose his job, if the kids don't stop talking about all that."

Another car splashed by, drawing their attention back to the steady drizzle.

***

Walt Taft was in trouble. The school board was mad at him, and the parents were even angrier. Still, he knew down deep, he was not going to stop doing his thesis on secret societies. It was a hot topic, and one that would probably get him a good grade, unless his supervising professor was a Mason, or a Rosicrucian, or the like. There was no turning back for him, regardless. The research would go on.

But first, he needed to narrow the focus of this thing. Others had done research on secret societies, so he needed to approach it from a different angle. Perhaps Jenny's observation about goddesses being ghosts was the way to go. The idea appealed to him, and eventually he settled on studying the possibility that ancient gods and goddesses could be living entities, and if so, having great influence on society, itself. "Actually, societies all over the world," he finally told himself. The young man dived right into those dangerous waters.

Days went by before he finally drew a deep breath and took a break. He looked around the tiny house he was renting there in Jericho Center. It was suddenly too quiet. He stood there, gazing out the bedroom window, slowly realizing there was something lacking in his personal life. It had been too singular, too lonely. He needed a companion, like a parrot or a dog or something. Several more days passed before he finally thought about the feisty Donna Roth. That thought turned into a fantasy that wouldn't quit, with glimpses of her as a fourteen-year-old Amazon, dodging the fearful arrows of abandonment, fighting for her own identity. So young. So pretty. So strong. One morning he arose with the desire to pursue this long-neglected friendship. But how to contact her? "Oh yeah, Jenny mentioned she was on the phone company's softball team."

On the same Saturday morning Jenny was chatting with the ladies on the nursing home porch, he made a call to the telephone company, getting the date of the next softball game. At two o'clock that afternoon, he took a seat in the bleachers of a small Burlington park. Dark clouds were closing in on the sunlight, but he spotted her coming toward the dugout with the rest of her team. "Aw crap," a nearby fan moaned, "they're calling the game. Too much rain on the way."

Walter had to think quickly, or he would miss this opportunity. He was at the dugout before she was, posing casually against the backstop webbing behind the catcher's plate. When she got close enough, he called out, "Hey! Is that you, Donna?"

The young woman stopped, squinting to see who was addressing her.

"Over here!" he yelled, waving a hand.

The athletic softball pitcher tucked her glove under her arm and approached the man. "Yeah?"

"Hey! You look great!" He waited for her to come closer. "It's me, Walter Taft." When she paused to focus, he moved toward her, reaching for a handshake. "Gosh, I don't know if you even remember me, but we were in the Home together."

Her mouth dropped open in recognition. The glove dropped to the ground as she reached out for a hug. "Oh my gosh, Walter! Oh my gosh!"

The embrace lasted longer than either one of them had intended.

***

The rain was falling steadily on Roth Ranch, driving the cattle to seek shelter under whatever trees they could find. Thunder, of course, had his pick from a whole grove of weeping willows, where he moseyed happily along, licking the occasional dribble off his wide nostrils. Mark Roth had already plowed the cornfield, so it was collecting rivulets of moisture in the furrows, in preparation for planting season. The soil was fragrant and fresh even at the edge of the large farmhouse porch, where Kathy and Mark were sitting, taking it all in. There was no conversation, just the gentle splashing of rainwater from the downspout on the outside of the railing. She sat with hands folded in her lap. No sense in asking the man how he was feeling — a bloody bandage above the pale face pretty much told the story.

The humming of a station wagon's engine announced its arrival just before it rounded the birches near the driveway. The Roths peered more closely, noting this was an unfamiliar vehicle. As it drew to a stop in front of the porch, they were surprised to see Jenny slide out, then hold the door open for a silver-haired woman. The car engine stopped as the two approached the steps. A moment later, Jenny was introducing Connie Collins and Greta Short.

"We just couldn't let this dear girl peddle all that way home in the rain," Greta explained, "especially since I had the station wagon right there." She pantomimed the next part. "So, we threw the bike in the back and trundled on up here."

"That was very nice of you, ladies," Kathy said. "Now, do you have time for a cup of tea and some cookies?"

The ladies were delighted, following her into the kitchen to help. Jenny turned to her uncle. "I'll get the bike out of the car, and then get out to help Eddie and Rhonda with chores. Are they in the barn?"

"Ay-yuh," he winced as he spoke.

She paused before going down the steps. "I'm so sorry you got hurt, Uncle Mark. Doc said you were chopping wood or something?" She wanted to hear it from his own lips.

"Ay-yuh, in a manner of speaking."

She let it go at that. Slipping out into the rain, she pulled the bike from the car and quickly wheeled it into the barn.

"Stop it! Stop it! I mean it, Rhonda. Keep away from me, you hear?" It was Eddie's frantic voice. Jenny looked up toward the swishing sound in the hay loft. There was a feminine laugh. "Stop it, or I'll belt you one, girl!" the boy yelled. This time it was a little girl's giggle.

Jenny let the bike fall to the floor. "Eddie? Eddie!" She was headed for the ladder to the loft. "Eddie!" She could hear more shuffling through the hay, then a howl.

"You pig!" Jenny recognized her roommate's shrieking. "Don't you ever try that again, you pig," the accusation went on. As Jenny's head cleared the top of the ladder, Rhonda came crashing toward her, wailing and crying. "Your little brother just tried to rape me, that pig." She pulled Jenny up from the ladder. "I'm telling," she sniffled out the words, "I'm telling." She kept the sniffling all the way down to the last rung.

By then, Eddie was at Jenny's side, face pale and sweaty. "Just the other way around," he panted as he tried to tuck the back of his shirt in. "She's *crazy*."

Jenny stepped to the edge of the loft. "Rhonda! Your folks have company. Now is not a good time to put on a big scene." Seeing the stepdaughter hesitate, she added the clincher: "I heard you giggling, and I will swear to it on the Bible... in court... in front of a judge and jury." She finished that threat as she climbed back down to the floor of the barn. There, she turned and spoke calmly: "You know what? I think we'd better get our chores done."

It wasn't long before the ladies and Mark had finished the tea and cookies, but a lot of conversation had taken place. In that process, it was discovered that Mark had actually been injured trying to chop up an old rocker in the attic. Greta's eyes sparkled at the thought of another antique find. "How old do you think it is?"

Mark shrugged. "Don't know, but it's too big to get through the attic door, anyway." He anticipated the next question. "Must have been put together up there, I guess."

Greta was even more interested. "Really? Oh my goodness! That is *so* intriguing."

"Greta collects rare antiques," Connie chortled to the Roths. "I swear, she would sell their business, the G and G Driving School, to own an oversized rocking chair, if it was a genuine antique."

"She's right. I probably would." Greta bent toward her hostess. "Oh, Kathy, do you suppose I could just take a look at it?"

Kathy looked to her husband who shrugged, again. "If you do take it," he said, "you'll be responsible to get it down from there." He nodded the go-ahead.

Minutes later, the three women stood in the dimness of the attic. "Sorry about the lights. We just need to put in new bulbs."

"That would help, for sure," Greta commented. "We're in no hurry. We promise to stand still until you get some bulbs. Would that be okay?"

"Oh sure," said the lady who wanted the nightly thumping to go away. "They're right down there in the linen closet."

As the two church ladies stood waiting under the rhythmic dance of rain on the roof overhead, their eyes became accustomed to the lack of illumination. Slowly, various pieces of furniture took shape from the darkness. There was a spindle-legged table with two books on it, a stack of eight or ten armless chairs, and what appeared to be a carpet rolled up and tucked into the snug space where the overhead beams slanted down to touch the outer edges of the attic floor. Five small boxes were pushed to one end of the attic, while the other end held the object of their curiosity. When Kathy got the two bulbs installed, their light revealed a large rocker, stained a dark shade of red. As the two shoppers moved closer, they discerned a delicate gold scrolling trim on the back and armrests, obviously amateurish, but still beautiful. When Greta reached out to wipe the dust off the trim, she was surprised by a loud crackling. "Ouch!" She drew her hand back, shaking it and rubbing the tips of her fingers. "That felt like an electric shock," she exclaimed.

Kathy didn't know what to say, so she lied. "We get a lot of electrical storms here on the ranch. We probably should check on the lightning rod. It could be sending the charge through this attic."

"So that would mean there must be metal of some sort in the rocker, itself." Greta's brows tightened before she bent to examine the rockers. "Hmm, I don't see any burn marks." She stood back up. "I'd like to research this for a couple of days, and then get back to you. Would that be alright with you?"

"Of course. And if you want it, you'll need to find a way to dismantle it." Kathy smiled apologetically. "Obviously, chopping it apart isn't working."

Connie did not speak up until the station wagon was all the way back to Jericho Corners. By then, there was a real rainstorm. Even though she was driving through a downpour, Greta glanced over at her friend. "Something on your mind, Connie?"

"Oh yes. Something is very much on my mind." She tapped the purse on her lap a couple of times. "Did you by any chance notice the two books on that table?"

"Nope. Too interested in the rocker."

"Well, I did." She shot a look of alarm to the driver. "Just keep your eyes on the road, though."

"Sorry."

"So, what I saw was two very old books." Her jaw went hard. "Too dusty to get the titles, but I definitely saw the word, 'witchcraft' on one of them, and there was some ancient deity pictured on the front of the other one." She shivered. "And that was no electrical shock that you felt. Lightning rods don't work that way."

"Okay, my friend, let's have it. What are you thinking?"

Connie Collins waited for Greta to pull out onto Vermont Highway 15, heading for Winooski and Burlington. The rain was now pelting the windshield, so Connie held her tongue until Greta increased the speed of the wipers. Then the silvery-haired lady spoke it out: "That chair didn't zap *you*. That was *you* zapping the *chair*."

"What? How do you figure that?"

"Okay, so maybe I should say, that was you zapping the spirit who was hanging around that chair."

Greta respected her friend's extensive experience in such matters. "You got that from those two books, right?"

"They alerted me, but when the *Holy* Spirit in you shot fire into that *un*holy spirit's personal space, I knew."

"Are you telling me, um, I'm trying to buy a haunted rocking chair?"

"Oh, I'm telling you more than that, my friend. I'm telling you that whole attic is probably an old gathering place for occult activity."

"Oh my," Greta whispered, "you just knocked me flat on my fanny. I need to really think about this."

And then, there was only the cadence of windshield wipers, marking, marking, marking the moment.

CHAPTER FIVE

Investigations

It was almost five o'clock that same Saturday evening. Walter Taft gazed across the Formica tabletop at Howard Johnson's restaurant out on Burlington's Shelburne Road. Donna was even more beautiful than he had remembered, in spite of the crumpled baseball cap and the smudge of dirt on one cheek. He had almost forgotten those Elizabeth Taylor eyes. Indeed, he was glad she had agreed to let him drive her home from the cancelled ball game, and glad she agreed to stop for a milkshake at this familiar landmark. She twisted slightly to spot the corner of Flynn Avenue, just south of where they sat. "I used to walk down that street to Champlain School," she reminisced, "from the time I was eight years old, until I started taking the bus to Edmunds High School."

He nodded. "In my case, I started taking that bus as soon as I came to the Home. I was fifteen."

"Really? So you were only in that place for three years? I thought it was longer than that." Her index finger tapped the top of the straw in her drink. "I'm surprised you even remember me; all you older kids were pretty tight." She took a small sip. "I probably shouldn't tell you this, but I thought you were so-o-o good looking." She laughed softly. "Do you know how much you look like Roy Rogers?"

He could feel the pleasure flush to the surface of his cheeks. "I have been told that, yes."

"And do you always blush like that, when it happens?" She was amused.

He pulled at his open shirt collar. "Nah, I really don't." He decided to flirt a bit. "Guess it takes a pretty girl to get me all flustered."

She laughed out loud. "Flattery!" He saw the shield go up. "Well, okay, I'll take a little flattery," she said, bending to take another creamy draw of the shake.

It was time to change to a lighter subject. "So, what have you been doing since you got out into the big, busy world?"

"Telephone operator. I love it, and I love being on the softball team." Her tongue slipped slowly across the bottom lip, catching runaway foam. "My next goal is to buy a car."

"Good for you. How close are you to accomplishing this lofty target?"

"Matter of fact, I'm looking at a couple of possibilities right now. If things work out, I should be a proud car owner within two weeks."

"Good for you." He had a sudden thought. "I have a friend who works at a used car dealership, right here in town. I would be glad to accompany you." He grinned. "Nothing like having a friend of the salesman along with you, to make sure you don't end up with a lemon." The brows went up. "What do you say? Could you use some help?"

She studied the top of the shiny table, before looking up. "You sure you wouldn't mind? I mean, I don't really know anything about cars..."

"I'm free every weekend," he reminded her.

"Are you? I thought you were busy writing a thesis, or something."

"I am doing that, but to tell the truth, things are getting a tad touchy concerning that matter. I could use a break."

"Yeah, I heard about your neighbors and the school board. Man, you sure stirred up a nest of hornets. How's it going? You been fired, yet?"

There was that sassy spunk, again. She was still the same little fighter. "Not yet. But I may have to move to the Bible Belt by next year."

"Oh gawd, I wouldn't wish *that* on *anybody*," she snapped. The surprise on his face brought her to a quick disclaimer. "Not that I don't believe in a spiritual world, or anything. But you're messing with some pretty big egos — the Masons are very powerful, I hear."

"Hmm, so you know more about this than I thought. Must be Jenny's been keeping you posted."

"Her and the Roths. Mark and Kathy."

He was surprised, again. "Oh! Right. Mark and Kathy are your uncle and aunt." His head rotated from left to right. "I guess you must know the daughter, Rhonda, then."

There was a ladylike snort. "Oh yeah, I know Rhonda. Boy oh-boy, talk about a handful."

"Is that right?" he asked carefully. "You must have known these folks for quite a while."

Donna took a long sip, sloshing it around in her mouth while deciding how to explain the situation. It went down in a lump, so she belched politely before she spoke. "Uncle Mark arrived in January of last year, bought the ranch and then had Kathy and Rhonda and his prize bull, Thunder, all arrive together a few weeks later. Then they approached Mrs. Bushey about taking all three of us kids to live with them. I was suspicious, because of my mom's will — us kids stand to get a pretty good sum, once she dies. So I asked if I could just make a few visits to the ranch to see how it felt. Of course, Mrs. Bushey and I thought it best that Jenny and Eddie not be aware. We didn't want them to get their hopes up."

"I see. And how many visits did it take for you to decide not to live there? Obviously, you never *did*."

The crafty investigator got a knowing look in her eyes. "I visited maybe six times over the next few months, and sure enough, I found out that all three of them were aware of my mom's will. Still, it wasn't the deciding factor in my choice. It was the petulant princess who sealed the deal."

"Rhonda?" The baseball cap moved in affirmation. "So what happened?"

"Had to be the center of attention, the favored child, and absolutely not to be outdone in any manner whatsoever. It was something else."

"How did you manage the problem?"

"I didn't. When that twerp found out I could throw a mean softball, she challenged me to a target contest — her with a slingshot, me with my pitcher's arm." He watched the competitive gleam fill those lovely lavender-blue eyes. "Only, she wouldn't let me use my softball, because it was bigger than her stones. Instead, she insisted that I only use the same size rocks that she did."

"You mean, you threw the rocks with your pitcher's arm?"

"That's exactly what I did." She pushed her cap back on her head and leaned toward Walter. "There were six empty aluminum cans lined up on the wood stack, and we paced back about fifteen steps, drew a line and took our places." She scrunched her shoulders like Rhonda had done that day. "Then she says, 'I go first.'"

"I bet she aced it," Walter ventured. "I hear she's a crack shot."

"Actually, she missed two cans."

"No kidding? And how'd you do?"

"I got all six." She smiled with satisfaction. "The big poophead was furious. I decided right then and there, I didn't need this in my life. I could get a good job and take care of myself." A slight shadow crossed her countenance. "On the other hand, Jenny and Eddie couldn't do that, and here they finally had a chance to get out of the Home..." Her gaze met Walter's, almost apologetically. "I just thought they might be okay, because they've learned to get along with so many maladjusted kids, you know?"

It was past six-thirty in the evening when he finally dropped her off in front of the Winooski Avenue apartment. Walter leaned just slightly toward her. "I'm so glad I caught up with you, Donna Roth."
She was quietly pleased. "Me, too."
"Does that mean I can go with you when you buy a car?"
She seemed to be even more pleased. "I guess that would be fine." She reached for the door handle.
"Wait! Wait!" He was out of the car and around to open her door before she could figure it out.
"A gentleman always opens the door for a lady," he whispered loudly.
"Oh." She slid out. "Thank you."
"May I walk you to your door, miss?"
She laughed out loud. "Oh, for Pete's sake, no, you don't have to do that."
"Very well, miss," he replied as he leaned against the car. "But I will stay right here until I'm sure you get all the way there without being attacked by a slingshot."
They were both laughing as she walked to the door, waved, and went inside.

Walter Taft stood there against the car for a moment longer, enjoying the fetching way she had just moved up that sidewalk. It was positively bewitching.

**

At the same time Walter was dropping Donna off, the Roth family was sitting down for supper. Both adults noticed the tension right away. All three children kept their eyes on their plates, slowly picking away at the meatloaf and string beans. "Would you like some homemade dill pickles?" Kathy asked. Eddie and his sister politely nodded and took a couple of spears from the cut glass dish, then passed it on to Rhonda, who wrinkled her nose and shoved it off to the side.

Mark took notice of that, but chose to overlook it for the present. He was more interested in the distress on the boy's face. "How's it going with my prize bull, son? You showing him who's boss?"

Eddie smiled weakly. "I'm trying, sir." The eyes went quickly back to the plate in front of him.

"Well, just don't back down. Thunder isn't as smart as you; just remember that."

"Yes, sir." His eyes remained riveted on the dinner plate.

The uncle paused, then reached for a biscuit. His words came slowly, like an actor who had learned how to deliver the next line in the script. "You know, I'm pretty damned proud of the way you jumped in there and learned how to work on this ranch." He spread blackberry jam on the fluffy slice cradled in his palm. "Ay-yuh," he drawled, raising the delicacy to his mouth, "damned pleased with you, boy."

The fourteen-year-old shot a grateful look to his uncle, then bowed down again.

It was time for Kathy to try breaking the silence. "You girls been busy today?" She saw the quick look between the two, followed by noncommittal humming. The woman turned to her husband. "Looks like we all need to pitch in for clean-up tonight."

"Looks like it," he agreed.

After dishes were done, Kathy ushered the two girls upstairs. There in the bedroom, she got the final word on the incident in the barn. Jenny repeated her stand on testifying in court against Rhonda. That was all Kathy needed. She ordered them both into bed, with the admonition that this matter not be revisited, ever again.

Meanwhile, uncle and nephew were having a chat on the front porch. Mark lit up his pipe, asking the question between puffs. "Something going on with you kids?" He wasn't settling for the evasive shrug. Extinguishing the match's flame with the shake of his hand, he pursued the answer. "Those girls giving you a hard time about something?"

Eddie knew he would have to spill the beans, so he cleared his throat and let loose: "Rhonda was chasing me, pulling on my clothes. Good thing Jenny caught her, 'cause I was gonna slug her a good one."

"You were gonna slug Rhonda? Why would you slug a girl?"

"She was pulling my shirt out of my pants, and laughing about it... chasing me in the hay loft."

Uncle Mark looked skeptical, so the boy got defensive. "You can ask Jenny."

"Jenny saw all this? What did she do about it?"

"Told Rhonda she heard her laughing, and it wasn't me trying to rape her — just the other way around. And then she tells her that she'll go to court and swear on the Bible that it wasn't me who was doing wrong."

"Hmm," the man hummed as he drew on his pipe. "So what did Rhonda say to that?"

"Nothing. Jenny just told her we should all get our chores done."

Mark Roth gazed out into the sunset for what seemed a long time. Finally, he leaned forward to address the young man. "I'm thinking Rhonda would have to do a lot of bee-essing to get out of this one, but just in case you're trying to pull the wool over my eyes, I need to remind you of some important facts." He stood up, towering over the kid on the porch swing. "If you ever get any ideas about doing such a thing to that girl, there will be severe consequences. I want to remind you that I am an Army veteran, I suffer from battle fatigue, I have a rifle and a shovel, and... they would never find you."

54

Meanwhile, uncle and nephew were having a chat on the front porch. Mark lit up his pipe, asking the question between puffs. "Something going on with you kids?" He wasn't settling for the evasive shrug. Extinguishing the match's flame with the shake of his hand, he pursued the answer. "Those girls giving you a hard time about something?"

Eddie knew he would have to spill the beans, so he cleared his throat and let loose: "Rhonda was chasing me, pulling on my clothes. Good thing Jenny caught her, 'cause I was gonna slug her a good one."

"You were gonna slug Rhonda? Why would you slug a girl?"

"She was pulling my shirt out of my pants, and laughing about it… chasing me in the hay loft."

Uncle Mark looked skeptical, so the boy got defensive. "You can ask Jenny."

"Jenny saw all this? What did she do about it?"

"Told Rhonda she heard her laughing, and it wasn't me trying to rape her — just the other way around. And then she tells her that she'll go to court and swear on the Bible that it wasn't me who was doing wrong."

"Hmm," the man hummed as he drew on his pipe. "So what did Rhonda say to that?"

"Nothing. Jenny just told her we should all get our chores done."

Mark Roth gazed out into the sunset for what seemed a long time. Finally, he leaned forward to address the young man. "I'm thinking Rhonda would have to do a lot of bee-essing to get out of this one, but just in case you're trying to pull the wool over my eyes, I need to remind you of some important facts." He stood up, towering over the kid on the porch swing. "If you ever get any ideas about doing such a thing to that girl, there will be severe consequences. I want to remind you that I am an Army veteran, I suffer from battle fatigue, I have a rifle and a shovel, and… they would never find you."

---

plates, slowly picking away at the meatloaf and string beans. "Would you like some homemade dill pickles?" Kathy asked. Eddie and his sister politely nodded and took a couple of spears from the cut glass dish, then passed it on to Rhonda, who wrinkled her nose and shoved it off to the side.

Mark took notice of that, but chose to overlook it for the present. He was more interested in the distress on the boy's face. "How's it going with my prize bull, son? You showing him who's boss?"

Eddie smiled weakly. "I'm trying, sir." The eyes went quickly back to the plate in front of him.

"Well, just don't back down. Thunder isn't as smart as you; just remember that."

"Yes, sir." His eyes remained riveted on the dinner plate.

The uncle paused, then reached for a biscuit. His words came slowly, like an actor who had learned how to deliver the next line in the script. "You know, I'm pretty damned proud of the way you jumped in there and learned how to work on this ranch." He spread blackberry jam on the fluffy slice cradled in his palm. "Ay-yuh," he drawled, raising the delicacy to his mouth, "damned pleased with you, boy."

The fourteen-year-old shot a grateful look to his uncle, then bowed down again.

It was time for Kathy to try breaking the silence. "You girls been busy today?" She saw the quick look between the two, followed by noncommittal humming. The woman turned to her husband. "Looks like we all need to pitch in for clean-up tonight."

"Looks like it," he agreed.

After dishes were done, Kathy ushered the two girls upstairs. There in the bedroom, she got the final word on the incident in the barn. Jenny repeated her stand on testifying in court against Rhonda. That was all Kathy needed. She ordered them both into bed, with the admonition that this matter not be revisited, ever again.

enough to upset the eight hundred pound demon in the room. Remember the witch doctor in Africa who hated — uh, I forget the missionary's name…"

"You know what?" he interrupted, "this is probably a good question for Pastor. We'll ask him what he thinks, okay? In the meantime, just fill me in on the rest of the details."

Her mind reconnected with the afternoon before. "Well, the rocker was in the attic, and when we got up there, Kathy had to go get light bulbs, so we had some time to look around. That's when I saw those books on the table, and there were chairs like, uh, like kitchen chairs, all stacked up, and boxes of more books and I guess there was probably more furniture, but I remember there was a rug of some kind, rolled up against the eaves or whatever they're called." She paused. "Come to think of it, that rug had to be round or oval because it looked like a soft beef burrito instead of an uncooked Barese sausage."

"What does *that* mean?"

"It didn't look like a tube. A square rug rolls into a long tube, with flat ends. This one had, like a tongue hanging out, like when you roll an empty corn tortilla."

He settled for that. "Okay, anything else?"

"Mmm," she thought out loud, "I know there was something, but I can't recall it right now." Her face brightened. "But Greta and I are going back out there, so I'll probably remember it then."

"Why would you even do that?" He was surprised. "Who wants to buy a rocker from a haunted attic?" Suddenly he had a bigger question. "By the way, do these people, the Roths, have any idea their attic has been used for occult rituals?" He corrected this statement immediately. "If, indeed, it actually has been."

She leaned toward him as though to impart private information. "A good question, hon." There was a straightening of the shoulders. "We talked for a while, down on the porch, before we went up to look at the chair, and it

With that, a fragile peace was established. All three children pretty much knew where they stood. But it was Eddie who seemed to come out ahead in all the ruckus. After his prayers, a smile stretched over his mouth as he added a side note. "Guess what?" he whispered to Jesus, "Uncle Mark is damned proud of me."

Mark and Kathy had waged a successful battle, which helped them sleep well that night. That, along with the odd fact that there was no bumping coming from the attic.

***

He was driving them to church in their sleek, black Studebaker Champion.

"Uh, wait. You telling me Greta zapped a demon out of a rocking chair?" Don Collins asked his wife. "I'm not sure that's biblical. We know that demons only possess people, not objects."

"The Bible tells us we have authority over the enemy: Luke 10:19," she reminded her husband. "Those things are hanging around, looking for bodies to make homes in, *and* they like to stay pretty much in the same geographic area, so I'm guessing there are a few hanging out in that attic. She just gave them a shove, I suppose."

"What does that mean? She told them to take a hike?"

"I don' know about that, but she *does* have the Blood Covering, and maybe that was what sent those scoundrels heading for the hills."

He laughed. "What an imagination! I swear, you don't usually come up with such far-out stuff, babe."

"Maybe it's not so far-out as you think. Don't forget, Greta is filled with the Holy Spirit. Sometimes His presence is seems the Roths only bought that place just over a year ago. I doubt they've been up in that attic more than once or twice. It's thick with dust... almost everywhere." She sensed he didn't want her to go there again, so she threw out the bait. "Of course, it would be good to have you come along, you know, to see what's going on."

"And just what do you think is going on?"

"Don't know, but those boxes could hold clues to the history of that ranch, and I know somebody who might know exactly what to look for. It's that history teacher, Walter Taft." She saw a glint of interest in her husband's eye. "So, will you come along?"

"I'll think about it," he promised, as he pulled into the parking area of the Swift Street Pentecostal Church.

***

By Monday evening, Walter and Donna were at the used car dealer out on Burlington's Williston Road. Walter had called his salesman friend on Saturday night, so there were several sedans ready for Donna to consider. She checked the looks while he checked the mechanics and after about three hours, she was the owner of a 1938 Ford Coupe. The sleek hood ornament was missing and those weren't white sidewalls, but the Miami Cream paint was still surprisingly untarnished. "Stored in a garage most of the year, by one owner who spent summers up here, winters in Florida. Used, but not abused," Walter's cheerful buddy had assured her. Walter followed her home, where she parked the sharp-looking car on the street in front of her apartment. He was glad to accept her invitation to come inside and meet her roommates, and then to give them the royal tour of all the ins and outs of Donna's new transportation. When he left at ten-thirty, Donna reached over and gave him a quick hug. "Thanks for everything. I don't know how to thank you."

He jammed his hands into his front pants pockets. "Well, you could be my date for the Jericho High School graduation festivities next Friday." Their eyes met. "That is, if you're off work."

"I'll check my schedule," she promised.

After a day shift at work the next Thursday, she showed up in front of the little house he was renting in Jericho Center. The cream-colored Ford came to a stop in the driveway. Before she was out of the car, he was opening the front door.

"Hey! Look at you, driving all over the place."

"Came to see my sister and brother," she lightly sang out. "Thought I'd drop in to see you for a minute, before going out to the ranch."

"Good." He motioned toward the house. "Would you like to come in?"

"Oh no," she answered casually. "I just wanted to thank you again for your help, and let you see how much I'm enjoying this new-found freedom."

"I'm glad." He thought she was prettier than ever. "So maybe you can come up and see them more often."

"Absolutely." She jiggled the car keys in her hand. "And I wanted to see if the invitation to the graduation ceremony tomorrow night is still open."

"Yes!" he answered quickly. "It sure is."

"Good." She stepped back toward the driver's door. "You can pick me up at the ranch, around six."

"Great."

She pulled the door open, then hesitated. "As a matter of fact, I'll be staying on through Saturday night, since my next shift at the company isn't until three on Sunday afternoon."

"Okay, so lots of time to visit, for sure."

"It might be fun for you to meet the prize bull, if you would like."

His laughter was more robust than he intended. "I would be honored."

She had called ahead, so Kathy had the guest room ready. Jenny followed Donna up there, sliding onto the large feather bed to watch her big sister unpack her overnight bag. "How long can you stay? Do you have time to give us a short ride in your gorgeous new car?"

"I can stay until Sunday morning; I have to be at work by three."

"You look so pretty. Is that a new dress?"

"Kind of. But now that I have car payments, I won't be buying a whole lot of clothes for a while."

There was a knocking on the doorjamb. "Hey, sis!" Eddie had missed her arrival, being busy with chores.

There was a quick hug, after which, she pointed him to a nearby chair, and for a brief while, the three siblings reconnected. It was much like the rare family visits in the Children's Home — all too short, and very intense — and then it was time to go down for supper.

"We could have used your help down here," the petulant princess whispered as she took her place at the table beside Jenny.

The Home kid was quick to handle it. "Aunt Kathy," she addressed the lady of the house, "thanks for letting me have time with Donna. I promise to make it up. We should let Rhonda have two whole days off from kitchen duty next week."

"Oh, I don't know if we have to do all that..." Kathy said, "but that's very nice of you, Jenny."

The out-maneuvered girl was doing another slow burn as Donna took the seat across from her. The burn would soon morph into fury as the conversation turned to the reason for the older sister's visit.

"So, you're going to the high school graduation tomorrow night," Kathy innocently commented. "We aren't going,

because we don't know any of those kids. Maybe next year."
She helped herself to the mashed potatoes. "So, who do you
know who's graduating?"

"Oh, I don't know any of them," Donna explained. "I'm
just going along as Walter Taft's date for the evening."

Rhonda's eyes went wide as her face turned bright pink.
The nostrils flared, the mouth opened.

It sounded like a gunshot out in the yard. As the table
jolted, Mark hit the floor, yelling, "Drop! Drop!"

But the rest of them froze, watching the water glasses slosh
and the silverware rattle across the smooth wooden table.

And then it was quiet.

"Earthquake," Donna mumbled. Nobody moved. "Just
wait, it could be just a small shock; that happens once in a
while."

"Should we go outside?" Eddie whispered.

His oldest sister hesitated. "I... don't think so." She held up
both hands to reassure them. "A real quake lasts a lot longer."
Her head tilted toward her uncle on the floor. "What's up
with him?" she asked Kathy.

"Battle fatigue," came the answer.

"You mean, shell shock?" Donna asked.

"Same thing," Kathy replied.

Donna seemed to listen for a couple of seconds. "Well,
okay, it was just a tiny jolt. We're good." She picked up her
fork. The others followed her lead, except Kathy, who stepped
over to help her husband onto his feet. As he rose, the rest of
the family politely looked to their plates, for his face was pale
and covered with sweat. The WWII hero turned away,
moving unsteadily toward the porch. His wife did not follow
him, for he had to deal with this humiliation in his own way.
Instead, she came back to her chair. "We'll all have to be real
quiet for a while," she said. "Whatever you do, don't drop
any dishes, or make any loud, sudden noises."

"Why? What will happen if we do?" Eddie asked softly.

"You don't want to know," Aunt Kathy answered.

CHAPTER SIX

Fighters

They were walking slowly back from the graduation ceremony, approaching the tiny house just up the hill from the historic Congregational Church on the village green. He was careful not to hold her hand, cautiously avoiding any encroachment on her carefully guarded personal space. Instead, he clasped his hands behind his back and strolled alongside, enjoying the melody of her voice in the cool, moonlit evening. Suddenly she stopped, her ruffled skirt fluttering in the pale light. "Am I talking too much? I mean, it was a really well-done ceremony, what with the music and the flowers, and the kids crying and hugging." It was almost an apology. "You know who came to my graduation from Edmunds? Jenny and Eddie and Mrs. Bushey."

"Who's Mrs. Bushey?"

"Director of the Children's Home. Only been there for a couple of years." She turned to continue the leisurely stroll. "I suppose I should be grateful there was *anybody* there, but all those other grads had parents and grandparents and aunts and uncles. You get the picture." She glanced sideways at her escort. "What about you? Who came to your graduation?"

He was surprised he didn't remember and told her that. "It just seems so far away, anymore. Did my time in the Army, then four years at UVM... it all tends to get lost, doesn't it?" He moved along beside her. "I guess I'm more focused on what's happening now."

"Like getting that thesis finished," she reminded him. "How's that going?"

"Hey, that reminds me: I got a call from this lady, Connie Collins. She knows Jenny, I guess. Anyway, she was wondering if I'd like to take a look at some papers and books from the attic over there at the ranch."

"Oh?"

"Well, you *know* I jumped at the chance. There has to be some history in those boxes, and I'm talking about *local* history." He bent closer, trying to see her face, but she was watching her step.

"So, will you actually take the boxes home and go through them?" she asked.

"If the Roths don't object... and why would they, since I might find a valuable document or something they could sell?"

"I see. That's a real possibility." She looked up, pointing to a white picket fence surrounding a house on the other side of the street. "Look at that. Straight out of a storybook."

"Yeah, and two very odd people who could be out of a storybook, as well." He brought his hands around to shove them into his jacket pockets. "He keeps to himself, and his sister, who lives with him, is a water witch."

She laughed. "No kidding! What interesting neighbors you have, Mr. Taft."

A few yards later, they reached the car at the edge of his driveway. He stopped. "I'd like to ask you in, but I don't think you would do that."

"Nah. Wouldn't look right." She smiled. "We'll just let your neighbors be the ones everybody talks about."

With that, she slipped into the passenger seat of his car, for the ride back to the ranch. As they prepared to back out onto the narrow street, she pulled her sweater closer over her bosom.

"Are you cold?" he asked.

"A bit."

He reached for the heater switch, then drew back to shift into reverse. When he twisted around to check the rear view, she noticed the Chevrolet medallion in the center of the steering wheel. "Hey, I never noticed before, but you drive a Chevy."

He grinned as the car moved slowly out of the driveway. "I hope that doesn't mean Ford owners can't be seen riding with Chevy owners," he chided.

"Nah. What's a little brand difference between friends?" she shot back.

He was encouraged to hear she thought of him as a friend. A quick glance revealed a small, quiet smile on her lips. *"Careful,"* he warned himself, *"keep it light; give her space."* He focused on the beams of light preceding the vehicle's forward thrust. "So, you had fun tonight, right?"

"I really did."

"Just checking, because you did invite me to meet Mister Thunder, and I would love to do that, but I don't want to wear out my welcome."

"Really? I don't see you wearing out any welcome. In fact, you should get there in time for lunch, and then we'll go see Thunder."

He thought quickly. "Actually, I should probably skip the lunch. Those three kids are in my class again, next year."

"So?"

"Teachers are admonished to not socialize with students. Familiarity often leads to lack of authority in the classroom, so we are asked not to do that."

"Hmm. I never knew that."

"Ay-yuh. Pretty standard policy. Probably a good thing, especially in Rhonda's case." He laughed softly. "Male teachers run into young flirts on a pretty regular basis. We're instructed to ignore it, and above all else, never be alone with those girls."

Donna turned her upper body toward the handsome teacher. "Wait a minute. Rhonda has the hots for you?"

"Unfortunately, it has been quite uncomfortable. She's very forward, and the whole class can see it."

"Well, school is out for the summer, so you can avoid that situation for a while." A serious scowl scrunched up her face. "But she's a hard one to handle."

"And that brings up a good point: Should I even be visiting at the Roth Ranch?"

She was surprised at her own reaction. "But... but I want you to come." There was a quick caveat. "We have fun together, you know? Why should Rhonda put a stop to that?"

"I hear you. But she needs to back off." He shrugged. "I don't know, but maybe your uncle or aunt could give her the word. What do you think?"

Donna reached over to pat his arm. "Don't give it another thought. I know exactly what to do, and nobody will have to be embarrassed."

"You sure about this, miss?"

"Trust me." There was a determined bob of the head. "All you have to do, is be at the ranch at one o'clock tomorrow."

***

Jenny was delighted to get the phone call from Essie that same Friday evening. "You're actually in Stowe visiting the Von Trapp family? Wow! How did *that* happen, Essie?"

"They heard we had to escape from Nazi Germany, just like they did. Boy-oh-boy, you should have been here this afternoon — the *stories* we shared."

"I can't imagine," Jenny exclaimed.

"Well, anyway, the reason I'm calling is that my *Vater* and *Mutter* heard that your uncle was fighting for their freedom, and they would like to stop and thank him, in person. We thought to stop by tomorrow afternoon. Do you think this would work for you folks?"

"As far as I know, we'll all be here, except maybe Donna. She's here, but out on a date with Mr. Taft, and who knows whether or not they might get together again tomorrow. She went to the graduation ceremony with him."

"Walter Taft is dating Donna? Oh, my gosh, kiddo. When did *this* start?"

"Um, he helped her buy a car, but I think this is the first official date."

"Donna has a car? Oh, my gosh." There was a quick pause. "Okay, here's my phone number. If it's not convenient, call me. Otherwise, we'll be there around two in the afternoon."

As she was writing it down, Jenny offered one more bit of information. "Rhonda is fit to be tied about Mr. Taft and Donna, so we'll need to avoid that subject in front of her. But, oh boy, am I ever glad you're coming!"

In a few minutes, the Roths had given permission for the visit, especially since this German family wanted to thank Mark for his service on their behalf. Jenny hurried upstairs to start packing, since she was starting her job at the nursing home on Monday, and there were too many other things also to be done. The suitcase could be filled and slid under the bed until Monday morning. Once packed, she could prepare for the professor's family visit. She was especially happy that they would get to share the cake which would mark her sixteenth birthday. "This will be my best birthday ever," she whispered as she hurried down the hall to the linen closet, where her beat-up suitcase was stored.

She yanked the door open to find Rhonda descending the rickety stairs. The girl froze before Jenny even asked it: "What do you think you're doing? We're not supposed to even drop those stairs down; they're too dangerous."

"The ladies went up them with no trouble," came the defensive answer.

"Doesn't matter. We're still not supposed to use them. What were you doing up there, anyway?"

"I wasn't up there. I only started to go up."

The Home kid spotted the fluff of dust clinging to one of Rhonda's tennis shoes, and pointed at it. "So, what's that? A dust bunny from under your bed?"

"That's exactly what it is, smarty-pants." She moved down to the last step.

"You've been up in this attic, and I'm telling your mother."

"I have *not!*" Her foot stomped heavily through the bottom tread, disappearing inside splintered, rotten wood. "Owie-owie-owie!" she screeched.

"Oh no," Jenny whispered. She looked around for something to loosen the painful vise-like grip on that ankle. As the screams grew louder, footsteps pounded in the hall.

"What is it?" Kathy yelled over the ruckus. Then the wooden spoon in her hand became a tool, prying and pounding the shards back from the flesh. It was over before they knew it, the foot withdrawn from the damaging grip, all scratched and red and definitely too painful to stand on. "Looks like you've got a sprained ankle," Kathy observed.

Mark arrived at the doorway, took one look and complained. "Aw, hell. I'm gonna have to patch that up before all those folks get here on Monday night."

"Maybe not, Uncle Mark. It's only the bottom step. They can just step right over it."

"Humph," he replied. "Nobody's gonna say I don't take care of my own property."

Somewhere around ten o'clock that night, Jenny heard Donna come home, climb the stairs and enter the bathroom.

Quietly, she slipped out of bed and into the hallway. When Donna opened the door, she pulled back in surprise, but suppressed the urge to cry out, for her sister was standing there, a silencing finger pressed against her lips. When Jenny signaled for her to follow, the two of them carefully entered the linen closet, where the broken stairs were still lowered, exposing the dark attic above.

"Thought you'd want to know about this," Jenny whispered to her sister. "I'm wondering if Rhonda knows something about all the thumping we had going on a week or so ago."

"There's been some more thumping?" The older girl looked concerned, then turned her sister toward the hall. "You get back to bed. I'll see what I can find out."

Jenny sneaked back under the covers, and buried her head deeply into the pillow. She slept hard, but it didn't help. She still awoke to the thumping, sometime around five in the morning.

***

He stood with one hand behind his back, a big grin on his face. "Happy birthday, sis!" He brought the surprise around front, holding it up for her to see. "I made you this!"

She took a breath, delighted. "A slingshot! I *love* it!" Eddie let her take it from his hand. "All I need is some rocks."

"You'll have to find those on your own," he told her. "What's for breakfast?"

Kathy came down the stairs. "Rhonda's ankle is too sore. She'll be spending the next day or so in bed, I'm afraid." She stirred up some oatmeal on the stove. "So let's go ahead and eat."

"Oh, that's too bad," Donna murmured. "We'll just have to bring her some birthday cake, later."

Jenny was pouring maple syrup on her bowl of steaming oatmeal. "If you folks don't mind, I'd like to wait for the Schulers to come before we have my cake."

"Good," Kathy said, "we can kill two birds with one stone."

"What does that mean?" the boy asked his uncle.

"Means she doesn't have to make cookies for company," Mark said, through a mouthful of toast. He lifted the glass of orange juice, took a swig, before putting it down. "Guess I'd better get that step repaired, while I have the time."

"I'll help you," the nephew volunteered.

Donna was helping Jenny with the dishwashing when they were finally alone. "So, what did you find out?" she asked her older sister.

"I'm not sure, kiddo. But *somebody's* been up there. There's footprints all over that dusty floor."

"Of course there are. The ladies went up to look at the rocking chair. It's an antique, I think, and Greta wants to buy it." She wiped the last bowl. "But there's a problem with getting it down from the attic; it's too big to get through that stairway opening." The cereal bowl was placed gently on the top of the other four. She was folding the dish towel as she disclosed the latest development. "And the thumping is back. Heard it above our bedroom ceiling early this morning."

Donna carefully emptied the dishwater from the pan, and wiped it inside and out, before sliding it into the cupboard under the sink. "Okay, tell me again, how long ago did it stop? Oh, and was it always in the same spot?"

The girl frowned. "I think it stopped about a week ago, and at that time, the noise was coming from the ceiling over Uncle Mark and Aunt Kathy's room."

"And this morning it was over the room you two girls share." She nodded to herself. "So whatever is thumping around up there is moving... all the way across the attic, in fact."

Jenny lifted the stacked bowls carefully into the cupboard off to her right. "Whoa," she exclaimed, "that's scary, Donna."

"What's scary?" Kathy's head appeared from behind the doorway into the living room.

Donna was quick on her feet. "Being sixteen," she lied. "Kind of moving out of our childhood when we get that old, don't you agree?"

Kathy moved toward the back door, where she could shake out the dust cloth she'd been using in the living room. "Oh, you young girls don't know the half of it. Enjoy yourselves while you can, that's what I say."

Once the woman was all the way outside shaking the dust from the soiled chamois, Donna cautioned her sister. "Just don't be talking about this to the rest of the family. Give me some time. I have a car, now, and can come up here more often. Just give me some time, okay?" Jenny nodded in agreement. "Great. Now, today is your birthday, and we both have company coming, so let's concentrate on having some fun."

Walter arrived promptly at one. Donna was there before he even opened the car door. "Hey there!" she greeted him. Then she bent in toward the open car window. "Don't worry about your high school students. Two of them are expecting a visit from old friends, so they'll be busy hosting, and the other one has a sprained ankle and is confined to her room."

"Are you saying Rhonda is confined to her room?" He eyed her suspiciously. "Please tell me you had nothing to do with that."

She laughed loudly. "Oh my goodness, Walter! You overestimate me." She stepped back to let him exit the Chevrolet. "Believe me, she did it to herself."

It turned out that the Schulers arrived a half-hour early, having miscalculated the actual mileage. Mark and Kathy greeted them hospitably, anyway. Essie hugged her dear pen pal, and even gave young Eddie a courteous European handshake, as did her eleven-year-old brother, David. The two boys became instant buddies, wandering on their own to collect rocks down at the river's edge, poking around the barn, and having pretty much their own private tour. Finally, they joined the rest of the group now gathered at the enclosure where they would meet the star of the show, Thunder.

He was every bit up to the encounter, moving along like a huge bundle of muscle, rippling slowly across the green carpet under a lacy-treed canopy. He moved amongst the trailing willow streamers, this warrior of the hour, royalty on review, his highly held crown of horns leaving no doubt that Thunder was indeed, master of his territory. Then he lifted his tail, pooped a steaming pile onto the ground, and moved on.

After the ripple of laughter, the tourists wandered over to the edge of the orchard on the other side of the barn to survey the goats, who cavorted charmingly amongst the visitors. Indeed, the professor, himself, joined in the fun, even following the frisky animals in and out of the old greenhouse and around the blossoming apple trees. He laughed, out of breath. "My friend," he said to his American hero, "this brings happy memories of my childhood!"

Swept up in the moment, Mark exuded a sudden burst of hospitality: "That's great. Feel free to come back for a visit, any time!"

The Schulers glowed and bowed a thank you.

"But I see you have four nannies and the buck. What? You have no kids this spring?"

"No. There have been miscarriages, I'm afraid. We're still figuring that one out." The host changed the subject. "But, let me show you more. We have only been here for just over a year, so our cattle herd only meets a head count of nine. But we're mighty proud of those ladies, if you would like to take a look."

As the tour of the ranch continued toward the upper pasture, Jenny and Essie went back to the house. In the kitchen, they caught up on some important subjects.

"Well, what do you think? Will Mr. Taft get fired?" Essie appeared anxious to hear the answer.

"I don't know. But there sure are a lot of folks mad at him. I heard him remind Donna, just a few minutes ago, that he's coming here on Monday night, to pick up some boxes from the attic. He figures there's a lot of local history in those cartons, and I'm thinking he's probably right, and if I know him, he'll just dig the heck out of that stuff." She pulled a glass from the cupboard. "You want some water?" Essie declined. "And so I'm thinking he's not going to gloss over things. He's going to pounce on them. That's who he is." She let the water run for a few seconds to let it get colder.

"Are you saying it looks like things could get even worse for him?" Essie wondered.

The birthday girl held the glass under the silvery stream from the faucet. "I guess so. I don't know, but if he uncovers dirt in this town…"

Essie leaned back against the kitchen counter. "You think he will do that?"

Jenny turned off the faucet. "Heck, yes. He's a fighter." There was a little sip. "He wants to make things right." Another sip. "He's the type that will get to the end of it. He wants the truth to come out."

The freckle-faced German friend waited patiently, watching Jenny take that final, long, full drink of water. "Guess we'll just pray for the best, for now," Essie concluded softly.

Jenny set her glass in the sink. "That doesn't sound too promising, you know."

"I agree. But this is part of the drama of life. What will happen, will happen." Essie stood up straight, ready to rejoin the other guests. "But keep me informed, would you?"

Eventually, the tour ended up inside the house. Birthday cake and drinks were served in the living room where Essie and her mother, Elke, could not say enough about the wonderful woodwork and the charming atmosphere. Flattered, Kathy took them upstairs with her, when she brought a piece of cake to the pouting Rhonda. They marveled at the bathroom which had replaced an extra bedroom, the view of the orchard from the guest room windows, and even got to peek into the linen closet, where dropped stairs pointed to a small opening into the cavernous shadows of the attic.

Once the ladies came downstairs, it was time to leave, but Professor Schuler had one more thing to do. He raised a glass to toast this American hero who had risked life and limb helping the Jews. "...and *Gott* knows, how many others." Before the four German guests got into their car, Herr Schuler stood at full attention to salute Mark Roth. Quiet tears followed warm hugs and then the Schulers departed.

Walter and Donna enjoyed a short conversation on the porch, before he left at four.

"This has been a special time," he told her. "I've enjoyed it so much."

"Good. So now I've repaid you for helping me buy a car."

He looked her in the eye. "Aw, come on... is that the only reason you invited me to come?" He regretted the question immediately, because that shield went up, again.

"Nah," she replied, "you're also a dead ringer for Roy Rogers."

She walked him to his car, where they said goodnight with a quick hug. As soon as his headlights disappeared around the stand of birches, she walked back to the house, where she quietly ascended the stairs and moved on down the hallway toward the guest room.

It should have been a peaceful ending to a wonderful day, but as night settled over Roth Ranch, five people slept fitfully. The thumping was back, more persistent than ever, now audible in *every* bedroom.

Mark Roth moved his pillow and a blanket out into the hall, where he lay in front of the linen closet door, his rifle by his side.

CHAPTER SEVEN

Puzzles

Before Donna left the ranch on Sunday, she pulled Jenny aside, slipping a velvet box into her sister's hand. "There was so much going on yesterday, I forgot to give this to you."

Jenny untied the blue ribbon and opened the box. "Oh wow! A watch!" She pulled the gold timepiece off the circular form that held it in place. "It's so pretty, Donna."

"Put it on," the older girl urged her. "See that? Doesn't that look nice on you?" There was a big hug. "And it's a twenty-one jewel. And it's a Bulova, see?"

"Oh my gosh, this is the best present I've ever, ever had."

"Good," Donna said, picking up her overnight bag. "Take good care of it. Don't get it wet."

"I won't." Suddenly she realized that Donna was leaving. "Um, it's only ten in the morning. I thought you didn't have to leave until one."

The young woman scanned the guest room, making sure she had not left anything. "I need to have some extra time." She seemed to have a sudden thought. "Hey, would you like me to drop you off at your new job? It's right on my way."

"That would be terrific! I'm all packed, sis."

Jenny followed down the hall, where Donna poked her head in to say goodbye to Rhonda. The dark-haired head acknowledged the farewell with a brief nod, Jenny grabbed her own suitcase, and the two sisters descended the stairs. A half-hour later, they were in front of Maude's Nursing Home.

"I wish you could stay longer," Jenny whispered.

"Don't worry," the reply came with a wink, "now that I have a car, I'll be visiting more often."

Donna waited until Jenny was inside, then slowly drove to the village green, where she made a left past the Congregational Church for a quick stop to see Walter. She noticed he was dressed for church. "I only dropped by for a minute," she informed him. He opened the door to let her into the house. "No, that's alright. We can talk right here on the step." He moved outside, closing the door behind him.

"What's up?"

"Remember yesterday, when we were walking up to look at that small herd of cattle?" He nodded. "Remember what I told you about the bumping noises we heard early that morning?"

"From the ceiling," he added.

"Right. Well," she shifted her weight to her other foot, "it was back last night, with a vengeance. In fact, it got so bad, Mark slept in front of the linen closet door all night, with a loaded rifle nearby."

"Oh-oh, that doesn't sound good." He stroked his chin. "Doesn't he have some sort of psychological problem, from the war?"

"Now you're getting the picture. He had a problem the minute he got off that troop train in Burlington. That's why he left for Texas, *alone*. Nobody wanted to be around that." She tugged the front of her cardigan closer together. "Anyway, that was before. My worry is that right now, he's showing signs of losing it, and I don't want that to happen to Jenny and Eddie."

"What do you think will happen?"

"To quote Kathy, 'You don't want to know.'" A crease appeared between her brows. "These battle fatigue guys have been known to kill 'attackers' in a split second. That's how they were trained, and how they stayed alive."

"Of course. I can see how that could happen. But do you honestly believe your brother and sister are in danger?"

It was a sigh of frustration. "I don't know what to think, Walter." She raised those glinting blue eyes to meet his concern. "I guess I just feel like I need to *tell* somebody." She blinked slowly. "I chose you."

***

Jenny woke up Monday morning, roused by an early light glowing softly around the edges of her only window's dark green shade. The tiny apartment was intended as housing for the nursing home's director, but Mrs. Hannity lived next door in her own cozy cottage, this being every bit as accessible in emergencies, and far more comfortable for her. So here was Jenny, in one room with a tiny bathroom — a commode, sink, and snug shower — but it was all hers, and she felt like a spoiled child. Her eyes blinked to focus on the delicate pale-blue flowered wallpaper, the worn white woodwork, the square etched-glass cover that clipped onto the light bulb in the middle of the plaster ceiling. "Thank you, Jesus," she whispered. For a few more minutes, she lay there, enjoying the blessing. Then she rose and made her bed and visited the bathroom and before she knew it, she was tying on her apron and heading down the hall to the kitchen.

Most of the morning was a blur of faces, trays, dishwashing, and mopping. At ten-thirty, she retreated to her room for private time. Then it was back to work at eleven, for more of the same. Her shift came to an end at three, when, once again, she went to her room for a visit to the bath, where she splashed water on her sixteen-year-old face. The sandwich she had brought with her from the kitchen went down with the hot tea seeped in a pink Melmac cup and saucer. When she returned the dishes to the kitchen, there was cool iced tea to be had. She poured some over ice, and took the treat out onto the large front porch, where she found a seat on that same spindled chair she had used during Greta and Connie's visit. She took a long draw from the refreshing brew, then leaned back to enjoy the fragrance of this summer afternoon.

The front door slammed her back to reality.

A fortyish woman with frizzy hair whipped out a cigarette lighter and touched the flame to the hand-twisted paper in her mouth. She pulled smoke from it, puffing it out with a vengeance. "Gawd! That bitch is gonna drive me to drink, I swear." She looked around for a place to sit during her break, her sights landing on the new worker who was staring at her with the big, wide eyes. She held the cigarette high in one hand as she approached what she perceived as the not-so-pretty and not-so-bright target. "You the new kid?" she asked as she slid onto the bench across from Jenny.

"Guess so," the girl cautiously replied.

"Yeah. Okay, we'll see how long *you* last." When Jenny did not respond, the bitterness came pouring out. "These old people are something else, you know? Mostly old women, if you want to get down to the facts. And old women are very, very demanding, kid. You might as well get used to it." She drew from the wrinkled thing in her mouth, then spoke through the smoky exhaling. "That bitch, Millie, is a good example. She can't shut up about having a three-minute egg. I mean, it's all she talks about, morning, noon, and night." The flick of a finger dislodged the ash at the end of the homemade cigarette.

"She wants it at breakfast?" Jenny inquired.

"Hell, no. She wants it at every meal. Throws a fit, every single, gawddim time!"

Even though she was not on duty, Jenny went to visit Millie at four o'clock, just an hour before supper was to be served in the dining room. She opened the conversation with, "I know your daughter, Greta." Before Millie went down to the supper hour, she was convinced that a three-minute egg was full of germs — bad germs — germs that could make people "sick unto death."

The staff was surprised at Millie's quiet demeanor during the dining room experience. The cook reported it to Mrs. Hannity, who traced it back to Jenny. "Alright, missy, it looks like you have earned a little bonus... and even on your first week with us," the lady said. "So, let me give you a week of free laundry services. They will even iron your clothes," she added. "And, if you don't need to go back to the ranch to do those things, you can spend your first weekend off, right here in Jericho Center."

Jenny was both relieved and flattered. She agreed to spend her first weekend in the comfort of her very own room.

It would prove to be one of the most important decisions of her life.

***

Monday evening couldn't come around fast enough for Kathy Roth. She had spent most of Sunday night out on the hall floor with her husband, reassuring him that, within twenty-four hours, the haunted rocking chair would be gone, and maybe all the other trash up there in the attic, and things would get back to normal. "No need to go shooting up your wonderful, old homestead, now, is there? Just wait a bit longer; Mark, it'll be okay, you'll see." So when the two cars came to a stop in front of the porch, she was the first one to greet the group.

Greta Short's husband, Gerald, was driving the station wagon. He was a tall man with a gentle smile. On the other hand, Connie Collins's husband, Don, was a stout, gregarious soul, with a pixie-like grin. The two couples waited for Walter to catch up with them on the porch.

"Is my car alright in that spot?" he inquired.

"It's fine," Mark assured him, before leading the group up to the linen closet, where the stairs were still lowered. "I'll go up first," the host announced, "to turn on the lights. Meanwhile, be very careful. These stairs are pretty old."

The two husbands inspected the rocker, agreeing it was worth about fifty dollars, if Mr. Roth would accept the offer. The fellow would have taken *five* dollars, but never blinked an eye. "Sounds fair enough," he murmured, "but you'll need to take it apart to get it through the stairwell door."

"Mmmm, not necessarily," Don Collins noted. He turned to Gerald. "What about that stair opening? Are those supporting beams?"

"Nope," came the soft answer. "I checked 'em out on the way up." He turned to Mr. Roth. "We can open up that space real easy, if you would give permission. Brought our own tools, and promise to put it all back together, once we're done."

"In fact, we'll make it even stronger, if you like," Don grinned. "What do you say?"

"Well, I'll be damned," the cattleman exclaimed, "I never thought of *that*."

It was agreed to move all of the boxes out to Walter's car, first. Once that was done, the four men went to work on the stairwell. Kathy had opted to get back downstairs before the carpentry began, but Greta and Connie chose to wander around the whole attic, murmuring under their breath. Once, there was a sharp zapping noise that caused the men to pause, but Connie waved them back to work, an unconcerned smile on her face. Within a couple of hours, the rocking chair was in the back of the station wagon, the two vehicles were winding up the hairpin driveway, and the Roths were fifty dollars richer.

But Connie Collins was very quiet where she shared the middle seat of the station wagon with Greta. The gregarious Don spoke up from the passenger seat. "So you ladies were right there on the job, casting out devils or whatever. We heard that electrical snap." But Connie did not respond. "Hey! Cat got your tongue?" he called out.

"Mmmm. I'm not sure," she replied. Greta signaled her permission, but Connie was still reluctant to get into it.

However, the married folks' radar was already up, and the husband was insistent. "As a matter of fact, babe, you've been pretty darned quiet all through the whole evening. What's up?"

Greta gave an encouraging nod. Connie was pretty much backed into a corner, so she spoke up. "Oh, I don't know if it's even important, but I did notice a couple of things while we were up in the attic. One was that there was a flashlight. That's the thing I couldn't remember before, Don. Seems odd that a shiny, modern flashlight would be needed in the attic, unless, it was used before the light bulbs were replaced."

"Ay-yuh," Don mused, "or it could have been left there by a real estate agent or somebody, and just forgotten."

"I suppose so. But my inquisitive mind doesn't feel comfortable with that conclusion." Connie's head wobbled with certainty.

"Okay, babe, I defer to your gut feelings." He grinned with the gentle driver, and pursued the conversation. "So you said you noticed a *couple* of things. What was the second thing you noticed?"

"Those two books were missing."

***

Walter Taft could hardly wait to check out what was in those boxes. He had hauled all five of them in from the car that same Monday night, planning on getting into this project the first thing in the morning. But this was truly a special occasion, and with that thought, he dug into a back corner of his kitchen cupboard and drew out a bottle of brandy. He poured just a couple of fingers tall, then he sat and stared at those cardboard treasure chests, lined up against one wall in his rented living room.

The phone rang.

"Hello, Walter? This is Connie Collins. Sorry to bother you so late, but I really need to talk to you."

"No problem," he lied, for his brain was feeling fuzzy. "What's going on?"

"It's about something in one of those boxes. A flashlight. Did you find it, yet?"

"No, ma'am. I haven't gotten into the boxes, yet. Figured I'd wait until morning, when I'm rested and ready, you know?"

"Oh, thank God." She seemed to take a second breath. "Now listen to me, because it's really important that you don't touch that flashlight. It probably has the fingerprints of whoever has been responsible for the noises coming from that attic, if it turns out to be an actual person. We need to know that."

He was surprised. "You know about the noise coming from the attic?"

"Yes, Jenny told Greta and me about it, when we gave her a ride home on the day we first met. I suspect somebody is up to something, but that's not what I called about. I called about the flashlight."

"Okay, the flashlight. Where is it, again?"

"It's in one of the boxes, Walter. You don't have to find it right now. The only thing is, when you *do*, don't touch it with your bare hands, okay?" She got specific. "So listen to me: There is a loop at the end of the flashlight handle, I think it's there so you can hang it up or something. Listen to me now… that's the only thing you can touch, okay?" She waited for his answer.

"Yes, ma'am, only touch the loop at the end of the flashlight."

"Good, Walter. That's good." There was another draw of air. "So when you pick up the flashlight by that loop, you need to drop it into a plastic bag. A plastic bag, Walter." She waited again.

"Yes, ma'am. I actually have some plastic bags, so, no problem."

"Thank God," she said, again. "Then you need to hide it, until we need it. We need it for evidence. At least, I think maybe we do." He heard her breathe out slowly. "You know what? Just do all that, and we'll see what comes up later. Is that okay with you, Walter?"

"Oh, I guess there's no harm in doing all that," he acquiesced.

Connie hung up the phone. "I just hope you can trust my instincts on this."

Don pulled her closer to him. "Wouldn't be the first time, babe."

***

On that same Monday evening, after the five treasure-seekers had left, Rhonda and Eddie got into an intense exchange. She had hobbled out into the hall and waited for him to come up to bed, knowing it was his habit to visit the bathroom before turning in, and she went into full Texas princess mode. "Hold it for a minute, greenhorn... I need to talk to you."

"Oh no you don't, Rhonda. I know better than to get within ten feet of you." He tried to get past her, but she blocked him with one jump of her body. He stepped back. "Cut it out, or I'll call your mother."

She laughed softly. "It's been a very late night. She's up to her ears in the kitchen." There was another hop, and passage down the hallway was impossible without physical contact. She enjoyed this moment of his frustration, but moved on quickly to her mission. "You need to stop Daddy Mark, before he kills somebody, you hear?" The lad's eyes froze under her icy stare. "You don't know what crazy things he can do. You need to get that rifle away from him — hide it, or somethin'."

"I can't do that. He's too quick and too messed up to know what he's doing. He could kill me, for Pete's sake."

"So? Are you man enough to protect the women on this ranch?" Her nostrils flared. "You're almost fifteen years old, for heaven's sake. Stop whining and grow up." She limped back toward her bedroom door. "You need to take care of this." The girl hobbled into her room. "If anything happens to me or my mother, it will be your fault. *Your* fault!"

He stood there, the door having been slammed in his face, and wondered whether there might be some truth in those words. By the time he got back from the bathroom, Mark and Kathy were upstairs, getting ready for bed. He got into his nightshirt, then listened at his door as his aunt and uncle got settled in front of the linen closet entrance. "I wish you would come to bed, Mark," he heard her say. There were frustrated words, more like grunts, coming from the man. "Alright then," the woman's voice replied, "I'll stay out here with you." At that, Eddie cracked the door open and slipped his head around the doorjamb. Aunt Kathy was dropping her own pillow to the hall floor. It was now or never, so the boy stepped out as though to head for the bathroom. When Kathy looked up, he waved desperately, pointing to the bathroom door. She checked her reclining husband and murmured something, then hastened along to step in beside the lavatory sink. "What is it?" she whispered.

"Things are getting pretty serious with Uncle Mark," he said in his best manly voice. "Maybe I should try to take that gun away from him, before he does something really bad."

She slapped one hand over her eyes. "Oh my gosh, Eddie, don't even think of such a thing. He'd shoot you before you even *touched* that weapon." The hand came down. "Where'd you get such a notion, anyway?"

He hated to admit it. "Rhonda."

"What? She knows better. She knows what to do when these things happen."

"Oh-kay… so what are we supposed to do?"

"If you hear yelling and gunshots, *hide*."

"Um, anywhere in particular?"

"Up to you, but I told Rhonda to slip out her window onto the porch roof and lie flat." Seeing his quick glance back toward his room, she tried to help. "Come to think of it, your window leads out onto that same roof."

"Yes, ma'am."

"Just make sure you close the window behind you, so he won't know you went out that way." She turned to leave. "And, for Pete's sake, lie flat where he can't see you, if he *does* look out there."

Eddie checked to see if the window would open, before he crawled under the covers. It was good to have a plan. Still, he wondered why Rhonda had ignored her mother's instructions, and urged him… no, tried to *shame* him into confronting his Uncle Mark. "*It's like she* wants *me to get shot*," he thought.

Nevertheless, he took time for his usual prayers before he turned over to find a soft spot in the pillow.

But he had one ear open, for the rest of the night.

Sometime around four Tuesday morning, Kathy awakened, her back aching from the hard hallway floor. Mark was lying sound asleep, his pillow propped up against the closet door. She moved slowly and silently to a more comfortable position and did a mental assessment: There had been no disturbances throughout the night. Mark was lying in a relaxed position, softly snoring. There was no stirring from the bedrooms down the hall. "*Could it be?*" she wondered. "*Could it be that there was no thumping from the attic last night?*"

She lay there quietly, waiting for what seemed a long time. When she glanced at her watch at the five o'clock hour, there had still been no disturbances.

Mark snorted, twisted his upper body into an upward stance, and looked over at his wife.

"Good morning," she sang out. "No banging around last night, honey. Looks like we are out of the woods."

He wiped the sleep from his eyes, slowly arriving at this possibility.

"Well, I'll be damned," he murmured.

CHAPTER EIGHT

Surprises

He got up early on Tuesday, anxious to inspect the treasure taken from the farmhouse attic.

The first box was tied shut with old string. Walter, wearing surgical gloves, checked that one out, first. Slowly, he pulled each item out and placed it on the carpeted living room floor: a set of *Nancy Drew Mysteries*, a copy of *Little Women*, a beaded child's necklace in a small envelope. "Obviously items belonging to a young girl," he told himself. "Something only a mother would keep." He continued by placing a blonde doll in wrinkled clothing alongside the books, followed by a paper bag containing crocheted baby tops and hats in various shade of pinks and yellows. At the very bottom of this carton, covered with dust, he found a child's finger ring of simple design, no stones nor inscriptions on what appeared to be a badly tarnished gold band. He slipped the ring into the necklace's envelope and then replaced all items. After he folded the top flaps closed, he labeled the box with a strip of white paper which read, "Young girl."

The second box was already open. The flashlight tucked into a top corner almost surprised him. "Okay, got to get this into a plastic bag and hide it." He took care of that task quickly, sliding the package into the back cupboard where he kept his brandy. Then he went back to work.

The open box contained more books, these being mostly instructions and recipes for some religious organization.

"Bingo!" he whispered. Upon closer examination, he determined they were connected with satanic rites. He went through them carefully, watching for names on the inside covers, or notes tucked in between pages. There were some marked margins, but nothing he deemed meaningful. Still, he perused the whole collection of seven books before replacing them in the cardboard container which he labeled, "Occult reading."

The third box was actually sealed with some sort of weathered tape, which he removed carefully, in case there were fingerprints or other evidence. Those pieces of tape were placed, using tweezers, in a large manila envelope. The pulled-back flaps revealed a folded newspaper, yellowed with age, laid out over the contents inside. Underneath, Walter found instructions for Patrons of Husbandry leadership. He recognized the sheaf of grain and the letters "P" and "H" on either side of it, even before he read the word "Grange" underneath. This shield was all too familiar to him. "Okay, so this person was involved with a local grange," he surmised. Digging deeper, he came upon what looked like aviator goggles. He smiled. "Hoodwinks! Wonder how they got their hands on those." Upon closer inspection, the glasses with the flipping lenses proved to be quite old. "Probably don't even use these things anymore," he guessed, lightly touching the velvet-lined insides of this antique, before placing them gently aside.

A silk cloth was next, proving to be a ceremonial apron, which, he guessed by the embroidered design, would have been worn by the Worthy Master. "Whoa! This is guy stuff, and the fellow was head honcho, wherever this place was." He sat back on his haunches to think. "*Okay, this could still be a woman's stash. She probably just kept all this stuff in his memory.*" Laying the shiny apron aside, he reached in and lifted out a drape which he recognized as part of an initiation ceremony, for which degree, he was not sure. It was placed on the carpet with the apron. A box of medallions and keepsakes of special occasions celebrated by the local, state, and national Granges was next. He thought these might have some value for the Roths. As he made a mental note of that, he reached in to lift a flat wooden box from the very bottom of the carton. Inside were all the implements of ceremonial rites performed during grange meetings: petite replicas of an axe, a plow, a spade, a hoe, a pruning knife, and a sickle. In the center of the lined box was a skeleton version of a five-pointed star. "Wow! Now this has to be worth a few dozen pennies."

He had just finished tagging this box as "Grange," when the phone broke the silence.

"Good morning," Donna said. "Let me guess what you're doing. Checking out those boxes, right?"

He laughed. "Guilty as charged."

"Anything interesting?"

"Oh yeah. Somebody was into both Satanism and Grange, if you can imagine that combination."

"Really! That's interesting." She cleared her throat. "Um, so I was going to see the kids this weekend up at the ranch. Any chance I could take a look at some of that stuff?"

He did a mental check. "I guess it would be alright. Have to be careful not to touch with bare hands, though."

"Understood." She changed the subject. "So you start your summer classes next week, right?"

"Right. I'll have my nose to the grindstone after that."

"Well, we could meet for coffee during class break, or something. All work and no play makes Jack a dull boy." He laughed again. "So, I need to get off to work," she informed him. "See you next weekend?"

"For sure."

The next box contained used candles in metal holders, and a variety of both metallic and glass vessels including a mortar and pestle. "For grinding chemicals and herbs, no doubt," he told himself. There were a couple of miniature statues of women in Roman garb, numerous chips revealing the plaster of Paris beneath. He set those aside and drew out a couple of old newspapers which had lined the bottom of the box. "No, wait. These are not for padding." He noted the careful folding to display certain stories. "Hmm," he noted, "both are about fires. One was a hotel, the other was… it looks like a big boarding house, or something." Closer scrutiny revealed that both fires occurred in Jericho, and both were of rather suspicious origin. "So, what do we have here?" He sat back against the wall and read the articles again. "Why did somebody keep these?" he wondered as he penned the label, "Ritual tools/Fires."

Suddenly he was hungry. In the kitchen, he put together a peanut butter and hot pepper jelly sandwich, which he washed down with a glass of milk. As he wiped his mouth with the back of his hand, there was a knock on the front door. A quick peek toward the window showed him it was Connie Collins.

"Walter, I'm so sorry to just pop in on you like this," she blurted out, "but I ran into Greta at the IGA store in Winooski, and she invited me to come along, and so, of course, I couldn't call ahead. She just dropped me off in front of your house, and went back to see her mother. I do hope this isn't an imposition."

"If it doesn't bother you to step around boxes, it doesn't bother me. Come on in."

Her eyes glinted at the sight of the opened containers. "Oh my. Oh my, looks like you've been busy." She adjusted her grip on the pocketbook in front of her tummy. "Anything interesting?"

He gave her a quick rundown, noting the woman's intensity. "So, I have only one more to go. If you have time, you can help me, Mrs. Collins."

The purse went flying into the nearest chair. "Oh, please call me Connie — I will need some gloves."

The last box proved to be the frosting on the cake. Connie's gray eyes widened as she fingered through piles of receipts

and important paperwork. "It's somebody by the name of Crocker. Yes, Timothy and Freda Crocker."

"I'm guessing these are former owners of the ranch property," he suggested. "It would make sense, since the sandy stretch of riverbank down where Thunder is pastured, is called Crocker's sand bar. Mark told us during the visit last Sunday." He moved up off the floor and slid into the easy chair opposite the couch. "And so, it figures that either Timothy or Freda — or both — were fooling around with some form of black magic, mixed with Grange rituals, or Freemasonry, or who-knows-what."

"So that attic was probably crawling with demons." The gray eyes blinked slowly.

"I don't know if I'd go that far," Walter cautioned her. Then his Roy Rogers twinkle came back. "I know a student whose grandpa is in the Masons. His name is Andrew. I'll see if he can get his grandpa to sit down for a beer sometime this week. If there's something we need to know, I have a feeling this old guy might just fill in the blanks."

"Good idea," she agreed. "Okay, I should go join Greta at the nursing home." She watched him label that last box, "Paperwork," then made a casual suggestion. "I don't suppose you'd like to give me that flashlight, for safe-keeping, would you, Walter?"

"I would be happy to do exactly that," he replied.

***

Andrew was forthcoming about his grandpa. "He might tell you to go to hell," the boy warned him.

"Not the first time I've been told that," the teacher informed the student.

The grandfather, named Ken Pearson, called Walter on Wednesday morning. "Guess you want to know about Tim

Crocker," he said. "Well, I'm the guy you want to talk to, because there's other folks out there who'll give you mostly gossip, and us former Grangers don't need that happening, for sure."

"Mr. Pearson, I understand you're now a Mason, but I was hoping you had some insight about the grange the Crockers attended."

"Ay-yuh. You came to the right person. Like I said, most people around here don't know the facts. I'm calling to set you straight, so I expect you'll listen careful and not go off the deep end about this stuff."

"I am listening, sir."

There was a lengthy clearing of the throat. "Well, as you may have guessed by now, Tim was Worthy Master in a local grange. I don't want to identify that particular grange, and I'm asking that you keep that information out of the theme paper, or whatever it is, that you're writing for UVM."

Walter did a quick mental check. "That would be fine. It is not relevant to the issue. No problem."

There was relief in the man's voice. "Good. Good. So, he was Worthy Master, but he was also into some witchcraft, and, for a long time, nobody but Freda knew about it." There was another clearing of the throat. "We don't know just how much she knew about it, but she kept it secret, and that was a bad choice... a really bad choice. People in this grange started having weird things happening, right in the middle of our ceremonies. I mean, the women who were in the roles of Ceres and Flora and Demeter, they would be reciting their lines, and suddenly, their eyes would roll back in their heads. This scared those women, and freaked out everybody in the assembly."

"Wow! I can't imagine how severely this must have disrupted your meetings, Ken. It must have been very difficult."

"That's probably what made us get to the bottom of all that. Freda. It was Freda. She would break down and cry out loud. Tim would call for order. Now, he was a slight man, small in stature, but he had a commanding presence. He would try to get the meeting back on track, yelling at his own wife, and some of the other women would calm her down." He sniffed as though wiping his nose. "That's what put us guys onto the problem: Tim had no control over his wife's weird reactions to the rolling, white eyeballs of those three ladies."

"Okay. So you decided to look into the situation?"

"Big time." Ken sniffed. "We sicced the women on Freda. It wasn't long before she confided what was going on with her man."

"Mmm," Walter responded, "and did she mention there were things going on in the attic?"

"Nah. We didn't have a clue about all that stuff. She just said he was fooling around with the devil, and she was scared he would go off the deep end, or something." He paused to get back to the point. "So, the rest of the officers got together and went to see Tim. He was fit to be tied; tried to deny everything, but we 'nailed him to the wall,' and had a special meeting later that same week, where we decided to get rid of him. Told him to take his Worthy Master trappings and get out of town before the sun went down, so to speak."

The wording was vague, but Walter got the message: Tim Crocker was dethroned in a local grange, and the whole thing had been swept under the rug. "I'm... curious, Ken. How did this go unnoticed by the upper echelons of the Grange organization?"

"I am not at liberty to say," came the reply. "What you need to understand, here, is that there was a breach of security in the Grange, and it was dealt with." The tone of voice went to a righteous tenure. "We were an honorable organization, Mr. Taft, and we did not tolerate deception, especially of the spiritual kind."

"Mmmm." Walter hummed slowly, making time to put the final question together. "I have no doubt that the Patrons of

Husbandry is an honorable organization, sir, but I am puzzled by the fact that they need to be secretive, in any way, since this opens the door for more deception, does it not?"

"What? I don't follow you, Mr. Taft."

Walter shifted his weight in the easy chair. "I guess what I'm saying is, if there are secret activities in an organization, there is the possibility of deception and even manipulation of its members, and yes, all the activities of that secretive society." He paused. "Manipulation and deception. Where is the honor in all that?"

"I don't know what you're talking about," the flustered grandfather replied.

"I'm just saying that secret societies breed an atmosphere of false superiority and authority. They really aren't any nobler than the general public. In fact, they are elitist snobs, who don't actually have any more 'superior' knowledge than the average Joe Public. They only want the rest of us to *think* so."

There was silence on the other end of the phone.

"Sir?" Walter waited, but there was no response. "I guess the only way to have all that authority and power is to keep all those Grangers sworn to secrecy." Still no response from Ken. "And what the *public* doesn't know, the *public* can't deal with. That seems to be the long and the short of it." The teacher wasn't sure Ken was still on the line, but he went for the final word, anyway. "That's why Tim Crocker got away with all that mischief. And what good did it do him? He lost all that power."

"Oh, he lost a whole lot more than that," the old man finally responded. "Killed hisself a month later."

***

Donna arrived at Walter's door early Saturday evening. This time she went inside, apparently unconcerned about what the neighbors might think. She was pulling on the surgical gloves when Walter brought up the phone call from Ken, Andrew's grandfather. "Oh my gosh, Walter! The man committed suicide? Where? On the ranch?"

"Yup."

The blue eyes stared. "Oh my gosh."

"They suspected some form of poison. His wife found him, dead in his bed."

Donna snapped the last glove into place. "That had to be awful."

"Something interesting, though. Mr. Pearson mentioned that the man was a talented woodworker. Apparently made a rocking chair, which he considered a special place, like a throne, or something. Bragged about it to his fellow Grangers, but nobody ever admitted seeing it."

He pulled out the box labeled "Young Girl," then sat back to watch Donna slowly go through the items. "I'm guessing he actually made it up there in the attic, because it was too large to fit through the opening down to the stairs."

"No kidding! I take it you saw the thing when you were up there, taking the boxes away." She was looking at the blonde doll, smoothing out the crumpled skirt, as he continued to tell her how the Shorts bought it, then got it down from there by doing the carpentry, themselves. At this, Donna looked up suddenly. "So, it's not up there anymore?" He shook his head no. "Well," she said, turning her attention back to the doll, "good riddance to bad rubbish, as they say." She closed up the first box and went to the one with the "Occult Reading" label. Suddenly she looked up. "Hey, you wouldn't have a cup of hot tea handy, would you? I'm definitely ready for one." The young man rose and prepared the brew, and when he came back, she was brushing the dust off the last book.

"Interesting stuff, but covered with soot or something," she remarked. He set the tea on the coffee table, then gave her a hand up to the sofa. She drew the teacup close her lips. "Mmm. Smells good!" After a lady-like sip, she inquired as to what was in the other boxes. He gave her a brief rundown, enjoying her presence. When he paused, she asked, "You folks took all of the stuff out of the attic, then?"

"No. There were some chairs and a rug and I don't remember what else. Oh, a table, for sure."

She took another sip. "Well, it looks like you're doing a great job, Walter. Too bad about the circumstances, though. Whatever happened to his wife — what's her name — Freda?"

"Right. That's tragic, too. She grieved for a year or so, then passed away from cancer. The daughter put the place up for sale, and the Roths bought it. End of story."

"Not quite. These boxes are opening up a whole new chapter, don't you think?"

"Maybe, Donna. Let's hope it brings a happier ending."

She set the cup down and leaned back into the cushions. "I don't know if I believe in happy endings."

"Oh, yeah? Why not?"

"I don't know. They just don't seem to happen."

He sat down at the far end of the sofa, making sure she had lots of space. "Alright, young lady. Let's see what it would take for you to have a happy-ever-after."

She tossed her soft brown pageboy hairdo. "That's easy: money." She wrinkled her nose. "Lots of money, for sure."

He feigned shock. "I don't believe you. Surely, you want something more heartwarming than hard, cold cash."

"Okay, I would settle for *soft, warm* cash... a lot of it," she sang back at him.

"Whoa! You need to remember what the Bible says: *"Where your treasure is, there will your heart be, also."*

"And that means my heart is centered on money, I guess." She looked a little guilty. "Aw, nuts. There goes my innocent, feminine image."

He laughed softly. "Not really. I don't believe that, for one minute."

Their gaze met for a few seconds before she said weakly, "I guess I should get going."

He walked her out to her car in an oncoming summer dusk. As she slid behind the wheel, his words slipped out before he could think about it. "Will I see you again, before you go back to Burlington?"

"Do you want to?"

"Absolutely."

She paused on purpose. "Well then, I guess you will."

***

Donna arrived to a quaint setting at the ranch. She joined the other four members of the Roth family for a quiet evening on the porch. Jenny had not come home for the weekend, but Rhonda's ankle had healed and she helped Kathy bring out bowls of popcorn and lots of cool ginger tea. Conversation was pleasant, punctuated by the rhythmic chirp and twitter of nature all around them. Somewhere around ten o'clock they all turned in for a peaceful night's rest.

Outside, the moonlit Vermont landscape slowly disappeared behind a bank of clouds. For the next few hours, the family slept soundly. None of them was aware of the sudden quiet which swept across the ranch, sometime in the dark of early morning. They did not rise at the sound of a phantom train rumbling along some nonexistent track. It was only when the rumbling and shaking grew louder that they lifted their heads from their pillows. But it was too late to run.

It was an earth-shattering blast from out of nowhere.

CHAPTER NINE

Quakings

"There's no service between Burlington and Jericho, or even Stowe," Essie Schuler reported as she laid the phone back on its cradle. "All the operator could say was that the Chittenden County Sheriff's Department is on the job, and so is the Vermont National Guard." She looked at her father. "*Vater,* doesn't the guard have a facility up there in the Jericho area?"

He answered in German, their native language, confirming the information. "They go up there for maneuvers and training exercises of some sort."

"Are they up there now?" the mother asked in her Bavarian dialect. Her husband shrugged. "They could help those people, not so?" she suggested.

"Who knows?" he replied. "It was like this during the 'forty-three bombing of Berlin — nobody could contact anybody."

"This is not Berlin," the daughter asserted. "In a few hours, things will start to get repaired. This is only an earthquake, according to the radio." She went to turn that thing back on. "Let's see if there's any more news. I want to know if Jenny is okay."

Speaking over the news chatter, the professor made a quick phone call. "Ach, so," he announced, hanging up, "the university has only slight damage. A few cracked windows and books on the floor. We should be able to start summer classes without too much delay."

"Books on the floor?" Frau Schuler got the picture immediately. "That means the library is probably a mess."

Essie looked up. "This is correct, *Mutter*. You should get right over there and start helping with the cleanup. This could get you employed at the library, come next September."

"Yah-yah," the mother agreed. "This could get me hired, for certain." She turned once again to her spouse. "Please, *Schatzie*, call and see when I should go over there."

"I think we can wait until we at least get daylight," he admonished her. "We have other things to be concerned about, remember?"

"Please! I want to hear the news," Essie begged. "I want to know if all is right up there at the Roth house."

"Oh, *mein Gott*," Elke suddenly recalled something important. "This could ruin everything."

"Maybe not, *Mutter*. I just need to talk to Jenny. Then we shall see what we shall see."

***

Walter Taft had heard the rumbling and bolted out of bed, grabbing his robe, shoes, and car keys before wobbling out into his driveway. When the blast hit, he was thrown against the side of his Chevy, where he slid slowly to the ground, dazed. He lay there until convinced the major part of the quake was over, then rose and slipped into the driver's seat. The ignition turned on the dashboard lights, where he saw the gas gauge registering almost a full tank. "*I need to check on Donna*," he thought. But he didn't want to do that in his underwear, so he went back into the house, threw on some clothes, and then pulled the car out onto the little street that led past the village green. There were no streetlights, nor any house lights, for that matter. It was a wonder he didn't run over Jenny on her bike, as she was pedaling past the high school. He pulled over and waited for her to catch up. "Hey," he yelled from his car window, "where the heck do you think you're going, young lady?"

"Home!" she yelled back from her slippery halt. "I have to get home!"

"No, no, not on a bike in the dark." He leaned out to make his point. "Tell you what, take the bike back to the nursing home, then we'll head for the ranch together."

She wasn't sure.

"It's only a few blocks back, Jenny. Take the bike back, and ride with me. It's safer."

She nodded, and a few minutes later, the two of them were moving up Browns Trace Road. Just a mile from the Roth Ranch on Lee River Road, they were stopped by National Guard troops. A fellow with captain's bars on his camouflage shirt approached them. "Sorry, folks. The road is impassable. There's a big chasm across it, and no way around it. You're going to have to turn back."

Jenny wept all the way back to the Center. There, Walter spotted a dim light coming from Doc Horton's office on the other side of the green. He drove over and tried the door. It opened into the oil lamp-lighted waiting room, which was packed with folks huddled around a shortwave radio. "You people have some news?" he asked. They looked up and nodded, then turned quickly back to the static of the newscast. In a moment, he caught Jenny's hand and pulled her into the room. "What?" she sniffled.

"Shhh," the teacher hissed, as they sat on the floor next to a small, cold wood stove.

Out on the Jericho Center village green, with the exception of the occasional headlights of passing vehicles, it was still pitch black.

There were no more shakings that night. The citizens of Jericho Township who managed to slip into an uneasy sleep were awakened at the crack of dawn by the sputtering of helicopters across the sky. It was a sign of hope, even though there was no electric or phone service. Over at Maude's Nursing Home, residents were finally calming down. Most of them did not recall the stress of the night before, much to Mrs. Hannity's relief. But she was definitely shorthanded, what with so many workers unable to get into town. "Jenny, I appreciate that you're still here," she told the weary youngster.

"Oh, that's okay, I couldn't have slept, anyway... even though I heard there were no serious injuries reported." She yawned. "Thank God for Doc's radio. It kept us all from panicking, I swear."

"*His* radio, and a few more. Folks around here still don't trust modern communications. Thank God for that!"

"Anyway, the sheriff's department has designated a detour around the break in the Lee River Road. Mr. Taft is driving up to the ranch this afternoon, and I get to ride with him." She smiled weakly. "And I don't even have to miss a shift to do that."

"Alright then, but try to get some rest. You're young, but you're not invincible, missy."

Around the corner and up the hill from the nursing home, Walter was hauling his weary body out of bed. He made it to the kitchen, where he found milk in a refrigerator that was still cold, and prepared a bowl of corn flakes. There would be no coffee this morning, but that was not a burning issue; he wanted to know how things were going at Roth Ranch. There was lukewarm water for a quick shower, but his shave was cool under a thick layer of mentholated cream. Finally, he dressed and went to the living room to grab his car keys and jacket.

He stopped in the middle of the room. *"What the heck is all this litter on the carpet?"* he thought. There were bits of string and paper along the wall opposite the sofa and easy chair. *"Are those drag marks all the way to the front door?"* It took a couple of seconds before he realized that the boxes from the Roth attic — all five of them — were gone.

"Oh no," he moaned aloud. "Oh no. Somebody took them. Somebody stole all that information." He dropped heavily into the easy chair, staring at the vacant area. "I can't believe it. How did that happen?"

Slumping back into the chair, he closed his eyes and tried to reconstruct the activities of the night before. "Okay," he finally concluded, "I was in such a hurry, I forgot to lock the door when I left to go to the ranch." He went further with the scenario. "Somebody came in the dark, and stole the boxes, probably while I was trying to get to the ranch, or when we were over at Doc's office, listening to the news." He sighed heavily. He had been negligent, to say the least. He would certainly have to answer to the Collinses, and to the Shorts, for with this theft, there were probably mysteries that would never be solved, like the cause of those suspicious fires in Jericho. But then, there was also his responsibility to the Roths, who may well have profited financially from some of those items.

"The Roths." He suddenly got their welfare into proper perspective. "If they're even okay. I need to address that issue first. I need to pick up Jenny, and get up there as soon as we can."

The detour road was rugged and full of irregular ruts stirred up by previous traffic by the time Mr. Taft's Chevy drove through. Still, the two of them arrived at the arched gate of Roth Ranch by early afternoon. As the vehicle wound down the hairpin curves, a helicopter rose noisily from behind the trees near Crocker's sand bar. Jenny bent forward. "Is that a sheriff's truck parked down near Thunder's enclosure?"

"Looks like it," the teacher noted. "Yeah, that's him walking toward us with your folks." They watched, as the lawman shook Mark's hand before getting into the official vehicle.

Mr. Taft pulled to a stop in front of the porch. When he looked up, the sheriff was driving toward him, the driver's window down. This new sheriff, Max Duncan, was only in his eighth month as head of the department, but he was right there, on the job. "Hey, folks!" he greeted them, poking his head out the window opening. He hit the brake. "You two relatives of the Roth family?"

"I am," Jenny replied.

"I'm a friend of the family," Walter explained.

Sheriff Duncan sized them both up before he spoke carefully. "Okay. Well, you need to know there's been an accident. The bull got stuck in the quicksand and Mr. Roth had to put him down."

"What quicksand?" Jenny asked. "There's no quicksand down by the river, or anywhere else on this place."

"Right. That's what your folks said. But it happens every once in a while, when there's a big earthquake. The water table rises and turns sand into mush. Animals and people get stuck in those places, because you can't tell until you're sinking and you can't get out." He pushed his official sheriff's hat back on his head. "In this case, the bull was too heavy. There was no choice." He glanced back at the four family members headed this way. "Now, on the other hand, we were able to remove the young man. We dropped a rescue team member down from the 'copter to loosen the quicksand then lifted the fellow up."

"What young man?" she asked. A quick look showed that Eddie was not one of the approaching Roths.

"Eddie? My brother, Eddie?" Her voice rose. "Where are you taking him? Is he going to be okay? Is he hurt?"

The sheriff looked away, then nodded toward the quartet that was almost alongside the two vehicles. "I'm going to leave that conversation for you and your folks, miss. Meanwhile, if there's anything else my department can do, let me know." He tipped his hat and drove away.

She was out of the car in a couple of seconds, zeroing in on Donna. "What happened to Eddie?"

The lovely blue eyes were glazed over, but Jenny persisted. "What happened to my brother?"

"What?" the older sister asked.

"Look at me, Donna. What's happened to Eddie?" She watched the words being formed, slowly and with great effort.

"He's dead."

***

On Monday morning, Walter headed for his first class at UVM. The past few days had been right out of a horror movie, and there were still electric outages and phone lines down, so he'd had no chance to tell Connie Collins or Greta Short about the missing boxes, let alone, the death of Eddie Roth. He left the Chevy in student parking and picked up materials from the bookstore, before finding a phone booth. Connie answered almost immediately.

"Mrs. Collins, this is Walter Taft."

"Oh thank heavens, Walter. Where are you?"

"On campus, ma'am."

"So they're still starting classes this week?"

"Yes, ma'am."

"Walter, I'm a fellow-teacher. You need to call me 'Connie.'" When he hesitated to reply, she thought to address the situation up in Jericho Township. "What's going on up at the ranch?"

"Bad news, there. I guess you may have heard on Sunday night news, there's been one death from the aftermath of the earthquake. Well, sadly, it was Eddie Roth, Jenny and Donna's brother." He heard the gasp on the other end of the phone line. "Ay-yuh. I guess they were all in bed when the quake happened. Had to make their way out of some lath and plaster rubble, but at least the old place didn't collapse around them. Anyway, it was too dark to do anything but wait for daylight, and when it came, the three kids set out to check on the animals. Mark and Kathy got busy trying to get some electricity and kitchen clean-up chores going. I guess Eddie found the bull, Thunder, had escaped from his pasture and charged straight for the river, where he got caught in quicksand." He paused. "Quicksand happens sometimes, after a major shift in the earth."

"Right. The newscast explained that. But they didn't say who had been trapped in it." There was a little cluck of her tongue. "I never thought it would be Jenny's brother." Her concern focused on the girl. "How is she doing?"

"In shock. But she's not staying at the ranch. That's another whole story. Donna feels neither she nor her sister should continue going up there. Something about insurance money. Like I say… another story." He took a big breath. "So, Connie, there is something else I need to tell you, and I'm sorry to say, it's also bad news."

"Alright, Walter."

"Um… during the chaos after the quake, I panicked and left my house unlocked for several hours." He bit his bottom lip. "Sometime that night, somebody stole those attic boxes from my living room."

He heard her take a deep breath. "Oh no! All of them?"

"I'm afraid so. I'm so, so very sorry. I feel terrible."

"Hmm," she murmured. "Any idea who might do that?"

"Definitely. Probably Andrew's grandpa, a guy named Ken Pearson." He shook his head, even though she couldn't see him do it. "All I have to do, is take Andrew aside and see if he can help somehow."

"I see. But right now, you don't even have telephone service. This could take a while, you know."

"Yes, ma'am, Connie."

"In the meantime, we do have the flashlight, and *now* we have a legitimate reason to check it for fingerprints. The person who was using it up in the attic is probably the same person who took the two books, and then those boxes from your house."

"What two books?"

"Whoops! I guess I forgot to tell you about those. Well, never mind. We can talk about that later. In the meantime, is there anything Don and I can do to help Jenny and Donna? We are Christian counselors, you know."

"I'm planning to have coffee with Donna sometime this afternoon, Connie. I'll let her know you've made the offer."

They met in a hamburger joint snuggled up against the Flynn Movie Theater on Main Street in Burlington. He could tell she had been weeping. "Did you make it in to work this morning?" he asked.

Donna leaned on the worn table between them. "Yup." She sniffed lightly. "I'm allowed some time off, but I asked if I could delay that until we get back the coroner's report."

"Ay-yuh, that's pretty standard procedure, I guess. How come you're waiting for it?"

"I asked Doc Horton how Eddie could drown in only eighteen inches of water. He said the kid would have either been out cold or dead before he went under." She touched the end of her nose with a crushed tissue. "He said he would look into it."

"Oh, that's right; he's the Chittenden County Coroner." Walter leaned across from his seat in the booth. "I assume you have a reason for all this?"

"There was a wound. I saw it. At the base of his skull." She motioned with one hand. "At the back of his neck."

He grimaced. "You think somebody stunned him on purpose?"

"Or maybe they killed him."

"But *why*, Donna?"

"Nothing new under the sun, Walter. It's money. In this case, insurance money."

"Okay... go on." He leaned back to listen.

She stared out the window. Across Main Street, a worker was mowing the grass at City Hall Park. "It's my mother's insurance money. We three kids are listed first. If anything happens to us, guess who's next in line?" She looked back at him. "Uncle Mark."

He frowned. "And does he know this?"

"All three of them, Kathy, Rhonda and him... they've known it all along. I found out when I was up there checking out the ranch before Jenny and Eddie moved in." She seemed to be double-checking her facts as her eyes followed a Burlington Transit bus moving past the window on its way to the bus station. "At least, that's what the lawyer told me."

"What lawyer?"

It was in the cover letter that came with my copy of the will. He said Uncle Mark had a copy of it."

"I see. Did you confirm this, though? Maybe your uncle never got his copy."

She nodded vigorously. "I did. I dropped a hint about the insurance one night while we were sitting on the porch, and Uncle Mark looked at Aunt Kathy and then he said, yes, they knew about it."

"Listen, Donna. We don't want to jump to conclusions, here. I mean, your mom is not wealthy; I doubt this life insurance is worth too much. Surely, not to kill for."

"Wrong. My dad took this insurance on her, a long time ago. Way before he even died. Not only is this a pretty good sum, but it might even make somebody move back from Texas, to make sure he gets his hands on it."

He suddenly saw the whole picture about not returning to the ranch. "Oh my gosh, Donna. Now I see why you girls shouldn't go back to that place. Is Jenny aware of all this?" She nodded no. "You must be terrified."

"Well, there's no running away if somebody has you in his crosshairs, but I sure don't want to make it easy for them."

He huffed incredulously. "I can't imagine somebody committing a triple murder for a measly few thousand dollars."

"Oh, they won't look like murders," she corrected him, "and we're talking *three hundred thousand* of those measly dollars."

CHAPTER TEN

Promises

Essie Schuler and her mother drove to Jericho to check on Jenny at the ranch, with the intention that she would help drive all the way to Stowe to also check on the Von Trapp family. After all, she had her student driver's license now, so more driving practice would be good. So, the same Monday afternoon Walter and Donna were having a conversation in downtown Burlington, the two Schuler ladies were driving through Essex Junction, along Vermont State Route 15, to make their rounds. They were able to avoid the fissure in Lee River Road, since it was on the other side of Roth Ranch. When they descended to a stop at the ranch house, the effects of the earthquake were obvious. Temporary fixes held the pasture fence together. The moan of an injured heifer rose softly from behind its protection. Piles of lath and plaster filled the grassy area between the porch and the driveway. "There must surely be damage in the whole house," Frau Schuler remarked. "This is not good."

"We must be patient, *Mutter*. We will see what we can see."

Making their way through the powdery path to the front door, the two knocked and waited.

Kathy's face was spotted with what looked like white flour. "Yes?"

"Hi, Mrs. Roth. I'm Essie Schuler and this is my *Mutter*. Do you remember us?"

"Oh yes." She opened the screen door. "I'm sorry, but we have quite a mess, here."

"No-no, please... we understand," the German mother reassured her. "We come only to check on everybody. Are you well?"

"Where is Jenny?" Essie asked.

"Jenny is at the nursing home, where she works. She lives there right now. Things are a mess, like I said."

"And the others?" The freckled face framed the concern in her young, pale blue eyes. "Your girl? And Mr. Roth? And Eddie?"

Kathy's chest moved with the deep breath. "Mark and Rhonda are fine. I guess you haven't heard about Eddie. I'm so sorry."

The girl's voice went up a whole octave. "What? What about Eddie?"

"He was... he was trying to save Thunder," came the trembling reply. "I'm sorry, but he couldn't do it, and he died — a real hero, miss." She wiped the corner of her eye with her dusty knuckle. "I'm so sorry."

"Eddie is dead? No!" She turned toward her mother's embrace.

"I'm so sorry," Kathy murmured, again.

Elke Schuler drove the detour route to the nursing home, where they found Jenny in her room. Tears and hugs eventually gave way to the trio sitting on the edge of her bed, the mother and daughter on either side of the grieving sister. "Jenny," the golden-haired mother said, "we are so sorry this has happened. We are from a war zone; we understand this feeling of helplessness. We know these times are too hard to even pray. We don't know how to pray."

"But Eddie really loved Jesus. How come he had to die like that?" As the grieving sister began to sob again, the mother's heart brought forth both English and German words of comfort: "We don't always have answers, *Mein Kind*. We can only let the Holy Ghost pray, instead of us. That's what we do. That's what we do." With that the woman placed her hand on Jenny's head and started praying in *another* language. It lasted for a few minutes, and then the girl felt a wave of peace, relaxing her whole body. The Schulers lifted her feet and stretched her out on the bed. As Essie pulled a blanket up over her friend, Jenny whispered, "I feel so much better. What was your mom saying in that German prayer?"

"Um, that wasn't German," her friend whispered back. "That was glossolalia."

"What's that?"

"We have to check on the Von Trapps, kiddo. I'll explain it later. Meanwhile, you just rest in the peace of God…"

***

Meanwhile, back in Burlington, the Collinses drove past Howard Johnson's restaurant and made a right turn off Shelburne Road onto Flynn Avenue. In a moment, they pulled into the Shorts' driveway. Don carried the potato salad around to the back patio, where Gerald was already flipping hamburgers. His cordial smile reflected the pleasant atmosphere on this late Monday afternoon. "Welcome to our first barbecue of the summer!" the host called out.

Don's elfish grin accompanied a similar greeting before the man-talk began. "Hey! Is that a new grill?"

It wasn't long before all four were seated at the picnic table. After saying grace, they commenced to enjoy the feast. Still the subject of conversation was centered on the quake.

"We sure were blessed that all we lost was our phone service," Greta commented as she passed the catsup to Don. "Some folks had actual damage."

"Most of the structural damage occurred more toward the east. Burlington just got a good shaking," Gerald added. He pressed a toasted bun around a juicy beef patty.

"Well, Don and I spent a few hours under the dining room table, I can tell ya," Connie stated. "It was the longest night I ever spent with my knees tucked up under my chin, and I hope I never have to do it again."

"That's what you'd call some serious cuddling," Don quipped as he winked at Gerald.

"So how come you didn't run outside?" Greta was curious.

Don came back with a chuckle. "What? And miss all that serious cuddling?"

"Don..." His wife displayed her stern teacher face, then turned the conversation toward another matter involving the earthquake. "Anyway, there was a lot of damage up at Jericho Township." She leaned toward her friend. "Thank God, Millie and the others were safe in the nursing home. But..." she dug her fork into the baked beans, "there was some stuff that happened during the blackout and the phone failure." She took a bite of the beans. "Um..." She finished swallowing. "You two remember those boxes we took out of the Roths' attic?"

It took only a few minutes to tell the whole story of the stolen items. There was a short time of weighing in of the implications of this theft, as the foursome ate quietly. Finally, Gerald asked the question: "You say Mr. Taft — Walter — says he knows who stole this stuff?"

"Yes," Connie answered. "In fact, I talked to him this morning. He believes it was the grandfather of one of his students."

"Will Walter Taft confront him, do you think?" Gerald asked gently.

"Probably, Gerald. If I know Walter, it will be private and he will leave an opening for the man to escape exposure."

Mr. Short leaned forward on both elbows. "Kind of makes you wonder why the grandpa would do such a thing, doesn't it?"

"Hmm," Don said thoughtfully. "Those Grange people take a lot of vows, from what I hear. Maybe he's just trying to protect somebody. Maybe he owes somebody his allegiance."

***

By Tuesday morning, Mark Roth was finally getting his act together. The battle fatigue had subsided just enough to allow some clearer thinking. He stood at the edge of the driveway and took score: Behind him, in the upper pasture, a mournful bellow reminded him of the most urgent task at hand. That one heifer definitely had a broken leg; she would have to be put down, and then butchered properly. There wouldn't be a complete loss, in that case.

But Thunder's situation was altogether different — his huge hulk would remain for the birds and wildcats to finish off. It could be some time before it could be extricated from its soggy prison. As devastating as that was for the man, there was more; only just a few hundred feet from there, the barn was filled with the fragrant chaos of a collapsed hayloft.

"Aw, hell..." he moaned, turning toward the ranch house. "And that's another thing," he said, gazing at the old homestead. "Got to get those upstairs halls reinforced, and then figure out what to do about those gawddim attic steps." He pictured those stairs, fallen into the linen closet below, jammed tightly in place, unmovable below the gaping black of the attic above. He shivered. "That's just gawddim creepy."

Kathy's call brought him back to reality.

"What?" he yelled back to his wife on the porch.

"We have phone service! It's back on!"

He waved an acknowledgment, then plodded toward the house, to contact the butchering team. "That's right. I can handle this." Suddenly he was a soldier, again. "I've been through tougher stuff than this. I'm up to the task. I can do this, standing on one leg, with one arm tied behind my back." He picked up the telephone like a general about to give orders for the next move in a battle plan. It was just a matter of a real man, taking real leadership. Kathy and Rhonda were depending on him.

***

Two other people had seen the wound at the back of Eddie's neck: the rescue worker, as he dangled in the harness to dig the body loose, and the sheriff, whom this shovel-wielding guardsman had motioned to. Max Duncan had acknowledged the enlisted man's signal and then moved on with his part of the rescue. It wasn't until he got back to headquarters that he put in a call to Doc Horton. "I think we may have a problem, here, Doc. There's a hole in the kid's head… Ay-yah, it doesn't look right. Think maybe somebody was throwing rocks or something. Anyway, just giving you a heads-up on this, because the sooner we have evidence, the sooner we can investigate." He waited for the doctor's reply. "Ay-yuh. You could be right, Doc. I'll see if there was insurance on the kid." Another brief comment from the coroner, and the sheriff ended the conversation with a repeated request: "I'll be waiting for your call… the sooner, the better, sir."

Deputy Smith looked up from a desk across the room. "You smell a rat, Sheriff?"

"That's what I do best, Smitty."

"Yes, sir." The younger man tapped a stack of papers into order. "That's how you got elected — keeping all those campaign promises alive and well." He grinned. "Of course, there's one promise you haven't kept, for sure."

"What's that, Smitty?"

"You promised you would stop calling me 'Smitty.'"

"Oh damn. Tell you what, give me a couple of days to get used to it." Sure enough, by Tuesday he had it down.

But he was still waiting for the coroner's report on Eddie Roth.

***

Walter went over the lesson plan he would have to complete in just a few weeks this summer. At the end of an hour, he was a bit doubtful about this whole thing. Still, he needed to get his master's. "Just in case I get fired from my position here at the high school," he reminded himself. "So, it's darned if I do, and darned if I don't." He stood up from the kitchen table, stretching toward the ceiling. "I should get out and walk a little, before I start tonight's homework." It seemed a good idea to wander down to the Jericho Center Country Store for a cool bottle of Pepsi. Sure enough, the stroll through the early evening was refreshing; a soft breeze moving the treetops in the waning daylight. Inside the store, he pulled the cold bottle out of the iced cooler and meandered past the canned goods toward the cashier. Suddenly, he stopped in his tracks. Andrew came around the corner, laughing at something someone behind him had just said. The student came to a stop at the sight of his teacher. "Hey, Mr. Taft!?" A quick look at the Pepsi opened the door for the conversation. "Out for a cold one, sir?"

"Ay-yuh. Out for a cold one," the man replied. Even as he spoke, a tall, distinguished gentleman with a neat, gray mustache which matched the thick head of hair, came to an easy halt beside the boy.

Andrew nodded toward the older man. "Mr. Taft, this is my grandpa."

Walter didn't know whether to be upset or delighted. The man was courteous, extending his hand to greet this upstart teacher, his eyes twinkling with amusement at the look on Walter's face. "I'm Ken Pearson."

Walter Taft shook the man's hand, a slow grin coming forth. "Call me Walter," he said.

The three of them moved slowly to the counter where a cash register was ka-chinging away. Walt turned to address the two following him. "How did you folks come through the quake last weekend? Everybody okay?"

"We have a family farm just this side of Jericho Corners. Got outside before the roof collapsed," Ken responded. "Got a tarp up the next day, and now we're working on the repairs." Walter shook his head in sympathy. "Oh, it'll be alright," the man continued. "At least nobody got killed. Not like what happened over at the Roths'. Sure sad about that boy."

Walter addressed the teenager. "Did you know Eddie Roth, Andrew?"

"Not really. He was a new kid. I just knew who he was, that's all." There was an awkward moment. "Anyways, it wasn't the quake that killed him. He got drowned in quicksand." He turned to Ken, "Right, Grandpa?"

"I don't know all the details, Andy." He patted the youngster on the shoulder. "We're just glad nothing happened to *you*, out all night with your friends."

The teacher noted the blush on the boy's face. "You were out all night, Andrew? I'm surprised. I figured you to be a lot more, um, refined." The remark was interrupted by Walter's turn to pay for his soda pop. He stepped aside, waiting for the other two to make their purchases, then led the way out to the parking lot.

As grandfather and grandson headed for a well-worn pickup truck, Walter continued the line of thought.

"So, what do young guys do, on these wild all-night forays?"

Andrew laughed. "Mostly go looking for girls, or drink beer, if we've got it. But mostly, we just talk about girls and sports."

Ken Pearson opened the driver's door of his truck. "He just takes this old bomb and stays out all night, but not very often, so we don't get too excited. Boys will be boys." He glanced around. "So, what're you driving these days, Walter?"

"A used Chevy. That's all I can afford."

Ken looked around the parking lot. "I don't see it."

"Aw, Grandpa, Mr. Taft probably walked over. He just lives up the road — you know — across the street from the water witch."

Walt Taft needed to get to his studies, but he just couldn't seem to settle down. Ken Pearson lived all the way up at the Corners, and he was at home the night of the earthquake. It didn't seem likely that the man could have stolen those boxes. "Heck, he didn't even know I lived in town; Andrew had to tell him."

The conclusion flashed before him; Andrew was not at home during the quake, and Andrew knew where his teacher lived.

***

On Wednesday, Jenny called Essie Schuler, right after getting off her morning shift. "You promised to explain that language your mom prayed over me."

"Of course." She seemed reluctant. "Are you sure you want to hear this over the phone? I could wait until we can converse, um, eye-to-eye. That might be better."

"No-no-no. I want to know about this, right now. It really settled me down. I actually slept through the night."

"You did? Oh, my *Mutter* will be glad to hear that."

"Good. Now, tell me about it."

"Wait," the strawberry blonde girl insisted. "I need to find a good place to sit down. You do the same."

"I can't," Jenny objected. "I'm in a phone booth."

"Oh my gosh, kiddo! This is long distance. You can't afford that." She thought quickly. "Go to the phone in the lobby of the nursing home — the one patients get phone calls on. I will call you there in fifteen minutes."

"But then it will be a long distance charge on your folks' phone, Essie."

"Don't worry. *Mutter* will be so happy you have slept through the night, it won't matter. Fifteen minutes, okay?"

Jenny was grateful to find the phone available. She picked it up and moved it as far as the cord into the wall would allow. She was sitting in a quiet corner when it rang. "I got it!" she called out. As soon as she heard Essie's voice, she turned to the questioning eyes in the home's dayroom. "It's for me," she sang out. Then she lowered her voice. "Okay, Essie, what is this glossy-ale thing your mother did?"

Over the next few minutes, the young German refugee explained that the Holy Spirit could pray through Christians, whenever things got too complicated or too overwhelming for them to pray on their own. "Too often, we get confused and don't pray for the right things... like we forget that we need to pray for God's will to be done, not ours. If we're upset or whatever, we get too involved with what *we* want, and that, as you Americans say, '...throws a monkey wrench into the whole works.'" She repeated the main point: "So the Holy Spirit can pray through a Christian."

"And what is that language called?"

Essie spelled it out for her. "If you go across the village green tomorrow, take a look in the dictionary, or ask the librarian to direct you to information about it."

"Okay."

"Did you write it down, Jenny?"

"Nope. Don't have to. It's 'glossy-ale- yeah'. I can remember that."

Her friend laughed. "Close enough. If the librarian is a Christian, she'll know what you mean. Otherwise, just ask for information about speaking in tongues."

"Okay." The student was getting down to particulars. "So how do we let the Holy Spirit talk through us? Is there something special we need to do?"

"Nope. Just ask God for the blessing of speaking in tongues, then open your mouth and puff out a few vowels and consonants, and the Spirit will take hold. It may not happen all of a sudden. Took me a few hours before I knew it was a real language. At first, it sounded like gibberish!" She laughed. "Just don't give up."

"So, both you and your mom have this, uh, blessing?"

"Yes, we do. All Christians can have it; they just have to ask God for it."

"All Christians? Really?" Suddenly, she sat straight up in her chair. "Wait a minute, Essie. You are Jews. You escaped from the Nazis and everything."

"No. That's not true. Only my *Vater* is a Jew. My *Mutter* is a German gentile, and a real Pentecostal."

"Wait," Jenny said again. "There are Pentecostals in Germany?"

There was that laugh, again. "Oh, you would be surprised. They are scattered all over Europe, but they are there, for sure."

"Oh my gosh, Essie. I never knew this. I sure never knew this about your family. You're actually half-Jew and half-Gentile, right?"

"Right."

"How could I know you Schulers so long, and not know all this?"

"Oh," came the answer, "there are a whole lot of other things you don't know about the Schulers."

CHAPTER ELEVEN

Burials

"I don't care *how* you do it; just get that dead animal out of the Lee River, without spilling any putrid blood, fluids, or body parts. Got that?"

Mark Roth sighed wearily. This was the third call from Vermont officials, warning him to get the job done. "Yes, sir," he replied.

"Good. You have two more days, then we start fining you."

"But it wasn't my fault, sir."

"Doesn't make any difference. The carcass is on your river bank, and you're responsible for any pollution of not only the Lee River, but the Lamoille, as well. That's a helluva lot of damage, Roth, so get a move on it." The phone slammed down.

"Which office was that?" Kathy asked from the top of the stairs.

"Doesn't matter. They're all saying the same thing: Move it, or pay fines until we do." He stepped to the foot of the stairs. "I think we're pretty much on our own, and we only have a couple more days to move Thunder's body."

"How can they fine us?" she asked. "It was an earthquake. Isn't this what's called 'an act of God,' or something?"

"You know, I think we've got a lot of state officials who really don't know how to handle this thing. A dead animal in the river is one thing, but one stuck in quicksand is another.

No, they just don't know how to get the problem solved, so they're dumping it on us."

"Well, that's not fair." She was dismayed. "It's not like we have a whole lot of money to hire somebody."

"I know." He shook his head. "But it looks like we'll have to do that very thing. We need somebody who has a big enough machine to dig around the body, without leaving the solid ground of the edge of the pasture." He swore under his breath before he turned to the living room. There, he picked up the telephone book and turned to the ads in the back. Almost immediately, he spotted the name of a large excavation company located in Barre. "Bet they work with the granite quarries," he mumbled as he lifted the black earpiece from its cradle.

The manager of Morrison Excavations took the call from his secretary. "Hello, Mr. Roth. This is Martin Morrison, and I was hoping to hear from you. I'm familiar with your situation. Been keeping an eye on how it was going. I'm guessing you need some pretty big equipment to do the clean-up."

Mark was surprised. "Uh, yeah. I guess we do, But I really need to inquire about the cost. I was hoping we could afford your services, but if not, maybe we could make payments or something..."

"Now, Mark — may I call you Mark?" He didn't wait for permission. "As I said, I've been watching this whole situation, and I think we may have an opportunity to do each other a favor. May I make you an offer, sir?"

"Uh, sure."

"You have a dire situation there, Mark, and all of New England is watching. Not only is there a problem with disposing of a dead animal in quicksand, but we also have, if you'll excuse me for being so blunt, the poignant situation of the unfortunate passing of your nephew. Again, with all due respect, Mark, this is a story that deserves to be on the front page of the *Burlington Free Press*, and maybe even a couple of

New York City tabloids. This would be great publicity for Morrison Excavations, Mark. And in return, we would charge you absolutely nothing. Zero bucks, Mark." He paused to let it all sink in. "So, what do you say? We can be up there by tomorrow afternoon."

"Well, I'll be damned," the cattleman exclaimed. "We've got a deal." It made no difference to him that Eddie's death would help advertise for Morrison's company. Further, Mark didn't mind in the least that the rest of the world would know how this company performed such an impressive recovery mission at absolutely no cost to the grieving Roth family. The problem would be solved and the state of Vermont would be off his back. The boy's demise just made a better newspaper story. It was what it was.

On Thursday afternoon, reporters and photographers were waiting as the Morrison flatbed trailer maneuvered down the tightly curved drive to unload the behemoth excavator at the riverside. Within a few minutes, the long, yellow neck was stretching out to where Thunder's form lay in the sudsy mud. Its bucket head sank powerful teeth into the murky water again and again, until the near side of the body was exposed. Then, with one great, clanking move, the jaws closed and the limp form came loose with a great sucking sound. Cameras clicked as a cheer went up.

Immediately, Martin Morrison was there, engaging with the press, making sure they got all the details correct. As soon as the huge bull's body was dropped into the burial spot beside Thunder's shelter, Mr. Morrison made one final grand gesture. Gathering the reporters at the edge of the deep grave, he turned to Mark. "Mr. Roth, it's my understanding that Thunder was a prize bull, and the apple of your eye. With that in mind, sir, I would like you to have something in remembrance of this special Hereford royalty." He signaled to one of his men, who had been busy down near the body. "Al! Come on up outta there!" As the man emerged, Martin got a big grin on his face. He reached to take the bloody, but neatly severed brow bearing Thunder's horns. "We thought you might like to hang these in a place of honor." Then, as cameras flashed and reporters clapped, Martin slowly placed the rag-wrapped gift into Mark's hands. The battle-fatigued veteran's chin quivered ever-so-slightly when he whispered his thanks. Finally, Martin placed a manly arm around Mark, for one more picture.

It was difficult to tell who was the man-of-the-hour — Mark Roth, Martin Morrison, or Thunder, whose death had led to this scenario. Meanwhile, due respect for Eddie Roth had been lost, somewhere between a recovery mission and a publicity stunt.

***

"Yup! Just what I thought."

Deputy Smith looked over at his boss. "What?"

Max Duncan shook out the carbon copy of the coroner's report. "Death by a blow that severed the spinal cord, just below the skull."

The deputy moved in closer, peering over the sheriff's shoulder. "That's what it says, huh?" He strained to read the blue-tinted print. "So what was the murder weapon?"

"It says it was an egg-shaped object, with a flat side that penetrated the spine, and lodged in the brain."

"So they got the object?"

"Nope. They figured it got sucked out when they pulled the kid out of the sand. He was lying face-up." Max pointed his finger at the print and repeated the shape of the object. "Egg-shaped, with a flat side."

Smith straightened up to consider that. "Sounds like a stone, or maybe the end of a pole... like maybe a metal fence pole."

"Metal fence poles are round, not egg-shaped," Sheriff Duncan reminded his deputy. "Nope, this had to be a rock. And of course, those were all around the murder scene — river rocks." He leaned back in his desk chair. "So what we're looking for here, is a killer who used a well-aimed rock to take down this boy."

"But why?" Smith asked.

"Aw, it's usually something to do with hiding evidence of another crime, or revenge, or money." He waved the copy in front of Smith's face. "Take your pick, mister."

Smith was a quick learner. "How about we just take a look at who was around at that hour of the day?"

Max grinned. "There ya go, Deputy." He tossed a notebook to his helper. "So, let's make a list." He rose from his desk chair, ambling over to the coffee pot located under the office window. "So, the first ones would be Mark, Kathy, and Rhonda Roth." He paused. "From Texas, by the way." He picked up the cup that was his. "What the hell were they doing up here from Texas, anyway?" He lifted the pot off the warmer and the hot, dark brew poured into the man's personal mug. "How was it going for them down there in cattlemen's country that they would even *think* of leaving?" He sniffed the fragrance from the cup. "I think we probably should run a little background on those folks. See what you can do." He took a sip. "And while we're at it, we should probably check out the older sister — what was her name?"

The deputy pulled out a slip of paper from his shirt pocket. "Uh... Donna. Her name is Donna."

"Okay. So let's get statements from all of them, as soon as possible."

"Like when, Sheriff?"

"I just told you, Smith: As soon as possible."

The deputy lowered his head. "Yes, sir, but you are aware that the funeral service for the boy is tomorrow, right?"

"Right. You'll need to cover for me."

"You're going?"

"Ay-yuh."

"May I ask what for, Sheriff?"

"Looking for rats, son. Looking for rats…"

***

It should have been a simple, private funeral service at the First Methodist Church in Burlington, Vermont, but the Morrison Excavation's high-publicity campaign turned it into a circus. Reporters' vehicles lined both sides of Beull Street and South Winooski Avenue, around the red sandstone and marble structure with the elegant asymmetric square tower. The quiet grief of the Roth sisters would now be exposed via the tabloids of America. Even the small contingency of Eddie's friends from the Children's Home felt the tension as they were escorted down to the front of the sanctuary. The Schulers came with Mrs. Hannity, followed by the foursome of the Collinses and the Shorts, all of whom kept their heads down, avoiding the press's bustle. Eddie's Sunday school teacher, Miss Green, managed a sideways glare at the intruders with their pads and pencils, as she moved down the aisle. Finally, the Roths entered from a side entrance and took their places in the front row. Walter was pleased that Donna had asked him to sit with the family.

The service was short, for there was not a lot of history to bring up for a youngster who was not quite fifteen years old. Still, the minister made the point: This boy was in Heaven. "He accepted Jesus as his Lord and Savior, and folks, that's all it takes," the preacher reminded the mourners. Somebody

sang a special song, after which, one of the Home boys read a poem. The congregation sang a hymn, and then pall bearers carried the casket out. People waited as the Roth family followed, eyes focused on the carpet in front of them. Then the press surged forward to file their stories. And all the while, Sheriff Max Duncan was watching from the back row, taking mental notes.

It was in the back seat of the long, black vehicle that Jenny leaned over to snuggle into her older sister's embrace. "Donna, I know our mother couldn't come for the funeral, but I really think we should at least try to tell her." She started to cry. "Please, Donna. I want to see Mama. Please, can't we go to see her?"

***

Walter got into the books the day after the funeral. It was Saturday, so he started early and kept at it all day. By that evening, he was ready for some supper. Seeing the refrigerator offered no quick fixes, he decided to go find a hamburger. The man was in the car before he realized he didn't want to do this alone. The key was in the ignition, but he needed to think about it. Shortly, he was back in the house, talking to Donna on the phone. "You working tonight?"

"Just got off a bit ago."

"I'm hungry. You want to go eat someplace?"

"You're coming all the way to Burlington to eat? Boy! You must be desperate."

He was, of course, but more for company than food. "I know a place that serves great burgers. What do you say?" She didn't answer immediately, so he pressed on. "Come on, Donna. It's Saturday night. They even have a jukebox."

She laughed. "You actually dance?"

"A regular Fred Astaire, lady. Try me."

He picked her up at seven and headed for an eatery in a mall on North Avenue. Upon entering, the couple was greeted by a waitress who led them toward a row of booths across the black and white dance floor. They asked for the one nearest the jukebox, which glowed with green and yellow lights against the back wall. "How've you been, Mandy?" he asked the attractive forty-something lady.

Mandy smiled. "Haven't seen you in a dog's age, mister. Thought you left town or something."

"And I did. Went to teach at Jericho High School." He reached out toward Donna's side of the table. "This is my friend, Donna."

"Nice to meetcha, Donna." She turned back to Walter. "Let's see... one cold beer, right?"

He addressed his date. "Here's the deal. I have one beer. Just one. And a glass of water with my hamburger. That's it for the evening."

"Oh? And that applies to me, as well?" She was amused, since she wasn't a drinker. "I'll take one glass of Coke, if that's alright with you."

"No limits on Coke." He reflected her amusement. "But you could get fat."

The burgers were large and smothered in French fries. They ate silently, enjoying the music blaring from the jukebox nearby. When they were finished, he raised his eyebrows as an invitation to dance. It was a jitterbug, first, then a fox trot, followed by another jitterbug, before they sat down for a short rest.

"I am so surprised," she commented. "How did you learn to dance like that?"

"Use to come down here with my college crowd, almost every weekend."

She tilted her head to one side. "Yeah? Did you have a girlfriend?"

"Nobody steady. I was too busy studying for all that." He took a sip of the beer. "So, where did *you* learn to dance?"

There was a wry smile. "Believe it or not, my mother taught me."

"No kidding? So she must have been pretty good."

"She should have been. She was a dance instructor. She loved it. Even taught while she was pregnant."

He nodded as he leaned closer to hear her over the music. She said something else, but he couldn't catch every word. "Hey, I can't hear you," he called out. He pantomimed for her permission to join her on the same side of the booth. She laughed and shook her head, sliding over to let him in. "Okay, start over," he said.

Anna had had her own dance studio for three years before she met a dashing military doctor, Captain Edward Roth. Their romance was fast and furious, lasting through the end of WWI and right up to the day the overworked fellow died of a heart attack. By then, there were three children. "I was eight when we learned that Mama was also sick. Headaches all the time, always throwing up. And it just got worse. She finally had to put us in the Home. And she paid full price for our board and room. We weren't charity cases, us three. We just didn't have anybody to keep us."

"What about your Uncle Mark?"

"He was too busy being a cowboy. Didn't have time for kids, not even any of his own. His first wife had two, um, what they told everybody were miscarriages. Personally, I think she died of a broken heart, but I can't prove it." Donna flipped her hair back with one hand. He caught a whiff of her perfume. "So, anyway, we spent a good ten years at the Home. Saw her once in a while at first, but now she's so far gone with the brain cancer, she doesn't even know her own children."

She was watching her own hands twisting the sweating Coke glass in its own puddle on the table.

He was watching *her*. "I guess that puts you in an uncomfortable position, with Jenny asking you to take her to see her mama."

She leaned back in the booth, looking at him with those sad, crystal-blue eyes. "Walter, I just don't want to do that. Our mother doesn't even know us. What's the point?"

He kept that eye contact going for a moment before he answered softly, something about burying the hatchet.

"I'm sorry," she said, bending closer. "I didn't hear you."

He was able to rephrase the thought as he moved nearer to her ear. "I said, 'Maybe the point is, she needs to get that mama-hug she's been missing for so long.'" Donna turned back to meet his gaze, just inches away. He lifted those Roy Rogers brows to emphasize the possibility. "Everybody needs that intimate connection, Donna. Everybody."

She turned away, her face hidden by the soft brown page boy's curtain. It was time for him to just sit quietly beside her.

The jukebox brought the latest rock-and-roll hit to a smashing finish. For a few seconds the arm moved out and another record dropped. When the arm came back down, Perry Como was singing Forever and Ever. Walter reached over to move the twisting fingers from the dripping glass. "Hey, it's getting late. How about one last dance?" Instead of the waltz, he chose to go with the high school staple — just swaying back and forth, and she let him draw her close. By the second time through the song, her head finally lay against his shoulder. He bent down, just enough to enjoy the fragrance of her hair. Suddenly, he wanted to drive both Donna and Jenny to White River Junction, for a hug from their mama. But he would ask Donna about it later. Right now, he was just glad he'd decided not to eat alone.

***

Greta was not happy. "I thought they turned that funeral into a circus," she told her husband. "All those reporters and cameras. Those people didn't even know the boy." She poured a second cup of coffee for Gerald's Saturday supper. "I tell you, I've been stewing about this all day."

"I could tell," he replied. "But, can't say I blame you. It should have been all about what Eddie was trying to do. Instead, it was all about some big adventure. What a shame, because he was a real hero."

"Yes, he was." She set the coffee pot down hard. "Sometimes people just stink, you know? It makes me wonder how God can love us at all."

"But He does, Greta, and we should be so grateful."

But the fretful wife would not be appeased. "And did you see that the county sheriff was there? What for?"

Gerald paused to pass his fingers across the crown of his head. "Now that one really makes me wonder. All I can think is, there's something fishy about that boy's death. That lawman wasn't there to socialize, let alone pay his respects. Ay-yuh. Something's up."

Greta repeated that opinion to her friend, Connie, after church the next morning. Connie seemed to think there was a lot more to the Roth Ranch picture than met the eye. "I'll talk to Don," she promised. "He knows how to dig into these things."

CHAPTER TWELVE

Max

Max Duncan was on the phone with the Burlington Police Department's Detective Division, also fondly referred to as "The Snoop Squad" by the rest of the force. "I know you guys are up to your ears right now, so if it's alright with everybody, I'll be happy to handle this investigation with my sheriff's department crew. I can tell you, it's pretty cut and dry, with only a few suspects. Somebody on the ranch had to have done it the morning after the quake. I think we can wrap this one up pretty quickly." He paused to listen, and then replied, "Sure. Sure. I'll keep you folks posted the minute I have something solid."

Because she hadn't been at the ranch when her brother died, Jenny would be less intimidated by his questions, so the sheriff decided to talk with her, first. Deputy Smith drove Max to Jericho Center, where the head lawman managed to get permission to talk with the girl in the privacy of Mrs. Hannity's office, on the condition that she — Irene Hannity — would be there to chaperone.

"Why are you interviewing our Jenny?" the woman asked him.

"Well, ma'am, we have discovered some serious irregularities in the death of her brother, Edward Roth."

"Irregularities?" she shot back.

He pinched his mouth into a circle, then released it. "There was a wound at the back of his head."

"What?" Jenny's voice was almost inaudible.

"What kind of wound? Was there an accident when they lifted him to the helicopter?" Mrs. Hannity surprised him with that one, but he recovered quickly.

"No, ma'am. The rescue guy pointed it out to me, before he signaled for the body to be lifted."

"You saw a wound? Are you sure?" Jenny was finding it hard to believe.

"Yes, miss. I saw it, and the coroner saw it, and the autopsy report shows that the young man died before he ever slipped down into the shallow water." He let those facts sink in.

Irene reached over to pat Jenny's hand. "There has to be an explanation for this, missy. Don't jump to any conclusions."

"Like what?" she asked. "Like, somebody hurt him, or even *killed* him?"

"Hold on, miss, nobody's saying anybody killed anybody. We just know he had a wound that killed him, and he didn't drown." He pretended to be curious. "My goodness, who would even want to kill your brother?"

She thought for a few seconds. "I... I don't know..."

"Probably was just an accident." Max seemed to have a sudden idea. "Unless there was insurance, or something." His eyes asked the question.

"Uh, no." The girl shrugged. "The only insurance *I* know about, is my mother's policy, where us three kids get something from *her* when she dies." Her face reflected relief. "And she's still alive. I hope to see her soon, in fact."

"Uh-huh." The sheriff seemed to be concerned. "And where is she right now, miss?"

"In White River Junction. She has a very slow-growing brain cancer. She doesn't even know us kids anymore."

"Aw, jeez, I'm sorry to hear that," he murmured, as he leaned back in the straight chair.

Mrs. Hannity's office chair wobbled as she wheeled it closer to her desk. "Okay then, Sheriff, I take it you are here to notify Jenny that her brother died of a wound... uh... where? On his head, or what?"

"At the base of his skull, on the back of his neck. Yes, ma'am, that's what I'm supposed to do. That's why I'm here."

"And what do you suppose she should do about that, Sheriff?"

He stood to his feet. "First, be aware. That's our duty, Mrs. Hannity." He placed his hat on his head. "And if there's anything she can do to help us determine whether there has been foul play, to get back to us." He was heading out the door. "After all, we want to do the right thing." He nodded his farewell to Jenny. "Please keep in touch, miss."

***

Deputy Smith steered the Sheriff Department's white pickup down the winding drive to the Roth Ranch house. "These folks know we're coming?" he asked his boss.

"Nope. They don't even know there's an investigation going on. All we're doing here is checking out the rescue site, okay?" He folded up the small notepad where he had made a few notes after talking to Jenny Roth. "Let's see what we can find out, before they feel like suspects."

Mark was in the upper pasture, tending his herd of Herefords. Upon spotting the official vehicle, he dropped everything and hurried across the field. "Hey!" His wave stopped them before they got to the front door. The rancher slipped between the fence rails and met the two law officers in the driveway. "What's up, Sheriff?"

"Good morning, Mr. Roth," Max said, with a friendly smile. "Don't want to bother you, but we need to check out some measurements of the rescue site... for our report. We need just a few minutes of your time."

"Okay, I can take you down, or you can go by yourself. Whatever you need."

"It might be helpful if you could be there in case we have a question." Max was still smiling.

The three men moved quickly to the river's edge, where the water level had dropped to almost normal. The sheriff turned to the deputy. "You got that tape measure?" Smith held up the large, metal tool. Max took it, pulled out the tab and handed the case to his helper. "Good. Now don't go too far too fast; we don't know how much is still quicksand." As Smith moved slowly across the river bank, Max began his investigation. "My god, mister, this was one tragic thing for you all to go through. How are you all doing?"

Mark's head bowed. "Aw, it's been pretty rough — especially on the girls."

"You talking about the two older ones, or all three?"

"All three... and, of course, Kathy."

"The boy only lived here for — what — four months?" He jostled the tape to keep it taut. "He must have been a special kid, to be liked as much as that."

"He was. And a damned hard worker. He worked with Thunder, so that tells you something." There was some admiration in the uncle's voice. "Ay-yuh, a damned hard worker. And plucky." His face went hard. "That's probably what killed him... going that extra mile."

Max motioned for Smith to move to the right. "What do you mean, '...that extra mile'?"

"If he'd just waited for me to get back with my rifle, well, things might have been different."

"Got that measurement?" the sheriff called out to Smith. Then he turned back to Mark. "You went to get your rifle?" There was a confirming nod. "Wait. I'm confused, here. Maybe you should tell me how you even found out the bull was stuck."

"Well, after the quake, we were pretty much trapped upstairs, in the dark. There was water running from broken pipes in the bathroom and all three of the women — Kathy, Rhonda, and Donna — were yelling and finding their way through the mess. Eddie was trapped in his room, but he managed to get out his window to the porch roof. He came back in through Rhonda's window, and met up with us in the hall." We just huddled there until daylight."

"Why didn't you get out through Rhonda's window?"

"Eddie said he barely made it. The roof was moving under him. I figured it was too risky. So we huddled and then it got light enough for us to find clothes. Eddie had to wear a shirt and denims from my closet. He rolled up the legs. Then he says he can hear Thunder bellowing, and he's going to go tend to him. Well, we had to dig our way down the stairs." He shook his head. "Gawd, I don't know how we *did* that, but when we got down into the living room, there was water coming through the ceiling and walls. So, I sent the three kids out to check on the animals, while Kathy and I tried to stop the leaks." He hesitated to go on.

Sheriff Duncan nodded an obscure direction to his deputy, who hid his smile and moved a few feet farther out. "So," Max got back to the story, "Eddie went to check on Thunder. And the girls...?"

"Rhonda went to the upper pasture to see about the herd, and Donna, she went to the barn to see if the goats were safe."

"You have goats?"

"Only five of them. Keep them in the barn at night, to protect them from predators."

"So, how did you know Thunder was in trouble?"

"It was Donna. She came running up to the house and I followed her back to the river, and there was Thunder, up to his briskets in water and quicksand." There was resignation in the finishing of the story. "I knew we couldn't save Thunder. He was too heavy, and panicked, eyes rolling and so tired. I told Eddie to just stay away from the quicksand, just try to talk gentle to the poor animal, while I went back to the house to get my gun. I should have known he would try to get to Thunder. I should have known..."

"Man, what a tragedy, Mr. Roth." Then the inquisitor pretended to have another thought. "So, when you left to get the gun, did Donna stay there with her brother?"

"No. She had to go back and let the goats out. The hayloft had collapsed, and they couldn't get out on their own. She was strong enough to lift and push them over the slippery hay."

"So Eddie was alone when he died," the sheriff concluded. "That fact, has to be hard to live with, for everybody." He signaled for Smith to come back. As the metal tape slowly retracted, he turned to the man beside him. "I just want you to know, Mr. Roth, that the sheriff's department extends condolences to you and your family."

Mark thanked him, then the three men made their way back to the vehicle. As they passed the stacked firewood leaning against Thunder's tilting shelter, Deputy Smith remarked, "Look at that!" He pointed to a row of tin cans lying on the ground at the bottom of the wood pile. "You do target practice over there?" he asked the rifleman.

There was a short snort. "Nah, that's where Rhonda practiced, before the quake. She's pretty good with a slingshot."

***

Deputy Smith wanted to ask the sheriff if they were operating within legal boundaries, not alerting the Roths about this being a murder investigation, but he had been the target of his boss's ire more than once, so he decided to keep his mouth shut. The task at hand was to spot Rhonda riding her bike somewhere near Jericho Center, where, according to

Mark Roth, she was headed to buy ice cream at the Country Store. At that site, there was no sign of her, so the two lawmen circled the village green. Smith spotted her sitting on the ground next to her bike, in what they noted was Mr. Taft's driveway. The truck drew to a quiet stop in front of the house before Max slipped nonchalantly from the cab, hitched up his pants, and wandered over toward her. He nodded courteously. "'Morning, miss. I'm Max Duncan. Remember me?"

"Yeah. You're the cop who was there after they found Eddie." She squinted up at him. "You looking for somebody?"

He turned the question back around. "Sort of. How about you?" All he got was a turned-away face, so he looked around, himself. "Waiting for your teacher to get home?" There was a twitch of the shoulders. "I just talked to your stepdad. He said you were going to get ice cream at the store. You already do that?" She looked down at the ground. "Nope? That's what I thought." He squatted down a few feet away from her. "So, you really came to see Mr. Taft, right?" She kept her eyes down. "Look, young lady, you can either answer my questions, or I can let Mr. Roth do the asking. Which do you prefer?"

She was exasperated. "I just wanted to ask him what he found in the boxes, that's all."

"What boxes?"

"The ones they took out of our attic." She looked up at the approach of Walter's second-hand Chevy.

The teacher drove slowly into the driveway, eyeing the situation. The words came as he exited the car: "Is there a problem, Sheriff?"

"I just need to ask this little lady a couple of questions. You showed up at just the right time. Now I have an adult to supervise the interview, if you would be so kind as to make yourself available."

Minutes later, Max asked his first question in the privacy of Walter Taft's living room. "Miss Roth, I have to inform you that your stepbrother, Eddie, apparently suffered some type of injury on the day he died." He signaled Smith to make notes. "Do you know anything about that?"

"What? No! No, I don't know anything about any injury. He slipped and drowned."

"I'm afraid not, miss." In the corner of his eye, Max noted the sudden stiffening of Walter's body. "The coroner reported a deep wound at the back of his neck, and the autopsy showed the boy did *not* drown." He shifted his weight to the other foot, looking down at her. "I've already talked to Mark Roth, and he and your mother seem to be in the clear. Maybe *you* can help, by telling what you remember about that morning."

Her story seemed to jibe with Mark's: She had gone to the upper pasture, found one wounded heifer who couldn't get to her feet, then pulled a partial bale of hay closer to the restless ones huddled under a tree.

She was stopped by the sound of a gunshot. Immediately, she ran to the river and there was Thunder, his noble head sunk into the foaming stream. "And... and Eddie was in a heap, underwater. Daddy Mark was trying to get to him, but he was sinking deeper and deeper. Mama Kathy was screaming from the front porch for him to stop before he got killed."

The lawman made a mental note that Kathy was up at the house, then moved on. "Where was Donna?"

"Just standing there, like a statue."

"Next to the river bank?"

"Well, uh, more over toward the barn."

The sheriff thanked the girl, who was only too happy to scoot out the door. He focused on Walter for a brief moment. "She said she wanted to know what was in those boxes you took out of their attic." He folded his arms. "What boxes would those be, Mr. Taft?"

The reply came carefully. "The Roths were cleaning out the attic. I was chosen to go through those containers, to see if there was anything of merit, and get back to them."

"I see. And where are those boxes now?"

"Well... I'm afraid they were stolen, right from this very room, the night of the earthquake." The teacher shoved his hands into his pants pockets.

Sheriff Duncan's eyes narrowed. "Hmm. So you can't show me these boxes, can you?" His thumbs hooked over his gun belt. "Pretty serious thing, having one of your cute female students waiting on your front yard. If I was you, I'd come up with those boxes in a hurry, before folks get the wrong idea."

Walter's face flushed with anger. "I told you, they were *stolen!*"

"Interesting thing about that, Mr. Taft: That was a few weeks ago, and nobody reported that break-in, let alone, the theft of any property. I wonder why that is."

Walter's hands jabbed inside the pockets. "I thought I could recover them, but now I'm not so sure."

"Oh, you did, did you? I assume you have an idea who took them?"

"Maybe. But I'd like to handle this by myself. I have an idea it was just what you fellows call 'petty theft.'"

Max Duncan nodded, and motioned his deputy to precede him out the door. There was one parting shot: "Just remember, mister, if those boxes turn out to have anything to do with the death of Eddie Roth, we can charge you with concealing evidence and obstruction of justice, and who-knows-what-else."

***

He was relieved when she picked up the phone. "Donna, you were right. The sheriff thinks there's been foul play in Eddie's death."

"I know," she replied. "Jenny called me and left a message at work." The older sister was at home, now, and more determined than ever that Jenny never set foot on Roth Ranch again. "It's the insurance money, Walter. That has to be it."

"I hate to think that, Donna. Like I said, it would be stupid to kill three people and think you could get away with it."

"But that's exactly what they have to do, isn't it?" She sounded frightened. "Maybe we should get to heck out of Vermont."

His heart sank. "Oh no, I hope it hasn't come to that." He reached for a straw in the wind. "Maybe we can figure this thing out. In the meantime, cooperate with the sheriff's department. The man only wants to know if you have an alibi. So far, Mark and Rhonda seem to be in the clear."

There was a short breath before she offered the next conclusion. "That leaves Kathy."

"Oh my gosh, Donna... I can't see her killing anybody."

"All the more reason to take a closer look," the woman reminded him.

"Okay, it's a notion, but a far-fetched one, if you ask me." He checked his watch. "I have a class at one o'clock. May I call you tonight?"

"I was hoping you would."

"Meanwhile, stay calm. We can do our own detective work. We can." He hung up and left the phone booth. It was an easy sprint across the campus green.

He never even noticed the white pickup parked on Colchester Avenue... the one with official lettering on the side doors. The deputy called in his report to the department's dispatch. The hollow reply bounced off the insides of the cab: "Subject has a one-hour class. Return to base for further instructions. Over."

Deputy Smith signed off and moved on.

Hugs

"We were right. There is something going on with that boy's death," Connie told the Shorts. The three of them were having cold drinks inside the screened patio of the Collinses' Winooski home as they waited for Don to arrive. It was their bowling night. Outside, the grass on Saint Michael's College grounds was finally a beautiful green. In a few days it would be July, and then the open spaces over near the football field would need watering. The three friends enjoyed the view as the conversation continued.

"We *knew* it!" Greta exclaimed.

"How did you find this out?" Gerald asked.

"Jenny Roth called me last night. She was so excited." Connie clasped her hands to her chest. "She's speaking in tongues! Can you believe it?"

"Wow!" the Shorts echoed each other.

"I know! And it happened because her friend, the little German girl — I forget her name — told her about it, and so Jenny got alone and opened her mouth, and I think she said, she 'blubbied-blubbied-blubbied,' until it started to get a few more syllables in there, and it all came together over a few hours." She laughed. "Can't you imagine this sweetheart hanging in there? But she said she just finally relaxed into it, and then it happened."

"Are you sure she's not just 'blubbying?'" Gerald wanted more proof.

"Oh yeah, because I asked her to pray for one of our clients, without telling her the situation, or the name."

The Shorts were listening intently. "So she said, 'I don't know that person, but the Holy Spirit does, right?' and I said, 'Right. Now ask Him to pray for that person.' And she did, and in a few seconds, all these lovely mutterings came over the phone, and it wasn't more than a minute before I could hear certain phrases and accented 'words' popping up throughout that prayer, and that was enough for me to know... this was a real language."

Gerald smiled. "Sounds like we have another prayer warrior for Jesus."

"Hallelujah!" Greta sang out.

The joy of the moment was cut short by the slamming of Don's car door. They leaned forward to welcome him as he came around the back to enter the patio. "Hey, folks. Sorry to be late. Had a drunk teenager throw up on my bus, so my clean-up took longer." He dropped heavily into the fourth chair.

While Connie hastened to pour her husband a cool iced tea, Gerald pursued the subject. "Anybody you recognize?"

"Nah. Looked like he was from out of town. Couldn't find the bus to Essex Junction. Said he had a ride waiting for him there."

"Did you let the cops know about this?" Gerald inquired.

Don took a long sip of the cold drink. "Nope. He was gone before I could do anything." He sniffed a heavy breath, then slowly let it out, ready to change the subject to happier news. "So, did Connie tell you about her young friend, Jenny?" He saw the smiles. "I guess we could all use some good news, right about now." The trio waited for him to continue. There was a small, wet belch before he went on. "I take it you three have been talking about the investigation going on, about the Roth boy, I mean."

"We were just getting to it," Connie informed him. "No details yet."

"Okay. Well," he leaned back and crossed his legs. "Seems there was a fatal injury before he dropped down into the water. Killed him, according to the coroner's report." He went on to give details, being careful to point out that this information was coming from Jenny, so it was second-hand. The Shorts sat silently weighing the situation.

"The question is," Connie interjected, "what sort of motive would we be dealing with, here? Jenny said there was no life insurance on her brother. In fact, she went on to say that the only insurance policy she knew about was the one on her mother."

"Was that policy to benefit all three of her children?" Gerald asked.

Connie got a sudden glint in her eye. "As a matter of fact, she did tell me that." She blinked. "Oh, my."

"Uh-huh. I thought of that possibility as I was on my way home," Don mused. "That would make the two girls suspects, but then..."

"They probably loved their brother," his wife concluded. "That usually happens when siblings are abandoned together." She let Greta fill the men in on Jenny's background at the Children's Home.

"I agree with that conclusion," Don stated. "So who else would benefit from that policy, if the boy was dead?" Nobody answered. "Ay-yuh. So maybe we should ask Jenny, when we get the chance."

"Think we should even get involved with this?" Connie was hopeful.

"Well, I think we should," Greta declared, with a shake of her light brown curls. "After the way that Texas bunch turned the poor youngster's funeral into a freak show. *Somebody* should take up the gauntlet."

"Is that what we're doing, my love?" Gerald's gentle smile was back.

Suddenly Greta slipped into mama bear mode. "Oh, I don't know. But we should do *something*. After all, what can they do to us?"

"I agree. What can they do to us?" the other mama bear addressed her husband, who was ready with the answer.

"They could charge us with interfering with an official murder investigation."

The two women exchanged a determined look. "Well then," Connie informed the two hesitant papa bears, "we'll just have to be very nice about it."

Greta sat up straight. "Right. We'll just have to be very, very nice about it." She dusted the problem off her hands. "Now, are we going bowling, or what?"

***

Donna was glad her roommates were not home; she preferred a little privacy while being questioned by the local sheriff. Even though he was professional and polite, a single trickle of sweat moved down between her shoulder blades. "I'm sorry to bother you, so close to your time of grief," he was saying, "but we have some disturbing facts concerning your brother's demise, and the sooner we get to the bottom of all this, the better. I'm sure you understand."

She acknowledged this with a short, quick breath, but said nothing, because his good manners did not hide the way his eyes scanned the living room, taking note of who-knew-what.

"Now, you told me over the phone that your sister informed you of the wound, and cause of death."

"Yes, that's right." She took a sip from the Pepsi bottle in her hand.

"I have to ask you a very important question, miss: What or who was the first thing that came to your mind when you heard this news?" He corrected himself immediately. "I mean, after the initial shock. What did you think? Do you remember?" Seeing the perplexity on her face, he apologized. "I'm so sorry, but if you need a few minutes, feel free. I need to get my notebook out, here." He deliberately took his time pulling the small spiraled rectangle from one pocket, then fidgeted through his pockets until he found a pen, all the time keeping his eyes on his own hands, apparently in no hurry. Finally, he looked up, leaning slightly forward in the overstuffed chair. "How're ya doing?"

She took another sip, licking her lips before answering. "Um, it's all so jumbled up."

"'Course it is." He stuck the pen inside the spiral hinge. "So just keep the thought in mind, and let me just see what we can come up with, okay?" He went into his investigator role. "So, who would want to hurt your brother, Miss Roth? Is there anybody who didn't like him or was mad at him, or wanted to get rid of him for one reason or another?"

Her eyes met his. "Oh. Oh, yes. That would be Rhonda, our step — um, Uncle Mark's stepdaughter." There was a second thought. "But of course, she didn't like Jenny, or me, either."

"Why not?"

"I guess we stole her position in the family, if you know what I mean. She likes being the center of attention. Gets real nasty when she's upstaged." There was a ladylike harrumph. "Uh-huh. She would like to see all three of us out of her way."

Max went quickly to the next question. "What would happen if all three of you were… to pass on? Any reason why she, or anybody else, would benefit from that?"

Suddenly she found her tongue. "Darned right. Our Uncle Mark would be the beneficiary of our mom's will."

Max seemed to be asking a casual question: "We talking about a lot of money, here?"

The conversation became more intense after that, Donna giving details she never intended to. So concentrated was she on nailing the trio from Texas, she got careless. The mistake happened out of the blue.

"So, how did you happen to be out at the ranch the night of the earthquake?"

"Oh, I went to the ranch to check on Eddie, but first I stopped to see my boyfriend at the Center."

"Okay. So nothing special. Just checking on your little brother. And a visit with... who?"

"My boyfriend, Walter. He's a teacher at the high school."

"Wait a minute. You're dating Walter Taft?"

And there it was. By the time Max Duncan left, forty minutes later, she had told him, not all, but most of what she knew about the boxes. She went immediately to the phone. Walter answered right away. "Oh damn," she greeted him, "I just told the sheriff about the boxes from the attic."

"Okay, and...?"

He heard the frustrated grunt. "Well, I don't know. Maybe he will try to... I don't know."

"You know what? At least now he knows those things are real. I'm glad you backed me up, miss. So don't let it throw you."

She moaned. "Oh, I don't know. I just don't know. Maybe I should grab Jenny and get out of the state of Vermont."

His heart sank, for this was the second time she had threatened to leave the area. "Remember, we agreed that you should just cooperate with the sheriff's department. Well, you're doing that. Why are you thinking of leaving, again?"

"The sheriff seems to agree that Uncle Mark's family is up here to get the insurance money."

"Did he say that?"

"N-no, but he *inferred* it."

He paused, buying time. "Listen, Donna. You need a break. You don't need to leave the state." A solution, albeit a temporary one, emerged, and he let it flow. "So, I have a great idea. You have grief leave coming, and you need a break. Next Saturday we slip into July. Let's pack a picnic lunch and drive Jenny down to see her mama. I'm sure Mrs. Hannity will be happy to let her have the day off. We can make the round trip in one day. We just have to start early, and we'll be back by sundown. What do you say?"

***

Anna Roth's health had deteriorated to where she had been moved to a comfort room. It was clean and bright from the July sunlight streaming through the window beside her bed. When Jenny saw the slim form propped up against the pillows, she approached slowly, careful not to disturb her mother. Up close, she took in the beautiful pale, porcelain face, framed by wisps of white hair. The eyelids, edged with long, dark lashes, were closed over the deep-set eyes. A breathing tube hung from the prominent nose, down across half-opened lips.

"Mama," she whispered. "Hey, Mama! It's us, Donna and Jenny." She waited, just in case there was a response. The nurse had told them there would be none, but she was still hoping. The girl looked down at the deeply veined hand lying close to where the sheet was tucked under her motionless form, then back to where Donna and Walter were standing close to the hallway door. "Is it alright if I touch her hand?" They nodded approval, and Walter pulled a chair close to the side of the bed, motioning her into the seat. The delicate hand was surprisingly cold, but Jenny lifted it into the warmth between her own two palms. As she held the velvet folds framing the long, limp fingers, she began to softly explain that Eddie was in Heaven, and would be waiting for her. At this point, Donna whispered to Walter, and the two left the room.

When they returned, Jenny's head was cradled under her mama's limp arm, and she was singing softly in an odd language. Donna approached her sister to comfort her, while her teacher friend remained by the door. He saw her come to a full stop, staring intently at her mother's face. Suddenly, Donna's hand went up over her mouth and her shoulders shook. He went to her immediately. "What?" he whispered. She pointed to her mother's smooth, white cheeks.

There were tears rolling down onto the pillow beneath Anna Roth's head.

For the first hour, it was quiet on the return trip. Jenny was snoozing in the back seat, lulled by the hum of Walter's old Chevy. Donna was staring out the passenger side window, touching her face with a tissue. He reached over and patted her hand once, and then, emotionally exhausted, she slipped into a soft snore. He glanced over, both amused and yet filled with compassion. It was the stop for gas that woke them both up. "Potty break!" he announced. He opened the doors for the ladies, and escorted them to the inside of the gas station, where he bought cool drinks which they took back to the refueled vehicle. In a few minutes, they were back on the road. Jenny finished her drink first, between happy comments about their visit with the long-lost mother. "I think she heard us. I think it was wonderful. Thanks for driving us down here, Mr. Taft."

Donna's thanks reflected a new softness in her eyes, before she decided to change the subject. "So, how's it going with your thesis, Walter?"

Her diversionary tactic worked.

"I've made really good progress, I think. I just had to determine where to put the emphasis. The subject of secret societies is very complicated, and it's really easy to get off on rabbit trails."

"So what did you decide to concentrate on?" Jenny asked.

"The flawed human being, trying to be the perfect hero." He chuckled. "Not exactly a new concept, but it seems to be the Achilles' heel in all these organizations."

"That means 'the weak point' in all these secret clubs," Donna called back to her sister.

Walter went on to explain: "Mere mortal man — from the Delphic Oracles and ancient Knights of the Whatever, on through the Jesuits and the Freemasons and the Mafia — has been a sad repetition of history. They all seemed to start out to do good, basically, humanity trying to fix humanity."

"And then what?" Jenny was trying to keep up.

"The sin nature, kiddo, that's what. They get too proud of themselves, 'cause they're the saviors of the world, so to speak. They are like Superman in duplicates. Next thing you know, it's the 'us four and no more' mentality."

Donna explained again. "They get conceited."

The teacher almost agreed. "Something like that." Suddenly he remembered a Bible verse from the book of Proverbs. "You know what they say, 'Pride goeth before destruction, a haughty spirit before a fall.'"

Outside the car, a descending dusk signaled they were running late. He turned on the headlights before finishing the thought. "Let's face it. Humanity cannot fix humanity, because humans are so *damnably* flawed. People seem to forget they are only people, and *not* God." His fingers tapped lightly on the steering wheel. "So they jump right in there, and they mess up, every time."

"Every time?" Donna was doubtful.

"Okay, it might take a while, but when greed or competition, or just plain, old jealousy get into the mix, good deeds get lost in the process. It becomes a whole new situation." He made a final point. "Take Ken Pearson, Andrew's grandpa, for instance. All he probably wants, is to be a good guy. He's just trying to do it without God, without the Blood of Jesus." He shook his head. "It just doesn't work, you know?"

Donna glanced over at the man. "*This guy is somebody special, for sure: polite, honest, protective, noble,*" she thought. It was almost too good to be true. *"Oh my gosh. He can't be for real."* Still, there was a check in her spirit. *"But then, a lot of things that happened today don't seem real either..."* She did a lot of thinking before they got back to Burlington.

It was ten o'clock by the time they reached her apartment. He walked her up to the door in the dark, holding her arm as they maneuvered the lumpy sidewalk. They were remarking about the success of the trip, both pleased with the day's events, as they reached the front door. There, she turned to look into his eyes. "I don't know how to thank you for today, you know that?"

"I am glad I got to be with you, miss. I just hate to see the evening come to an end."

She was cautious. "Are you flattering me, Walter Taft?"

"Not at all. As matter of fact, if your little sister wasn't sitting back there in the car and watching us, I would ask for a goodnight kiss."

She looked down. "Why would you ask for a goodnight kiss, Mr. Taft?"

He stepped closer, taking her hands in his. "Because I'm crazy about you, Donna."

It was more of a deflection than a cute comment. "Wait. Doesn't that sound like something out of a class B movie?" she murmured.

He drew her hands to his lips. "I don't give a damn what it sounds like. I just know I'm in love with you."

He pressed her fingers into the cushion of his mouth, then dropped them gently. "Goodnight, Donna Roth. I'll see you in my dreams... and I mean *that* line, too."

He was halfway back down the sidewalk before she called out, "Wait! Wait a minute, mister! What kind of a guy tells a girl he loves her, then doesn't give her a goodnight kiss?"

He couldn't get back there fast enough.

CHAPTER FOURTEEN

Discoveries

"You know where we forgot to look?" Deputy Smith asked his boss. "In the barn."

Max Duncan rolled his eyes. "Aw, hell, you're right." He scratched his head. "Don't know how I missed that one."

"Think we can find another excuse to go out there?"

The sheriff pulled out a stick of Wrigley's gum and slowly unwrapped the foil. "Oh, I usually can come up with something." He folded the sweet stick into his mouth and began to chew slowly. The deputy watched him crush the wrapper, then toss it into the wastepaper basket in the corner. "Now why would we need to get inside that damaged barn, Smith?"

"I guess maybe to clean it up, or something. That would be legitimate... if we weren't lawmen."

Sheriff Duncan chewed faster, as a glint appeared in his eye. "Exactly. To clean it up. Or better yet, to head up a group of volunteers to do that very thing."

"Got anybody in mind, Sheriff?"

"Gimme a couple-a days, son."

It was the same Saturday that Mr. Taft drove the Roth girls to White River Junction to see their mother, that Sheriff Duncan showed up at the ranch to help clean up the barn. He had called ahead, of course, explaining that a work crew from the county jail was looking for a project, and if Mark was willing, everybody could help out everybody else. Mark was delighted to get the assistance. He was standing in the middle of the mess when five prisoners, two deputies, and the sheriff came marching from the small bus in the driveway. He greeted the sheriff with a handshake. "Sure appreciate you coming by."

"We are at your service, Mr. Roth. Where would you like us to start?"

Over the next three hours, heavy beams were moved, hay was restacked and the outside door for the goats was fully repaired. Kathy furnished cold water and homemade cookies at break time, but she kept Rhonda hidden in the house. At four o'clock, the group said its goodbyes and returned to Burlington. The five inmates prepared for evening chow and the sheriff's department crew disbanded for the day. Before Max left, however, he signaled Deputy Smith to hang back, for a private word. "I see you got the sling shot. Good work." He stuffed another stick of gum into his mouth. "How did you manage to keep it?"

"Asked the missus — Kathy — who it belonged to. She said Eddie had given it to Jenny for her birthday. So I asked if Jenny would like to have it, and she said, 'You might as well take it to her, because she and Donna don't want to come back here to the ranch, for sure.'" He smiled. "So I told her we would be happy to get it to the girl, and slipped it into my back pocket."

"Without leaving your own fingerprints on it, I hope," Max said.

"No problem." The deputy was proud of himself, until he saw the triumph in the sheriff's eyes. "What?"

Sheriff Duncan pulled a cloth bag of river rocks from inside his jacket. "I snitched the rocks that were hanging right beside the sling shot, just before we left. These babies will have fingerprints all over 'em!"

Smith sought to get the attention back on his own accomplishment. "So, how about we dust the actual weapon for prints and go from there? I mean, it's not like somebody was hiding it, or something."

Max's reply was almost sarcastic. "Hey! That's interesting, isn't it? Almost like somebody left it right out there to be noticed, you know?" He was holding out an evidence bag for the sling shot. "Where is it?" Smith turned his backside around, and the sheriff pulled the thing out of the pocket, holding it by the plastic bag. "Yup, this thing and the rocks, right out there where we could spot them; so we should keep that thought in mind."

The deputy turned back around to face his boss. "That, and one other thing," he added. "Who was in the barn when the boy was killed?" There was a short pause. "I believe it was his older sister, Donna. Am I right?"

"Interesting thought," Max noted, "but so much time has elapsed since the murder, *anybody* could have planted the rocks and weapon on those nails, to set her up."

"Or to set up the younger one, Jenny."

"No, Smith. Jenny was not there at the time of the killing."

"Oh. Right. I forgot."

"Exactly. You forgot that, and you forgot the rocks, as well. That's why I'm the Chittenden County Sheriff, and you're not."

***

The next morning, Walter encountered Mrs. Hannity in church. She asked how the trip had gone.

"Very well." He was surprised she had not talked with Jenny. "She will tell you, better than I can, what happened with her mother. It was like a miracle, I swear."

"Talking about a miracle, let me tell you what happened to *me* yesterday." She stepped to one side of the center aisle of the sanctuary, motioning for him to sit down for a minute. "Are you aware that I live right next door to the nursing home?" He nodded as he took a seat. "Okay, good. So I got off work last evening and hurried over to my front door, anxious to kick off my shoes and all that, and I almost fell over this cardboard box, sitting right there on the step. At first I thought it was trash, but then I saw it had a label on it, so I picked it up and brought it inside." She lifted her shoulders in a short motion. "So, I was in a hurry to get comfy, and just let it sit there for a half-hour or more, until I finally decided to take a look." She shook her head as though to sort out the next few words. "It had this label on it, 'Young girl.'"

Walter felt the blood leave his face, but he said nothing. "And I'm thinking," she laughed as she spoke the words, "who in the world that might be, but I went ahead and opened it up, anyway." Her hands clasped together in delight. "And, oh, the treasures inside that package!" Her eyes sparkled like a child on Christmas morning. "My books! And my doll! And the necklace and the ring, and all the rest of the things in that box… all memories from my childhood at the farm!" She shivered with pleasure. "I just couldn't believe it. I just kept touching those things, and I was crying, Mr. Taft. I was actually weeping."

"My-oh-my," the man softly commented. "What a delightful surprise. And do you have any idea where this box came from?"

"It *had* to have come from the farm. I guess maybe it was in with all that stuff in the attic. I just left it there. I guess I forgot about this box."

"Are you talking about Roth Ranch, by any chance?"

She seemed surprised. "Of course. That was my childhood home." She leaned forward to look into his face. "Oh my. You haven't been here all that long. I guess you didn't know that my maiden name was Crocker." She sat up straight. "Nobody ever told you, right?"

"Ri-i-ght," he replied slowly. Suddenly he seemed to be enjoying the story. "So, any idea who left the box on your step, or was this just a gift from some suitor, or what?"

She almost giggled. "I have no blooming idea. None. I just can't figure that one out. I mean, how did they get the box out of the attic?" There was a spontaneous pop of the eyes. "Say, you don't suppose the Roths found it and just dropped it off, do you?"

"Hmm. I rather doubt they would mark the thing as 'Young girl.' After all, they would have to know it was you, don't you think?"

"Mmm," she hummed thoughtfully. "And why would they be secretive about it? Now, that's a good question. Especially if they knew how much it meant to me, to get all those precious memories." Her head tilted to the right. "No, this had to have come from someone who knew what all this meant to me." She smiled. "I have to conclude that this was a kindly gesture, by someone who meant well." The smile faded. "I wonder why they were so secretive."

He stood up. "Hey! Maybe you'll get a phone call from them in the next day or so. Maybe they just didn't have time to stop and visit, or whatever." He patted her shoulder. "Do me a favor and let me know who it was, would you? Maybe this isn't all that much of a mystery."

But he knew very well, he was being a sly phony; it certainly was a mystery, and he certainly wanted to solve it.

***

157

"That's the same kid who threw up on my bus," Don told Connie. He motioned toward Andrew, who was riding his bike past Maude's Nursing Home.

"The one who was drunk?" she asked. Don acknowledged that with a quick nod. "Hmm. So he really *was* expecting a ride when he got to Essex Junction." The two of them watched from the home's porch, as the youngster slowed down and stopped to talk to a gentleman who happened to be out for a stroll. "Oh look, Don! He's talking to Walter Taft."

But he wasn't looking at that. "Here's the sheriff, right on time," he notified her.

"Good. Maybe now we can get some idea about who left that flashlight in the Roths' attic," she murmured as Max and Deputy Smith exited their vehicle. But the sheriff came to a sudden stop, his eyes on the two conversationalists a few yards away. Andrew spotted the lawman and said something to Walter, then mounted the bike and left. Walter turned to see Sheriff Duncan motioning for the teacher to approach him.

"Glad to bump into you, Mr. Taft. I have an appointment with some folks here at the nursing home, and I think you probably should be in on it." As Walter joined him to approach the porch, Max signaled Smith to stay with the vehicle. "Thanks for meeting me here," he said to the Collinses. The four of them took seats right there at the south end of the verandah.

"We're glad to do it, Sheriff," Connie said. "We even got to visit with Millie for a few minutes. And, of course, we're anxious to know what you came up with on the flashlight." She turned to Walter. "You remember how I said we now have a legitimate reason to check for fingerprints? Well, I turned the flashlight over to Sheriff Duncan, and he's here to give us a report. Isn't that nice of him?"

Walter addressed the sheriff. "You checked it for fingerprints? Good. What did you find?"

The lawman tilted his head as though he didn't like what he had to say. "You probably won't be too happy about this, Mr. Taft."

"Oh?" The teacher sat back in the porch swing. "It's only a flashlight, Sheriff, and *anybody* could have left it in one of those boxes."

"True," Max replied, "but we know now, that it wasn't just anybody." He folded his arms. "Your girlfriend's fingerprints are all over it."

"Donna's prints are on that flashlight?" Connie seemed disappointed. "Well, she was at the ranch a lot, so I don't see what's so significant about that. She probably was up there — maybe only once, for all we know — and she forgot to take it back downstairs."

"That's right," the boyfriend answered quickly. "No big deal, as far as I can see." His mouth went hard for a second. "Uh, how did you happen to have her prints on file?"

"Oh," came the smug answer, "we have our ways of getting evidence."

"Like picking up the Pepsi bottle she just drank from, right?" The sheriff had no comment, but Walter answered his own question. "Did it when you interviewed her at her apartment."

The front door opened with a push of Mrs. Hannity's hand. "My-oh-my! What's all this?? Looks like Old Home Week out here!" Her smile was welcoming, even though she folded her arms. "You arresting somebody, Sheriff?"

"Not yet," he joked back. "I've been up this way all morning, and these good folks agreed to meet me here, for a real quick meeting." He looked around. "And I guess we have done that, unless anybody has a question."

No one responded, so he stood to his feet. "Oh!" He remembered something to tell the other three. "Now that I know for sure there are some missing boxes, I'll file a written report, so I'll need signed statements from you folks." He was halfway down the sidewalk when Mrs. Hannity called out.

"Sheriff Duncan! I think I should tell you… somebody left a box on my doorstep a couple of nights ago."

"Oh, crap," the teacher thought, *"I'm about to get caught with my pants down…"*

***

"So, your *Mutter* heard you praying, right?" Essie wiped the doughnut crumbs off her mouth, using the paper napkin with bright, orange pumpkins stamped along all four edges. "I mean, she actually *cried*!"

Jenny choked up. "She did. We saw the tears trickling down her face, so she got *something*."

"Please, I would remind you both," Frau Schuler admonished, "this was the Holy Ghost language she heard… not what *you* were praying, Jenny, but what *He* was praying."

Jenny glanced around the diner-style restaurant, then bent closer to the woman. "Okay, tell me how that works, again."

"Of course." She brushed a strand of strawberry blonde hair away from her face before taking a sip of hot coffee to wash down her bite of spiced doughnut. "Remember that when you speak in tongues, it is not you who is speaking. It is always the Holy Ghost, who knows *exactly* what to pray for." She caught the girl's eye. "You understand, correct?" Jenny nodded. "Very good. And the Holy Spirit will either pray in an *earthly* language that you do not understand, or He will pray in a *heavenly* language, which you will not understand, either."

"Wait. Wait. I'm confused. Is He 'Holy Ghost' or 'Holy Spirit'?" Jenny held her doughnut in mid-air, poised for its next dunk into the hot chocolate.

"The same," Essie volunteered. "Same thing."

"Same *person!*" the mother explained. "He is a real person. In fact, part of the Trinity."

The dark tresses moved in acknowledgment, and the doughnut got dunked. She lifted the dripping delicacy to her lips, then murmured through the drool. "So, um... my mama... she heard the perfect prayer, hmmm?"

"Correct," Essie's mother replied.

The three of them settled into enjoying their doughnut treats in The Harvest. They took in the delicious fragrance of artfully displayed goodies decorating the top of the long lunch counter, all reflected in the large mirror that ran along the wall above it. It had been a fun shopping trip, with both teenagers finding a sweater or blouse for next school year. Jenny was glad to be earning her own money, at last, and she said so, right there in the restaurant.

"Of course. We understand," the German mother smiled. "You are becoming your own person, now. That is excellent."

"Mrs. Hannity says I can stay right there and work after school for three hours a day." She put out the qualifier. "Of course, that means no after-school activities, but I guess I can live with that, to have my own room and everything." She licked the lingering flavor off her lips. "Not like I have any family left to impress." Her head bowed. "All I have is Donna, now."

"Oh-oh!" Essie's exhortation was immediate. "You forgot — you have Jesus!"

"Yup. Yup, you're right. I do have Jesus." She blinked slowly. "Just wish I could feel a hug, that's all."

The little German girl held up a teaching finger. "Hey, He can actually do that, you know." She turned to the woman. "Right, *Mutter?*"

Frau Schuler rotated the cup in its saucer. "This is correct. But it is not always a physical/spiritual thing; sometimes those hugs come in the form of kindnesses from human beings... you understand?" She smiled with the next reminder. "You are part of the family of God, child. The Holy Spirit gives us hugs all the time — remember this!"

"Yeah?" Jenny wanted to hear more, but the place was getting busy, and they would have to vacate the table. As they made their way to the car, however, she asked Frau Schuler to tell her more about this third Person of the Trinity.

It was a long, informative trip back to Jericho Center, where the Schuler ladies left to continue on to Stowe, for an overnight at the Von Trapps' Lodge. There were some folks Jenny knew out there on the front porch, but she was too tired, physically and emotionally, to stop for a visit. Instead, she entered through the side door into the kitchen, then showered and prepared for a full workday on the morrow. Her prayers were much the same as when she was in the Children's Home, but now followed by a whisper to the Holy Spirit.

"I never thought of You as being God — you know — part of the Trinity. I'm really sorry for that. It wasn't very respectful. I will try to do better, Sir." Suddenly, there was moisture in her eyes. "I never knew how much you cared about us — each one of us, who belongs to Jesus." There was a quick sniff. "Frau Schuler says You're a real Person, with real feelings, and it really matters to You how we're living our lives." She sniffed, again. "She says You are The Helper, who comes alongside us, and points us toward Jesus. You show us the way to our Savior, day after day. But You don't take away our free will." She cringed at the next thought. "I don't know about other people, Holy Spirit, but I do know about myself — not paying attention to what You were trying to show me, acting like I'm the boss, instead of listening for You to lead me. I know I have frustrated You so, so much." Now the tears were real, burning inside the eyelids. "How could I do that? How could I hurt You like that, my Helper?" The realization hit hard. "Oh my goodness; Oh my goodness. You are a *person... a real person!*"

At that moment, a warm, shimmering presence trickled over her kneeling body. She delighted in this lovely surprise until it subsided, and it was time to slip into bed. But as she did, the Spirit prompted her to utter one last communication, this time to Jesus. "I know you love me, Lord, but could I just ask... why Eddie had to die like that? Wasn't he also in the family of God? I... really would like to know about that."

There was only silence, but somehow she knew her prayer had been heard. The answer would come when the time was right.

***

Meanwhile, back out on the front porch, Walter Taft was pulling up his britches, so to speak. "Mrs. Hannity, I owe you an explanation, for sure." Out of the corner of his eye, he noted Sheriff Duncan returning to the front steps, pausing to listen. "I actually knew about the origin of that box, but it had been stolen from my home, and I guess — no, I *hoped* you could lead me to the thief."

The sheriff stomped up the steps. "Damn you, Taft, why didn't you let me in on this?"

"Thought it would be better if there weren't any officials involved, at least, not at first." Walter nodded reassuringly. "I would have let you know what I found out, for sure."

"Maybe you should have thought twice about that, mister. That's interfering with an investigation." Max glared at the teacher.

"I was under the impression you had not yet filed a report, Sheriff. Didn't you just say you would need statements when you did that?"

The lawman's face turned red. "Just watch your step, Taft. From now on, the sheriff's department is in charge of this thing." He turned to Mrs. Hannity. "Fill me in."

The Collinses were surprised to learn that she was the daughter of Tim and Freda Crocker, previous owners of Roth Ranch. Don telegraphed a call for silence to his wife, with a hard squint of the eyelids. No need to let the sheriff know how much *they* knew. After all, there may still be a need for some undercover work.

Mrs. Hannity concluded her short story for Max. "Well, I just think that was the sweetest thing, somebody bringing those long-lost items to my doorstep. I don't know why they didn't let me know who they were, unless maybe they're the one who stole it from Mr. Taft."

"Pretty good guess," the sheriff murmured. Then he got serious. "Alright, ma'am, you need to think about who this goodhearted thief might be."

"Somebody familiar with your past, for sure," Don asserted. "Got any ideas about that?"

She laughed. "Quite a few folks, I guess. Not many folks move away, because they love this town." The brow wrinkled thoughtfully. "I probably need time to think about this. God knows I've been curious about it, myself."

"I suggest you start with your early childhood. Who was around then, and still is today?" Connie asked. "Who would know that you'd be delighted to get those old memories back?"

"I went down the list at least a dozen times, I can assure you, because I wanted to thank them." The nursing home director shook her head. "Nope. I just need more time."

"Then we'll leave it at that, at least for now," Max Duncan said. He turned to Walter. "You got anything else I need to know about this situation, mister?"

"Not that I can think of, Sheriff."

"Tell you what, I'm going to hold your feet to the fire, if I find out otherwise." He descended the porch steps. "Keep that in mind, Mr. Taft."

The four of them watched Sheriff Duncan's vehicle move slowly away. Then Mrs. Hannity asked the burning question: "You said there were five boxes, Walter? What was in the other four?"

He rolled his eyes toward the porch ceiling. "Um, mostly just a lot of junk. You got the important stuff, for sure." He met her gaze. "But, technically, those things belong to the Roth family. They were abandoned by you way last year." He saw her acknowledgment. "Of course," he reassured her, "if there is anything…"

"Say," Don changed the subject, "it's getting late. We should be getting along, babe." Connie nodded. He spoke to Walter. "Walk us to our car, would you? We want to hear about your thesis, if you have a few minutes."

The three of them said goodbye to Mrs. Hannity, who hastened to return to her duties. As the trio moved toward the street, Don murmured, "Wow! Nicely handled, mister."

"Not a bad job, yourselves. He has no idea how much you know. That frees the both of you up to do some pretty intense snooping." He glanced over his shoulder. "I'm thinking we need to have a list of all residents for the last — what? — fifty years? Think you two can handle that?"

The impish smile crept across Don's face. "No problem. In fact, we have a few ideas of our own."

"Great," the young man said, reaching for a handshake.

As the Studebaker moved away, Walter turned quickly on his heel setting a good pace toward his home up the hill from the village green.

He needed to call Donna about her fingerprints. Surely, she had been looking for that flashlight, while checking out those boxes in his living room. That had to have been the reason why, on that particular day, she didn't care what the neighbors thought about her being alone in the house with a man.

CHAPTER FIFTEEN

Desperation

Andrew was curious about the meeting that had taken place on the nursing home porch. He had been standing under a tree a couple of hundred yards away, while that had been going on. When all participants dispersed, he turned back toward the village green and rode around to the back of the library. It was getting late in the afternoon, but before he returned home up close to the Corners, he needed to see what he could find out. Finally, he spotted Mr. Taft heading home, obviously in a hurry. Quickly, the teenager steered the bike around the opposite side of the green, to purposely intersect the hasty steps of his teacher.

"Hey, again, Mr. Taft!" he called out, skidding to a stop. "You look like you're in a hurry. Something wrong?"

Walter looked up in surprise. "Hi again, Andrew. You on your way home?"

"Just about. But say, you don't look too happy. Something must be up. What's going on?"

Walter stopped in his tracks to address this curious youngster. "What makes you think something is up?"

There was a shrug. "Just thought you looked kinda uptight," came the answer.

"Oh, well, nothing you should concern yourself about, for sure." He waved toward the main road. "You should probably get going." But as the teacher started to walk away, the student put out the big question.

"Does this have anything to do with those boxes?"

Walter came to an abrupt stop. "How did you know about the boxes?"

The boy grinned. "Jenny told my girlfriend, who works with her at the Home."

"Oh, I see." Walter was curious. "Who's your girlfriend, Andrew?"

He laughed and replied coyly. "I'd rather not say." He pushed the bike closer to Mr. Taft. "So, I guess I must be right, then — the meeting was about those boxes, right?"

The man decided to give the boy some of his own medicine. "I'd rather not say," he said, as he resumed his rapid stride toward home. He didn't bother to look back, until he turned in at his driveway. There he came to a stop, noting something a bit odd: Andrew had reached the main road, but instead of turning right to head toward Jericho Corners, he had gone to the left, toward the library side of the green.

"Where are you going, you sly kid?" he wondered. For a moment, he stood and watched, but the boy was soon out of sight. He wondered if he should go back down there to see what the teenager was up to, but immediately thought better of it, because it was more important to talk to Donna. Inside, he made the call.

There was no answer.

***

The morning after the meeting on the Maude's Nursing Home porch, Don Collins was on the phone with his lawyer acquaintance, John Courtney, over in Montpelier. After a few courtesies, the Christian counselor explained the situation in Jericho Center. Mr. Courtney was interested and promised to get back to Don as soon as possible.

Connie made the next call. "Hi, Greta. Got a minute?" At the end of that conversation, punctuated by husbands calling out their opinions in the background, it was agreed that all four of them would meet with the lawyer, whenever he was ready.

Surprisingly, John got back to Don that same evening. "Ay-yuh, we've handled things like this before. I double-checked with my Uncle Doug — he's the real boss, you know — and he gave me the go-ahead. Lucky for you, there's a break in my schedule."

"Excellent!" Don declared. "When can we get together?"

"How about tomorrow at two, right here in my office?"

"We'll be there, sir." He hung up the phone. "Tomorrow at two, in Montpelier," he told his wife.

"Well, I can make it, and so can the Shorts, but how about you? You have a three o'clock shift."

"Um, about eight in the morning, I will have an urgent family emergency, and need to see a lawyer."

"Whoa! Are you stretching the truth, Donald Collins?"

"Maybe just a tad, babe. But I absolutely *do* have to see a lawyer about a matter in the family of God."

***

The night before Don's call to John Courtney, Walter was informed by one of her roommates that Donna was working the late shift. His urgent calls had not been answered for several hours, so this news brought on more irritation. "Would you ask her to call me, first thing in the morning?" There was a perfunctory "Sure," before the speaker hung up. Not at all satisfied that the message would even get to her, he endured a restless night.

In the morning, he resisted the urge to call too early, since she had worked most of the night and was probably still sleeping. At nine o'clock, he finally picked up the phone. Again, there was no answer. "Probably too early. She's probably still sleeping." He decided to work on his thesis, which was nearly completed. It was, he thought, the perfect distraction from all the questions in his mind. But he was wrong. *"What was she doing up in the Roths' attic: Why did she use a flashlight, instead of turning on the lights? Why didn't she tell him she was looking for the flashlight that day she went through the boxes right there in his living room?"* He swallowed hard, acknowledging she had deliberately misled him.

He called again at ten. This time the same voice answered. "Oh damn, mister, I forgot to tell her. And, yeah, she's out right now. Oil change for her car, I think. Gee, I'm sorry. I'll tell her as soon as she gets back. Or not, if I'm out. Tell you what, I'll leave a note for her on the refrigerator. Again, I apologize."

He hung up, frustrated but hoping to hear from her before too much longer. He dived into the task of finishing up that important paper, submerging himself for hours in the puzzle of human nature. When the phone rang, he grabbed it. "Donna?"

"No, it's me, Jenny. I just wanted to let you know I'm on my way up to the ranch."

"What? What for?"

I just got off work, and I'll be back before dark," she assured him.

Walter looked at the clock, surprised that it was already three in the afternoon. No, you shouldn't be going up there, especially alone. Why in the world would you do such a thing?"

"I just need to do one thing: I need to get my birthday present from Eddie. I left it in the barn. I can just take it and leave. That's all I'll be doing, honest. Just a quick in and out. And I should be back by seven at the latest, and it will still be light. It doesn't get dark until nine o'clock now. Anyway, I just wanted to let you know." And she hung up.

He stared at the mouthpiece. "No!" He was almost out the door before he realized that, if he left, he would miss Donna's call. He had waited all night and half the day for that call. It took a few deep breaths before he decided to let Jenny take her chances. "Oh God," he prayed, "keep Your hand on that dumb kid."

***

Max Duncan was still seething over Walter Taft's deception about the box found on Mrs. Hannity's doorstep. He arrived at work with more than the usual chip on his shoulder. "Smith!" he snapped, "what do we really know about that damned schoolteacher, anyway?"

The deputy looked up from the sign-in sheet. "Nothing that I know of, but I can check on that."

The sheriff tightened his gun belt with a decisive tug. "Good. I've had about enough of that S.O.B."

"Yeah," the underling replied, "he's getting to be too much of a distraction in this murder investigation."

"Exactly." Max took a moment to lean back in his desk chair. "We need to concentrate on that, instead of chasing missing boxes... at least for now." He tossed his hat onto the desk. "So, what've we got on who killed that kid, so far?"

"Suspects are, firstly, his big sister, who was out in the barn at the time, no witnesses. She's probably number one on the list. Then there's the hotshot slingshot performer from Texas, uh..."

"Rhonda."

"Yeah, Rhonda. And the aunt, who was supposedly in the house at the time." He looked doubtful. "That's a real stretch."

"So the only other one on the premises was Uncle Mark. But he had a rifle, not a river rock." Sheriff Duncan paused for a moment, then suddenly reached for his cap. "Time to hit the road," he announced. "We can think about this while we're on patrol."

Smith grabbed the keys and followed his boss out the door. "Not much to go on," he grumbled.

***

Meanwhile in Montpelier, the meeting was very informative. Johnny Courtney surprised them with a plan already in place.

"I made a call to some friends in Burlington, the Smiths. He's a retired detective from the Snoop Squad at the Burlington Police Department, and she's a published writer and former reporter for the *Burlington Free Press* — Ed Smith and Sophia Pizarro Smith. They're perfect for an undercover operation."

"Operation?" Connie had asked.

Mr. Courtney bent his lean body forward. "Exactly what we need." He sat up straight, again. "Somebody needs to interview all the folks who were in Jericho Center the night of the quake, so we figured out a way to draw them out of the woodwork." He grinned. "Sophia will pretend to write a book on the effects of the quake on these particular people. First, she'll get the word out by talking with a few of the town fathers, and then maybe a notice on the bulletin board over at the Country Store, with a date and location." He tilted his head confidently. "Most locals can't resist being mentioned in a book, especially if they love to tell a good story." He noted the approving glances between the two couples. "And they'll talk a whole lot more freely to a book writer than they would to a sheriff, don't you agree?"

"Excellent!" Greta commented. "Sounds like a great plan."

"So, how long will this take? Any idea?" Gerald was thinking ahead. "We need to get this done before Max Duncan shows up and folks stop talking."

"That's right, Mr. Short. So, the two of them will be starting tomorrow."

A murmur of delight filled the office.

Indeed, it had been a successful meeting; now all they had to do, was wait.

***

Jenny decided to take the old road they had used as a detour right after the earthquake, since it was actually shorter than going along Browns Trace and then onto Lee River Road. It was certainly much rougher going, with all the deep ruts and jagged rocks scattered throughout. She progressed steadily over the rugged terrain, steering carefully at first, then relaxing into the bumpy ride and enjoying the artistic tangle of the roadside vegetation. It was while she was admiring the treetops on her right that the bike hit one of those protruding rocks and jumped high into the air before landing with a crunch in the middle of a deep rut. "Oh no!"

She dismounted and checked the bicycle for damage. All she could find was a dent in the brake chain's cover. She re-tucked her pant legs back inside her socks, then mounted the bike and checked the brakes. All seemed in order, so she sighed in relief and continued her journey. But she kept a sharp eye out for rocks from then on.

The brakes worked fine as she descended the serpentine driveway down to the ranch. She noted the repaired fence and piles of rubble on the lawn ahead of her. And then she saw Rhonda, standing at the end of the sidewalk near the driveway, apparently trying to repair the wheel of a lawnmower. She slowed her bike to a stop.

"What are you doing here?" the Texas princess growled softly.

"Came to get my present from Eddie."

"What? That piece of junk?"

Kathy's greeting from the front porch interrupted Jenny's reply. "Oh, my goodness! Jenny!" She waved to her. "Come on in."

"Uh, I really can't stay, Aunt Kathy. I have to get right back."

The woman approached, wiping her hands on her apron. "Oh, not even for a cool drink? Look at you... all sweaty and dirt on your dungarees." She came to a stop near the girls. "What happened? Did you fall or something?"

"Nah. My bike hit a bump and I had to check it out. Got a dent in the brake cover."

"Oh my. Too bad your Uncle Mark isn't here. He could fix that." She smiled. "The insurance finally came and he went in to pick up some repair supplies."

"Hmph, I could probably fix that thing," Rhonda said. "Why don't you go down and get your birthday present, and I'll take a look at it. Probably just a dent, anyway." She drew out a screwdriver and bent down to inspect the damage.

"Birthday present?" Kathy was puzzled.

"A slingshot. I hung it in the goat pen in the barn."

"Oh. Oh dear. I'm afraid it's no longer there," the woman said. "It was removed when prisoners cleaned up the mess from the quake. The deputy said they would get it to you." She tried to make it right. "Now listen, you've made the trip up here, and the least I can do is get you a cool glass of water, and heaven knows, now is the time to visit the restroom — am I right?"

Jenny had to agree, and the two of them went into the house. When she finally got back onto her bike, Rhonda was just rising from her inspection of the damage to the brake cover. "Don't see anything you need to worry about," she reassured Jenny. "Just a dent in the casing, as far as I can see."

Jenny was surprised at the girl's concern, but thanked her. "Appreciate it," she said. "I know you must have a lot of chores to do around here, what with Eddie and me both gone, so I really do appreciate it."

A sullen look washed over the princess's face. "Maybe you should get back here and do your share. After all, you're still in Daddy Mark's custody. He can make you come back here anytime he wants, and I think he should do that. It's not fair that Mama Kathy and I have to do so much work." She glared at the girl. "And we don't draw a paycheck, like you, either. We *work* for our board and room."

Jenny's head bowed, but she said nothing. Rhonda's eyes were moist with hatred. She threw down the screwdriver, and stomped away toward the house.

For a moment, Jenny felt sorry for her. Then she realized the Texas tyrant had just threatened her — Uncle Mark could, indeed, make her come back to the ranch. Suddenly, she couldn't get out of there fast enough. Checking that her pant legs were tucked in, Jenny mounted the bike and peddled as hard and fast as she could, getting a good start up that long hill. About halfway, she gave up and pushed the thing the rest of the way to the road. She was only a couple of miles down Lee River Road, when she needed to slow down for a chipmunk, skittering across the road. It was then that she noticed the brakes were not catching evenly. She bent down to see what was happening, just in time to see the chain snap out onto the asphalt.

The blaring horn and screeching brakes brought her vision up to a red flash. The impact somersaulted her body across the hood, crashing feet-first through the windshield.

CHAPTER SIXTEEN

Women

"I *told* you they wanted to kill her! I *told* you that, Walter Taft! And you *still* let her go up there, and all by herself! By herself?" Donna wiped her eyes with a tissue. "I can't believe you did that. I thought I could trust you."

"Look, I know this isn't much of an excuse, but I had waited for a whole twenty-four hours for you to call me back, and I didn't want to miss that call." He sat down heavily in the metal chair. "I needed to ask you about the flashlight."

"What about it?" Her voice suddenly changed.

"Your fingerprints are all over it."

For a couple of seconds, she seemed to have nothing to say, then she spoke up casually. "Oh, I can explain that, but this is neither the time nor the place. My little sister is at risk, here. All we know is that she's still breathing. If she survives this, authorities could make her go back to the ranch, because she doesn't have proper supervision, don't you realize that? Then we won't have any way to protect her."

"We may have to prove she's in danger up there," he said. "That shouldn't be too hard, what with that big insurance policy."

"Maybe you're right. That may just be the break…"

The door into the waiting room opened, filled with the form of a young doctor. His face mask drooped down under his chin as he spotted the two of them. "Are you the Roths?"

"I'm Jenny's sister."

"Well, your sister is one lucky young lady. We've done x-rays and the whole gamut, and all we found, so far, is a few abrasions. Although," he hastened to add," there is one sizable gash in one forearm."

"Oh, thank God," Donna choked out.

"Of course, there could be internal injuries that don't show up on an x-ray, so we're keeping her at least overnight. We'll see how she feels in the morning."

"Of course," Walter said.

"Can we see her?" Donna asked.

"Sure, but she's still groggy, so don't expect much conversation. And don't stay too long." He turned to leave, but had another thought. "You have somebody to take her home when it's time, right?"

"Yes," they answered together.

Jenny was lying flat under a white sheet, her head cradled in a thin pillow. Her eyes were swimming as she returned their visual contact. "Hey," she whispered, "I'm so sorry."

"Well, at least you weren't killed," Donna murmured back. "I don't think I could have survived that." She noted the bandaged arm. "Looks like you've got a major boo-boo, there."

"Yes, and I'm so sorry."

Walter moved in. "Can you tell us what happened?"

The girl licked her lips. "Brakes."

"Your bike had no brakes?" He needed to hear it clearly.

"Yes, and I'm so sorry."

Donna nudged Walter out of the way. "What happened to your brakes: Did somebody touch them?"

"Yes, and I'm so sorry." Her eyes swam for another few seconds.

"Who touched those brakes, Jenny? Try to remember. Who touched those brakes? Was it somebody at the ranch?"

She blinked and the eyeballs rolled one more time. "Rhonda. Oh, I'm so sorry."

Donna threw a confirming eye signal to Walter, then refocused on her sister. "Well, don't you worry, kiddo, I'm going to try to get custody of you, and you won't have to go back there, ever again." She bent to leave a kiss on the scraped forehead. "Is that okay with you?"

"There was a crooked smile. "Yes, and I'm so sorry."

"We understand. You're really sorry," Donna patted the top of her groggy head. "So you can stop saying you're sorry."

"But, it got all bloody."

The two of them suddenly spotted the personal belongings bag on the bed stand. Donna picked it up and saw the blood-soaked watch. She looked back into Jenny's gyrating gaze "You talking about the watch?"

"Yes, and I'm so sorry."

"Aw, kiddo, what are you so sorry about?"

The lids closed to keep the room from spinning. "You told me... not to let it... get wet."

The two of them were walking down the hall toward the hospital exit.

"It could have been a lot worse, but then, I *did* pray for her."

"You did? What did you pray?"

"For God to protect that dumb kid."

"Huh," she conceded. "Looks like it worked." There was a pause. "But I still can't believe you let her go up there. I just can't figure where your head was."

"It was on *you*, for Pete's sake. I just told you that."

The exchange continued to gain intensity, so much so, neither one of them spotted the uniformed figure approaching them in the corridor.

Sheriff Duncan had been on the scene a few minutes after the truck driver brought the injured girl in to the emergency room at Fanny Allen Hospital. Having finished interviewing the fellow, he was making his way back to talk to Jenny, when he bumped into Donna and Walter hurrying down the hospital hallway. He noted the heated conversation before he lifted a staying hand. "Hey, you two. Listen, I'm sorry about what's happened, but I need to have a few words with you, before I talk to Jenny Roth."

Donna was suspicious. "Why do you need to bother her? Hasn't she had enough for one day?"

"Just part of my job, Miss Roth." He motioned the two of them toward a bench along the wall. This won't take long." The couple took a seat. "So," he said, flipping open his little notebook, "according to the driver, the girl was looking down and drifting into on-coming traffic when the accident occurred. Any idea why she was doing that?"

"She'll tell you, herself. Her brakes were failing. She was looking down to see what was happening," Walter informed him.

"That right? Any idea why they failed?" He watched their reactions carefully.

"You'd better ask Jenny that question," Donna suggested.

"Why? Something fishy going on?"

"I don't know, Sheriff." She grimaced. "Maybe."

"Like what?" he persisted.

"Jenny says Rhonda was messing with the brakes, up at the ranch." Walter put it out there. "And then the brakes failed out there on the road. So yeah, I'd say there was something fishy going on."

"Uh-huh," the lawman said as he made a note. "Anything else?"

"You might bear in mind, these two sisters stand to inherit a goodly sum when their mother passes on," Walter continued. "You do the math, Sheriff."

Max Duncan hummed, seeming to recall something. "Now, according to the driver of the truck, she was into the wrong lane, for sure. He was helpless to prevent the accident. In fact, he threw the bike into the back of his pickup and drove her straight to this hospital. I would say that was a pretty smart thing to do, seeing as how it would have been a while before anybody could get an ambulance on the scene. I would say this fellow had his wits about him, and did the right thing." His brows went up. "Wouldn't you agree?" Seeing the acknowledgment, he finished the thought. "In fact, I would say this guy was like a hero in this whole thing."

"Ay-yuh, I suppose you could say that. Every second counts," Walter Taft agreed. "We should probably thank him." Donna was nodding in agreement, so he sought the information. "I'm assuming you have this guy's name and phone number."

The sheriff scribbled the information on a page of his notebook and handed it to Walter. "I believe you can reach him at home," he suggested, with a sly smile, and then he marched down the hall toward Jenny's room.

Donna was curious. "So who was this alert driver? What does the note say?"

Walter smoothed out the small page, and looked up. "Aw, for Pete's sake," he said. "It says, 'Mark Roth.'"

***

The Smiths were in the Center around noon on that sunny July day. Sophia thought it was more like an author to wander into the Country Store and strike up a conversation with some of the locals, even though Ed was more in favor of talking to the town fathers, first. "If we have a culprit in *that* close-knit group, they could put a stop to any interviews, in a hurry," she had reminded him. It turned out, she hit the jackpot, right in front of the Pepsi cooler. An elderly gentleman in a blue and green plaid shirt nodded a friendly greeting to the lady in the yellow summer dress. "Mornin'."

She returned the greeting with a wide smile. "Good morning!" There was a quick swish of her skirt as she motioned around at the scene. "What a great store! There must be a lot of history in this place."

He nodded. "You bet. Lots of it."

She fixed that smile on him. "You look like you might be a native of Jericho Center. Am I correct?"

"You are," he replied.

"So, I bet you would be familiar with some of that history, am I right again?"

There was a bit of pride in the answer. "Absolutely." He sized her up. "You interested in history?"

"I am." She laughed softly. "I write books about historical events and places." She let that sink in, while she seemed to be looking over the potential all around her. "Matter of fact, I'm doing a book on the earthquake that just took place up here."

"That right?" There was glint in his eye. "What for?"

"It's my understanding, " she told him, as she rested her pleasingly plump body against the side of the cooler, "that you folks were a prime example of stalwart Vermont character, the way you all went through that very dangerous situation." She smiled, again. "I love stories like that. In fact, I *write* stories like that."

The glint was still in his eye. "Well, you've come to the right place. We've got all kinds of stories about that night. Matter of fact, I was right in the middle of the whole thing, myself."

She made wide eyes at him. "Really, sir? Are you saying you, yourself, have a few things to talk about?"

He pretended to bow a humble head. "Well, I was all night over at Doc and Cindy Hortons' place on that fateful night," he stated dramatically. "I have a great memory, miss, if I do say so, myself."

"Oh my, sir... may I ask your name?"

He reached out for the handshake. "Malcolm J. Burke, at your service."

"Well, Mr. Malcolm J. Burke, would you consider the possibility of being in my book?"

He feigned reluctance. "Aw, I don't know..."

"Tell you what, we can go across to the village green and have a little talk, and then we can decide. What do you think?"

"Mmmm, I guess that wouldn't do any harm."

"Good," she replied as they started to stroll toward the green. "So, who are Doc and Cindy Horton?"

"Well see, old Doc has been our medicine guy for years around here, and Cindy is his wife, and also his office nurse, and also his secretary..."

Ed Smith watched the two take a seat on a bench at the edge of that wide patch of neatly mowed lawn. "Oh for Pete's sake," he said, staring out through the windshield," she's landed one, already. What a woman." But there was no time to be wasted. He needed to get into business mode and start wandering around, just looking for possible crime sites. It would take him some time to locate "hot spots" before sauntering into the scene of Sophia's "interview" and introducing himself as her husband, and her official photographer.

***

When they left the hospital, Donna and Walter had a lot of things to talk about, but she was due to take on the midnight shift at the telephone company, and so all that had to be postponed. A quick call to the hospital, before she went to bed the next morning revealed that Jenny was doing as well as could be expected, and the doctor would determine whether or not she could come home that day.

She was awakened by her roommate at ten that morning. Walter informed her that the doctor was keeping Jenny for one more day, to determine whether there were internal injuries. If all went well, she could go home the next day. But there was a hitch: she would be signed out by her uncle, who had custody. This was necessary, to avoid making waves in the social worker circles.

Donna's hands were tied. She started to cry. "I can't let this happen. I can't." She could hardly get the words out. Her roommate waved apologetically as *she* went off to work, and Donna Roth was alone to deal with this shock. "No!" she screamed into the mouthpiece. "No-no-no-no." The sobs were audible.

"We'll be there when he gets there. Maybe he'll let us take her back to the nursing home." It was a futile attempt to comfort the woman, who was trying to talk through the tears. "No, Donna, it's worth a try; the man can't be a complete degenerate — he brought her straight to the hospital, remember?" But she was still crying, unable to get any words out, at all. It was clear that she was having a meltdown. "Donna. Donna, listen to me. I'm cutting my next class. I'll be there in ten minutes." She was still crying. "Ten minutes, Donna. Be there to open the door for me, okay?" He wasn't sure she heard him, so he repeated it in a loud voice: "Donna! You need to open the door for me! I'll be there in ten minutes! Ten minutes!"

He was, indeed, on her front step in ten minutes, pounding on the door. He breathed a sigh of relief when she opened it, still clad in her cotton pajamas, her face twisted in distress. He reached out to her and she collapsed in his arms. He held her just long enough to pass on some strength, then swept her up and took her over to sit beside him on the sofa. She buried her head in the hollow of his shoulder, releasing a moaning from deep down in her soul. He felt the total collapse of the spunky little woman he had loved for so long. "Donna," he said softly, "I'm here. I'm here."

And then he let her cry until she could cry no more, lying weakly against the warmth of his comforting presence. At length, there was a long, quivering sigh. He kissed the top of her fevered head and waited.

"I guess I deserve this," she whispered.

He reached for a tissue on the lamp stand nearby. "What are you talking about?" he asked, wiping her face. She took the tissue from him, patting under her nose, shaking her head in resignation before burying her face back into his shoulder. He stroked her hair. "Got something you need to tell me, miss?"

She moaned, again. "You're not going to love me anymore."

"Oh?"

"You'll' never trust me again, Walter." There was a muffled groan. "I wouldn't blame you one bit." She lifted her head to kiss him on the chin. "I'm so sorry." She kissed him there, again. "I am so darned sorry, please believe me."

Suddenly, he was returning her kiss holding her close, and she was responding, and everything was spinning.

The footsteps on the doorstep preceded the key turning in the lock. When the roommate came in, Walter was sitting on the sofa, wiping his mouth with the back of his hand, and Donna was on her way to put on a robe. "Hey there," he mumbled to the lady. "I was just going to use your phone to call the hospital. Would that be okay?" When she nodded approval, he pulled out the number for Fanny Allen, connecting immediately with the nurses' station. Suddenly, he slammed the mouthpiece into its cradle. "Donna!" he shouted.

"Get dressed. The doctor has changed his mind. They're discharging Jenny right now. Mark has signed the papers and they're getting her dressed!"

***

Connie and Greta checked at the nurses' station for directions to Jenny's room. "Just follow those two," the woman answered, "but remember, four people at a time, and no more." The ladies hurried to catch up with the woman and teenager ahead of them. In her typical fashion, Greta called out to the leaders. "Hey there!" She waved to them when they turned to acknowledge the voice. "The nurse said to just follow you to Jenny's room." As they caught up, she introduced herself. "I'm Greta, and this is my friend, Connie."

"Oh!" Essie recognized the names immediately. "I'm Jenny's friend, Essie, and this is my *Mutter*, Elke Schuler."

There was a courteous bow from the German lady. "Oh, of course, Jenny has spoken of you." She turned to lead the way. "It looks like we have just time to say 'Hello,' because they are processing her to leave the hospital even as we speak."

"Is that right? We didn't know that," Connie said.

"Well, at least we get to talk to her for a minute," Greta reassured herself. "I don't know about you, Mrs. Schuler but I want to know what happened."

"Please, you may call me Elke," the woman replied, "and, yes, we want to hear this, also."

Connie scooted to catch up with Elke. "So you two have some suspicions about this so-called accident, as well?"

The German lady came to a sudden halt. "We do. Jenny has told us she never wanted to go back to live there, because her brother's death was very suspicious." She looked at the other three in the tight circle that now blocked the hallway. "Do we all have these same feelings?" Three heads nodded in agreement. "Then we must ask her some questions, not so?" When the nods were repeated, she strode purposefully to the second door down on the left. "Here we are," she suddenly whispered. "So, we ask questions, but we do not frighten the girl, agreed?"

Jenny was sitting on the side of the bed, where a nurse's aide was helping to put on her shoes. Quiet greetings and casual conversation prevailed until the young candy striper had left the room. It was Essie who took up the questioning. "My gosh, kiddo, what happened?"

The four ladies listened while Jenny noted how her bike brakes had failed, after Rhonda had fiddled with them, and now she was scared to death to go back to the ranch, but had been informed that her Uncle Mark had custody of her, and she had no choice. The tears welled up. "I hate that place."

"Whatever possessed you to go there, in the first place?" Connie asked.

"I wanted to get the slingshot Eddie gave me for my birthday."

Greta jumped in on that. "Even when you knew that you were in danger?"

"Well," she replied sheepishly, "I thought the Holy Spirit would protect me."

"Ach so," Frau Schuler hummed in a mixture of English and German. "Now I understand." She looked the girl in the eye. "Holy Spirit does advise us, but we are to use our common sense, *Kind*! You have free will, do you remember this? And He can only *prompt* us to use wisdom."

"That's right," Connie added. "The Holy Spirit is not going to overrule your decisions." She touched a finger to her own temple. "But I do see that *somebody* did protect you at the moment of the accident. Think about it: You could have been killed. No, you *should* have been killed. Instead, you suffered only minor injuries. There must have been a couple of angels on duty. Think about that."

The arrival of the wheelchair interrupted any further discussion. In a matter of minutes, the five of them were standing outside the hospital's main entrance, and Mark Roth's truck was pulling up to take the girl back to the ranch.

"Wait a minute! Hold it, right there!" Walter and Donna were running toward the truck. "We have something to say about this," Walter continued.

"Yeah," Donna agreed, as she pulled her bathrobe tighter over her pajamas.

Mark turned off the engine and slipped out of the cab. "What the hell...?"

The younger man was out of breath, but spoke up, anyway. "You... you'd better listen to what... we have to say... before you take that girl away."

Mark looked at the man, and the disheveled older sister beside him. "What's sticking in your craw, you two? I'm responsible for this kid, and she's coming back to the ranch with me, and that's all there is to it."

"Not if you're smart," Walter shot back. "That girl had brakes tampered with up there at your precious ranch, by your stepdaughter, only minutes before the accident. The sheriff has Jenny's statement confirming that, and she also told Donna and me the same thing."

"And," Connie spoke up boldly, "Jenny just told us four ladies the very same thing."

"What are you talking about? I haven't heard any such nonsense." Mark glanced around at the accusing faces. "The kid is probably still under the influence of pain pills, or something," he pointed out.

"No, I'm *not!*" Jenny insisted. "I know exactly what I'm saying, and you can even ask Aunt Kathy. I was in the house with her and when we came back out, Rhonda had a screwdriver and was tinkering with the brake chain case." She sniffed, on the edge of more tears. "You just ask her. You just ask her. She'll tell you."

"If I were you," the young teacher cautioned the cattleman, "I would think twice before taking this kid back to a place where her life is probably in danger. After all, there are six witnesses here, right now, who will swear that you refused to protect this minor from bodily harm, or even death."

Mark Roth's face went pale. His back was against the wall. It took only a few minutes before he agreed to let Donna take her sister back to the nursing home, for her own safety. When he finally took the discharge paperwork and drove off, all seven of them heaved a sigh of relief.

The three of them stopped at Donna's apartment so she could get dressed, before heading to Maude's Nursing Home. They left Jenny under the watchful care of Mrs. Hannity, then headed for his little rental. Once inside, he pulled Donna to the sofa.

"Now, my love," he said firmly, "you have some explaining to do."

CHAPTER SEVENTEEN

Strategies

The four ladies had stood there at Fanny Allen Hospital's entrance, watching Walter's car drive away, with Jenny safely inside. It hadn't taken long before Connie expressed concern that Mark Roth would think it over, then contact social services in order to explain his decision. "They will probably send the girl back to the Children's Home, just to be on the safe side, until her eighteenth birthday."

"Oh, rats," Greta had said. "That's what it'll come down to — the Home or the ranch."

"This is true," the German lady had acknowledged, "and so, we must address the basic problem: We need to make the ranch a safe place." She had looked at her watch. "I see it is almost noon, and I have hunger. I invite you to join me at The Black Cat restaurant in Burlington. I find it most enjoyable and we can make some plans while we eat."

"Plans?" Connie wasn't following this quick-witted lady.

They waited until the waitress in the dark uniform, lacy cap, and ruffled white apron had taken the order before Frau Schuler laid out the strategy. "It is, as my American friends like to say, 'a long shot,' but I think we should give it a try." There had been a quick wink. "Perhaps we can dislodge any evil spirits in that household, by bringing in a good, big dose of Jesus." Three faces were looking rather doubtful. "Oh, I see you have questions. No problem. We just need to offer some help in the repairs. I think Mrs. Roth would be delighted to have a helping hand. Once we are there, we do whatever we can do and we talk about lovely things, as we show the love of God." There was still some doubt. "Ach so, what do we have to lose?"

Frau Schuler made the phone call that afternoon, and she was right. Kathy was delighted, since she was ready to paint the woodwork in the living room and had already purchased the wallpaper, which would go in place next. She would, indeed, need some help. She even asked how soon they could all come.

***

"You're probably going to drop me like a hot potato," she said. "And I wouldn't blame you."

"Why? Did you kill somebody?"

Her lavender-blue eyes widened in shock. "What?! No! Why would you even say such a thing?"

"I don't know... Maybe just to get that one out of the way."

"You thought maybe I had killed someone? Really?" Suddenly, she made the connection. "Oh, Walter, you don't really think I would kill my own brother."

"No, not really, but that would probably be the only reason I would drop you like a hot potato. But then, I would have picked you up again, to try and figure it all out."

She paused to think that one through. "Oh."

He tried to give her a starting point. "So, why are your fingerprints all over that mysterious flashlight?"

"Okay, yeah, those are my prints, alright. I, uh, I was up in that attic a lot, before Eddie and Jenny ever came to the ranch." She saw the question in his eyes. "Well, I think I told you that Mrs. Bushey and I agreed... Um, you remember her don't you — the director of the Home?"

"Barely. She started there the year I left, I think. But go on."

"Well, I asked if I could visit the ranch a few times before it was decided Uncle Mark could take all three of us up there. So, I did." She shivered. "I just had a bad feeling about that place, the very first time I went there. It wasn't just that I found out they knew about the insurance policy... no, it was more than that. Couldn't put my finger on it, until the second visit." She curled her legs up under her, and leaned forward. "Have you ever had a creepy feeling about some place? I mean a *really* creepy feeling?"

"Can't say I have, but know other people have talked about that." He took in the beauty of her earnest face. "So, what did you do about it?" he asked.

"Started poking around the place, whenever I thought they weren't watching."

"Find anything?"

"Took me a while, but..." she needed to explain how it happened. "See, when I visited up there, they would put me in the guest room. I guess they wanted to make a good impression, because they could have very well put me in with Rhonda, but they didn't." She slipped into a teacher voice. "As you probably remember from when you took the boxes from the attic, the guest room is located right beside the linen closet, where the attic stairs drop down. They warned me that the stairs were old, and often dropped down, so I shouldn't go in there without turning on a light because I could bump into the steps and get hurt." She seemed to double-check her memory, then took a breath and went on. "Now, I had seen this the very first time I visited, because Aunt Kathy had to show me where to get an extra blanket, and guess what else? There was a door between the guest room and that closet. If I wanted to, I could go into the linen storage without bothering anyone else." She tilted her head to see if he was getting all that. He nodded. "And so it was a little cool that night, and I went through my private door to get a blanket, and sure enough, stubbed my toe against those steps."

"And you decided to go up into the attic?"

"You're getting ahead of me, but yes, I did go up. But first I grabbed my flashlight from my suitcase."

"Why did you have a flashlight in your suitcase?"

"I'll tell you why," she said with a determined wiggle. "After that first visit, I made up my mind to protect myself from whatever was so creepy in that house."

"Mmmm," he hummed.

"What? You think that was stupid? Well, I sure didn't feel stupid. I was glad I had it with me, especially once I got up those stairs." He could see she was picturing the dark attic. "I shined the light on all that stuff — and I mean there was a lot of stuff. At first, I just stood there and moved the light beam from one thing to another, over and over." She shrugged and gave herself a hug. "Then I got too cold. I needed to grab a blanket and get back into bed." She rubbed her upper arms, still in hugging mode. "But as I turned to go back down, I saw these books on the table. I shone the light on them and saw a couple of titles that were very, very intriguing." She shivered. "I grabbed them, and headed back downstairs." There was a regretful nod of her lovely head. "That was my first mistake."

"Going up into the attic," he assumed.

"Nope. Taking those two books."

"Really? So what were they about?"

"I thought you would like to know, so I grabbed them before we left my place today, after I got dressed." She reached for a paper grocery bag and slid the two worn hardcovers out. "I'm so sorry about this," she whispered as she handed them to Walter.

He read the titles aloud: "*The Art of Witchcraft*, and *Hecate, Goddess of Witchcraft*." The man looked at the woman he loved. "What did you do with these, Donna?" He turned them over carefully in his hands. "I know you. This was not just casual reading, now, was it?"

She bowed her head. "No. No, it wasn't." Her voice was barely above a whisper. "I studied them, and I... used them, to try to scare those people into going back to Texas. I knew my brother and sister should not be moving in, but I didn't want to tell Mrs. Bushey what I was reading and planning, and before I knew it, she gave permission for those two innocent kids to move in." She wiped something from her eye. "I was just too late. I should have started before he brought Eddie and Jenny to the ranch." There was a small sniff. "It just took a lot of studying, and so I wasn't able to start until the first night I knew they had moved in." She started to explain how a spell could be cast from a distance, even all the way from her apartment in Burlington, but he interrupted her.

"Wait. Are you saying you're responsible for the banging on the ceilings?" He stared at the books. "You learned how to do that, from these books?" She nodded her yes. "Oh my god, Donna, what have you opened yourself up to? You have no idea what this crap can do to a person, to a family, to a whole town, for Pete's sake."

Suddenly, she curled into a ball, the crying muffled by her own body. He slipped the books onto the cushion beside him and reached to hold her. "Okay, okay, we need to get a handle on this." He lifted her chin. "Listen, if there were directions for that kind of spell, or whatever it is, there must be directions for lifting it, right?" She blinked hopefully. "So, let's not go to pieces just yet. Here," he let loose of her and held up the two books. "We'll just scour these pages until we find the answer." He handed her one of the books. "Here, you take this one home to study, and I'll keep this one."

"Yeah? You think we can do this?" She was wiping her face with the back of her hand.

"Well, we can give it one hell of a try." He flipped the pages of the book in his hand. "Are they still hearing all that thumping, do you know?"

"I don't know. I haven't heard any more about it."

"Alright, we can check on that easily enough. My biggest concern is that you're not in danger. The spirit world is very real." Suddenly, he remembered. "Oh man. What am I thinking? I'll just pray for you, right now. I'll plead the Blood over you. Better yet, *you* plead the Blood of Jesus over yourself, and I'll stand in agreement."

She looked worried. "Um, I haven't been in touch with God, for quite a while. Do you think He'll even listen to me?"

"Are you sorry about this stuff you've done? And are you sorry you've not been in touch with God like you should have?"

"Yeah," she admitted. "I'm sorry about a lot of things."

"Okay, just tell Him that, and ask for His forgiveness, and then ask for His protection."

"That's it?" A crease appeared between her brows. "Seems too simple."

"Oh, it's not just mouthing the words, miss. You need to really be sorry, and change your ways. You can't have all the benefits without honoring the Benefactor." He made sure she understood. "You need to start a new relationship with Jesus. Are you ready to do that?"

She got it. "You know what, Walter? I *am*. I'm ready to get my life back on track with Him."

He saw the tears, again, and put his arm around her. "Alright then, go for it."

She set her jaw firmly and closed her eyes. "Dear Jesus..." she prayed.

In a few minutes the prayer was completed. He gave her a quick kiss on the forehead and leaned back into the cushions. "Okay, now I feel better."

She heaved a long, slow sigh. "Oh my goodness. So do I." Her head leaned back into the softness behind it. "I should have done that a long time ago."

Walter smiled. "It was there inside you for a long time, that's for sure. Once we accept Jesus as our Lord, the Holy

Spirit hangs in there, through all the bumps and bruises, waiting for you to get back to the reality of your salvation." There was a quick clap of his hands. "And now we can really get back into fighting this witchcraft thing." He lifted the book he had chosen to study and read the title again. "*Hecate, Goddess of Witchcraft*. Guess I'll have to put it off until I finish typing up my thesis, though." He flipped through the pages, coming to a sudden stop. "Hey, what's this?" He pulled out a paper, folded in half, and tucked between the pages of the book. Donna wasn't surprised.

"Oh, I never paid any attention to it. I guess somebody marked that page with it." She peered over at the worn sheet of paper. "What is it, anyway?"

He opened it carefully. "Huh. It's a marriage certificate. Old."

"Oh yeah?" She was momentarily delighted at the thought. "Whose marriage?"

He read it, then read it, again. "Oh my gosh, Donna. It's the Crockers' marriage certificate. Oh my gosh."

"Really?" She cooed softly. "How sweet. Let me see it." But he pulled it back from her reach.

"Not 'til I read it to you," he insisted. He waited for her to settle back into the soft cushion, then spoke slowly and clearly: "This is a real certificate, dated and everything. The groom is listed as Timothy K. Crocker and the bride is listed as Freda A. Schuler."

"Schuler?" she puzzled. "Where have I heard that name before?"

***

Sheriff Max Duncan and his deputy had answered a domestic disturbance call up toward Stowe, and were returning through Jericho township, when Max decided to make a stop. The matter of who killed Eddie Roth was still a high priority on the lawman's agenda. Jenny and Eddie's fingerprints were the only ones found on the rocks and slingshot, so there was no evidence there. Further, there was still the mystery of the missing boxes. He decided to interview Mrs. Hannity again; this time about the events during the early morning earthquake. "Maybe we can pick up on something about those stolen boxes, if we come from that point of few," he postulated.

"No appointment?" Deputy Smith asked.

"Nah. Let's see if we can surprise some information out of her."

She was surprised, especially when he showed up at the supper hour, busy time at Maude's Nursing Home.

"Is there something wrong, Sheriff? I wasn't expecting you today, was I?" She had hustled the two men into her office.

"No, ma'am, and I apologize for the inconvenience, but we need some information that you might be able to help us with. So, we happen to be up this way on another call, and it was the perfect opportunity to get together for just a few minutes. We sure appreciate your cooperation."

"I see," she replied. "And what is the information you need?"

"Well, ma'am, everyone here was pretty much awake and aware of the goings-on in the community during those first few hours after the earthquake, what with having to take care of all your patients. We hoped you might have noticed any unusual traffic or presence of strangers coming in and out of your facility, or maybe on the street."

"Oh." She stopped to think, her eyes focused on the ceiling. "Well, in the nursing home, here, we only had Doc Horton, who came over right away. He sedated the ones who needed

it, then left some pills for any who might need them later."
She looked down at the sheriff. "I really don't know about
what was going on outside. Just a few cars or whatever,
moving slowly, as I recall." She turned her attention to the
deputy. "We were all worried about aftershocks, or
whatever... I'm sure you can understand that."

The deputy nodded sympathetically, but Max did the
talking. "Of course. So you were probably watching for some
rescue vehicles or something like that. You know, maybe
looking up the road toward Jericho Corners, right?"

"Why, yes," she suddenly remembered. "That's where I
figured they would come from."

"Anybody else watching for those rescuers? Maybe
somebody who works here?" He folded his arms and leaned
against the closed door.

"Let's see." There was a slight frown. "There were only two
of us on duty overnight, myself and Bella." She looked up
again. "That poor woman was up to her ears, but she did well.
We're lucky to have her."

"So she was in the building all that time?" Max didn't want
to miss a thing.

"I think so. She was flitting all over the place, until
daylight." Mrs. Hannity was proud of the woman's
dedication. "I'm telling you, I don't think she even hit the
restroom for about four hours."

The sheriff's brows moved only slightly. "That's a long
time." He grinned at the deputy, then got back to business.
"So, who is this 'Bella'? I don't believe we've ever interviewed
her."

"Well, she's quite a character. But she's a good worker, as I
just said." She paused. "So, do you have to talk to her?"

"I'm afraid so, ma'am. She could have the very information
we need, you know?" He stood up straight. "Is she here right
now?"

The woman was reluctant to lose any more help in the
dining room. "Yes, but could you just wait for another half-

hour? Tell you what, join us for a cup of coffee and some dessert. Now, wouldn't that be nice?"

He wasn't into being nice, but being the savvy lawman that he was, he knew he could observe the woman as she scurried around the dining room. He sent Deputy Smith out to listen for dispatch in the car, and ambled into the buzz of suppertime at Maude's Nursing Home.

***

"Oh, I remember where we've heard that name before," Walter said. "Wasn't that the German couple who dropped by on the same day you introduced me to Thunder?" He saw the recognition in her eyes. "Yeah, the little freckle-faced girl — what was her name?"

"That would be Essie. She and her mother were at the hospital, remember? With those other two ladies."

"Yeah, Essie. I guess she and Jenny are pretty close friends." He double-checked his facts. "Doesn't she have a younger brother?"

"Right. I forget his name, but he and Eddie hit it off, right away." Her face clouded over. "Too bad that friendship never got a chance. Eddie could have used a friend up there; he was so isolated — a prime target, for sure." Her mouth went into a quick pinch and release. "Unfortunately, I had my head in the sand, and didn't pray for his protection." She let loose an exasperated huff.

"Hey," he said, reaching for her hand, "you need to quit that stuff. What's done is done; now we pay attention and find out who did this awful thing to him."

"But I should have pled the Blood over him. I should have prayed over both of them." The thought hit her. "Oh, man, I can still plead the Blood over Jenny, right?"

"You can," he reassured her.

"Then help me do that; stand in agreement, okay?"

She prayed fervently for her sister's safety, and then slipped into Walter's embrace. "What would I do without you, Walter Taft? I swear, you're my hero."

"Whoa! That's a pretty big role to fill. Are you sure you won't settle for me just being your boyfriend?"

She laughed against his chest. "My boyfriend? I thought you said you were in love with me, you rascal."

He stroked her shoulder as he answered. "I am." He kissed her temple. "But I'm being careful. I don't want to end up with a broken heart, or whatever it's called."

She lifted her head to look into his eyes. "You think I'm going to dump you?" She was incredulous. "And here, all this time, I thought *you* would get fed up with all this family drama, and drop *me*!" She closed her eyes and leaned her forehead against his chin. "I've been waiting for you to send me packing, since this morning. I thought you would get away from my deceitful self, the minute I told you about the books and the attic and —"

He lowered his head, just enough to press his mouth against hers. The kiss was hard and persistent, until he pulled back just enough to speak. "I just need to know if you love me, Donna Roth."

"Oh, God help me, if you ever leave me, Walter. Right now, I can't imagine life without you beside me."

"That's all I need to hear," he whispered. And then he kissed her like he never dared before. And then he did it again. And once more. But then he got the message, as all guys do, that things could really get out of hand. "Uh, we'd better slow down, miss, before I make you a tainted woman." She pulled back, her eyelids seductively lowered. "In fact," he said softly, "I think it's high time I proposed." He let go of her, sliding to one knee in front of the sofa. "Marry me, Donna. Please say yes. You know we belong together. Please marry me."

She squealed the happy answer and he swept her up off the sofa as if to carry her over the threshold. In a moment, he was in the center of the room, twirling her around and around, until, with a laugh, he dropped her back onto the cushions. "So we need to get a marriage license. When will you be off work, so we can get over to city hall?"

"Um, tomorrow afternoon, at three?" She wasn't sure. "Are we in a hurry?"

"Oh yes, we're in a hurry. Two reasons: One, I can't keep my hands off you, and two, once we're a married couple, we can apply for custody of Jenny."

"What? We can get Jenny? Why in the world didn't you tell me this, before?"

"I wanted to make sure you were in love with me, first. I wouldn't want you to marry me, just to get custody of Jenny, now, would I?"

In a few minutes, they were checking on Jenny over at the nursing home. The girl was resting her bruises in her room. When they told her they were getting married, she was overjoyed. "May I come to the wedding?" she asked. They reassured her that she could be maid of honor, which brought an even bigger sparkle to the girl's eyes. They left her without mentioning the possibility of getting custody of her. There was no sense in getting her hopes up. After all, life had been pretty unpredictable for the last four months.

As they slipped back into the car to get Donna back to Burlington, Deputy Smith took notice from his seat in the squad car. He made a note that the couple had parked off to the side of the building instead of out on the street. He wasn't sure that meant anything important, so there was no need to interrupt the sheriff, who was busy at this very moment, interviewing a lady named Bella, up there on the front porch.

The first thing he noticed about Bella, was her intensity. She focused on the task at hand, and didn't like it when somebody else got in the way. She was also slightly built, with frizzy hair and a stern countenance, and after she had lit up a hand-rolled cigarette out there on the porch, she proved to have a mean mouth. "What the hell do *you* want? I haven't done anything."

"I understand you were on duty when the earthquake hit. Thought maybe you could tell us if you noticed anything out of the ordinary."

She looked at the sheriff like he was a dumb kid. "Well now, I would say just about every goddim thing was out of the ordinary, in the middle of an earthquake."

"Just fill me in on what happened over the next four hours or so." He would ignore the sassy mouth for the moment. Cocky people tended to get impressed with themselves, and usually spilled the beans before they realized it. This one was a prime candidate. "Maybe you could start by telling me what happened right after the quake."

She took a slow draw on the cigarette, picking loose tobacco off her lower lip as she exhaled. "That's easy. Doc Horton showed up, did his thing, then left. Said he had a shortwave radio at his office and his wife was hosting some folks who were listening, so if anything came up, he would let us know."

"I understand you were real busy with upset patients, but were you expecting a rescue team to show up here in the Center?"

"We were hoping. Glanced out the window a couple of times." She took a seat on the porch swing.

"Notice any traffic, at all?" He drew out the little notepad.

"Well, that stupid kid, Jenny, jumped on her bike to go up to the ranch where her brother and sister were staying overnight." She snorted her contempt. "You'd think she would stay here where she was needed, but it turned out, she came back and got in the car with that teacher. I heard later, they got turned back and went over to Doc's office to listen for news on that radio."

"Who told you that?" It was a possible connection.

"Aw, for Cry-sake, I don't remember. Too much going on." She flicked the ash off the end of twisted paper.

"Got any idea who else was over there at Doc's?" He poised the pen over the lined paper.

"Not sure, but probably the usual locals." She was moving the swing just a bit.

"Like who?"

She squinted as she made a guess. "Probably Malcolm. He's usually right in the middle of things."

Sheriff Duncan found Malcolm hanging around the front of Jericho Center Country Store. He had a brief conversation that proved to be fruitful. Seems the older man and his buddies had spent most of the four hours right there in Doc Horton's office that fateful morning. "And," the man smiled, "turns out, we're all gonna be in a book that's being written about the quake."

"Oh? Somebody's writing a book about the quake? Who might that be, Malcolm?"

The old man smiled, again. "Her name's Sophia Somebody. She's been interviewing us guys for about a week, now."

"Is that right? My goodness, where would a person conduct such detailed interviews, in this small village?"

Malcolm nodded across the green. "The librarian is letting her use the children's corner. It's always noisy over in that section, anyway."

"Well, that's pretty exciting! I wouldn't mind talking to her, myself. Got any idea when she'll be back?"

"Nah, but she used to work for the *Burlington Free Press*. I bet they could give you a phone number, or something."

The sheriff called in on the car radio, and got an answer before he and his deputy had reached Essex Junction. "Alright, now we got something. She's married to a retired Snoop. This has to be an undercover operation of some sort."

"Think so, Sheriff?"

"I'd bet my badge on it. It's your old man, kid. So now we need to have a chat with the detective squad in Burlington about Ed Smith and who he's working for." He looked directly at the deputy. "And *you* are ethically bound to not inform your dad about this, understand?" He turned to the passenger window. "We finally got a bit of a lead."

"I get it, Sheriff — you smell a rat."

"More like a rat's *nest*..." He yawned. "Head back to the office, Deputy, I'm done for now. I need to sleep."

Indeed, it had been a long, complicated day for everybody.

CHAPTER EIGHTEEN

Treasures

The investigation was going well for the Smiths. There were so many interviews that the flattered townsfolk had, indeed, talked the librarian into providing a corner for them in the children's section. About the fourth day into the project, somebody mentioned they had seen "...some idiot in a beat-up truck, creeping along with its headlights off, but with all the strange stuff going on, I didn't think much about it. Just noticed it was light colored." Sophia went through her list of contributors, just in case someone else had seen the same pickup. It turned out that another person remembered it being in back of the library while it was still dark, but it wasn't there in the morning light. "I think we might have something here," she told Ed that night. "Why would anybody be driving in the dark without headlights, especially when there's been an earthquake?"

"Maybe they didn't want to be seen?" he joked. He took another bite of the pizza, and then asked through the drooping mozzarella, "Anything else?"

"Aw, I don't know. Maybe. Like, the doctor wasn't there for most of the time."

"Guess he had to go over to the nursing home." He licked a thin strand off his bottom lip. "Anybody say how long he was gone?"

"Nope. Didn't think to ask that one." She leaned back and stretched. "I could check with Malcolm on that one, because he was there the entire time. I've got his phone number." She checked her watch. "It's only six o'clock. I'll give him a call."

Ed listened from the kitchen table. The call was short and sweet. When she came back, he motioned for her to take the last wedge of pizza. "So?"

"He says the doctor didn't show up until just before daylight. Said the old guy looked bushed."

"Must have been a long, hard night over there, with all those old folks scared out of their gourds," he remarked as he went to the refrigerator for a beer. He had a sudden thought. "What do we know about the good doctor, anyway?"

She swallowed. "Not much." She anticipated his suggestion. "Why don't you do a little tailing for a couple of days?"

He flipped the cap off the beer. "I'd be delighted."

It was close to eight-thirty when the phone rang. He recognized his son's voice. "How's it going, kid?"

"Hey, Dad. I've got a problem."

"Yeah?"

"The battery in my car is dead."

Ed stopped the conversation immediately. "No sweat. I can be there in a half-hour."

There was a shuffling on the other end of the line, before the son got back to the father. "No, wait. My neighbor just came by. He's going to give me a jump. Thanks, anyway."

Ed hung up. "Oh, crap."

Sophia looked up from her typewriter. "Okay, I know that look. You just got a coded message. What's up?"

"We've been fingered."

"Aw, nuts. By who — I mean, by whom?" She watched his face carefully.

"Well, who the hell does my boy work for, huh?"

"Waddaya know about that: Max Duncan is worse than the damned Mafia, I swear."

"Whatever. The jig is up. Time to report to John Courtney."

She was slipping into bed when she remembered something else. "Hey, bambino," she whispered, "you asleep yet?" He grunted. "Okay, one more thing. I remember one of those guys talking about the death up there at some ranch. He was saying how those Masons stick together, and they really get things done. I asked what he meant, and he said the contractor from Barre and the local Masons got together on that one. Said there was a real good old boys' thing going on, right there in Jericho township." She tucked the covers under her lovely, plump body. "Don't know if this means anything, but he made a big deal out of the fact that Doc Horton was a 33rd degree Mason, or something. Does that make his wife a member of the Eastern Star?"

Ed turned over to stare at her. "Good gawd, Sophia! Don't you remember what Courtney said was in those boxes? We need to make sure he gets that information in our report!"

***

The four ladies arrived sharply at nine in the morning, dressed in work clothes that showed these volunteers meant business. The Roths had pushed the living room furniture into the center of the room, where it half hid under a paint-splattered sheet. Obviously, Mark and Kathy had already repaired and painted the ceiling. Kathy had paint buckets and brushes all ready. "It's woodwork," she pointed out as she handed out damp wipe cloths, "but we don't have to worry about getting paint on the walls, since we'll be papering over that area."

Connie pulled the plastic floor cover closer to the mopboard. "I brought tape, if you want to keep a nice clean line at the edge of the floor."

"Good thinking!" Greta exclaimed. "I'll take some of that."

The two Schulers claimed the ladders. "We'll get the tops of the doorways and windows," Essie proclaimed.

"That leaves the mantle. I can handle that," Kathy added.

In a few minutes, all five were fast at work. "How was the drive up here?" the hostess asked Greta, who had driven the work crew up in her car.

"It was actually pretty nice," Greta answered.

"Yah-yah! It's always nice in the mornings," Elke added.

"The air is still so fresh, before the July afternoon heat sets in," Essie noted.

"Can you believe it's almost August?" Connie's voice bounced from low in a corner.

From the other side of the furniture barrier, Greta called out, "Hey! Don't rush us into the next month too fast. I want all the back porch time in my rocking chair that I can possibly get."

Kathy looked down from her perch at the top of the fireplace mantle. "Rocking chair? Are you talking about the one you bought from us?"

"I am," the woman replied. "I absolutely love that big old thing."

Frau Schuler looked down from her ladder. "You bought a rocking chair from this ranch? How nice. Was it an antique?"

"Bet your bottom dollar, it was." Greta wiped the edge of the brush along the rim of the paint can. "I love to collect antiques."

"Oh my," Elke said sadly. "I think I'm a tiny bit jealous."

Kathy tossed her a quick glance. "Why? Are you a collector, too?"

"I guess you could say that." She pushed a strand of the strawberry blonde hair back behind one ear. "In fact, you wouldn't have any more of that type of furnishings for sale, would you?"

Kathy stopped to think. "You know, there's still a table and some chairs, and even an old rug, up there in the attic."

"Oh my," the German woman said, again." I wonder if we could take a look, when we get finished here."

"Sure. That's okay with me," Kathy happily replied.

The painting was finished by noon, whereupon, Kathy served tuna sandwiches and iced tea. Elke hastened to help clean up the kitchen, anticipating the visit to the attic. Kathy led the way, passing Rhonda's open door. The girl was lying asleep on her bed. "I wondered where she was," Essie whispered.

"That poor girl is exhausted," Kathy whispered back. "She's pretty much taken over all the chores here on the ranch. I wish we could hire some help, but that's just not possible right now." By this time, she had reached the door to the linen closet. "Now, these stairs have been repaired, but please be careful, anyway."

Connie and Greta, who had chosen to revisit this intriguing storage area, followed the other three. The two ladies exchanged a knowing look, recalling that those five boxes had been stolen. But Kathy was preoccupied with making a sale, giving no hint that she was aware of that theft, so neither one of them brought up the subject.

"So, we have this table, and those stacked chairs, and of course, the rug." Kathy was moving toward the rolled-up item snuggled at the edge of the attic floor. She bent down, attempting to move the dusty thing, but it seemed wedged tightly in the crack where the slanted ceiling met the floor.

"Here," Elke Schuler said, bending down to take the opposite end. "Essie, you take the other end for Kathy." The daughter obeyed, and the rug came loose with a dull snap. Elke stood up. "We need to get it over to that space, so we can open it up." Again the Schulers grabbed the heavy thing and pulled it into place.

"Let me go get a broom," Kathy suggested. "It's absolutely layered with filth."

"No-no, this will be fine." She signaled to her daughter, and they began to unroll the rug.

"It's got a gold edge." Essie squinted in the dim light of the bulb just above her. "Looks like wheat or something." The unrolling continued slowly for the fibers were deeply embedded. "It's blue," the girl continued.

"Wait! Stop!" Her mother bent down for a closer look. "Oh my, oh my." She looked up at the other ladies. "Do you see it?" She moved a pointed finger along the weave of the back side. "Look. It's handmade."

Greta gasped. "How could I have missed that?" She shook her head in frustration. "Okay, looks like you have found a real prize here, Elke. You'd better take it, *or I will.*"

Essie resumed the unrolling with greater care. "Blue background, and some star-shaped thing in the middle."

"That's a spin-off of the Grange ceremonial rug," Connie informed the others. As the girl gently pulled the rest of the thing open, the Christian counselor continued: "Not accurate, but probably wasn't intended to be."

"What do you mean?" Greta wanted to know.

"Well, for one thing, the usual sheath of grain is missing, replaced by a satanic pentagram — a five-pointed star in a circle — and look: right in the center of that star, there's an all-seeing eye inside a triangle."

Essie looked up. "Um, excuse me, Miss Connie, but isn't there one of those 'all-seeing' eyes on the American one-dollar bill?"

"There is, Essie."

"Then why is that symbol on this rug... satanic?" She waited for the answer.

Connie tilted her head to one side. "I don't know, Essie. That would be a good study for someone who is curious enough to follow up on it, don't you think?" Having bounced that ball back onto the youngster, she turned back to the rug, itself. "So, what do we have here? A handmade rug, with mixed spiritual symbols. I guess the question we have before us is, where was this rug-maker coming from?"

"Ach so!" Frau Schuler exclaimed. "This is all very interesting, but not of great importance to me. I see an earnest attempt by a sincere crafter, to create her own artistic statement."

"Why do you think this crafter was a woman, Elke?" Connie's instincts were perking just below the surface.

The German lady took another look at the back of this heavily woven artwork. "You may very well be right about that, Connie. This whole thing is very heavy. It may have been done by a man... but who really knows?" She attempted a casual chuckle. "It is still a nice piece of work, and," she turned to Kathy, "I would like to offer you a hundred dollars for it." She barely paused to let the woman think about it. "I can give you a check right now. You can have the money in the bank before the sun goes down."

It ended up with Frau Schuler purchasing not only the handcrafted rug, but the spool-legged table, for a total of one hundred and seventy-five dollars.

The two items were placed in the back of Greta's station wagon, and plans were made for the four volunteers to come back for wall papering the following morning. During the trip back to Burlington, Connie mentioned she would be meeting her husband at the Shorts' home, so they dropped the Schulers and their antique treasures off at the professor's residence near UVM, before heading out to Flynn Avenue.

"Hey, how did it go up at the ranch today?" Don asked, as the two ladies ascended the stairs to the back porch. Gerald looked up to listen.

"I guess the shortest answer would be," Connie replied, "we were supposed to go up there to spread the love of Jesus, but all that got done was getting the woodwork painted, and Frau Schuler buying two items from the attic."

"And they would be?" Gerald asked.

Greta dropped down into the rocking chair. "Aw, just that old table, and a handmade rug with satanic symbols."

"Holy cow!" her husband exclaimed. "Did she know what she was buying?"

"Not sure," Greta replied. "But she seemed to be real happy with it."

"That doesn't add up," Connie murmured from where she had sat down beside her husband. He moved over on the caned settee's flowered cushion. "That woman is a Pentecostal believer. Jenny told me she learned about speaking in tongues from this lady." She directed the question to Don. "Why would a tongues-speaking Christian want a satanic rug, handmade or otherwise?"

"Good question." He paused. "And one I can't answer."

"Another mystery," Greta said, wearily.

"Another?" Gerald wondered, but then he got it. "Oh, you're talking about the stolen boxes." He sat up straight to ask the next thing. "Speaking of which, did Kathy Roth ask about them?"

"No, and we thought better than to bring it up," his wife replied. "Personally, I hope she's forgotten about them, what with the earthquake and all that happened."

"Well, it's only a matter of time before the sheriff thinks to interview the Roths about this case of theft. And believe me, he will," Don stated. "I think you ladies should bring up the subject as soon as possible. We don't want anybody going to jail, if we can prevent it."

Greta stopped rocking. "Don, if you don't mind me asking, why are you so hung up on figuring this case out before Max Duncan does?"

"Like I just said, Greta, my gut feeling is that this was not a malicious act, and nobody should have to go to jail over it. We only need to get to the bottom of it, before the sheriff does any unnecessary harm."

"And we need to be very nice about it," Connie reminded her. "Otherwise, we could be charged with interfering with an official investigation."

"Right. I remember that part." She started rocking the big chair, again. "So, what about the Roths being told that those things were stolen from Walter Taft's house the morning of the earthquake?"

"I vote that you ladies get that information to Kathy when you go back tomorrow," Gerald said quietly.

"I agree," Don added. "You may come up with some evidence, who knows?"

Greta looked over at her friend. "Okay, I guess we have our assignment for tomorrow, Connie."

"Uh-huh, and we'll need to be very nice about that one, too."

***

"We have to wait three days," Walter told Donna. "I guess you'd like to have a wedding dress or something," he continued as they left Burlington's City Hall. "Want to look for one, right now?"

"We'll go to the Bee Hive and to Abernathy's," she quickly stated.

"As long as it's white. You have to have white," he reminded her. The Bee Hive had nothing in white, but the bridal department at Abernathy's was more than accommodating. The gracious clerk pulled out a white linen two piece suit, and a small white hat with a tiny veil wrapped around the front. Then, out of nowhere, white high heels appeared, practical, of course, so she could wear them to work. "Now all you need is a bouquet and a couple of rings," the delighted employee remarked.

"Rings!" Walter touched a finger to his temple. "We need rings."

"Do we have the money for that?" Donna asked, timidly.

"I have some savings. I can get the cash tomorrow."

"And will there be enough for a bouquet, Walter?"

He looked grim, but pulled her hands up to kiss her fingers. "How about one beautiful red rose? From me to you."

"Wait!" The alert lady behind the counter reached over for the phone. A short, pleasant conversation took place, and when she hung up, she was smiling. "You two know where Donahue's Greenhouse is in Essex Junction?" The couple nodded together. "Good. They're friends of mine. You're getting married on Saturday morning, right?" Another nod in unison. "Great. You can pick up a nice little bouquet of six red roses, with baby's breath, lace, and a white ribbon, on Friday night." The engaged twosome looked like they probably still wouldn't be able to pay for it. "It's all paid for — my wedding present to you!"

Donna squealed and they all hugged.

The next day, Walter dashed from his afternoon class to meet Donna at the jewelry store. After they bought the cheapest set they could get, they hurried back to her place, to invite a few friends to the wedding. She lifted the phone, but then hesitated. "Oh my gosh, Walter. Where are we getting married? Do we even have a preacher?"

He laughed. "We talked about that last night, remember? We'll get married right there at the village green, in the historic Congregational Church, and the pastor said he would be happy to perform the ceremony."

"We did? Oh, for Pete's sake, Walter, I've got too many stars in my eyes. I can't even think straight." She covered her face. "I've... I've never been in love before. I'm a complete dingbat!"

He gently took the phone from her. "Here, my darling lady, let me make the first call, okay?" She shook her head, and then went into the kitchen to find a cup of coffee.

"Hello, Connie. This is Walter Taft." She recognized his voice. "Yeah, I'm calling to invite you to a wedding." He laughed. "Yes, Donna Roth and I are getting married day after tomorrow." He was giving her the particulars when she suddenly interrupted him, to say Don wanted to talk to him.

"Hello, Walter. Did I hear the conversation correctly? You and Donna are getting married?"

"Ay-yuh, you heard it right. This Saturday morning, at the church there in Jericho Center."

"Wow! Kind of sudden, isn't it? I mean, folks usually go through some premarital counseling before taking such a serious step." He cleared his throat. "Don't want to pour cold water on anything, but it sounds like this is... well, rushed, you know?"

"Sure. I can see where you might be concerned, but Donna and I have known each other for a long time. That young woman is the love of my life. I treasure her more than anything else in this old world, believe me." He knew the man wanted more than the ranting of a guy in love, so he went to something more practical. "We go back together at the Children's Home, did you know that?"

"I see." He seemed to be looking for the next words. "I'm assuming you have your reasons, Walter. Connie tells me you're a pretty level-headed young man. She says you're a great teacher, and getting your master's. That sounds pretty responsible. Still, if I thought it would do any good, I would advise you two to take a step back and think a little longer about this, but," he chuckled, "I'm old enough to know when to butt out. Hey, we would love to be there. Did you say ten o'clock?"

After all the phone calls were made, Donna started getting ready to go to work. He hung around until it was time for her to leave, chatting with the roommates, who were anticipating the wedding. "Wasn't that nice of the lady at the nursing home to offer the dining hall for a reception?" one of them remarked. The other piped up, "And that German lady is making a wedding cake. Hey, that ought-a be good, ya know?"

He followed her out to the car, drawing her close for a goodnight kiss. "Just think of it, Donna. Two days from now, we won't have to stand out on somebody's front yard to kiss goodnight."

"Mmm," she cooed. "It'll be you and me and the bedbugs."

He laughed. "No bedbugs in my bed, I guarantee."

"Good. I'll settle for nice, clean sheets."

"Oh my gosh!" he thought, *"I completely forgot about that..."*

CHAPTER NINETEEN

Thursday

The same Thursday that Walter and Donna bought their wedding rings, the four volunteers had arrived again, at nine o'clock sharp, to wallpaper the Roths' living room. Kathy had set up a long table in the kitchen, an archway away from the furniture huddled in the middle of the newly painted room. On the kitchen work table, all the elements of the trade were assembled — a pan of warm water, a wide brush, scissors, and dry cloths to wipe the edges of each strip as it was pressed firmly onto the wall. When Kathy rolled out the actual wallpaper, Elke Schuler was ecstatic. Her compliments came out in German, but she quickly corrected them in English. "Oh my, oh my, Kathy. So beautiful! So perfect!"

The rest of the women took in the dusty deep blue background, filled with swirls of tiny blossoms and delicate leafing. "Whoa!" Greta exclaimed, in her usual robust manner. "You really hit the jackpot on this one, Kathy Roth." She gave her hostess a firm look. "You sure you haven't done this before?"

Kathy blushed with pleasure. "Aw, it wasn't just me; Rhonda has a real talent for this kind of thing."

All eyes had turned toward the Texas princess, who was starting out the door to do more chores. It was Essie who spoke up. "Rhonda! Where did you learn how to decorate?"

The girl shrugged. "I don't know. I just read magazines. I get ideas."

Suddenly, Mark Roth was standing behind her, just outside the front door. "Hey, you going to help me with these cows, or what?" he bellowed.

She bowed her head and slammed the screened door behind her.

Kathy had not seemed to know what to say, so went back to the task at hand. Before long, the five women had become a team, and by noon, the work table was cleaned up, hands were washed and lunch was served out on the large front porch. Sometime around one-thirty, the women wandered back into the newly papered room. It had been entirely transformed. The four helpers were standing there admiring the change, when Kathy brought up a whole new perspective. "I'm having a hard time," she said softly, "understanding why you ladies would even come up here and help — and God knows you have gone above and beyond the neighborly thing to help get this house back into shape."

"Ach so," Frau Schuler answered. "We are Christians. This is what we do, not true?" Her hands went up in a worshipful gesture. "We love Jesus, and we want others to see Him in us." Her smile was sincere. "So, we do this, and we are happy to do it. Now, you must just enjoy His love being poured out on you and your family."

Connie and Greta were stunned. Here was a woman who had just purchased a satanic rug, talking about the very real love of Jesus. Still, they saw the melting of Kathy's heart. She was weeping.

"You are good people," the tearful woman pronounced. "My family needs more of you folks in our life, that's for sure."

Connie saw the opportunity, and moved forward to encircle Kathy in an honest embrace. "Listen, Kathy, come back out onto the porch. Greta and I have something to tell you. Maybe then, you'll have a different outlook on people who love Jesus." She steered her back out the door. "We're not perfect. You need to know that." She pulled the woman to a seat beside her on the porch swing. Her nod brought Greta to take her place on the other side of this Texas mama.

"Something has happened, and Greta and I have not told you about it. We thought we could take care of the problem before you and your family would have to deal with it."

Kathy looked first at Connie, then to her left, at Greta. "This sounds serious," she said.

"Maybe, but then again, maybe not." Connie swallowed hard. "You remember those boxes we gave to Walter Taft... to see what was in them?" Kathy slowly acknowledged this. "Well, it turned out, the morning of the earthquake, somebody stole them from Walter's house."

She waited for the little Texan to process the information. "And?" Kathy finally asked.

"We're still trying to find them, but no breaks so far," Connie sadly informed her.

"I see." It was like she suddenly thought to ask, "So, do we know what was in those boxes?"

"Oh, some books, and some paperwork, and there was a box that we later found out contained some personal items for Mrs. Hannity, over at the nursing home." She looked Kathy in the eye. "Did you know she was the only child of the Crockers?"

"Why no," the surprised lady replied. "We had no idea. But then, we never went through all that stuff up there in the attic. We had a lot of other things to do, to change this place from a farm, to a ranch."

"Of course. I understand. But Greta and I wanted you to know that these items have been stolen, and we are trying to recover them. We even hired a lawyer."

"Is that right? Oh my goodness."

"We're waiting to hear from him, even as we speak," Greta assured her.

"So, alright then," the rancher's petite wife pronounced. "We wait. That's all we can do."

On the other side of the screen door, Essie and Elke stood quietly, hearing every word.

***

"Well, I can certainly say you two came up with some important information," John Courtney said, as he leaned against the front of his desk. He adjusted his slight-but-sturdy body into a more comfortable position. "Good work. You had a limited time, and you made the best of it."

Ed and Sophia finally relaxed into their chairs.

"Now, let's see what we have, here," the lawyer said. His attention went back to the Smiths' note, where he gave the paperwork a quick shake to flatten the folds. "To add it all up, we have seven locals who told their stories, two of which noted a beat-up, light-colored pickup. The first witness noticed it was moving along near the village green, with no headlights. The second one noted it parked behind the library while it was still dark, but not there at daylight." He looked up. "But neither one of these men knew whose truck that was. This tells us, it was probably an out-of-town driver, which brings up the question of what was that person doing in Jericho Center, the night before the quake?" He tapped the papers in his hand. "I would venture a guess, that person just got caught up in the circumstances, but didn't want to be noticed."

"Exactly," the detective agreed. "So, the first thing we noted in the report was sneaky behavior by an unknown driver. And with a truck. Of course, that would be the ideal vehicle to load five boxes onto, in a hurry, and then get away... to the back of the library. Unfortunately, we got fingered before we could check out the basement of that building."

"There's a basement?" John zoned in on that. "Does it have an outside door?"

"Like I said, we lost our cover, so we never went back to check on that." Ed looked at Sophia. "Did anybody in your group mention anything about that?"

She frowned thoughtfully. "No... nope. Nobody talked about there being a door there."

"But you conducted most of these on-going interviews inside the building, right?"

"Yes, sir. In the children's section, near the back windows..." Her voice trailed off, as she struggled to recall something. "In fact, I remember there were a couple of cars parked back there." She gave a slight shrug. "I'm thinking one of them was probably the librarian's. But I'm only guessing."

"Do you remember what building was next door?" the handsome fellow asked. "Like maybe somebody from there was in the habit of parking out there in back. After all, it's a public library."

"Oh, that's easy," Ed spoke up confidently. "That's Doc Horton's office."

"Office and residence," Sophia corrected the information.

"Is there parking in front of that office?"

"Oh yes, Mr. Courtney. Probably room for three or four cars, I would say." She was glad to talk about something she was sure of. "Of course, those spaces would probably be saved for patients, and it's pretty likely that Doc and his wife would park around back."

"Doc is married? I thought he was an older man," the man remarked, checking his notes.

"Ay-yuh. She's also his office nurse, in case we didn't include that in the report." Ed wondered just where the lawyer was going with this, but then John was moving down the page as though searching for something. At the top of the second page, he poked his finger at an item of interest.

"I see you have been told that Doc Horton is a 33rd degree Mason." He emitted a low whistle. "Those guys pull a lot of weight, right up to the state and national levels. Were you two aware of that?"

"Not really," Sophia admitted. "But it was mentioned that this Barre contractor and the local Masonic Lodge, up there in Jericho Corners, well, they all worked together to get that bull out of the quicksand."

John nodded. "I can believe that." He lowered the stack of papers in his hand, to stare out at the sunny sidewalks of Montpelier. At length, he came back to the conversation. "Well, even though we know there were some historical records from an old Grange organization in this area, the link is weak, when we try to tie all that in with a few powerful Masons. What motive would they have, to steal a few boxes of mostly private records and receipts? I guess the strongest lead is the mysterious truck driver." Suddenly, he was laughing. "I seem to have no choice on where to get that information." He looked at his watch. "I should be getting a call from Sheriff Max Duncan any time, now." He laid the report on his desk. "That guy has *already* gotten the lowdown on you two, and knows I hired you."

A few minutes after the Smiths took their check and headed for home, Johnny Courtney got Don Collins on the line. "Guess we've gone about as far as we can on this one," he informed the man. "Max has you in his sights. I suggest you cooperate, because he has the resources to get some answers. Anyway, here's what we have…"

The morning sun was just breaking through the blinds in his office windows, so he reached out to close them. It would get a lot hotter as this Thursday in late July progressed.

***

Max Duncan was onto the new information furnished by the Smiths like a hound dog on a fresh scent. There was no time for throwing fits at all that Johnny Courtney and his religious foursome had done. Better to just take the Smiths' leads and follow up on them. So, by seven in the evening, his deputies had narrowed the search for a light-colored pickup down to one. "Belongs to Ken Pearson, up in Jericho Corners," the report came back.

"Got a phone number for that household?" Max asked. He jotted it down, then placed a finger on the cradle to end that call, before letting it loose. He gave the number and waited. "Hello. This is Sheriff Max Duncan of the Chittenden County Sheriff's Department. I need to speak to Mr. Ken Pearson." The older man came to the phone. "Yes, sir. Mr. Pearson, do you own a pickup truck?" The man answered to the affirmative. "Could you tell me where that truck was on the morning of the earthquake?" There was a small pause. "That's okay, take your time." He waited again. "Yes, it was a while ago, but we usually remember stuff that happens during things like floods and fires and earthquakes. For instance, where were all your family members during the actual earthquake? Surely, you remember that."

The conversation ended fifteen minutes later. The sheriff turned to Deputy Smith. "Looks like we got a teenager who was out riding around in that truck, just before the quake. His grandpa doesn't know exactly where the kid was, but said he would ask him. I told him I had a better idea: I would be up to talk to the boy in about half an hour." He placed his hat on his head. "Let's go."

The nervous lad was waiting on the front porch when they got there, the grandfather hovering close by. "You understand, Andrew is a minor, and I have to be here to supervise this," Ken Pearson said.

"Of course," Max acquiesced, but he took a wide-legged stance in front of the youngster, to establish a superior position. "So, Andrew, we can make this short and simple, or we can take you in for questioning. What will it be?"

"Wait a minute," Ken objected. "Are you saying he's a suspect, or something?"

"I'm afraid so, Mr. Pearson. He was seen driving near the village green at the Center, right after the earthquake, and then we know he parked the truck over behind the library while it was dark, and removed it before daylight. Yeah, he's a suspect in a burglary at his own teacher's house, and he got away with it, because of all the chaos." He saw the teen's face go white, and knew he was on the right track. "What do you have to say for yourself, mister?"

Andrew glanced at his grandfather. "I'm so sorry. I'm so sorry. I hoped you would never know." Deputy Smith drew out a notepad and waited. "Could we make sure nobody else is listening?" the young man asked quietly.

Ken looked around. "Let's just walk out to where you parked the squad car," he suggested. "That way, you can order the nosey neighbors to keep their distance."

The deputy noted a few clusters of curious folks beginning to gather down near the road. "He's got a good point, there, Sheriff." Max gave the nod, and Smith moved out ahead of the other three, motioning for the onlookers to get back to their own business. Ken and Andrew leaned up against the car, but Max took his command position, hands clasped behind his back, a couple of feet in front of the two.

"Alright, let's have it," the sheriff ordered the boy.

"It was… it was before the quake. I was parked behind the nursing home."

"I don't think so," Max corrected him. "There's no space back there for parking."

"Uh, yeah. There's an alley. They have to have it, for fire safety or something." He wiped the sweat off his top lip. "So, anyways, he caught us." He shivered. "Talk about embarrassing."

"Who caught you?" the sheriff asked.

"The doctor." Ken Pearson's attention piqued at his grandson's words. "Doc Horton. Just came up and pulled the door open. No knock, no nothing." He wiped under his nose, again. "It was *embarrassing*, man."

"Wait a minute," Max interrupted. "You saying you had a girl in there?"

"Um, not exactly a girl. She's older. We get together once in a while. I get some experience, and she enjoys herself. Sort of an understanding. No ties."

"And who is this older woman?" the officer pressed in.

"I'd rather not say. No reason to get her into trouble."

Max laughed in derision. "I'll find out, sooner or later, so you might as well spill the beans right here and now."

"No, I don't think so, sir. If you do find out, at least it won't be me who tells. A guy needs to have some self-respect, you know?"

Sheriff Duncan laughed again. "Look, I already know it's that frizzy-haired chain smoker. She's in hot water for lying to me about not seeing anybody hanging around that night." He brought his arms around to fold them in a further authoritative stance. "So, Doc Horton caught you, in the act, so to speak. What did he do?"

"Swore. Then told me to get my butt down to the schoolyard and wait for him there."

"What did he say to Bella?" He knew the man could have gotten her fired, but did not.

"Told her to get back on duty, and that's what she did."

"Then what happened?" The lawman was hard on the scent.

"He showed up at the schoolyard, told me he was very disappointed in me, but that, if I did him a favor, he would never tell a soul." The two law officers waited. Andrew looked up into his grandfather's sorrowful face. "Doc told me he needed to have some boxes moved from Mr. Tate's house, over to the library basement. Said it had to be done in secret, to protect some innocent people. Said he would let me know when to do it, then told me I should get home."

"And did you go home?"

He hung his young head. "Nope. Hung around, hoping to meet up with Bella when she got off shift in the morning." He brushed his hair back from his forehead. "Didn't know there would be an earthquake."

"Where were you, when it hit, son?" Ken asked quietly.

"Back in the same alley behind the home. I figured if he wouldn't tell about the first time he caught me back there, he wouldn't tell about the second time. Besides, me and Bella had some unfinished business, if you know what I mean."

The three older mean shook their heads at such youthful gall. "Alright," the sheriff finally asked, "why did you go rob the place after the earthquake? He said he would tell you when to do it."

"Oh, he did. After he took care of the scared patients, he spotted me out there and got into my truck. 'Drive over to Mr. Taft's,' he said. So I did. We loaded the boxes into my truck, and took them over to the library basement." He stood up straight. "And that's all I know."

The sheriff signaled his deputy that the interview was over, and gave one last admonishment to the other two. "Just keep quiet about this whole thing, until I tell you otherwise — I mean that," he said as he slipped into the passenger side of the car. "Just keep your mouths shut." Deputy Smith started the car, and slowly backed it out onto the road.

"Aw, Andrew," his grandpa opined, "look at what you've done. And all because you couldn't keep your pants zipped up."

CHAPTER TWENTY

Interviews

In one last gesture of Christian good works, the four women came back to the ranch on Friday morning, this time to tidy up the floor and move the furniture back into place. They came at a later hour, figuring it would not take long, and sure enough, all of the big pieces were moved into place by eleven-thirty. They were getting the small items arranged on end tables, bookshelves, and the mantle, when Sheriff Max Duncan knocked on the door. He apologized for not having called first, explaining this was just a stop along the way to another call at the Center, and he hoped he wasn't disturbing anything important. The fellow was followed closely by Mark Roth's entrance, since he had seen the lawman drive up and go into the house. "How's it going, Sheriff?"

"Not too bad, sir." He shook the cattleman's hand, and turned to survey the ladies' activities. "My goodness, what do we have here — a renovation team?" The volunteers stopped, thinking this was official business, and Kathy would send them on their way. But Max continued, admiring the handsome room as he spoke. "Very nice. Very nice." He motioned for them to continue. "Don't let me get in the way. I just had a couple of questions." He spotted the two Schulers, and tipped his hat. "Don't believe I've had the pleasure. You are...?"

Frau Schuler bowed her head in a formal greeting. "I am Elke Schuler, and this is my daughter, Essie."

"Alright. And I'm Sheriff Max Duncan." He went on, his best manners paving the way for some serious answers. "New to the area?"

"Pretty much," Elke replied.

"How do you like Jericho? Are you finding it a good place to live?" he inquired politely.

"Oh, we don't live here," Essie blurted out the information. "We're from Burlington. My *Vater* — that's 'father' in German — is a professor at UVM."

"Oh, really? A professor of what, if I may ask?" No sense in passing up the perfect opening to get the details.

"He's a biochemist," the daughter replied proudly.

"Is that right? That's pretty impressive." He tilted his head. "And do I detect a slight accent, there?"

"Yes. We're from Germany." She picked up a tiny ceramic figurine, as if to examine it for cleaning.

He addressed the mother. "On some kind of exchange program, are you?"

"No," Elke answered softly. "We are now United States citizens."

He smiled. "Well, isn't that great! Congratulations, and welcome to America." He turned his attention to the two Roths. "So, let me get to the point. I see you are busy." He drew out his trusty little notebook and flipped it open. "I really need to be brought up-to-date on the boxes that Walter Taft got from your attic."

"Yeah, Kathy tells me those got stolen," Mark noted. "What the hell for?"

"That's what I'm trying to find out." He glanced over at Connie and Greta. "It's my understanding that you ladies and your husbands were here when those cartons were handed over to this guy. Is that correct?" The two women nodded. "So do any of you happen to know what was in those boxes?"

"I don't have a clue," Mark grumbled.

"I think probably it was mostly paperwork and books, but I'm not sure." Max noticed Kathy's glance toward Connie.

"So, um, it's Mrs. Collins, right?" She nodded. "So, Mrs. Collins, were you aware of the contents in those boxes?"

"We didn't open anything," she slowly replied. "We just helped Walter to load them into his car."

"I see. So when did you decide I needed to check on fingerprints on the flashlight?" He sat down and waited for her answer.

"Right." She thought quickly. "So, Walter found it in one of the boxes. It looked too new to be part of the storage stuff. He hid the flashlight, thinking it could be important in some way." She cleared her throat. "Then, when that stuff got stolen, we thought we could find the thief, or maybe a clue, or something. That's when we decided to turn it over to you."

"We?" Max squinted suspiciously.

"Well, of course, Walter was very open about where the flashlight was found. So Don and I felt it was time for professional action."

"And just how were *you* involved?" he inquired of Greta.

"We're close friends. We agreed you needed to get a look at the flashlight."

"What flashlight?" Kathy asked.

"It was found in one of the boxes," Connie explained. "It turned out to have Donna's prints on it."

"What the hell does that mean?" Mark was frowning. "She was up in the attic?" When no one responded, he swore again. "What the hell for?"

Connie attempted to smooth it over. "Most likely, she only wanted to explore the place. After all, you folks were planning on having all three of those children move in with you." She smiled weakly. "You can't blame her for being curious."

"Speaking of being curious, Mrs. Collins, it's difficult for me to believe that you folks didn't go poking through those boxes, yourselves. I'm going to assume you probably did, and in that case, I will ask you again: What did you find inside of them?"

She was getting backed into a corner, but she didn't want to lie. "Well, if I —"

"Hold it!" Mark moved in to take a large pair of steer horns from Essie, who was having difficulty managing the heavy thing. "I'll take that," he called out, slipping his strong arms under the clumsy trophy. The man turned to place the prized piece up on the mantle. "When I get money enough to get a plaque, this is going up there over this fireplace, in a place of honor. Meanwhile, it just sits up here." He turned to the girl. "Don't be messing with things you can't handle."

Before Essie could reach a full blush, the screened front door burst open. Rhonda stood there, tears running down her sweaty face. "Daddy Mark," she sobbed, "you have to come help me. I can't do this all by myself. Two of the heifers got out."

The cattleman swore again as he followed her out, the door slamming behind them.

Kathy hurried over to peer through the screen. "Oh dear," she said, before turning her distressed face back toward the others. "Oh dear…"

Connie seized the moment. "Oh my, we should get going; you have your hands full." She addressed the sheriff. "I'm sorry we weren't much help today, but we're very confident you'll get to the bottom of this." Without missing a beat, she called out to the other three helpers, "Okay, let's wrap it up, and get out of the way."

Max Duncan assessed the drama all around him, and decided to give up on any further investigating, for the moment. He bid a hasty adieu to Kathy and went out the door. As he drove away, Connie and Greta sighed in relief, for they had avoided some persistent questioning, without making anybody mad.

Indeed, they had defied the law, and managed to do so while still being — as Connie had said — "very nice about it."

It took a bit longer for the ladies to get on their way, however, because when they got outside, two red and white young Herefords were standing in front of Greta's station wagon. She was quick to respond. "Okay, girls, we need to get those youngsters back into their enclosure." She surveyed the situation and took charge. "Connie and Elke, you take the left side and Kathy and Essie, you take the right side. We're forming a funnel toward that gate over there. See it?" The four herders saw the target, where Mark and Rhonda were standing, exhausted. "I'll move the car along, so they have to move ahead of me, while you keep them headed toward that opening."

"How do we do that?" Essie called out.

"Yip! Don't yell, because you might spook them. And flap your arms," Kathy answered, "and if that doesn't work, yip and flap your skirts."

They approached from the rear of the station wagon, while two pairs of bovine eyelashes fluttered over clueless stares. Greta slipped into the driver's seat, started up the engine and gently nudged the two cows ahead. Kathy motioned to her husband and daughter to get back and be ready to close the gate, and the yipping and flapping began. Maybe it was the feminine connection, or maybe the two heifers were used to being herded, but the task was completed in about ten minutes.

Seven sweaty people ended up on the porch, gulping down cold lemonade.

"Oh my gosh," Rhonda was laughing, "you women sure looked funny, with all your skirts up in the wind."

Mark wiped the smirk off his face. "What the hell, it worked, didn't it?"

"It did, and I think we made a new breakthrough in the art of herding cattle, today. We should mark it down in history." Kathy was chuckling, herself. She looked at Mark. "I think we should hire them on permanent, don't you?"

"No thanks," Connie declined the offer. "I'd be worn out before lunchtime, for sure."

"Speaking of lunch time," Greta rose from her chair as she spoke, "we need to get going. We have to get ready for a wedding in the morning." As she gathered the glasses, Kathy asked for details.

"Who's getting married? Anyone we know?"

Greta looked at Connie, hoping she would think of something quick, but the woman, again, would not lie. As her friend took the empty glasses into the house, she just came right out with it: "Donna and Walter Taft."

Kathy was surprised. "What? Donna's getting married? We didn't know anything about it."

"Well, it was pretty sudden. We were *all* taken by surprise," Connie explained.

Greta came back out onto the porch during the awkward silence. "Ready to go, ladies?"

Mark rose with a grunt and headed down the driveway toward the barn. "Come on, Rhonda, we have chores to do before lunch." The Texas princess was no longer smiling.

"It's because of me," she complained. "They want people to think I killed Eddie."

"Oh, I don't know about that," Connie murmured, rising from her seat.

Rhonda jumped to her feet, but had one last shot before following Mark. "But I didn't. It was her, Donna, who was down by the barn when he died. I saw her when I got down there... standing like a statue, not screaming or crying or anything. Now, who does that when they see their little brother under muddy water?"

"Um," Greta ventured, "maybe somebody who was in *shock*?"

Still, all four were very quiet on the ride back home.

***

Sheriff Duncan was still grumbling to himself about the mess up there at the ranch, when he pulled into Walter Taft's driveway. "Well, let's see if I can surprise some information out of *this* guy," he moaned.

When Walter answered the door, he was holding a toilet brush in one hand. "Guess I caught you in the middle of some cleaning chores," the lawman said, with a forced grin. "But this won't take long." He followed Walter's motion toward the overstuffed chair, removing his hat as he took a seat. He noted the distinct odor of bleach, and decided to use this to keep his interviewee off balance. "How's the water up here in the Center? Does it leave a ring in the toilet? If you folks are on well water, that's pretty much a given. Lots of minerals in Vermont soil."

Walter stood there, a confused look on his face. "Yeah? Never thought much about that."

"Guess maybe you've got a lot of other things to think about, these days. How's it going on locating those boxes?"

"Um, nothing new."

"No? Well, I'm not surprised. Folks are pretty closed-mouthed around here, especially when it comes to family secrets and all that. I'm wondering if there might be something like that, stuffed inside of at least one of those cartons. What do you think?" Walter shrugged. "I figure somebody's got some dirty laundry they want buried or burned in the trash. Think that might be a real possibility." His eyes were moving around the room as he spoke. "Got any ideas on that?"

The teacher was still standing. "Haven't had time to mull that one over, Sheriff. I've been pretty busy."

Max stood up, as if to leave. "Right. So I won't keep you." He acted surprised, as if he'd just noticed the typewriter. "Hey, is this that paper you're doing on the Masons? How's that going?" He picked up the top sheet of a stack of typed work. "Man, you know you're walking on thin ice, here, don't you?" He flicked a finger across the page. "This is forbidden territory, Mr. Taft. You could lose your job."

"You may be right," the man answered. He checked to see if the brush was dripping on the carpet.

"I guess you probably know Doc Horton is a 33rd degree-er," Max dropped the bait. Sure enough, Walter's surprise left him speechless, mouth wide open. "Or maybe you don't," the lawman continued. "Well, okay then, maybe I just did you a favor. You owe me one, mister."

Suddenly Walter was laughing. "Oh, I don't know, Sheriff. I won't be changing my mind about my thesis. It's a matter of ethics, you know? Secret societies are a weird mixture of charity and chicanery, and the sooner the rest of us become aware of this, the better." He stepped over to open the door for his departing guest. "Now, if you'll excuse me, Donna and I are getting married tomorrow morning, and I want to bring her home to a clean house."

Max Duncan's whole body went stiff. "The hell you say! You're marrying Donna Roth?" He shook his head in disbelief. "My gawd, Taft, don't you ever stand still? First this thing about secret societies, then sticking your nose into this business of the boxes, then trying to solve the theft behind my back, and now you're marrying the chief suspect in the murder of Eddie Roth. Are you a glutton for punishment, or just plain crazy?"

***

Friday afternoon was turning into evening, but the sheriff didn't want to leave Jericho Center without taking care of one more piece of business. He drove quickly to Doc Horton's office on the other side of the village green. A sweet-faced older woman looked up as he entered. "Oh, hello, Sheriff." She nodded toward the doctor's office. "Go ahead in," she said, turning back to her paperwork.

Inside, Doc Horton peered through the gold-rimmed glasses, his yellowish eyes glinting with purpose. "I see you got my message," he said. "Have a seat."

"I didn't get any message," Max informed the man in the white doctor coat. "I'm on my own today, so I may have missed it. They usually repeat unanswered calls every ten minutes or so, depending on how urgently..." His voice trailed off. There was no need to explain such things to someone who was a suspect in a robbery. "So you called me? What for?"

"I wanted to be sure you understood about the boxes." The man leaned back in his desk chair. "It's important that we have a little conversation."

The sheriff didn't like the sound of that, so he went into confrontation mode. "Right. You entered a private residence and took stuff that didn't belong to you. That's called 'theft.'"

The physician's slender hands folded across his aging midriff. "Oh, that's not what I'm saying, sir. I'm not saying I did any such thing." It was a faint smile. "I just wanted to make you aware of some facts about those particular missing items."

The lawman leaned forward. "Listen, Doc, I have a witness that you actually stole the damned things and hid them in the library basement. I could order that basement cleaned out, right now. I could see what's in there within the next hour. So, don't play games with me."

The faint smile disappeared. "I have no intention of playing games, sir. I intend for you to take what I say very seriously." His fingers were tapping in place. "So I suggest you listen and listen very carefully."

"Doctor Horton, you need to be real careful right now. It almost sounds like you're threatening an officer of the law."

"No threat, sir, just facts." His fingers went back into a loose clasp. "We were all surprised to know those things were still in Crocker's attic."

"Roths' attic," the sheriff corrected him.

There was an irritated jerk of the head. "Whatever. We all still think of it as the Crocker place." He got back on track. "Tim Crocker had a, shall we say, a rather interesting past, just before he died. There's a good chance, those boxes contain items that could cause a lot of unnecessary pain and suffering to a whole lot of nice people. Lives and reputations could be ruined, if it all became common knowledge. I feel it was actually fortunate that those boxes disappeared like they did. And, if you knew the facts, I think you would agree."

"Are you telling me, you took those things, just to protect some people?"

"I'm not telling you I took anything, at all. I'm just informing you of the real situation, and," his hands loosened, then closed, again, "advising you that some things are just best left alone."

"You want me to drop the investigation?" He chuckled. "I couldn't do that, even if I wanted to. We have a whole lot of people who know about those missing boxes. There's no way you or anybody else can wash this whole thing away."

"You'd be surprised, my friend. It's been a while since those things disappeared. My guess is that you'll probably find the empty cartons, somewhere over in the county dump, by now. If there was anything to hide, it probably got destroyed by now, don't you think?" The faint smile came back. "You probably ought to make that trip to the dumpsite. Then we can put an end to the mystery."

Max Duncan stood up. "Even if I did that, it wouldn't be the end of it. You forget about Walter Taft. He knows what was in every box, and he doesn't keep his mouth shut. He may be looking at the world through rose-colored glasses, but he's honest."

"Don't worry about the noble Mr. Taft. I can handle him."

As Max was going through the doorway, he turned around to tell the fellow he was dead wrong, but stopped at the sight of Doc Horton's wide, triumphant grin. "What?" he asked.

The gold-rimmed glasses glittered. "I guess you're unaware that I'm on the school board."

CHAPTER TWENTY-ONE

Vows

The wedding took place on Saturday, July twenty-ninth, with only a fifteen-minute delay. "That's a miracle, right there," Greta remarked from her place in the pew. It had, indeed, been a busy morning, what with getting all things into place, but the church's organist played soft music as Walter's car salesman friend walked Jenny down the aisle. The best man was decked out in a loud plaid jacket with a donated red rose tucked into his lapel, while the maid of honor moved gracefully alongside, in a blue lace dress borrowed from one of Donna's roommates. She carried one long-stemmed red rose with a narrow white lacy ribbon, and Jenny had not felt that special, in all of her sixteen years. Once they took their place beside the sweaty-faced groom, all guests rose to their feet and the Wedding March announced the arrival of the bride.

She was beautiful, of course, in the white suit and veiled hat and the bridal bouquet of red roses. But there was more to the moment: Walter watched her approach, moving slowly toward him, all alone, no father or brother or trusted family member to give her away. "*Oh, Donna,*" he thought, "*you won't be alone like this anymore. No more trying to manage life with that feisty attitude. Now it's you and me — you and me and God, Donna.*"

The reception was held in one corner of the nursing home's dining room, where Mrs. Hannity had managed to find white tablecloths to hide the regular Formica-topped tables. Frau Schuler's three-tiered wedding cake sat in the place of honor, surrounded by pale blue paper plates and napkins. The Schulers were joined by Gerald and Greta Short, and the Collinses. It was Gerald who surprised the wedding couple with the cash gift collected from the guests; it was Don who slipped the minister a fifty-dollar bill. The patients who were out in the dayroom wandered in to extend rather confused congratulations, then a lot of cake served up, before somebody noticed that the bride and groom had disappeared.

But nobody wondered why...

***

"There's too darned much door-slamming going on around here," Kathy announced over supper that same Saturday night. "This place has turned into a regular snake pit, full of worked-up rattlers. A person doesn't feel peaceful in their own house, for heaven's sake."

Mark glared at her over his glass of cool water. "What the hell are you talking about?"

"That." She pointed her fork at him. "That attitude, right there." She set the utensil sharply down on her plate. "You're mad, mad, mad, all the time. You get up mad in the morning and you go to bed mad at night." She watched his mouth drop open, and then she turned to the smirking girl across the table. "And you're just as bad, so don't think *your* behavior has gone unnoticed." She sat up straighter. "Now, I know we are all tired. We're all overwhelmed. But that doesn't excuse us from being loving and respectful to each other." Her voice trembled as she let it all out. "After all, we're a family, and right now, we're all we've got. Jenny doesn't want to live with us, and Donna didn't even ask us to be part of her wedding."

The woman looked directly at her husband. "You should have walked that girl down the aisle."

"She didn't ask me," he reminded his wife.

Kathy addressed Rhonda. "And you should have been a bridesmaid or something, and I should have been Mother of the Bride..." The glistening of tears kept the other two from lashing out; instead, they fixed their eyes on their plates as she murmured, "Those two don't want to have anything to do with us."

For a few minutes, there was only the sound of forks sliding across plates and quiet chewing. They had never heard Kathy speak up like this, before.

Then Rhonda found her tongue. "I couldn't care less. One of them is a lazy stuck-up, and the other is a murderer. Good riddance, if you ask me."

Kathy swallowed and licked her lips. "And that's another thing. You need to stop saying Donna is a murderer, or whatever." She lifted her cup of coffee. "There is not one shred of evidence that she's any such thing."

"Oh yeah? Let's just talk about that." Rhonda ticked off the list on her fingers. "Number one: She was the only person down there when it happened. Number two: She's not good with a slingshot, but she can zing a rock into a target like it was a bullet. I've seen her do it, more than once. Three: Insurance money. It now goes to only two kids, instead of three. And four: She didn't even cry. Just stood there." The daughter rose to clear her place from the table. "So add it all up. She did it."

Mark was not satisfied. "Can't prove a damned thing, Rhonda."

"That's why I think we need to have the sheriff come back and take another look, Daddy Mark." She waited for him to answer.

"We *do* need to get this settled," Kathy prompted him.

The man sighed. "I guess it wouldn't hurt to have him take another look around," he said.

Satisfied, the girl turned to head for the kitchen sink.

"Just a minute, young lady," her mother called out. "We're not finished with the 'grouch and slouch' conversation." Kathy leaned back in her chair. "We need to make a fresh start. No more slamming doors and bad attitude. Do I make myself clear?" She turned to find Mark with his mouth open, again. "And, yes, Mark Roth, I'm talking to you, too." His face was turning red, but she kept going, anyway. "I want to have peace in my home, and I want it now."

Suddenly the man made a mental shift. He gave a quick nod to his stepdaughter. "You heard your mother. Get your head on straight. Now, clear the table." He signaled his wife to follow him into the living room. There, in front of the mantle, he peered down into her sweet, round face. "What the hell is the matter with you?" There was a quick sniff through the flaring nostrils. "And this better be damned good."

"Things are getting bad around this place. It's like we never smile any more. We need to start over."

"What the hell does that mean? You want to move back to Texas?" He ran his fingers through the graying hair. "No way in hell we can do that."

"Mark," she said as she reached to touch his arm, "listen to me. There's more than one way to start over. We can do that without even moving. We just make a fresh start at being a family." He was obviously confused, so she slowed down. "You know, I was being just as bad as you and Rhonda, until those nice ladies came to help with the living room." It was like a light went on in his eyes. "I was so relaxed while they were here, and then after they left, I was so… peaceful. I can't think of a better word, Mark. I was so peaceful!" She looked right at him. "Isn't it interesting that those ladies came into our life, because of an earthquake?"

He missed the point.

"So, what'er you thinking? You need some friends?" He shrugged. "That's okay, especially ones that will help get things done around here."

"Well, that's kind of what I'm thinking, but I'm pretty sure all three of us need to make friends. We need friends, Mark. We need to be friendly with good people like them."

He went into the logistics. "Don't those people live way the hell over there in Burlington?"

"Yes. But not all good people live that far away. I'm sure we can meet some that live in, say, Jericho Center or thereabouts."

"And just how are we going to meet these folks?"

"Well, I don't know how you want to do it, but *I* have decided to start going to church, like those ladies do."

"Aw, hell," he moaned.

"And I'm taking Rhonda with me."

"Aw, for gawd's sake, Kathy, I swear, you've lost your mind."

***

As the "on-call" doctor for Maude's Nursing Home, Doc Horton could pretty much set his weekly visits for whatever suited his schedule. The fact that the Hortons and Irene Crocker-Hannity had a long friendship helped a lot. Doc and Cindy knew that she was away at business college when her father, Tim Crocker, had died. "It was suicide," he had told the girl, and she believed him, for he was, after all, the coroner and he had filed the report. The reason for the taking of his own life, Doc had told her, was that the man had been suffering from depression, and nobody really knew how bad it was, until it was too late. Her mother, Freda, had grieved so hard, there were not many opportunities for loving, healing moments, before the young girl had to return to pursue the business degree. Cindy Horton had stepped in to comfort and support the woman, but she died of cancer, and Irene became a bona fide orphan. Then there had been the marriage to

George Hannity. The good doctor had the privilege of walking her down the aisle, but even *that* happiness had ended in the tragedy of war.

Now, as he walked the short distance from his office to the home she ran, he tried to remember if Irene had ever been up in the attic, or aware of meetings held up there. These were subjects he and Cindy had avoided for years, but now, things were different. There had been boxes and other items up there in that attic that they had not been aware of... things that Freda never mentioned... things that Walter Taft now knew about. "And who knows how many others may have seen?" he thought out loud. Yes, he would have to see what she remembered, first, and then go from there.

He asked the question casually. "I understand you got a box or something left on your doorstep a few weeks ago." He watched her take a seat at her desk. "The sheriff told me about it. Seems he thinks it's part of some things that were in the attic of your folks' farmhouse. I guess you left some stuff up there when you sold the place. Did you do that on purpose, or did you just never know about all that junk?"

"You know, Doc, I was really surprised to get that box. And no, I wasn't aware of any stuff left up in that God-forsaken hole in the ceiling." There was a little shiver. "I always thought of that place as dark and creepy. I went up and peeked at the scary shadows *once*. That's when I was probably six or seven years old. Hey, I steered clear of those stairs, for sure. Never went up there again."

"Hmm," he mused. "The word is, there were some furniture — chairs, I think — that indicated there may have been some sort of meetings up there. What do you think about that? Think there were gatherings up in that place?"

Her eyes widened. "Oh my goodness, no! Not that I ever knew about. But I guess that could have happened, maybe when I wasn't home." She thought quickly. "And when I was home, I slept in the bedroom with the window looking out over the porch. It was on the same side of the hall as the bathroom. Do you remember the inside of the house, at all?"

"Vaguely." He crossed his legs. "I never went up more than that second floor." He smiled. "Remember when you had the measles?"

She laughed. "I was an awful-looking mess, wasn't I?"

"And your poor mother couldn't keep you down. Cindy managed to rein you in, but you always *were* a going concern. No wonder you turned out to be such a good business woman." He stood up, satisfied she knew nothing important. "Okay, just wanted to double-check whether you needed help to get back anything you needed. Too bad that stuff got stolen, but it could be worse. There could have been jewelry or something."

"Was there?" She rose to open the office door.

"Nah. If there had been, there'd be a whole lot more investigating going on. I guess there was just a bunch of paperwork and receipts. Anyway, that's what I heard." He kept it casual, even going on to make his weekly rounds, as though nothing unusual was going on.

But he still had to deal with Walter, and whoever else had seen what had gotten into those stolen cartons.

***

The Shorts and Collinses seemed to be at a dead end, since the undercover team, the Smiths, had been exposed. The four of them were standing out in front of the Swift Street Pentecostal Church, waiting for Sunday morning service to commence. "So," Don was saying in a low voice, "Connie and I were adding things up and we came to some conclusions: Connie is the only one of us who has seen what was in the boxes, but all four of us saw stuff in the attic. I am concerned that she might be a target, because she knows too much. The same goes for Walter Taft." He shifted his weight to the other foot. "I guess you've heard the old saying about there being safety in numbers, so I feel like the more of us who know the facts, the harder it will be to deny them."

"So," Connie said quietly, "I want to make sure the three of you know, as well." She dug into her purse. "I made a list, as well as I could remember. Here."

Gerald took the list and tucked it into his suit pocket. "You realize that this could get pretty sticky, don't you? I'm talking about being called down to police headquarters or worse. And," he pointed out, "it could all be considered second-hand information."

"Don't forget Walter," Don reminded the man. "He can verify most, if not all the things on that list."

Gerald was still not comfortable. "Go over this thing one more time. Just why are we being so persistent in checking out this theft?"

"Sure." Don probably needed to make that clarification, for all four members of this small team. "We know there was satanic ritual mixed with Grange activities up in that attic, topped off by a suicide. I doubt that Sheriff Duncan knows this, but I would bet my bottom dollar that the thief knows all the details. Honestly, I think there was, or now is, a cover-up. And we do now know that Doc is a 33rd degree Mason. Maybe he was trying to keep bad history out of the public eye."

"But why didn't he get rid of those boxes a long time ago?" Greta asked.

"My guess is because he didn't know they existed. Freda Crocker could have assembled all that material, out of respect for her late husband, or maybe with the intention of hiding it… take your pick." He needed to make one more point. "Just remember, these exclusive societies Walter is writing about — the Freemasons, the Grange — all involve vows of secrecy."

Connie interrupted her husband. "Oh look! They came!"

The other three turned to watch Elke and Essie Schuler approaching.

"Yay!" Greta exclaimed as she waved to them.

"We invited them yesterday morning, at the wedding," Connie murmured through her welcoming smile.

"Good. That's good," Don replied. "But we don't discuss this matter while in the presence of others."

Nevertheless, the six of them ended up in a wide corner booth at Ralph's Diner, right after church. The coffee was fresh and pancakes shimmered under a coating of real Vermont maple syrup. Essie couldn't stop talking about the church service. "Best one we've been to, in a long time, right, *Mutter*?"

"For certain," the mother agreed. "I think we have found a new church."

"And your husband? Will he join us?" Gerald inquired.

Frau Schuler laughed. "No-no. My husband is a Jew." She enjoyed the look on all four faces. "He celebrates the traditional Shabbat." She blew across her steaming cup of milky coffee. "He is from the old school, and so, of course, our son attends with him."

"That must be interesting, navigating two extremes like that," Greta spoke her opinion.

"It is, but we have managed to overcome most of them," Elke assured the lady.

"You know what they say," Essie piped up. "'Love conquers all.'"

Greta couldn't resist asking the next question. "And what did he think about the rug and table you brought home this week?"

"He was very pleased with the table," the German lady answered. "But I didn't show him the rug. In fact, I burned it. Too much of the devil in that thing."

"You burned it up? Wow!" Greta forgot to slip the forkful of pancake into her mouth, letting is float in mid-air. "You burned up a hundred dollar rug? That's like burning up a hundred dollars in cash."

"I think that is certainly one way of looking at this," Elke replied. "Or we can see it as having paid a hundred dollars to get rid of something very evil."

"Oh," Greta said flatly. Then she shoved the dripping bite of pancake into her big mouth.

***

It involved getting up early to get Sunday morning chores done, then getting a whiney teenager to dress up for church, and even putting up with a grumbling husband, but Kathy managed to get into a nice dress and a string of pearls and get the two of them on their way. The red pickup slipped into a parking space not far from the front door of Jericho Center's First Congregational Church, in time for them to find a seat about halfway down the aisle. Kathy held her head high, nodding at perfect strangers as she guided her daughter into the pew. Rhonda kept her eyes toward the floor, hoping she wouldn't see anyone she knew. It didn't work.

"Okay," her mother whispered, "might as well quit pouting and look like you belong here." She motioned toward the front. "That's Mrs. Hannity, who sold us the ranch, and she's sitting right beside Jenny."

"You didn't tell me that little brat would be here," she hissed.

She tapped her knee against her daughter's, right beside her. "Ignore that. Just be your lovely self."

Somehow, they made it through all the standing and sitting and head-bowing and singing. And then the minister was headed back down the aisle to the front door, where he stood poised for the usual handshake ritual. "Relieved that the ordeal was finally over, Rhonda turned to follow her mother, the two of them mingling in the slow-moving crowd. As she strained to see how much longer it would be before they could get out of there, the familiar figure of Walter Taft came into view. She blinked. Then she squinted to be sure of what she was seeing. Sure enough, Donna was moving along beside her new husband.

"They were sitting back there, through the whole service," she realized. It made her furious. Kathy saw her daughter's lips form a silent curse, whereupon she followed the girl's line of sight and spotted the new bride and groom.

She touched Rhonda's arm. "Not one squeal out of you, young lady," she whispered.

By the time Kathy got to shake the minister's hand, the newlyweds were halfway home, Walter's arm around Donna's waist as they strolled toward the tiny rental. The man-of-God was politely inquiring as to whether Kathy and Rhonda were just visiting in the area, so she played the obedient, shy daughter until the cordialities were finished. "Please come back and see us," the minister called out as they started for their truck.

Rhonda climbed in and glared through the windshield as the happy couple moved along. *"That bitch. That stinking murderer. She doesn't deserve Walter Taft. One of these days, she's gonna get caught, and then,"* the Texas princess promised herself, *"I'll get to watch her dangle at the end of a rope."* The very thought made her snicker out loud.

"What's so funny?" the mother asked.

"Aw, nothing. Just felt like laughing."

But Kathy decided they would try a church up at Jericho Corners, next time.

CHAPTER TWENTY-TWO

Partners

After church that Sunday morning, Mrs. Hannity invited Jenny to take a slow walk around the edge of the village green. The girl was delighted, readily answering the woman's casual question as they left the front doors. "Wasn't that a lovely little wedding, yesterday? Were you happy for your sister?"

"Oh my gosh! I was so happy. I've never felt so gorgeous. And Donna was so beautiful." She turned to look into Irene's face. "I've never seen my sister so happy, either. Did you see how her whole face was just glowing?" She laughed. "Oh my gosh! That must be what it's like to be in love, you know?" There was a short shiver. "That's must be what it's like, right? I mean, you should know, right? You're married..." Her words faded at the sight of Mrs. Hannity's tight-lipped countenance.

"Right. I should know." The nursing home director pulled her purse up under one arm, tugging the strap up over her shoulder. "And I can tell you, I, myself, was walking on air. I was so in love with my Georgie, I could hardly swallow in his presence." She jerked her head, just slightly. "I'm sure all those folks around me thought I was a complete ding-a-ling."

"He sure is handsome. I've seen his picture on your desk. He's in the Navy, right?"

Again, the lady's head jerked just a tiny bit. "Technically, yes, he is." She felt the quizzical glance from her teenage companion. "I guess nobody's told you...?" Acknowledging the nod from Jenny, she hastened to explain. "He was in Pearl Harbor when the Japanese attacked. Over twenty-four hundred U.S. military were killed there. Most were identified, but a lot of them were not. My Georgie was one of those." She was watching the path ahead of her. "He's still listed as MIA — Missing In Action."

Jenny stopped in her tracks. "I, I'm so sorry. I didn't know about all that. I just saw the picture and you're wearing a wedding ring, and..." There was a choke in her voice. "Wow. I just had no idea. I'm so, so sorry."

Irene Hannity patted the girl's shoulder. "Not your fault. And," she chose to lighten up, "isn't it nice to know that my private life isn't being discussed by my employees, or the locals!" The two of them moved along in silence until Irene made an effort to ease out of the subject. "So, you can imagine how uplifting it was, for me to find that box of memorabilia from the farm, right there on my doorstep." When Jenny emitted a sympathetic hum, she went on. "I have no idea who put it there, but it was a bit of sunshine shining into my life, I can tell you. Almost like they knew I needed to have a stronger sense of who I was, and who I am now."

"But your time with George, that was precious, too," Jenny pointed out. "That is a big part of who you are, don't you think?"

"It was," Mrs. Hannity admitted as they approached the nursing home's rear entrance. "But nine years is a long time to hold onto desperate hope."

"How do you do it?" Jenny asked.

Mrs. Hannity stood still and thought for a moment, before she answered. "Well, I keep real busy, and I go to church a lot."

***

After Jenny got back from her after-church walk with Mrs. Hannity, she went on duty in the dining room. During her break that afternoon she was notified she had a long distance call on the dayroom phone. It was Essie. Jenny pulled the phone into a corner, for privacy.

"Are you on break?" Essie asked.

"For about ten more minutes. That's fine. What's up?"

"*Mutter* and I were talking about how lovely you looked at the wedding yesterday. And how the color scheme turned out to be red, white, and blue. Wasn't that something? Almost like we planned it!"

"I didn't even think of that. Oh my gosh. That is so neat. And even the paper plates and napkins fit right in."

"And *Mutter's* wedding cake had blue flowers spritzed on it."

"Are you sure she didn't check with Mrs. Hannity on that matter?"

"No," the German girl insisted. Then her tone changed. "How *is* Mrs. Hannity doing today? Is she okay?"

"What do you mean?" Jenny wasn't sure how to answer her friend.

"So, I guess you didn't know about her husband. He's a missing-in-action sailor. So I was wondering how she did, attending a wedding. That had to be hard."

"Essie, I didn't know about him until today. When did you find out about it?"

There was a slight pause. "Um, I guess you forgot we're all friends with the Trapp family. We've made several trips up there, together."

"Oh. Well, she was a little sad, I think. But she tries to look at the happier things that come along in her life. You know, like the box of her childhood memories that got left on her doorstep." She nodded, even though her friend could not see her. "Yeah, I guess she'll be okay."

"That was something weird, wasn't it — the way that box just showed up like that? Did she even know about it being up there in the farmhouse attic?"

"Funny that you should ask that. She told me this morning, she had no idea any of that stuff was up there."

"Really? I don't know… if it was me, I would want to know what else I had left up there, that's for sure," the freckled one said.

"Oh, she knows, now. Doc Horton said he talked to the sheriff and the sheriff told him it was just a bunch of paperwork."

"Oh my gosh, Jenny, that's no fun. I was thinking there might be something more interesting." She went on to another subject. "So, I was wondering about something else. Have you ever been out in that old greenhouse? I was wondering if there might be plants or something… maybe even some roses. Wouldn't that be nice?"

"Nope. Never wanted to go in there. Too old and dirty. And I doubt there are any good plants left in there, anyway."

"Yah-yah. You're probably right. Even the apple trees are in bad shape. You'll probably end up making applesauce, instead of pies." She giggled. "Just make sure you don't get any worms in it!"

Jenny checked the clock. "Well, on that happy thought, I will say goodbye. My break is nearly up, and I still have to hit the restroom."

"Hey, go for it. I'll talk to you soon."

Essie hung up the phone and turned to report to her parents who had been sitting quietly nearby. "It's just as we suspected," she said in her native tongue. "Irene did not know about those boxes, and neither did the doctor."

"I see," the professor answered in High German. "It may be for the best, in her case. On the other hand, if he took those boxes, he probably now knows what was in them, and has probably destroyed crucial information. This is frustrating, for we need to have more proof." His visage went grim. "I'm thinking I may have to bluff the man into making a move."

***

Earlier that Sunday morning, Max rolled over in bed. It had been a long Saturday night in Chittenden County, and this was supposed to be his day off. The morning sun was not a welcome sight — the birds were noisy, and he had a lot on his mind.

He lifted the sheet to scratch where it itched, then flopped onto his stomach to bury his head under the edge of the pillow. "This thing up in Jericho is getting to be a pain in the butt," he whispered. "A double whammy, what with the kid getting killed, and then Doc and Andrew stealing those boxes." It occurred to him that both problems had something to do with the Roth Ranch, just about the same time he became aware that he needed to visit the bathroom. Priorities being what they were, he didn't get back to the ranch connection until he was staring at himself in the medicine cabinet mirror. "That place was just a nice farm in a quiet Vermont countryside, until the Roths showed up. Then two kids move in with them, and one of them gets killed, and the other moves out, eventually ending up accusing that Rhonda girl of messing with her bike brakes, and — as if that wasn't enough — the local doctor steals some mysterious boxes that came from the Roth attic." He checked the stubble on his chin, looking himself in the eye, again. "So, it was all good until the Roths came to Vermont. Too bad they came to Vermont. Why in hell would they even want to come to Vermont?" It was like an alarm went off in his head. "Oh, crap. It's the money. It had to be the insurance money." He looked down into the

252

sink. "I wonder whose idea it was to leave Texas. That might answer a whole lot of other questions."

The phone rang from the other side of the studio apartment. One of the on-duty deputies made a hasty apology. "Hate to bother you on your day off, boss, but this note was left on my desk. I'll just give you the message, and you can take it from there."

"Go ahead."

"It says, 'Could you please take another look at what happened to Eddie? Our family is suspicious about who did it. Call me when you can.' It's from Mark Roth."

"*Speak of the devil,*" Max thought. "Okay. Got the phone number there?"

"Yes, sir." He gave the number, then added one more thing. "Deputy Smith saw the note, and said he would be glad to assist on this, if you wanted to follow up."

"*Nobody like a brown-noser,*" Max reminded himself. "Oh yeah? Well, just tell him I can..." he suddenly remembered that a second officer might bring more cooperation when the questions got too personal for the Roths. A quick glance at the clock on the bedstand showed the ten-thirty mark. "...tell him to be ready in an hour. I have a feeling those folks are anxious to get down to some serious talking. I'll call the Roths and get things rolling. I want to be at their front door by one."

They arrived at the ranch only a few minutes after Kathy and Rhonda got home from church. The ladies were still in their Sunday best, so when the five of them walked down to the river, the dress-up shoes were kept clean by carefully guarded steps. Indeed, they came to a stop before things started to get soggy, letting the sheriff and Mark go on ahead. Deputy Smith hung back there with the two of them, ostensibly to make idle chatter. He chose the subject of the nearby woodpile. "So, this is your target practice site?" he inquired through his most engaging smile. "A pretty good set-up, for an amateur." He winked at Kathy, but they all knew he was teasing Rhonda.

Flattered by the attention, she took the bait. "Yeah?" She shook her dark curls. "You handle a slingshot, do you?" Encouraged by what she thought was a contrite expression on his face, she let him know she was no amateur. "I happen to be one of the best in the country. I won prizes in Texas," she addressed her mother without looking at her, "didn't I, Mama Kathy?"

"Yes, you did, girl."

"I could have gone national, even international, but you need a manager for that." She shrugged. "We didn't have the money for a manager, let alone for the travel expenses."

The deputy wanted to sound impressed. "Well, I'll be. I stand corrected." He moved in for a closer inspection. "So, you hit these tin cans, huh? From how far away?"

The conversation continued for a half-hour or so, when the two men returned from the river's edge.

Rhonda couldn't wait to ask, "So, did you figure out how she did it?"

Max cleared his throat. "I may have a clue. But I need to check on a couple of things, first." He turned to lead the little procession back toward the house.

"I *knew it*," she exclaimed gleefully. "She can throw a stone like a bullet. Did Daddy Mark tell you? I've seen her do it." She skipped along beside the sheriff. "*And* she was the only one down there when it happened, for sure."

"Rhonda," Mark called out, "Sheriff Duncan knows what he's doing. He needs no help from you."

"I just wanted to make sure he knows she can throw like that," she said, slipping into a pout.

The Sheriff's Department vehicle had not even reached the top of the hairpin driveway before Max asked, "Okay, so what did you find out?"

"My gawd, boss, that kid is *so* full of herself. It was like, as they say, 'taking candy from a baby.'"

"Good. So what have you got?" Max grabbed his notebook. "Aw hell, I've only got two pages left."

"Write small," the deputy suggested.

They were traveling along the River Road as he gave all the information. "She could have gone into some serious competition, if they'd had the money. Then, the mother said, they heard that Anna's kids needed a home, and Rhonda always wanted siblings, and so she begged her parents to move to Vermont, where they could all be a 'family.'" He paused. "May I give *my* version of the story?" His boss waited, pencil poised. "The kid needed money to compete, found out about the insurance policy and made up her mind to get in on it, even if it meant leaving Texas."

"And just how did she learn about the insurance?"

"Mr. Roth is listed on the policy, next in line, after the kids. That means he probably got a notification, if the lawyer was doing his job."

"Ay-yuh," Max recalled, "the older sister, Donna, said something about that, when I interviewed her in her apartment." He made a quick note. "I forgot about that." He blinked. "So it was Rhonda who wanted to move to Vermont. Interesting." Then he put the pad down on his lap. "Tell you what else is interesting. When I asked Mark Roth if Eddie had had any run-ins with anybody since coming up here to Jericho, the only ones he could remember were a couple of squabbles between him and — guess who? — Rhonda." The brows knit together for a second. "Let's see, something about 'boy stuff' in the hay loft, and then she was pelting the bull — what was his name? Oh yeah, Thunder. Roth said he took her slingshot away for a while, and that was the end of that."

"Whoa. May I offer my interpretation of *that* situation, boss?" He took the shrug as permission to speak. "So, she was trying to get the bull to attack the kid, right? I wonder why?" He shifted his buttocks in the driver's seat. "Probably not to kill him. That would be too risky. Nope, my bet would be that she just wanted him injured, so he would have to stay on the ranch, and eventually, inherit his share of the money." Suddenly he thought of something else. "Hey! Did these people from Texas know how sick... or not sick... Anna Roth was?"

"Good question." Max made another note. "That would figure in the decision to move from Texas, like so damned suddenly. I think those three kids were in the home for about ten years. Where the hell was Mark Roth all that time?"

"Maybe that S.O.B. had money in the back of his mind, when he decided to move to Vermont," the deputy postulated. "Maybe he didn't have to be begged to make the move, like they would have us believe."

"So how does the mother fit into all this? She doesn't seem to have a motive to do anybody any harm," Max wondered.

"Well, the daughter is a schemer, the husband has battle fatigue, and Mrs. Roth is, I guess you could say, the moderator in this volatile situation." He glanced at his boss. "Maybe she just has to keep the two of them from destroying the family circle."

"Huh," Max grunted. "So, in the middle of all this, there's an earthquake, and in the end, Eddie Roth dies of a fatal wound at the base of his skull, obviously made by a river rock. The question is: Was the rock shot from a slingshot, or from a deadly aimed pitch?"

Deputy Smith didn't have an answer for that; instead, he had a suggestion. "Alright, so there was a murder. We know that. What we don't know, is who benefited from it? If it was Donna, his older sister, what did she have to gain? On the other hand, if it was the self-centered brat, what did *she* have to gain?"

Max rose to the challenge. "Let's see... if it was Donna, she would have one less sibling to share the insurance money with." He tilted his head. "But the murder was impulsive, on the spur of the moment. It was a rare opportunity. An earthquake and some quicksand." He went a bit further. "And there was only a matter of a few minutes to think it through and actually do it, before her uncle came back with his rifle."

"But she could have done all that, right?" Smith checked to see if his boss was tracking this correctly.

"Or," Max conjectured, "the girl, Rhonda, may not have really been in the upper pasture, like she keeps saying. Maybe she was down there, and saw that Donna was in the barn taking care of the goats, and did the deed, before pretending to just arrive."

"Um, no, boss. She said she heard the rifle shot before she went down to the river." He tried to soften the fact that he had just corrected his superior. "Of course, that's what she *said*. You may be right." He had another thought. "Wait. What did Mark Roth say about that?"

The sheriff sighed. "I believe he said he and Donna were the only ones down there, when he shot the bull."

"Yes, sir. So that's probably how it really was. After all, the kid was already under water, and Mr. Roth had tried to pull him out, but couldn't get close enough."

"Right!" Max suddenly recalled. "And Mrs. Roth was yelling at him, from the porch, not to go in any deeper."

"She was yelling from the porch?" He glanced at the sheriff to get confirmation. "So, do you think she may have seen her daughter running from the upper field?"

The sheriff's shoulders slumped. "I don't know, Smith, I just don't know."

"Well, sir, I only bring that up, because it seems to me, that if Eddie is now conveniently out of the way, and if she could prove that Donna was the only one who was there when it happened, then maybe — just maybe — Rhonda would be rid of two of the kids who stand between her and that insurance check."

His boss slapped his own forehead. "Oh shee-it. Of course. And then she tampers with the last kid's bike brakes. Her own mother saw that, not just the girl, Jenny." He relaxed back into the passenger seat. "I think maybe we need to check out this conceited Texas slingshot champion."

"Ay-yuh. That little braggart claims she's a crack shot, as far away as two hundred yards. That's with some kind of ball they use in competitions."

"That right, Smith? I wonder how far she could send a river rock?"

"I suppose it depends on how close she could get and still be hidden behind a tree or something, Sheriff."

"That's true, Deputy." A smile spread slowly across his lips. "She didn't even have to go all the way down there, now, did she?"

There was silence in the cab of the official pickup as it moved steadily toward Essex Junction. The deputy had learned to be quiet during these times when Sheriff Duncan went into a period of contemplation. It usually meant the man was onto something really important. When Max told him to head for Burlington, he lowered his head and set his sights on the new destination. Sunday traffic stirred up summer dust from the roadside, but the two lawmen rolled down the windows, anyway. Soon they would pass through the five-way traffic circle of the village, and as they approached the Winooski River Bridge, it would get increasingly humid from the heavy, moist air rising from the nearby expanse of Lake Champlain.

Deputy Smith pulled the truck into the parking lot of Battery Park, high above the edge of the lake. "So, why did you have me buy ice cream bars from Colodny's Market, then drive us across the street to park here?" he asked his reluctant mentor. "Are we on a stake-out or something?"

"Kind of, Smith," the sheriff informed his driver. "We just solved a murder. Now we have to figure out how to prove it." He began to unwrap the icy treat. "We don't go home until we do that." He pulled the sticky paper loose. "I figure we might as well come up with a sure-fire plan, while sitting in a park and eating ice cream."

"I'm not sure I follow…"

"Look at it this way: We're too far from home to just put it all off until tomorrow, and head back to bed. That's pretty big temptation, when it's supposed to be your day off." The bar was poised in front of his mouth, but he had one more thing to say. "Now, how are we going to corner that sharpshootin' Texas filly?"

***

Monday morning's dawn was yet to break over Jericho Center, but Walter was already awake, his face pressed against his bride's shoulder. He was still enthralled by the fragrance of her soft skin, by her smooth curves that led to the silky depths of the marriage bed. She was finally his, and he was hers, and it was a new world, filled with love, in every sense of the word. In a few minutes the alarm would ring, and it would be time to get back to the world of making a living, but for now, he lay quietly marveling at the gentle rhythm of her breathing.

When he got out of the shower, she was in the kitchen, making coffee, resplendent in one of his old, baggy undershirts. "Hey, where did you find that?" he laughed.

"Under the bed," she said, stretching the bottom edges like a skirt across her knees. "I figured you wouldn't mind."

"I warmed up the shower for you," he said, with a playful pat on her bottom. "I'll make breakfast. You get ready for work."

They drove in together, in his old Chevy. He dropped her off at the telephone company and went on to his first class. At noon, they met to share a sandwich on a bench in front of her building. "Did you call Don Collins, yet?" she asked between bites.

"Yup. Told him we wanted to use the wedding gift money to hire a lawyer." He wiped his mouth with the back of his hand. "He said we need to talk about that." She handed him a paper napkin. "So, I'm not sure what's going to happen." He dabbed the flimsy thing against his lips. "But he knows we're serious about getting custody of Jenny."

"You know, I was wondering about getting that sheriff to testify for us. Jenny told him she didn't want to go back to the ranch." She blinked her lavender blue eyes. "That might help, don't you think?"

"Let's see what Don has to say," came his cautious reply.

They stopped at the Collinses' home in Winooski, after he picked her up from her shift. Connie answered the door and bid them to have a seat in the living room. The window blinds were closed against the August afternoon heat, and an electric fan whirred from one corner of the room. The two of them watched a magazine flutter as the rotating breeze moved across the coffee table in front of their sofa seats, until their hostess came back in from the kitchen with a cool pitcher of lemonade. "Don should be home any minute," she told them. "He's bringing pizza."

"Oh, I hope you didn't do that for us," Donna objected.

"No-no," Connie brushed that notion away with the flip of her hand. "We do this whenever I don't have time to get supper." She looked at Walter. "Would you believe that we teachers at EJHS are already having meetings to get ready for the new school year?"

"I expect a call any day, now." He stretched. "And I still have another two weeks of classes at UVM."

"Right. And that reminds me: How's it going with the thesis?" She poured him a glass of the cold refreshment, pretending not to notice the look that passed between the young couple.

"Pretty close to finishing." He nodded his thanks as he took the drink.

"Also, pretty controversial," Donna remarked.

Connie poured the second glassful as she spoke. "I suspected it would be." She handed the beverage to Donna. "Are you prepared for the repercussions?"

He shrugged. "Probably not. God only knows what's going to happen."

"Good point," Connie reminded him. "God *absolutely* knows, and He can handle it."

"Pizza delivery!" Don yelled, as he pulled the back screen door open.

Connie pointed to the dining room table in its little alcove between them and the kitchen. "Bring your drinks and have a seat." In a few minutes, the cheesy treat was pulled from the box, and four diners were busy licking fingers and snatching mozzarella strings off the edges of piping hot wedges.

"Have you been waiting long?" the bus driver asked.

"Nope. Only a few minutes," Walter answered.

Don turned to his wife. "Did I miss anything?"

"Mmm… we did talk about his controversial thesis," she let him know.

"So I *did* miss something." He looked at Walter. "Why is it controversial? You calling somebody bad names, or something?"

The Tafts laughed together. "Worse than that," Donna murmured.

"He's writing about secret societies, Don. Like the Masons and the different types of granges — stuff like that." Connie wound a cheese string around her finger. "Did you forget, hon?"

"Okay. Gotcha." He loosened his bus driver's tie. "So, what are you saying, that they're all phonies, or what?"

"I don't think they see themselves as any such thing." Walter stopped eating. "They are deadly serious about possessing some kind of mysterious 'truth' — something beyond what the rest of us could ever understand. And they hide behind a lot of good works, to carry on some very evil secret activities."

"Ay-yuh. I can see where you might step on a few toes... very powerful toes, at that." Don took another bite, chewing thoughtfully. "Now correct me if I'm wrong, but don't these organizations deny the one true God? I seem to recall that they allow all religions, but forbid any one in particular be superior to the others."

"That's pretty much how they present the false notion of inclusive love," the younger man stated. "But the bottom line is that they teach that human beings can solve human problems, if we are all humble and loving, and follow a few wise leaders."

"Except, these leaders are the privileged few who *say* they know the 'truth.'" Donna tried to recall how her husband had explained it to her. "But they, themselves, have been fooled, degree-by-degree, as they rose to those leadership positions, and don't realize they have been deceived, inch-by-inch, into believing in something that was not at all the *real* truth." She looked to Walter to pick it up from there.

"They end up putting Satan — or Lucifer, as they call him — on the same level as Jesus Christ. They really believe that those two are brothers, along with Buddha and the rest of the gang."

"But," Donna hastened to add, "the emblems and logos for these secret societies are mostly goats and all-seeing eyes and satanic stars, and skulls, and, well, things we think of as Halloween trimmings." There was a smart jerk of her light brown curls. "Now, *you* tell *me*: Does that sound like godly clubs for godly people?"

"Nope." Don picked up his glass of lemonade. "But here's the thing, Walter. You probably aren't the first one to come up with all of this. There probably have been other attempts to get this information out to the general public, and yet, those societies continue to exist." The high school teacher nodded his head in agreement. "Which tells me, they were either silenced or laughed out of the room."

"Yes, sir." He looked over at his beautiful new wife. "And that could very well happen."

Mrs. Taft reached over to touch her husband's hand. "But at least you will have tried... at least you will have tried."

There was a moment of silence. Then Don needed to get to the original reason for the Tafts' visit. He leaned back in the dining room chair. "So, you two want to get custody of Jenny. I am so blown away by that!" He grinned. "I mean, you're just starting out life together, and here, you're adding a teenager to your household. You sure you want to do that?"

"She's in danger if she goes back to the ranch," Donna reminded him. "We'll snuggle her into that tiny house, whatever it takes, even if she sleeps on the floor."

"Oh my gosh," Connie interjected, "whatever you do, don't say that to the social worker." She pushed back a strand of her silvery hair. "No-no. You need to present a picture of security... her own room, a healthy environment, in every way. Otherwise, they will opt to send her back to the Home." She hunched forward, intent on a plan. "You may have to move."

"Whoa." Don held up both hands. "Remember this: Jenny is old enough to where they will ask her what she wants to do," he reminded his wife. "We've seen this all work out, many times, and yes, they will ask her what she wants." He looked confident. "I think we all know what her answer will be."

"But they will still want details on where and how and all the safety measures, Don. You know they'll look into all those things. They don't just let a teenager decide to sleep on the floor or whatever. No, the girl is technically still a minor."

"Okay," Donna concluded, "it would be best if we didn't have to deal with social workers. It would be better if we could just work something out with Uncle Mark. All we need is official papers, signed by all of us, right?"

"It's been done that way before," Connie noted. "The problem might be that your uncle may not want to cooperate."

Mrs. Taft shook her head vigorously. "So we really *do* need to have a lawyer to stand up for us."

"Not necessarily." Don pinched his lips together before he continued: "Sometimes, when you're making a deal with someone, you may have to 'sweeten the pot' a bit." He picked up another wedge of pizza. "Let's take a minute to think about that. Now, what is it that Mark Roth wants, more than anything in the world?"

"Money," Donna announced, without a second thought.

"No, wait." Walter took a quick sip from his glass. "That's not really what most men want. They want respectability, a good reputation, good standing in the community." Don smiled at this young man's insight. "Yes, all that can come with having money, but having big bucks can't really bring the genuine thing," Walter concluded.

"You just hit the nail right on the head, Walter," Don murmured through the pizza crust. "But let's turn that thought the other way around. Suppose you offer to help him *keep those things*, by letting Jenny go, for her own peace of mind and happiness. You could point out how that would make Mark Roth a big man in the township of Jericho, Vermont." He envisioned the next part. "I can hear Jenny saying only nice things about that fellow, instead of telling folks she was afraid to live with him. Her uncle would have a choice, and my bet is that he'll choose being a hero, rather than a villain."

"Wow! I would never have thought of that," Donna whispered. She turned to her husband. "Do you think it would work?"

"Hey, it's worth a try," he answered.

"Stop me if I'm wrong, Don," Connie told him. Then she addressed the Tafts: "I suggest you talk to Jenny, first. She needs to know you really want her, and she needs to know how to handle those folks at the ranch."

"Good advice," Don agreed. "So, what do you two think? Want to give the man a chance to be a hero?" The newlyweds looked hopeful. "Good. In the meantime, you just hold onto your money. After all, it was a wedding gift."

CHAPTER TWENTY-THREE

Lawyers

Professor Abraham Schuler stared across Doc Horton's desk. "I regret that it has come to this," he said, in his best English.

"Regret? What do you regret, sir?" The gold-rimmed glasses glinted in the colorful August sunset outside the office window. "I don't believe you have ever been a patient of mine," his words tumbled between a nervous chuckle, "so this certainly can't be a doctor-patient thing."

"In a manner of speaking, it actually is, sir."

"Very well. And just who is this patient?"

"It was my older sister, Freda Crocker." He watched the doctor's countenance go gray. "Surely, you remember her — lovely golden hair, a fetching German accent? Ah yes, I see that you do." He went to the next point. "She was a German war bride, who came to Jericho as Mrs. Timothy Crocker, and who, I'm sure you recall, was a talented gardener... even an accomplished botanist." He observed the shield go up, as the older man's face turned to stone. "Can you imagine my joy, that my Jewish sister had escaped Hitler's murderous agenda? Indeed, it gave me hope, as a young educator, myself, that I might well find that same freedom." He loosened the stiffness in his own shoulders. "For several years, we kept in touch, by airmail and even the occasional overseas telephone call. It was difficult, for I had a new bride, and we kept moving from one district to another, to keep ahead of the..." He stopped himself, to get back to the task at hand. "My wife and I are aware that Freda was involved with you."

Doc Horton straightened into a commanding position in his desk chair. "That's right. I remember her well. She suffered from, for lack of a better word, a nervous condition, brought on by her husband's erratic behavior." He paused, apparently searching for the right words.

The professor cleared his throat loudly. "Please excuse me, *Herr Doktor*. That is not what I meant when I said my sister was involved with you." He caught the sudden panic in the practitioner's eyes. "You see," Abe Schuler murmured softly, "we had a lot of correspondence, and you were mentioned frequently. Ach so... my sister was in love with you, not true?"

The yellowish eyes narrowed behind the glasses. "I can assure you, mister, that those were the ravings of a woman in the midst of a nervous breakdown. I will not be held responsible for any such thing." He rose to usher the man out of his office, but the professor did not budge.

"I think it best, if you sit, *Doktor* Horton, since there is still more I will say to you." He stayed in his seat, keeping eye contact with the doctor, until the man dropped back into his desk chair. "I must inform you that my family knows all this, and we now know it was you who stole the attic boxes from the teacher's home, on the occasion of the earthquake."

"Who told you such a thing? That's a lie!"

"No one told us; it was just logic. You needed to cover up how Timothy died." Again, he watched the man's face harden. "We waited to be sure, but then you showed us that Freda had told us the truth." He leaned forward to make sure the doctor heard him. "It was *not* a suicide." Professor Schuler did not back down from the icy stare. "It was *not!*" He lifted a teaching finger toward the man behind the desk. "Timothy Crocker was *poisoned,* with a pesticide from the greenhouse, and you knew it, and you falsified the autopsy and the coroner's report, or whatever you call them in this country — and you did it, to hide the identity of the killer."

Doc Horton shot up out of his chair. "The hell I did! What a filthy bunch of crap! I'll see to it that you, and anybody else who tries to do this to me, you'll all rot in prison."

"I doubt that, sir," the educator replied. "Freda never told you about the information stored in the attic. My family believes she kept that from you, to make sure you did not blame her for her husband's death. After the murder, she lost trust in her lover, who also was cheating on his wife." Doc Horton gritted his teeth, but before he could say anything, the professor slammed him with the clincher: "And you proved your guilt buy stealing those boxes." He smiled again. "Tell me, sir, did you find any incriminating evidence, or was it a waste of your time and effort?"

The accused man's face was bright red, as he slammed a fist on the desktop. "Get your sorry ass out of my office, and don't ever come back."

"Ach so, this is the answer of a guilty man, I perceive." Abraham Schuler stood up to finish the story. "And you didn't do it to protect our dear Freda; you did it because Timothy had become an embarrassment to the Grange, and yes, ultimately to the Masons in this state." He moved to open the office door. "By stealing those boxes, you have torn the shroud of secrecy aside, and you have done it to your very own self."

The triumphant smile on Schuler's face drove the doctor one step further. "Get the hell out! I'm not telling you again. I'll have you and your whole family deported, you slimy son-of-a-bitch!"

Unfortunately, these last words were heard by two people out in the waiting room. One was Mrs. Horton, and the other was a fellow by the name of Malcolm J. Burke.

Across the village green, Mrs. Hannity was confused. "I had no idea you felt that way about the Roths," she said to Jenny. "You're actually afraid to go back there?" Jenny confirmed it with a quick nod. The woman turned to Walter and Donna. "How long has this been going on?"

"It's a pretty long story," the older sister replied. "But Walter and I are convinced Jenny is in danger, should she be forced to return to that place."

From where he was leaning against the office wall, Walter explained further: "We wanted to inform you that we intend to get custody of Jenny, but we also need to ask if she could remain here at the nursing home until we can move to a larger house."

"Of course. My offer to let her stay even after school starts still stands. We agreed she could work here after school, for her board and room." She looked across the office to where the girl was seated. "I really enjoy this young lady, you know? We all like her, and I'm sure it will be fine."

"That's a great relief," Walter told her. "Now, we'll see if Mark Roth will go along with this change in custody thing."

"Why wouldn't he?" Irene Hannity wondered. "Seems like, if somebody doesn't want to live in the same house with you, you'd be happy to accommodate them." She had a second thought. "Unless he has some other reason for her to have to be there." Noting the quick look between the three of them, she decided to let it go. "Anyway, it's time to make evening rounds and tuck our folks in."

Jenny and the Tafts stood to move toward the office door, but the girl suddenly turned to go back and give her boss a hug. "Thank you," she whispered. Then they were gone.

Irene took a moment to ponder the situation. "Boy-oh-boy... who would have thought the old place would turn into a 'house of horrors'?" But then she rose from her chair, laughing out loud. "Well now, that was exactly what I *did* think, wasn't it? I didn't want to go back there, either." Mrs. Hannity was still chuckling as she closed the office door behind her.

She didn't notice her uncle, Professor Abe Schuler, driving quickly past the building. If he kept a steady speed, he would get back to Burlington just after dusk.

***

"I don't think we have enough evidence to get in touch with the Snoop Squad. Not yet," Sheriff Max Duncan told Deputy Smith. They were getting ready to pay a visit to Roth Ranch. "But by the time we get done up there today, we should have plenty. He strapped his holster into place, looking out at the bright Tuesday morning sunshine.

"I hope this works," Smith said.

"It will." Max placed his official hat on his head. "Let's go."

They were still on the River Road when they heard the call from dispatch. A car was in the ditch just west of Jericho Corners. One passenger. Apparently there all night. Max took the mike. "That's a ten-four, dispatch, five minutes away."

They were surprised to see Andrew standing beside his grandpa's beat-up truck, parked awkwardly on the side of the road. The boy waved his arms for them to stop. "It's down there!" He was pointing to a gray sedan lying on its side, half-hidden under a couple of sumac bushes. The two lawmen moved quickly down to find a fortyish gentleman peering out through the driver's window, obviously trapped by the damaged door.

"Are you hurt?" Smith called out to him. The man pointed to the foot jammed between the brake pedal and the floor. "We need an ambulance, Sheriff."

"Wait a minute," Max yelled up to the teenager. "You got something we can pry this door open with?"

Andrew came down to hand a crowbar to the deputy. Sheriff Duncan was surprised. "You actually had this in your truck?"

The kid grinned. "Didn't know it was there, but the toolbox in back of the seat was tipped over, and there it was."

In a few minutes, the man was safely removed from the wreckage, able to limp up the bank and get seated in the Chittenden County truck. It was time to make a report.

"Do you want medical attention here, or would you like to call someone to take you to your own doctor?"

"I will call, if you don't mind."

"Max noticed the accent; this fellow was not from the States. Alright, sir, but first I need your driver's license and proof of insurance. The name caught his attention. "Schuler? Is that the way you pronounce it?" he asked, casually. He pretended to scrutinize the license, buying some time to put it all together.

"You visiting here in the States, Mr. Schuler?"

"No-no. I am a professor at UVM."

And there it was: This guy belonged to the two gals he had met at the Roth Ranch house. Max took the proof of insurance paper from the deputy, who had retrieved it from the wrecked car's glove box. "Okay, looks like everything's in order." He handed the two items back to the professor. "So, just exactly what happened here? Why did you end up down there in the bushes?"

Professor Schuler explained that he was driving home from a meeting in Jericho Center, when a fast-moving pickup had attempted to pass him, but got too close, causing Herr Schuler to pull the sedan's steering wheel hard to the right. "Then it was sliding and bumped over some rocks. It landed down there, where nobody could see." The man rubbed his ankle. "I sounded the horn, but it did no good."

"The other driver did not stop?" Max was making another note.

"I regret to say, he did not."

"Did you get a look at him?" The man nodded a no. "How about the pickup — can you describe it?"

Abe Schuler eyed the truck that Andrew had parked just a few feet away. "It was much like that one."

"I see." He let that go for the moment. "You don't have anybody mad at you, do you?" He saw a flicker of something in the instructor's eye, but he let that one go, too. "Now, Professor, I have to ask a couple more questions, and I don't mean to be nosy or rude. I simply need to get all the facts into my report. Do you understand?"

"Of course."

"Good. Now, please tell me where you were, before heading home."

"At the doctor's office."

"Doc Horton's office?" The man nodded in agreement. "You sick, or was it just a social call?"

The lips went tight. "I think we could say it was a social call, yes."

"No alcohol consumed?" Another nodded no. "Have you been friends with Doc for a long time?"

"Ach, no. We have a mutual friend or two."

The sheriff acted like he was suddenly enlightened. "Oh, of course. You must be a Mason." Abe indicated this was incorrect. "No? Well, then, you must be a Grange member." The German sat up straighter, as though to shed an unwelcome cloak. Clearly, the gentleman was uncomfortable. "Hey, Smith, did you call for a tow truck yet?" The deputy signaled that he had. The sheriff turned back to Herr Schuler. "Okay, sir, just sit tight and we'll see about getting you home." With that word of assurance to the professor, Max walked up to where Andrew was leaning against the old truck. He lowered his voice. "You out raising hell last night, kid?"

The boy blinked. "No, sir!" Max didn't look convinced. "No, sir, and I can prove it. I didn't even have the truck last night. My grandpa got a call and took off like a shot. He didn't come back until early in the morning... at least, that's what my mom said."

"Okay. So, what're you doing now?"

"On my way to Burlington. Going to a ball game, later."

"Good. Give this guy a ride home. He's got a sore ankle and he's very tired. You should be very nice to him."

Sheriff Duncan waited until those two were on the road, then remarked to his partner, "I think we need to have a little talk with Ken Pearson, Andrew's grandfather. Seems he went speeding down this road last night, in that old truck, and was out until late."

"Why would *he* want to scare a guy off the road?"

"Two things, Smith. He's a close friend of Doc Horton, who the professor seems to have a problem with. And then, he also happens to be a Mason."

"So you think the professor might have made somebody mad?"

"You know what, Smith? I think we'll just put off our chat with Rhonda Roth, for a day or so. She's not going anywhere. Instead I think we should pay *Doc* a visit. If anything happened in that office, we need to know what it was." He pulled out a stick of gum. "Ay-yuh. We should strike while the iron's hot."

***

Mark Roth was irritated to be called from the middle of morning chores, but figured he owed Martin Morrison the courtesy of returning his call.

"Morrison Excavations. How may we help you?" Mark identified himself and the secretary quickly got the boss on the line.

"Mark! It's Marty! How the hell are ya?" He didn't wait for an answer. "Hey, I've got a proposition for ya, something we could both make a few bucks at, if we handle it right."

"Oh?" Mark was no longer irritated. "Well, let's hear it."

"It's about that grove of apple trees out behind your house. I noticed it when we were over there helping you with the quicksand problem." It sounded like he was holding a cigar in his mouth. "I got to thinking, this could be a pretty nice enterprise for Morrison Excavations, running an orchard. Of course, we won't make money on it, but it would make us look more involved in the agriculture community in the state of Vermont, and besides that, we need a tax write-off, know what I mean?" Mark grunted his acknowledgment. "So, I would like to offer you five hundred dollars for a five-year lease on that patch of land. What do you think?"

"Mmmm," Mark hummed back. "Of course, you know there's a greenhouse and a watering system that goes with all that?" He hummed again. "Maybe we should think about a higher fee, Marty." There was silence on the other end, for the businessman knew Mark was about to negotiate. The cattleman went for it. "Tell you what, my friend, you did me a big favor taking care of Thunder, so I'm willing to let you lease that land for only six hundred, and a four-year lease. And to sweeten the pot, you can bring in your own equipment and update that whole orchard, any way you want. What do you say?"

"I'll have my lawyer draw up the papers and see you in a couple of days. How's that?"

You've got a deal, sir." Mark hung up the living room phone and turned to see Kathy standing there.

"We've got company," she said. "It's Donna and her new husband, and they have Jenny with them."

The knock came on the front door before the Roths could collect their thoughts. "I'll get it," she whispered.

After a polite greeting, the three guests entered and followed Kathy's invitation to have a seat. Mark recognized their presence with a perfunctory nod.

Walter cleared his throat and took the lead. "Donna and I need to take just a few minutes of your time." He looked at Mark, then Kathy. "It's about you having custody of Jenny." The Roths exchanged a quick look.

"What about it?" Mark asked cautiously.

"Well, now that Donna and I are married, we would like to take custody of her."

Another quick look was exchanged by the Roth adults, then Mark leaned back against the wall near the phone. "What for?"

"Jenny feels very uncomfortable living here, because of what happened to Eddie." Donna sat up straight as she spoke. After all, she wasn't really lying. That part was true.

"Oh, of course," Kathy said softly. "That makes sense." She turned to her husband. "We can understand that, can't we, Mark?"

"Thank you," Walter hastened to follow up. "We *thought* you would see how much it would bother her."

Mark looked at Jenny. "Is that true, girl? You get the willies living here on the ranch?"

"It's only because of Eddie," Kathy reminded him. "Isn't that right, Jenny?"

"Yes, ma'am." The sixteen-year-old then addressed her uncle. "I don't want to hurt anybody's feelings, especially since you took us out of the Home, and all that, but now that Eddie got killed here, well, I just don't want to be around this place." The tears were coming, as she twisted a tissue in her hands. "I know I owe you a lot, Uncle Mark, but I just need you to be my hero… one more time."

His eyes seemed to stare right through her, then finally blinked. "It's okay, kid. You've got a little battle fatigue, that's all." He studied the floor for a couple of seconds. "I guess we can let you go live someplace else."

Walter stood up. "Mr. Roth, it takes a big man to understand this situation. You have my utmost respect." He drew forth some paperwork. "You may want to have a lawyer take a look at these. You need to sign her over to our care."

Kathy reached over to take them. "I don't think we'll take too long to get this done, uh, is it 'Walter'?"

"Yes, ma-am."

"Okay, Walter. We should get back to you in a few days." She smiled at Jenny. "You know you're always welcome to come back and visit, don't you, honey?"

The grateful girl gave her Aunt Kathy and Uncle Mark a hug, and the three of them left.

"Well, Mark, I think you handled that very well." She gave him a pat on the arm.

"Aw, just one less mouth to feed," he groused.

CHAPTER TWENTY-FOUR

Rats

Frau Schuler jumped up from her chair at the sight of her husband coming through the front doorway. "Oh, *mein Gott!*" she blurted out her Bavarian German. "Where have you been?" she cried out against his shoulder. "I was about to call the police!"

"You did not call them last night?"

"They make you wait for twenty-four hours, or something like that." She kissed him quickly on the cheek. "Why are you limping?"

Essie came bounding down the stairs. "*Vater!* What is? What is?"

"Be careful, *mein Kind,*" he cautioned her as he folded his other arm around her, "you are slipping out of your High German."

She laughed incredulously. "I don't care. Just tell us what happened."

He filled them in on the whole story, from the office visit to the accident.

"It's a wonder you weren't killed," the wife remarked.

"A miracle, *Mutter* — that's what it was. We were praying so hard..."

"Where is the boy?" the father asked. "At school?" The two ladies nodded to confirm that. "Good. He does not need to hear what else I have to say." He moved to sit on the sofa, his darlings on each side. "Let's review the situation: The *Doktor* knows that we have letters from Freda, accusing him of poisoning Timothy and falsifying the paperwork. He denied it, of course, but I could see he was terrified. I am sure we have touched an extremely sensitive spot in this man's history."

"I bet he wishes he never stole those boxes, *Vater*. He opened a whole new can of worms when he did that." Essie folded her arms. "If he knew what Aunt Freda wrote in those letters, he would have a fit."

"Oh, he has no idea how much she told us — how Tim had a heart attack in the attic, and how she dragged his body down to the bedroom." Elke was picturing it in her mind. "She actually dragged him. He was a small man, despite all his violence."

"She called Doc, because he was the only *Doktor* in the area, and that rotten man of medicine used the opportunity to trap his mistress in a prison of silence," Herr Schuler murmured. "Made sure Tim was dead by giving him a shot of poison — probably pesticide — then threatened her if she ever told anybody about their relationship, he would have the body exhumed and accuse her of using her own gardening ingredients to kill her crazy husband." He shook his head in disbelief. "How evil people can be. It is not just in the Nazi party." He took a big breath. "Ach so, even though I accused him of poisoning Timothy, we really have no evidence of that."

"But we do have the letters," Elke reminded him.

"Right now, the *Doktor* does not know where we have hidden Freda's letters," Abe Schuler reminded his ladies. "But when we have to present them as evidence, I believe he will pull every political string he has, to make them look phony. Remember, not only is he a medical *Doktor*, but he is a very powerful man — a 33rd degree Mason." We could have a very long, expensive court battle, as we try to clear Freda's name."

"Ha! He may be powerful, but not so smart," the daughter noted. "After all, he was dumb enough to steal those boxes. We know this, now, and this shows he's involved in hiding something." Essie felt quite confident as she spoke. "And the cover-up is how Timothy Crocker died. That's pretty serious. It's hard to believe, but I think he will be caught," Essie stated.

"You may be right Esther, because people *do* get caught... especially those who think they have already gotten away with it. They get careless, they get cocky, they get drunk and start bragging. And then, when they realize they've been caught, they *lie*." He drew his arms back, to clasp his hands over his knees. "People will lie, to protect what they treasure the most — their reputation, their money, whatever — and that's a fact." Abe looked first at his wife, and then his daughter. "I also think the man is about to get caught. So, eventually, we have a decision to make: Do we try to take him to court on charges of murder and tampering with evidence, or do we 'strike a bargain,' as the Americans like to say?"

"But first, *Vater*, we need for somebody to arrest him, not true?"

There was a glint in his eye. "When he questioned me about the accident this morning, the sheriff seemed a bit too interested in what I *didn't* have to say about *Doktor* Horton." He wobbled the clasped hands like a teacher making a point. "I got the distinct feeling he was going to see what the good *Doktor* had to do with me being run off the road like that."

"Does, the sheriff know Doc stole those boxes?" Essie asked.

"I don't know, but that lawman smells a *Ratte*, I think." He laughed softly. "Ach so, it wouldn't surprise me if he was in that rodent's office, before the day is over."

***

279

Ken Pearson was just getting up when Sheriff Max Duncan knocked on the door. The bloodshot eyes told the lawman that Ken hadn't slept well enough, nor long enough. He asked the question as he took a seat across the breakfast table, where the tired grandfather was downing a second cup of coffee. "Late night, Mr. Pearson?"

"Guess you could say that," he said over the rim of the cup.

"I can, because your grandson told me you jumped into the truck and took off like a bat out of hell." He noted the man's silent displeasure. "Only reason he told me, was I accused him of running somebody off the road early last evening. He said *you* had the truck and were gone until early this morning." Max got to the point. "Mind telling me where you went?"

"Is this an official investigation, Sheriff?" Ken set the cup down.

"I hope not, Mr. Pearson. I would hate to think you deliberately caused an accident. In fact, I tend to believe the opposite. I'm guessing you were just in a big rush, and that's what I'm really curious about: Where the heck were you going, in such a hurry?

The grandfather rubbed the sleep from the inner corner of his eye, then wiped that finger on his shirt front. "Got a call from a friend; needed to get to Barre."

"An emergency, I presume, sir?"

Ken shifted his behind in the chair. "Ay-yuh. A friend needed some help."

"What friend would that be? Somebody in Barre, no doubt." Max drew out the small tablet and fumbled for a pen. When he looked up for an answer, the color was rising in Ken's face. The fellow was going to try and lie about this. Max cleared his throat. "I would advise you to think carefully before you answer that question, Mr. Pearson, because, sooner or later, I will find out the truth." He tapped the pen on the tablet. "Better to get it over with right now, than to play cat and mouse with a police officer, don't you think?"

There was some hemming and hawing, but the older gentleman finally decided to come clean. "I needed to talk to Marty Morrison."

"That sounds familiar. Is this the guy who has the excavation business that helped the Roths remove their bull from the quicksand?" Ken nodded in agreement. "So, what was his emergency?"

Ken Pearson looked miserable, but he answered, anyway. "It wasn't his emergency." There was a long, weary sigh. "Doc Horton asked me to talk to Marty about an important job." He looked up, knowing the sheriff wanted to know what it was. "Doc discovered some dangerous chemicals in the Roths' greenhouse and wanted to get them removed as soon as possible."

"Okay." Max took a slow look around the kitchen, before he came up with the next curiosity. "So what was the big hurry?"

"Doc said somebody could get killed up there. Said the whole orchard had to be cleaned up, stat."

"Uh-huh," the lawman mused. "Must need to get that done... how soon?"

"Immediately. But of course, it'll take a day or two before Marty can get all that equipment up there."

Max made a mental note of that.

***

Mrs. Horton, who was also Doc's nurse, informed Max that the doctor was over at the nursing home, making rounds. The sheriff signaled Deputy Smith to go over to the Country Store to pick up a lunch snack for the two of them, and then turned his attention back to the gray-haired wife. "I hear there was some excitement over here yesterday." Seeing the reluctance in her face, he attempted to make light of it. "Professor Schuler is quite a character, wouldn't you say?"

"I guess so," she said through a weak smile. "They say there's one of those in every family, so I guess we can't complain too much."

"You folks related to the Schulers, ma'am?"

"In a distant sort of way. Doc stepped in after Tim and Freda died. He's been like a father to Irene."

He nodded as if he already knew that. "Oh yeah, I forgot she was Tim and Freda's daughter. And, let's see, the Schulers are related to the Crockers... how?"

"Freda was a Schuler. The temperamental professor is her younger brother."

He touched a finger to his temple. "Right, right. Got it now." He glanced around the waiting room. "You two have been a big help to this community. I hear a lot of good things about the Hortons."

Her smile widened. "Thank you. It's nice to hear something good. It's not always like that, you know."

"Well, as long as nobody else heard anything yesterday, there should be no mention of the incident, Mrs. Horton."

"Oh dear." She suddenly looked concerned. "There *was* somebody else here. Malcolm Burke."

"Malcolm?" Max deliberately frowned. "Oh no. What did he hear, do you remember?"

She was embarrassed, but said it, anyway: "Professor accused Doc of stealing those boxes, and Doc told him to get the heck out, or he would have the whole Schuler family deported."

Sheriff Duncan stepped up to her rescue. "Don't worry, ma'am. I'll try to have a word with Mr. Burke." He went on to change the subject, "So, Doc will be a while at Maude's?"

"Yes. You could probably catch him as he leaves, in about fifteen minutes."

Max met Deputy Smith at the store entrance. "Hey, boss," Smith whispered, as he handed the sheriff half a sandwich, "I just had an interesting conversation with a guy named Malcolm J. Burke." He grinned. "Says he heard Doc Horton threaten to kick somebody out of the country."

"I already know that, Smith." Max took a bite out of the egg salad-on-white lunch.

"Okay. But did you know Mr. Burke was a member of the same grange the Crockers attended? He had some pretty interesting stuff to say about that."

"I'm listening," the sheriff answered through the mouthful.

"Seems there was some voodoo going on, the ladies got scared and there was a ruckus, more than once."

"Uh-huh. And?" He sucked the mayonnaise off his lower lip.

"More than once, Doc Horton had to take Mrs. Crocker home, to allow time for Mr. Crocker to cool off, and — get this — he had his wife, Cindy, stay and calm down the other ladies, and she rode home with one of them."

"More than once, huh?"

"Yessir. More than once. Malcolm was very specific about that."

"Hmm," the sheriff said, as he chewed the last bite of the squishy sandwich, "sounds like the mice will play while the cat's away."

***

Doc Horton was unusually busy during his house call duties at Maude's Nursing Home, so the sheriff and his deputy hung out in Irene Hannity's office while waiting for him. She stopped by to make them welcome.

"What's up with you two?" she quipped. "Did I get a parking ticket or something?"

"In Jericho Center? I don't think so," Max joked back. "Nah, we're just following up on your uncle's car accident last night."

She frowned. "*What* accident?" She took a quick breath. "Is he okay?"

"Sore ankle, but that's about it." Max hastened to let her know the car probably just needed a new door, which could take a couple of days. "So, you probably won't be seeing them too much, for a while."

She listened while the two men furnished the details, and then asked cautiously, "Who would want to run Uncle Abe off the road?"

"Don't really know, yet." Max paused, to get the next comment just right. "I don't suppose you've noticed anybody being a real grump this morning? We figure it was somebody who was mad at him."

"Ay-yuh," the deputy noted. "It pretty much makes sense, don't you think?"

She decided to sit for a minute. "I guess it does, but the only ones who are grumpy are the same people who are almost always grumpy."

"Like who?" Max asked.

"Oh... like Bella. She's a good worker, but not very happy." Suddenly she laughed. "And there's Doc, but that's pretty normal for him, too."

"Would you say he's more grumpy today, than usual?" The sheriff let her think about it a second. "I mean, he gets mad at people, too."

"What? Well, maybe, but not mad enough to push somebody off the road." She rose to his defense. "I've known Doc since I was seventeen or eighteen. He may be gruff, but he has a heart of gold. Why, he walked me down the aisle when I got married, and before that, he stepped in to help when my father committed suicide. He and his wife, Cindy, were at my mother's side when *she* died, for goodness sake."

"Right." Max redirected his attack. "I stand corrected." He telegraphed his concern with the humble tilt of his head. "Um, may I ask, Mrs. Hannity, how your mom died?"

"Of course. She died of stomach cancer. Doc said she worked with too many chemicals, and poisons, or whatever, out there in the greenhouse... probably by wiping sweat from her mouth, or something." Her voice was softer as she finished the thought. "Guess we never think about how we can damage our very health, just by some innocent action, you know?"

***

Sheriff Duncan's sudden decision not to interview Doc Horton just yet caught the deputy by surprise. Instead, the duo headed for Burlington and the Gove Court home of the Schulers'. "We need to know what the fight was about, Smith. Otherwise, we might lack some ammunition to bring that swelled-headed Mason to his knees."

Mrs. Schuler led them into the tiny living room, where the professor sat, one foot elevated.

"How're you doing, sir?" Max inquired.

The man adjusted the ice pack on his ankle. "I think I will be walking quite well, in a day or two, thank you." He went right to the point. "So, you have some questions, no?"

"We do," the sheriff conceded. "It has come to our attention that you and Doc Horton had an argument in his office last evening, just about thirty-five minutes before your accident." He looked directly at the man. "We need to hear your version of the story." Out of the corner of his eye, he saw the wife stiffen in her chair.

"And am I obligated to speak to you without a lawyer?" the careful question came.

"No, but I find it interesting that you feel you may need one." The eyebrows came together. "Why would you need a lawyer, sir?" This time, the woman bowed her head to stare at her folded hands. "I do want to inform you that we have two witnesses who overheard the fact the doctor threatened to have your whole family deported. That sounds pretty serious to me." He pushed his hat back on his head. "Almost sounds like there might be some blackmailing going on."

Abe Schuler straightened up, adjusting the sore ankle as he did so. "Ach no! I did not go to do harm, I went to determine his guilt, and that is exactly what I accomplished. He *did* steal those boxes, and he did it to hide his role in the death of my sister's husband."

"So, Mr. Croker did *not* commit suicide?" Max asked.

"Absolutely not: We — our family — have my sister's letters, to prove it." He leaned forward. "That's what he is so angry about; why he threatened to have us deported. He poisoned Timothy, and he knows *now* that we have Freda's letters to prove it."

"She accused him, or what?" the lawman dug deeper.

"She described the whole thing," Mrs. Schuler's words burst forth. "But he did not know this until yesterday. No-no. Think about it carefully: Before he knew about the letters, he *learned* there were containers found in the Roths' attic, he stole the boxes to make sure there was no evidence that would convict him. He told on himself."

"Then, last evening, he learned about the letters," her husband added. "And now, he is panicking." He lifted a commanding fist. "You just watch, Mr. Sheriff. You just watch what he does over the next few days and weeks. He will make sure to cover his cowardly backside."

"What do you think he'll do, Professor?"

"That I cannot tell you, but there is one thing I'm certain of: He will try to make it look like Freda killed her own husband. He will do that."

Max nodded an exit mode to Deputy Smith. "Okay, I'll certainly take your advice, sir. Meanwhile, please remain available for further contacts with the Chittenden County Sheriff's Department. There may be more you can do to straighten out this situation."

"Of course," came the polite German reply.

They were almost out the door before Max remembered something else. "Say, Professor, may I ask how long after Tim Crocker's poisoning, did your sister die? And what did she die from?"

Elke was quick to answer: "Two years later, from stomach cancer. Why?"

"Who determined the cause of death, do you remember?" He watched the couple reach the same shocking conclusion.

"*Doktor* Horton," they whispered together.

Sheriff Duncan used the Schulers' telephone to warn Mark Roth. "Do not allow any work to be done in your orchard, and especially in the greenhouse. There is an investigation going on, and that area probably contains crucial evidence." He waited until Mark stopped swearing. "I'm sure you don't want us to slap an official order on you, Mr. Roth. It might look like you, yourself, are trying to hide something, you know what I mean?" The pause was short. "That's what I thought. So, it will take a few days before we get a team up there. In the meantime, stay out of that area, and keep your goats out of there, also." Another short pause. "Oh, I don't know, but you do have the lower enclosure, where Thunder used to be." He shifted his weight. "Oh, I'm sure they'll be okay there. And, by the way, you should expect those goats to be tested, because there's a good chance they've all been eating stuff tainted by chemicals." He stood up straighter. "What? Miscarriages? Okay, be sure you get that into the report, Mr. Roth."

The sheriff led the way out the door. "Smith," he ordered over his shoulder, "we also need to get moving on the murder of Eddie Roth. I told the Snoop Squad this would be an easy wrap-up, and it's already the middle of August."

"So we need to concentrate on the kid's murder, instead of the missing boxes?" the deputy asked.

Max came to a sudden stop, turning to look his helper in the eye. "I'm not sure. Have you noticed there's a connection between those two things?"

Smith was paying attention.

"It's those damned Masons, for God's sake! Don't you see it?" Max did a visual check to make certain Smith was thinking along the same lines, then went on to clarify his conclusions. "Maybe they didn't intend for it to happen, but they were involved in both situations." He moved forward, sliding into the passenger seat. When Smith got around to slip behind the wheel, he finished making the point. "In the murder, that organization came through with all sorts of help in doing the cleanup at the river bank, and then, when it came to the stolen boxes, they came together again, to hide evidence. It's the same bunch." He pressed his lips together. "Same bunch, different public images."

Smith started the vehicle. "Ay-yuh, same thing, only different." He pulled out onto the five-way intersection and turned left toward UVM and Winooski. "See, the way it looks to me," the deputy explained, "they used the boy's death to glorify the work of the Masons, and, *at the same time,* they were still an organization that was hiding behind secret oaths and activities. So even when they were doing good, they were scamming the public, hiding behind that phony 'superior' image, you know?"

"Okay." The sheriff was listening.

"And now that same group is trying to hide evidence that might incriminate one of their own. Getting rid of the attic stuff and then trying to get rid of the pesticides just shows more sneaking around, if you ask me. Where's all that uppityup, inside knowledge of the 'truth,' now? So, yeah, they're just as crooked and flawed as the rest of us."

For a few minutes, it was quiet. Then the sheriff laid a hand across his own forehead. "Aw, for gawd's sake," he whined.

"What is it, Sheriff?" the driver asked.

"That damned teacher is *right*. These people are two-faced, manipulating shysters. And all the philanthropic activities they take part in, do not excuse one ounce of the underhanded — no, *highhanded* — manipulation of the general public." He slapped his thigh. "They are a massive collection of hypocrites. Good God!!"

"Yessir. They probably think we're all *so* stupid, fawning over all their good deeds, bowing down to their great wisdom and mercy." He shifted down, and the engine ground down Colchester Avenue, in second gear.

"But you know what makes me *really* mad, Smith?" He paused to make it a more dramatic point: "Walter Taft is right."

"No kidding, boss, the guy turns out to be onto something."

Max Duncan went on to finish his statement. "The sad reality is, if those secret societies get their way, that important paper he's writing for UVM will probably end up in a trash pile, somewhere in the county dumpsite, where it will be torn to pieces by junkyard dogs, and nibbled into oblivion by hungry field mice."

CHAPTER TWENTY-FIVE

Home

It was almost as if Anna Roth knew what was going on. Donna and Walter were celebrating their success in getting custody of Jenny, although knowing they had only a few weeks to secure proper housing for this minor child. The Collinses and the Shorts were helping, combing the countryside for an affordable rental close to Burlington, where Donna worked. Walter was already looking for a teaching position in that area, for two reasons: He needed to work nearer to his wife's workplace to cut down on travel expenses, and he wanted to get out from under the tyrannical rule of the most powerful Jericho School Board member, Doc Horton. It was already the third week of August. Walter was finished with his summer classes, and had submitted his thesis on "The History of Secret Societies." It was a frantic Sunday afternoon, when they got the news... Anna had passed on, peacefully, just before dawn.

That quickly, the search for housing went from rental to ownership, opening a whole new search. Of course, it would take time for the insurance money to come through, but Don Collins figured the Tafts could arrange to rent the new property until the payment arrived from the insurer. Jenny cried a lot that week, while Donna leaned on her husband's strength, and by the next Sunday, they had settled on a small bungalow, just three houses down from where the Schulers lived, on Gove Court.

"It's only a block from the Burlington Transit bus route to Edmunds High," Donna reminded her sister. "And you can finish high school with your friend, Essie."

"That's perfect!" Jenny exclaimed. She had started high school at that very location, just before she and Eddie had left the Children's Home. She hugged her brother-in-law. "Now I can do this, because you're not my teacher, any more."

And indeed, he was not. In fact, he wasn't anybody's teacher any more, since he had given notice at Jericho High School. Now, he sat amongst the mover's cartons and sighed in relief. It was going to be good to get away from Doc Horton and all that stuff about the stolen boxes. Still, he knew that situation was not entirely over yet... He knew too much.

But then, so did the Collinses, the Shorts, Andrew and his grandpa, and even the two law officers. All of these people knew that Doc Horton was in deep trouble, and that was tantamount to declaring war on one of Vermont's most powerful secret societies.

***

Across the street, just three houses up from the Taft bungalow, Professor Abraham Schuler was driving his brand-new 1950 Ford into his driveway. Before he even drew to a stop, Elke and the two children were coming off the porch, exclamations pouring forth with each light-footed step.

"Oh, so beautiful!" Essie called out, taking in the magical gleam of the black four-door sedan.

David spun around the vehicle like a top, enthralled by the chrome strip of the divided windshield, a silvery line which continued down the center of the hood to a smart ornament, then flared out across the front bumper. He noted other strips glistening along the sides of the car, and then the matching orbs inside the whitewalls beneath. "*Wunderbar!*" he shouted to his father.

Elke just stood there, hands over her delighted smile, until Abe approached her and gave the German version of a passionate hug. "We have payments of twenty American dollars each month," he proudly announced. "I am thinking we are now *real Americans!*"

Their very first road trip was a visit to Stowe, where they engaged once more with the Von Trapps. Of course, there were several short rides, since that was a large family, and then there was the usual pitching in to help their hosts in the dining room and kitchen that evening. When things finally settled down, there was music and stories and fond memories of the homeland, now forever changed. "But we are so blessed, to be here in the United States," Essie had spoken up during a solemn moment.

"Ach so!" the youngest Von Trapp boy shouted. Then he and David went into a silly dance, whereupon, both Maria and Elke took their young sons by the scruff of the neck, and guided them toward bedtime preparations.

The professor took advantage of this mothering move, to lean forward and issue a whispered request into the ear of his host. "I would have a word with you, please, as soon as we end this evening's festivities."

Thirty minutes later, in the cellar of the Von Trapp Family Lodge, Abe watched his friend open the newly installed safe. The kindly man reached inside and pulled out a package of letters, neatly tied with a slender yellow ribbon. "Here they are," he spoke quietly to his guest. "Do we have a camera?"

"We do," Abe replied. "It shouldn't take too long."

Indeed, the professor would secure the evidence he needed, get a good night's rest, and be back home by Monday afternoon. On Tuesday, he would have a trusted student in the photo lab at the nearby business college print out some very important shots of Freda Crocker's letters… in duplicate.

***

It was the same Monday — the third week of August — that Professor Schuler's family got back from Stowe, when Max finally made that official visit to Roth Ranch. "Time to get this murder solved," he said to his deputy. He had the office call ahead, so Mark Roth was at the front door when the two lawmen arrived at ten o'clock that morning. He ushered them into the attractive living room, where, as requested, both Kathy and Rhonda were waiting. This visit, the sheriff had no friendly smile.

"So, I have a few questions, and would appreciate prompt and truthful answers." He looked around the room. "I will eventually get the truth, so we might as well get right to it, and not waste my time, nor yours."

Mark didn't like the sound of that. "Wait a minute. Should we have a lawyer here? What kind of questions are you talking about?"

"Well, for one thing, Mr. Roth, have you allowed anyone to move soil in your orchard?"

"Of course not. You pretty much ordered me to put a stop to that." He huffed out the rest of the story. "That made some people pretty damned mad. I owed them a favor, and I had to renege on that. Pretty damned embarrassing, I can tell you. A man is only as good as his word, you know. These guys are really pissed."

"What guys are they, sir? Anybody I know?"

The rancher twitched into a defensive position, then sat down in an overstuffed chair. "Mr. Morrison, the excavation guy who got Thunder's body out of the quicksand."

"That's only one guy. Who else?"

"Uh, he didn't really say." Mark was confused. "What difference does it make?"

"I'm not sure yet," the sheriff answered. "Just thought maybe you would know, since you seem to be so embarrassed about it." He signaled Smith to take notes. "Alright then, you don't really know who else is mad at you?"

"Aw, I guess there's a bunch of fellas that belong to the Freemasons, or something. He said they would not be happy with how ungrateful I was." Mr. Roth's shoulder sloped.

"Did he threaten you, sir?"

The cattleman's long legs moved slowly out in front of his sitting position. "Aw, hell, I don't know."

Max moved carefully to the next subject. "Well, let's talk about how Morrison Excavations actually got your prize bull's body out of the riverbank." He looked upward, picturing the rescue. "That was quite an operation, wasn't it? A lot of publicity about that, and the funeral for Eddie, wouldn't you say?" Mark nodded in agreement. "But at the end of the day, it turned out that the *real* story, was that Eddie had sustained a fatal blow at the base of his skull, and that blow, according to the county coroner, was the real cause of death." He paused to lick his tongue slowly across his teeth. "Sad, isn't it, that this young kid gets killed, and nobody seems to know why, or how?"

Suddenly, Rhonda came to life from her seat on the sofa. "Well, I can tell you a little bit about that," she snapped. "He was killed by his older sister, for the insurance money!"

"Rhonda!" her mother objected, "you have no proof of that."

The girl leaned forward, intent on making her statement. "I already *told* you! She was the only one down there, when

Daddy Mark went to get his rifle. She was the only one *down* there!"

Sheriff Duncan turned to Kathy Roth. "Did you call to your husband, from the front porch, to stop him from going any farther into the quicksand to help Eddie?"

"I... I did," came her careful answer. "Why?"

"At that time, do you recall your daughter being in the upper pasture with the cattle?"

The woman frowned, trying to recall. "I don't remember."

Max pressed in. "After Mr. Roth got his rifle and went back down to the river, did you notice where your daughter was?"

"Hold it!" Mark didn't like what he was hearing. "Don't answer that, Kathy." He moved forward in his seat, to look Max in the face. "Where are you going with this, Sheriff?"

Max was ready. "Alright, Mr. Roth, you told me, yourself, that Rhonda had a couple of run-ins with Eddie, one of which, where she intentionally trained that bull to hate the boy. You had to take the slingshot away, remember?" He accepted the man's acknowledgment. "And we have no witness that she was actually in the upper pasture between the time you left to get your rifle, and came back to put Thunder out of his misery." He drew a long breath, before he said it. "This young lady is a slingshot champion, who can hit a target from as much as two hundred yards, if she has the right ammunition, and even if she has to use a river rock, she could have struck her target."

"That's enough!" the mother objected. "Why should she ever do such a thing? *How* could she do such a thing?"

"She could have done it, by hiding behind the trees, like she did, training Thunder to mistrust his caretaker," the lawman replied. "And she would have done it, because she wanted the insurance money, to finance her career as a champion in the slingshot competition." He looked directly at Kathy. "You know how much she wanted that, didn't you?"

"Oh no," she stated, "not that much. Never. I don't believe that for one minute."

There was a gasping denial from the girl. "No-no-no-no!" Her face was white with fear. "No, I didn't. No, I didn't do that. I was in the upper... I was not down there until after Daddy Mark shot Thunder." There was a short, frantic breath. "I wasn't down there. Only Donna was down there. She was the only one. Just her and Eddie and Thunder." There were real tears coming. "I swear, it was Donna. It *had* to be!" The words came between frantic sobs. "She was... she was there. She... she could throw a river rock like a bullet... like a bullet... she did it... she had to, she had to!" The overwhelmed girl collapsed against her mother's shoulder.

"What the hell are you doing?" Mark was furious. "I should kick your sorry asses out of here, you know that?" He stood up. "In fact, that's what I'm doing right now." He swooped the air with a finger toward the front door. "There was no one down there when I left to get my rifle, except Donna, Eddie, and my frantic prize bull!"

The sheriff thought the interview was over, and it was a failed one, at that. But there was a soft hum from his deputy, which brought everything to a standstill. "Sheriff," Smith said quietly, "what shape was the river rock that killed the kid?"

Max dug quickly for the answer. "Okay, it was, according to the report, 'oval-shaped, and flat on the impact site.' Why do you ask?"

Deputy Smith looked up at the steer horn trophy on the mantle, and then moved over to inspect the ends of the sawed-off tips. "Like this?" he asked.

Mark Roth let the lawmen take the trophy in for the Snoop Squad to compare with the fatal wound at the base of Eddie Roth's skull. It was a complete match. In addition, traces of the boy's blood were found on the tip of the bull's right horn. The frantic Thunder had only tried to protect himself, having no concept of the compassionate young fellow, who was speaking softly, and attempting to stroke a helpless animal.

As these things fell into place the next few days, Deputy Smith reached for a conclusion. "So, there was no murder at Roth Ranch, after all?"

"Oh, I wouldn't exactly say that," Sheriff Duncan replied.

***

The news spread quickly. Donna and Jenny were both relieved and embarrassed. They discussed making a trip up to the ranch, to apologize, but Walter convinced them it would be better to just let it go. "No need to bring up things that those folks didn't even know you thought about them." And the same reasoning prevailed up at the ranch, where Rhonda went into a silent sulk. Not only had Donna been proven innocent, but Anna Roth had died, and the insurance money was no longer an issue. It was going to be life on the ranch, whether in Vermont, or in Texas. She began to express her frustration by pelting the apple trees with rocks, but Kathy and Mark put a stop to that, forbidding the girl to go into the tainted orchard. "How do we even know it's poisoned?" she objected.

"That's what we're told," Mark answered. "It has something to do with those damned boxes that got stolen."

"What about them, anyway?" the girl persisted. "Why did they get stolen? What was in them? All I ever saw was a bunch of books and old papers."

Kathy was surprised. "You went through those boxes?"

"Yup. Well, not all of them. Just the ones with the witch books and the ceremonial junk from a grange, or something."

The two parents exchanged a look. "Come over here and sit down, young lady," Daddy Mark said, pointing to the porch swing.

After a few minutes, the Roths were quite enlightened. Mark rubbed his chin as he spoke. "Looks like somebody's hiding bad history, if you ask me."

"Mmm," Kathy agreed. "And I don't think we need to get involved. This is something that probably involves Mrs. Hannity, the lady we bought this place from." She rose to get back to work in the house. "We need to back off," she shot over her shoulder.

"Yeah, well," Mark called after her, "I still want my land back." He turned to Rhonda. "We'll just see about this."

"Yes, sir, Daddy Mark. We either get our land back, or we go back to Texas, right?"

The man let out a low moan. "Come on, girl. We've got chores to do."

***

The Tafts held a barbeque on Labor Day weekend, in their new backyard. The Schulers, Collinses, and Shorts were there. Irene Hannity was invited, but it was a busy time at Maude's Nursing Home, so she couldn't make it. It was a happy gathering, with the new housewarming gift of a croquet set providing much of the entertainment. The warm sun faded as the afternoon grew later, and the eight adults sat in webbed folding chairs, watching the three youngsters in another round of mallet-smacking fun. The professor, decked out in traditional lederhosen — leather shorts with embroidered suspenders — was enjoying the last of the genuine imported German beer, courtesy of his host. It was then that Irene's name came up in the quiet conversation.

"Too bad Irene couldn't make it," Donna commented. "She's done so much for Jenny, and we really wanted to thank her, right along with you folks." She twisted the empty plastic picnic glass in her hands. "It's been a rocky six months for her, for sure."

"But Jenny has grown throughout that whole thing," Connie noted. She addressed the German lady. "She speaks in tongues because of you, Elke. That was a major stabilizer after Eddie's death, and then during her time with her mother. Oh my, singing in tongues, and the tender tears of her mama."

"Gott is good," Frau Schuler replied. "He was watching out for Jenny, when she went to work with Irene, not true? We should remember that the child was spared the calamity of the earthquake at the ranch, because Irene invited her to stay at the nursing home that weekend." She shook her head wisely. "That was not a coincidence, I think."

"Ach so," Abe Schuler interjected. "Irene, herself has not had an easy time, either." He hooked his thumbs under the straps of his lederhosen, then made visual contact with the schoolteacher. "Did you know, Walter, that she is my niece?" The young host raised his eyebrows as a noncommittal courtesy, since he wasn't sure of what the professor really knew, either. "Yes, indeed," the older educator continued, "she lost her father before she even got married; her mother died shortly after that wedding, then her husband went missing in action during the terrible attack on Pearl Harbor."

"Oh my goodness," Connie murmured, glancing over at Greta. "We didn't know that. How tragic."

"So, you can see where Irene gets all that compassion," Elke noted.

Don made a quick decision to see what else the Schulers knew about Mrs. Hannity. "Well, that certainly shows how much it meant to have that special box of memoirs from the Roths' attic." He took a sip from his plastic glass. "She seemed so pleased. Too bad she didn't know who left it on her doorstep."

There was a quick glance between Herr and Frau Schuler. The man unhooked his thumbs and emitted an ironic chuckle.

"That is no mystery to *us*. We are her closest family. We know."

Four heads bent closer, but it was Don who asked, "And would that be something you could share with us?"

"Why not?" the professor said. "We have nothing to hide. The man is a scoundrel, and we have confronted him, already." He went into teaching mode. "Ach so, the very saintly *Doktor* Horton is the thief, sir. There is no doubt."

Gerald Short took the lead, this time. "No doubt, Professor?" was his gentle query. "How can you be so sure?"

"We have letters," the man replied. "Letters from my sister, Freda Crocker." He leaned forward, tugged at his knee-high stockings, mentally assembling his presentation. "Yes. We have copies of these letters, and we have the originals. And these letters tell us that Timothy Crocker did not commit suicide. He was murdered by the esteemed *Doktor*."

The other five appeared to be speechless, so Greta stepped in. "Your sister, Freda, told you this?" Herr Schuler affirmed this with a solid shake of his head. "How did she know? And why didn't she notify the authorities?"

"Because she was having an affair with this noble man of medicine." His head bowed. "Yes, how sad." His head raised to finish the story. "When she tried to break it off, he threatened to blame her for the murder." He blinked sadly. "She was his unwilling mistress, until she died of stomach cancer, a couple of years later." He looked around, one face at a time, seeking a sympathetic response.

"Oh my goodness," Connie said, again. "If you have these letters, this should all come together, and the man should be charged."

"Uh, babe," Don held up a staying hand. "You forget that the suspect in this theft is a very prominent member of the Freemasons."

"Your husband is right," Herr Schuler assured her. "But if the local law officers put all our evidence together, we may defeat that whole organization, at least on this one matter."

He sat up straighter. "Let me say right now, that the sheriff is aware of the letters and the confrontation between the *Doktor* and me. Part of the reason we were so happy to come here today, was that we hoped we could determine your willingness to testify, and put that man in prison… and keep him from publically accusing Freda of murder." He folded his hands on his lap, asking one last thing. "Will you share what you know about the boxes with Elke and me? Was there anything in there that would prove Freda's innocence, that would absolve her of killing her husband?"

There was a short silence. Then Don spoke up. "All we know is that there was evidence of Tim's involvement with witchcraft, and he was mixing it with the Grange rituals, or ceremonies, whatever you want to call them. We know he was exhibiting erratic behavior, and Freda was at the end of her wits. If what you say about her having an affair with Doc Horton is true, we can certainly understand how she would have turned to him — or any other sympathetic fellow — for emotional support."

"Listen, as sad as that would be, there is something else that was going on," Connie chimed in. "It was that *satanic connection*." She wobbled her head at this powerful liaison. "Timothy opened the door to evil powers that overwhelmed him and his secret society activities. He got in, way over his head, and when Doc Horton got in on it, so did he. He may be a 33rd degree Mason, but he's no match for the principalities that rule in Satan's kingdom."

"That's exactly right, Connie." Walter could not resist highlighting the main point of his thesis. "People like Doc and his buddies all want to be heroes, but they just aren't up to it. No elitist club can make them heroes, either. Humans can't fix humans, nor correct the human condition. Not even Eddie, who was probably the most noble of them all." He set his jaw, speaking emphatically. "Only Jesus Christ can do that, and only Jesus Christ is the *real* Hero!"

Everyone but Abe Schuler nodded in agreement. Instead, the man went back to the immediate task. "I am asking this next question, to get some reassurance about my sister, so please be patient with me." He looked directly at Walter. "Would you be so kind as to share with me, what was in those boxes?"

The host leaned back in the lawn chair. "I was trying to avoid hurting anybody, because I suspected there was stuff there that was inflammatory, and now I see I was right. I didn't want to tell Sheriff Duncan what all that stuff was, because I was hoping to settle things quietly — if there was actually anything to settle."

"So, my sister's situation *was* revealed in those materials?"

"No, Professor." Walter looked at the other two couples. "I think we can all agree on that." The Shorts and Collinses agreed. "Mostly, it was stuff that showed Tim's involvement with the spiritual dark side."

"How do you know that Freda was not involved in the witchcraft?" Elke asked.

"The grandfather of one of my students, Ken Pearson, filled in the details of how Tim was ousted from being Worthy Master, and how that particular grange hall had been disbanded."

Professor Schuler had noticed the other two couples seemed to know what was in the boxes, as well. "Am I correct, that you are all aware of the contents of these stolen goods? How did that happen, if I may ask?"

"Safety measures," Connie answered. "If one of us had an 'accident' there were five of us who had back-up lists."

The German gentleman seemed to be a bit surprised, but he sat quietly listening, as the group told how they had hired a lawyer and an undercover team, to find the stolen boxes. "*Mein Gott!*" he declared, when they finished filling him in on their escapades. "You folks are like the FBI, I think."

CHAPTER TWENTY-SIX

Secrets

He was off the hook with the Snoop Squad, so Sheriff Max Duncan turned his full attention to Doc Horton and the stolen boxes. It should have been a matter of petty theft, but the suspect was so arrogant, the lawman smelled another rat. They were once again sitting in the cab of one of the department's official trucks, gazing out across Lake Champlain from Burlington's Battery Park. Max slowly unwrapped his ice cream bar as he spoke. "Okay, let's add it all up. We know for a fact, that Doc and Andrew stole those things and stashed them in the library basement shortly after the earthquake. We also know there's a small wood stove in the waiting room of his office. When I finally questioned him about the missing items, he suggested I check the county dumpsite 'for empty cartons,' I believe he said."

Smith pulled the paper back from the top edge of the cold treat. "Sounds like he burned what he could, then dumped the cartons." He had a thought. "Probably made sure the cardboard got soaked, in order to remove any fingerprints."

"Probably did. Had enough time to do all that, before I was finally onto him."

"Did his wife see him burning that stuff?" The deputy took a bite off one corner of the bar. "I don't see how she could have missed that — the weather was too warm for using the stove for heat, right?"

"Doesn't matter. A wife can't be forced to testify against her husband." Max assessed where to bite into the creamy chocolate. "Anyway, she's not the type to make waves. I could see that when I talked to her. She just wants to be a good nurse and live a quiet life in a quiet town."

"Wait a minute. If her husband is so high up in the Masons, isn't she also active in, um, what's the women's group called? Oh yeah, the Eastern Star."

"Probably, but I know some of those ladies. There are a couple who are regular wallflowers, just standing there beside their bellowing husbands, like good little wives. Trust me, she fills the bill."

"Any other suspects?" the deputy wanted to know.

"Nope. Just those two, and the kid probably didn't have anything to do with destroying all that stuff," Max noted. "When he came clean, he came clean. He would have included that, if he'd been guilty of it. He was scared out of his shorts, remember?"

There was a moment of serious munching of the frozen treats before Smith had another idea. "Maybe Doc buried the stuff up there in the Roths' orchard. After all, he asked that excavator guy — Morrison — to make a deal and go up there to dig up the place."

The sheriff stopped eating, to think about that. "He might have stashed it up there, but I doubt it. He wanted to get rid of the poisons left in the greenhouse, I think. And probably the pesticides that are in the top layers of the rest of the orchard. The Roths have goats grazing there, and he says the nannies are dropping kids long before they're full term. That tells you something about the soil and weeds."

"Oh," his partner grunted. "So what *about* the Roths? Do they have any idea what was in their attic?"

"They do now, but I doubt they were aware of any oddities before they had Taft take them home."

"I suppose they weren't aware of the pesticides in amongst the apple trees, either." He licked a drip from the edge of the bar. "Heck, I bet they didn't know that Freda lady was a scientist, either."

"She was a botanist," Max corrected him. "Grew hybrids, I think."

"Well, my question is, do you think they would testify about the poisoned orchard the Mason buddies wanted to destroy?"

"Probably only under subpoena. Roth doesn't want trouble with the Masons."

"Right. He would like to have Doc exonerated, so he leases his land to Marty Morrison."

"Whether or not we prosecute this case, he may get his land back," the sheriff clarified the issue. "That could very well happen, so why would he even want to get involved? Nah, he would have to be subpoenaed." He took another short munch. "I'd rather have willing witnesses, you know?"

"Hmm," Smith mused, "probably pretty much the same situation with the grandpa, Mr. Pearson."

"Probably. And then he's a Mason, as well." He licked his lower lip. "Now, on the other hand, the kid might want to make a deal to testify, for a lighter sentence or fine."

"So Andrew is a 'maybe.'" Smith pulled the sticky paper back farther. "And what about this Malcolm guy? Think those allegations about an affair are true? And if so, could Freda's death also have occurred at the hands of Doc?"

Max brightened a bit. "Now, there's a thought: Probably needed to be sure she never spilled the beans."

"Okay, so that's one willing witness, boss." Another bite slid into his mouth. "Mmm!" He had to squish the cold on his tongue. "What about Walter Taft, and his undercover friends?"

"Taft can only testify about what was in the boxes. Same with his friends — those who know. As for the undercover team, they can only repeat what Malcolm and *his* buddies told them. More likely a waste of time."

"Aw crap," the deputy moaned. "We don't really have much to charge the guy with — only petty theft, and he'll just get a slap on the wrist."

"Probably," Max agreed. "And the judge is probably a Mason, as well."

The two lawmen slowly finished their ice cream, and then it was time to get back on patrol. As they were pulling out onto Battery Street, the boss snapped his fingers, just inches from his own chin. "Of course! That's it!" He grinned at Deputy Smith. "The only real evidence is the murder victims, themselves."

"Okay...?" Smith waited for the rest of it.

"We need to exhume those bodies!" Sheriff Duncan concluded.

***

"They need to get those awful chairs out of the attic, and then write scriptures on the beams and ceilings," Greta told Gerald.

He observed the Bible in her hands. "I think you are talking about Matthew, chapter twelve."

"Right." She paraphrased the three verses: "About the man who cleanses his 'house,' then backslides, and the former occupier — a demonic spirit — returns, bringing seven other spirits which are far more wicked."

"Well, you and Connie kind of did that cleansing, when we got the rocking chair out, and Walter took the boxes home. Why do you think it needs to be done, again?"

"Because nobody in that household is saved. Kathy seems to be on her way to that, but Mark and Rhonda are blatantly stiff-necked. Either one of them could unknowingly open a door, by taking drugs or getting into some sort of sexual sin, and — boom!" She stroked the pages of that open book. "The thing is, not to get too hung up on demons; seeing them in every closet. But to bear in mind that they are out there, just on the other side of the veil, waiting for somebody to open up a door through which they may enter the earthly realm and create chaos… to their great enjoyment."

"I see," he said, slowly. He waited for the neighbor's dog to stop barking, sliding forward on his favorite back porch seat. "What you're saying is basically true; demons tend to hang around their old haunts even after they are silenced, and God knows, there were a lot of them up in that ritual-filled attic. But our concerns might be misconstrued by the Roth household as just plain, old interference."

She smiled. "That's why I was hoping you could come up with a way we could do this."

He smiled back. "You know how I hate to put the cart before the horse. So, we need to get those folks saved, before we get the attic saved!" He appreciated her chuckle. "It comes right down to evangelism, don't you agree?" She did. "Okay, got any ideas how we can get the horse in place?"

Her eyes brightened. Kathy is looking for a church. She tried the one in Jericho Center, but Rhonda was not so happy there." She had a second thought on that. "Of course, all the people Rhonda was unhappy with, except for Mrs. Hannity, have moved out of town." She patted the book. "Too bad they don't have a youth group."

"Now, there's a thought, hon. Maybe somebody from our church could offer to organize one up there."

The neighbor's dog let out a series of raging barks, then responded to a sharp command and slinked into its doghouse.

"Or, we could just invite them to a barbeque or something," he suggested. "It would be a lot simpler."

"Oh, that sounds like a great idea. How about next weekend? I could call Kathy right away."

"Sure. That settles that." He slid back into his chair, folding his hands over his belt buckle.

She saw the bemused expression. "What?"

"Oh, I was just thinking," he said, crossing his ankles, "what you should do about that rocker you're sitting in." She frowned. "Now, let me finish, Greta." He took a breath. "You prayed over that thing and silenced at least a couple of demonic presences, would you agree?" She responded with a reluctant nod. "So, what happens when you pass on to Heaven, or for some reason, the chair becomes the property of a non-believer, who commits a sin and opens the doors for those things to come back and do their noisy rocking chair thing, again?" He watched her jaw gently drop. "Think about it: Demons cannot possess *things*, only bodies. They can only *haunt* things, like a house or a garden, or even a baby carriage. Now listen, if they can come back into the area of the attic — in larger numbers, by the way — they can come back to haunt that old rocking chair, also in greater numbers."

She was speechless.

An hour later, Greta had recovered from the demon lecture, and asking the Roths to a backyard gathering after church next Sunday. Kathy responded with pleasure, but noted there were too many daily chores for the family to be away for that many hours, even on a Sunday. "Well, then, could we bring the picnic up to you on Saturday, instead? That way, we would come in work clothes, and help with a few chores."

"Oh my," the woman responded, "that would be a special treat, for sure."

"Let me see if the Collinses can come along," Greta added, with a laugh. "We'll make a real day of it."

The four of them arrived at seven in the morning. Food was put into the kitchen, and then each one of them was assigned to help with various chores until the noon hour rolled around. Mark was in his glory, taking the leadership role he had held in the military. He was actually smiling as he washed up at the kitchen sink.

"Now, Mark, you need to do that upstairs in the bathroom," his wife admonished him. "We're real busy here."

The meal featured Italian sausages, topped high with a selection of condiments — a treat for the beef-eating Roths. A cold macaroni salad came alongside a luscious mixture of fresh greens laced with Italian dressing, and dessert was pistachio ice cream. Kathy added homemade pickles and her special Company Cookies. As they sat down to the feast-laden table, Gerald said grace by making a simple remark: "Thank God for good food and good friends, right, folks?"

An hour later the three men were sitting out on the big porch, resting their full stomachs, Mark puffing away on his pipe, when Don asked Gerald about the upcoming guest speaker at church. "Is that tomorrow, or not 'til next Sunday?"

"It's tomorrow. Interesting guy, Mark." The cattleman listened politely as Gerald went on. "He's been a missionary in North Africa for the last ten years."

"Hmm," Mark hummed through his pipe stem. "Sounds like he didn't know there was a war going on."

"Oh, he knew there was a war going on, for sure. If the witch doctors weren't after him, the Nazis were, and sometimes it was the both of them." The man's gentle smile relayed his admiration. "He was rescued a couple of times by American forces. I'm looking forward to hearing the whole story."

Don cleared his throat. "As a veteran, you know what it is to really earn your stripes, Mark. I'm thinking you might really enjoy hearing this guy."

Kathy pushed the screen door open, leading the ladies out to join the conversation. "Hearing what guy?" she inquired.

Don explained, while the women took seats, then Kathy commented: "That *would* be interesting. We should try to make it."

Mr. Roth drew smoke from the pipe and stared out at the upper pasture. "Got our hands full, right now. Need to find us a bull, get the herd built up. Hope to lease out some land, get some income to hire some permanent help." He puffed once more. "Got too much going on, right now, but appreciate the invite."

It was a solid decline, so the guests drew back, even though Kathy seemed distressed, fiddling her thumbs nervously in her lap. There was a little more conversation and then it was time to depart.

As the car commenced the winding drive up to Lee River Road, Kathy turned to her husband. "After all we got done this morning, I would think we'd have time to attend one church service. It would have been so interesting, and probably would have done the three of us a world of good, just getting off this place for a couple of hours." She rose to go into the house. "That's a big part of your problem, Mark Roth. You have no desire to look past your own wounds and opinions." She pulled the screen open and motioned for Rhonda to get inside to help. "Well, you can sit here and grouse all you want, but Rhonda and I aren't going to do it with you. She and I will be going to hear that man's talk."

"No you won't, woman," he growled. "You won't be taking that truck anywhere."

She stood up very straight. "I already hid the keys, Mark. Tomorrow, Rhonda and I will be going to that church service, and you'd better not try to stop us." She glared defiantly as she switched to military lingo. "Do I make myself perfectly clear, mister?"

When the door slammed in his face, Mark Roth stood in shock. He had never beaten a woman in his whole life, let alone shot one. He was furious, but helpless. He stomped off to the barn, muttering over and over, "Well, I'll be God-damned."

And, by his own choice — at least for the time being, he *was*.

A few days later, Greta asked her husband to cut up the demon-attracting rocking chair and incinerate it in their backyard burn barrel, piece by piece. Gerald was proud of her decision to sacrifice the nicely decorated antique, but there was more. "That's fifty dollars going up in smoke, kiddo. That takes a lot of dedication."

Greta smiled faintly, thinking of Elke Schuler, who had, in the burning of that one hundred dollar rug, demonstrated *twice* as much dedication.

***

"No matter how we handle this," Sheriff Duncan said to his deputy, "she will have to know all the bad details. So this will not be easy for anybody."

"Yessir," the patrol partner agreed. "Do you want me to come in with you?"

"Oh yeah. She's going to need more than just my word for it; you'll need to back me up, and you'll need to have your notes handy, so she can see the series of events." He patted his pocket, making sure he had his own notebook ready. The walk along the sidewalk that led to Maude's Nursing Home's front porch seemed extra-long, and Irene Hannity opened the front door before the two men had even climbed the front steps. "Thanks for calling ahead," she said, ushering them once again into her office. A clock on the wall showed they were right on time for the seven o'clock appointment. Before she closed the door, there were whispered instructions for no interruptions, then she reached over and pulled the cord to shut the venetian blinds, eliminating any distractions out there in the cool September dusk. There was a wave of her hand toward a small sofa. The official duo sat gingerly on the front edges of the cushions. Seeing this, Irene pulled her desk chair into a more intimate circle, sitting down directly in front of them. "I can see by your faces, you weren't kidding when you told me we had a serious matter to discuss." She folded her hands on her lap. "What do you need, gentlemen?"

Max took the lead. "We need to start by talking about the stolen boxes." He pulled out his spiral notebook. "We have done a thorough investigation, and we now know they were stolen from Mr. Taft's home by Doctor Horton."

Her eyes focused on the sheriff's face. "Doc Horton? *My* Doc Horton? Are you sure?"

"Yes, ma'am. We have a witness."

"And just who would that be?" she challenged him.

"The teenager who helped him do it. Kid named Andrew, one of Taft's students."

There was a short huff. "I don't believe it. Can you prove this?"

Deputy Smith pulled out his notebook, flipping to a tagged page. "Here's my record of his initial confession. You can see the date and the place where that occurred." He watched her take a closer look. "And he also signed an official statement."

"And what about Doc? Did he sign a statement, too?" Both men shook their heads no. "So there you are! The kid is probably lying."

"Well, if he was lying, he did a thorough job of it, giving some very specific details, and standing right there next to his own grandfather," Max stated. "Why, he even apologized to his grandfather, right in front of us."

She folded her arms. "Okay, so let's see what the youngster said. What were the details?"

"This won't be pretty. You sure you want those details?" Max had hoped she would skip this part.

"I'm tougher than you think, Sheriff. Shoot."

He told her about Andrew and Bella getting caught, Doc's offer to cover for the kid if he would go along with doing Doc a favor, and the theft that took place in the aftermath of the earthquake. She sat stone-faced through all of it. "Well," she finally concluded, "I can fire Bella, and suspend Doc, but I'm not going to help you do *him* any more harm. After all, it was so sweet of him to let me have my memories back. I am grateful that he didn't destroy those." There was a soft cluck of the tongue. "No, no harm to him. I'll gladly give him a good letter of reference."

"Uh, you might want to think that one over, Mrs. Hannity. You don't know why the man stole all those boxes." Max waited for her to see there was more.

"Okay," she finally said. "Why did he steal them? My guess is that he wanted to protect *me* somehow."

"It looks like he was trying to keep you, and who knows who else, from certain information that might be found in all those books and paperwork." The sheriff drew out his list of the contents, incomplete though it was, to show her what he knew.

She actually took the notebook, scanning down the lines. "I left all that in the attic? I had no idea." She looked up. "Where is all this stuff now?"

"When I confronted him with this theft, he laughed and told me I should check the county dumpsite for empty cartons." Max's eyebrows and shoulders moved up and down in sync. "We think he probably burned everything."

"So, you're saying he was getting rid of something? Like what, Sheriff?" She noted the quick glance between the men. "I take it, there's a lot more that will be hard to hear. Well, I'd better know all of it, or I won't make informed decisions. Let me have it."

"Yes, ma'am. So, we have a witness that your father, when he was head of the grange, was mixing those ceremonies with satanic rituals and curses." He waited, letting her digest that part. "A lot of the books in those boxes were about occult recipes and practices. Another box contained Grange paraphernalia. But anyway, this same witness reported erratic behavior during the Grange meetings, where your mother would break down. She was taken home on many occasions by Doc, to keep her from being harmed by your unstable father. The same witness accused Doc and Freda of becoming involved." He paused, not sure how to put the next thing out there. "So, apparently, your mother was writing letters to your aunt and uncle in Germany, where she not only admitted to the affair, but accused Doc of creating your dad's 'suicide.'"

Her mouth drooped before she asked. "Uncle Abe has letters from my mother? And they say all this?"

"Yes, ma'am." Max looked at the floor. "And there's more: When Freda tried to end the affair, Doc threatened to charge her with Tim's death."

"He could have done that," she noted softly, "since he was both the attending doctor and the coroner."

"Exactly." Max tapped the closed notebook on the palm of one hand.

Irene sat staring at her own shoes for a minute. When she lifted her face, the eyes were filled with tears. "This is heartbreaking, you know." The two lawmen politely kept their own sights toward the floor. "I just can't believe all this. Are you sure you can prove that he killed my dad?"

"Your mom's letters told how Tim had a temper tantrum and passed out from a heart attack in the attic. She said she dragged him down to their bed, so no one would see what Tim had been doing up there. She called the only doctor nearby — Doc — who took the opportunity to put the crazy man out of his misery. He injected Tim with a diluted solution of one of her pesticides or fertilizers... she wasn't sure which one." Max made eye contact. "That's what your mom said in one of her letters. That's according to your aunt and uncle."

"They never told me all that." She stared at the ceiling. "Although, they seemed very interested in being friends with the Roths." She suddenly stiffened. "So exactly what did the Roths know about those boxes? Were they in on this, also?"

"No, they actually found out, long after the things were stolen from Taft. And now, they don't want to get involved with any investigation, because of the Mason clique here in the area." Max stopped, to let that bit of information get absorbed.

"Oh my gosh. This is really bad. I had no idea. All that evidence... what are you going to do with Doc?"

"Unfortunately, Mrs. Hannity, we have all these witnesses and evidence, but we can't prove a thing. The fact is, we cannot get a solid case against Doc Horton, and even if we did, the sentencing judge would likely be a Mason, and would not make an example out of Doc, who is a 33rd degree-er."

"So you're telling me that you can't even arrest him?"

"Oh, we could hold him as a suspect, but we have no solid proof. The defense could claim the witnesses and letters were all questionable, doubtful, or part of conspiracy to undermine the reputation of Freemasonry. Remember, Walter Taft was writing his thesis on secret societies, and the Masonic pattern is the basis for a lot of other ones. That could be very damaging." He watched her slump back into her chair. "There is only one way we can prove that Doc actually killed your dad."

"And that is?" She was really listening.

"We would have to exhume Timothy Crocker's body," Max informed her.

Her hands went up to cover her face. "Oh my dear God. Oh no."

He let her take a few stabilizing breaths, then gave her the final line. "It's the only way we can establish that Doc actually gave him that fatal shot, and then falsified the paperwork. And the only person who can and *must* give permission for us to take a look at that body, is *you*, Mrs. Hannity."

Her hands dropped down. "That's not true. A judge can order that."

"Not if he decides there's not enough cause, and especially if he's targeting a high-standing fellow Mason." His expression was firm. "It has to be you, and you have to make a *lot* of noise about it. Otherwise, we have no case. It would be a waste of time and money to pursue justice in this matter."

She stood up to slowly wheel her chair back to the desk, where she seemed to freeze in place for a very long time, her head bowed and eyes closed. At length, she addressed them without looking their way. "I'm going to need a couple of days to think this through, gentlemen. A couple of days, at least. I'll get back to you then. Thanks for coming by."

"Yes, ma'am," Max replied as the two of them rose and quietly exited the office. Outside, Deputy Smith questioned his boss. "Are we sure there's no one else who can order the exhumation?"

"Aw hell, Smith," Sheriff Max Duncan reminded him, "I don't know. Whatever works, okay?"

***

Mrs. Hannity spent the night praying and working through the shock and grief, at least to the point where she could begin to think straight. By seven in the morning, she had made up her mind. Knowing the Schulers were early risers, she called them first. Uncle Abe came to the phone immediately, listening intently as she recounted her interview with the sheriff. When Irene expressed her concern that things had gone too far and too long, he had to agree with her. "At least we know that *Doktor* Horton will not try to blame our Freda for Timothy's death. It would cause too much trouble for him. One thing I do regret, dear Irene, is determining whether that terrible man might also have killed your *Mutter*. We are not convinced that she got stomach cancer by working in the orchard. But, that may be something we will never know."

"Uncle, please forgive me, but I simply can't bear any more bad news about my family. I need to get away from all that for a while. In fact, I am resigning from my job, leaving Jericho Center, and I will not pursue action against anybody. I think it's best to move on and let the past go."

The Schulers agreed that the worry about Doc was over; he could no longer harm Freda, without bringing up suspicions as to his own part in the both of the Crockers' deaths. As soon as Irene hung up, Elke hastened to let the Tafts know. Walter was relieved that Doc's back was finally against the wall. He made two quick calls to the Shorts and Collinses, who all agreed Doc was pretty unlikely to make any more waves, and God must be trusted as the final judge. As the last phone call ended, Don had a final piece of news. "By the way, Walter, Connie says one of their teachers at Essex Junction High School is retiring in January. She says you're a shoe-in for the position and you should go for it."

At nine, Irene applied for a position at Northside Nursing Home on North Avenue in Burlington. They were delighted to hear from her, since they had been trying to recruit her for over a year. It was understood that, while it was necessary to go through the interview process, she was guaranteed the job. At nine-thirty, she called the owners of Maude's Nursing Home, and gave the required two weeks' notice.

Sheriff Duncan was having a busy day and did not return her call until late afternoon. Her message to him was clear and simple: "This family has had too much tragedy already. We won't exhume any bodies, if I have anything to say about it. In fact I will resist any efforts to do such a thing. I'm asking you and any other authorities to just let it go." Recognizing the futility of the situation, the frustrated lawman pulled the file, even while still on the phone, and marked it "Family refuses to press charges." Then he reassured her, "Mrs. Hannity, I am moving this investigation into the cold case file. It will remain there until there is reasonable cause to reopen it… which will be very unlikely." She thanked him and went back to work. The only one left to speak to, was Doc, himself.

He came in late that day, seeing patients right after the supper hour. She sent word that he needed to check in with her before leaving the premises. He knocked on the office door at six forty-five. "Come in," she called out, and when he saw the look on her face, he knew it was all over.

"You were my hero," she murmured.

"I can explain," he started to say.

"Don't bother. I've heard too much, already." She tapped a pencil on the desk pad. "I'm asking you to take a month's leave, until I move into my new job. There's a new doctor in Essex who will cover for you until you come back. Your patients still trust you. They're elderly and handicapped and they need that comfort. See to it that you don't let *them* down, would you? As for *our* relationship, it is beyond repair. I have decided not to drag you into court — although God knows you deserve it. I want no further family-type contact with you. I will miss Cindy, but that's just the way it has to be." She motioned him toward the door. "Now, get out of my office, and don't come back to this facility for a whole month."

When she left work that night, she grabbed George's picture off the desk. In her little cottage, she slipped it and her wedding ring into a large manila envelope, and dropped it into the bottom drawer of the nightstand beside her bed. Then she wrapped herself in the bedspread and cried into her pillow until sleep brought relief. It was a temporary fix, of course, but so was everything else in this world.

Across the village green, the Hortons finally relaxed over a light supper in their upstairs quarters.

"Thank you for your faithful support," he said to his sweet-faced wife. "You know that man was crazy as a loon. You know I did what I had to do."

"Of course," she answered, "I really believe in justice. All that lying and sneaking around and doing wicked things needed to stop. He deserved everything he got." She smiled. "How about a piece of pumpkin pie and a nice cup of tea for dessert?"

"Sounds wonderful," he said.

And then Mrs. Horton went into the kitchen, where she slipped a golden slice onto his plate, and poured her husband a very special cup of tea. Before giving it a stir, she added just a pinch of a special ingredient from an unlabeled little jar on her spice rack. It was the same blend of spiced tea she had served her husband's mistress, for the last couple of years of *her* life. "*Of course, Doc is now a lot older than Freda had been when she finally passed on,*" she reminded herself, "*so he probably will die a lot sooner.*" She again took up the delightfully innocent smile, and set the lovely treat in front of her yellow-eyed chameleon... the one wearing the special ordered, gold-rimmed glasses.

THE END

From L. E. Fleury's *Junctions Murder Mystery Series*:

Book One: LOST

Book Two: HAUNTED

Book Three: PORTALS

Book Four: CHAMELEONS

Book Five: DAMAGED

Stay tuned for more to come!

Made in the USA
Middletown, DE
28 July 2024